DUKE OF A GILDED AGE

SUZANNE G. ROGERS

IDUNN COURT PUBLISHING

Duke of a Gilded Age, Copyright © Suzanne G. Rogers, 2013

All Rights Reserved. Except as permitted under the U.S. Copyright Act of 1976, no part of this publication may be reproduced, distributed, or transmitted in any form or by any means, or stored in a database or retrieval system, without prior written permission of the publisher.

This book is a work of fiction. While references may be made to actual places, persons, or events, the names, characters, incidents, and locations are either from the author's imagination or are used fictitiously and are not a resemblance to actual living or dead persons, businesses, or events. Any similarity is coincidental.

Idunn Court Publishing
7 Ramshorn Court
Savannah, GA 31411

Published by Idunn Court Publishing, June 2013
Revised Second Edition Published August 2020

ISBN: 978-1-947463-11-0

This book is licensed to the original purchaser only. Duplication or distribution via any means is illegal and a violation of International Copyright Law, subject to criminal prosecution and upon conviction, fines and/or imprisonment. No part of this book can be reproduced or sold by any person or business without the express permission of the publisher.

Published in the United States of America

❦ Created with Vellum

This book is dedicated to my mother,
Carolyn Scott Rogers,
who always supported me...and taught me how to be a lady.

CHAPTER 1
THE TENTH DUKE OF MANSBURY

England • June 1890

The elderly housekeeper escorted Mr. Oakhurst through Caisteal Park's imposing entryway, past a walnut staircase with elaborately carved banisters, and down a wide corridor.

"I've heard your daughter is to be congratulated on her recent engagement," she said.

"Ah, yes. Thank you, Mrs. Blount." Mr. Oakhurst's tone and somewhat grim expression revealed his feelings.

"You're not happy with the gentleman?"

"To all outward appearances, Sir Errol seems a respectable sort, but he's new to Mansbury and nobody knows him well." Mr. Oakhurst shook his head. "I fear Annabelle has rushed into this engagement too quickly."

"Perhaps a change of scenery would do her good," Mrs. Blount said.

"That's not a bad idea. An extended stay with my sister in London may give her a fresh perspective."

"London may not be far enough."

Just outside the paneled double doors, the housekeeper hesitated. "I'm sorry about the warmth inside the library, Mr. Oakhurst, but His Grace frequently feels chilled these days. He insists on having the fireplace lit, even though it's June."

"I'll manage, Mrs. Blount."

"His Grace has been in one of his moods," she said, low. "The poor man wouldn't eat anything yesterday or this morning."

"Did you send for a surgeon?"

"His Grace wouldn't let me. Perhaps you can make him see reason?"

Mr. Oakhurst tapped his leather satchel. "I'm his solicitor, not a miracle worker. Nevertheless, I'll do my best, Mrs. Blount."

The housekeeper pushed open the doors to the library. Septimus Parker, the tenth Duke of Mansbury, sat in front of a tall marble fireplace, facing the dying embers of a fire. An enormous oil painting was hung over the mantle, depicting the late ninth Duke of Mansbury, his now-deceased wife, and his two children, Septimus and Frederic Parker. In the portrait, Septimus was nearly a grown man and his younger brother was a baby.

Mrs. Blount cleared her throat. "Mr. Oakhurst is here to see you, Your Grace."

When the duke made no indication he'd heard, the housekeeper exchanged a worried glance with Mr. Oakhurst.

"Er...just ring for tea when you're ready," she murmured before disappearing down the hall.

Mr. Oakhurst glanced up at the portrait as he approached his employer. The age difference between the two sons depicted therein never ceased to impress him. It wasn't surprising, really, that Septimus and Frederic Parker had never been close.

"Good afternoon, Your Grace," he said. "I've good news. I managed to trace your brother to America, where…oh, dear."

Shocked, Mr. Oakhurst sank onto the leather-covered footstool. From the blue pallor of his countenance and the stiffness of his posture, it appeared Septimus Parker had long since passed away.

∼

THE OCEAN BREEZE, full of promise, whipped the ribbons on Belle's straw hat to and fro. Beaming with excitement, she stood at the ship's railing as the ocean liner sailed into the port of New York City. Although the transatlantic crossing had taken a little over a week, more than one passenger was on deck, eager for the journey's end. All eyes were trained on the rapidly approaching landmark situated on Bedloe's Island in New York Harbor. The graceful lines and dull copper color of the Statue of Liberty, dedicated a scant four years ago, was spectacular against the azure August sky.

Her father joined her just then. "Now *that* is a pretty sight."

"Why, Lady Liberty is taller than Saint Mary-le-Bow Church in London!" Belle exclaimed. "She's simply marvelous, isn't she? Very inspirational."

"Indeed, she is."

The tide was cooperative and their vessel sailed up the North River, amidst yachts, fishing boats, and steamships of all sizes. The skyline of Manhattan struck Belle as beautiful.

"So many lovely buildings, don't you think, Papa?" she asked.

Mr. Oakhurst pointed. "That spire is the Trinity Church,

and it's the tallest structure in the city at the moment. But when the World Building is completed, *it* will be the tallest."

"Is that the domed one a little farther north? Why it's touching the heavens!" She giggled. "Will clouds will ever get caught around the top, I wonder?"

"I wouldn't think so. And I expect very soon someone else will build something even taller. There's a competitive spirit in this Gilded Age of America."

Belle gave her father's arm an affectionate squeeze. "Oh, Papa, I can't believe we're here at last. Thank you for allowing me to sail with you. I know you paid for my ticket out of your own pocket."

Her father favored her with an indulgent smile. "I could hardly leave you home alone and unprotected while I sailed to America and back. The lovesick Sir Errol might have induced you to elope in my absence."

"Papa, Errol is a hopeless romantic who would never ask me to do anything so improper! He even gave me a packet of seven different love poems before I left, to open each morning at sea." Belle sighed. "I wish he were here."

"I'm glad he isn't."

She gave him a startled glance. "You don't like him?"

"It's not that, Annabelle. My only concern is for your happiness."

"Errol makes me happy."

"How well can you know the man in a few short weeks? My dear, I worry you haven't had the chance to meet many gentlemen. It's my own fault, of course, for having chosen to be a solicitor and not a barrister. Then you could have been presented at court and moved in society like your mother did."

"The distinction between solicitors and barristers is completely unfair, in my opinion. Why should you be barred from the gentry class just because you get paid directly for your services, while barristers get paid through solicitors?"

"Because payments to barristers are considered gifts. Fair or no, I'm considered to be 'in trade' and there's nothing to be done about it. Your mother married down when she married me, perhaps, but she married for love. We were very contented, and I'd like to see you similarly situated."

"Don't concern yourself, Papa! If you had been a barrister, you would have spent all your time away in London, pleading cases in court. Besides which, Errol is everything I desire in a husband. He's high-minded, sophisticated, mannerly, has exceptional taste, and is in possession of a title. Furthermore, I met the Duke of Mansbury on several occasions. If he represents the Upper Tens of society, I'm content with far less."

"Septimus Parker was eccentric, and it's sad, really, that he died alone. I regret I couldn't locate his brother sooner."

"The Duke of Mansbury drove his only brother across the Atlantic Ocean with his ungenerous and spiteful nature, so it was his own doing!" She paused. "I suppose I should thank him, though."

"What do you mean?"

"His disagreeable disposition has resulted in an unusual adventure of which few could boast."

"Do you mean our quest to locate the eleventh Duke of Mansbury?"

"Indeed I do, and a nobler cause was never undertaken." Belle's tone was serious but she ended her sentence with a wink.

"That is so."

"Will Lord Frederic sail with us on our return voyage?"

"I think we may dispense with his courtesy title now and call him His Grace. To answer your question, I can't say for certain, since he didn't respond to my cables. He and Lady

Frederic may have extensive property to dispose of and therefore I can't predict when he will finally take up residence at Caisteal Park. It's quite possible you and I may sail back to England alone."

"I wouldn't mind that in the least. I expect we'll find the new Duke of Mansbury just as disagreeable as his elder brother."

∼

WESLEY LEANED against a wooden pillar inside the tiny garden apartment, waiting for his mother to finish tying string around a large paper-wrapped bundle. Matilda Parker gave him a disapproving glance.

"You shouldn't slouch, Wesley." The woman's cultivated English accent was at odds with her inelegant surroundings.

"If I don't slouch, I end up hitting my head on the pipes."

"It's your own fault for growing so tall."

"I can't help it!"

Matilda flicked Wesley a teasing glance. "I'm not serious! Any mother would be proud to have such a tall, strapping son. You may have just turned twenty years old, but to me you'll always be my little boy."

"If it's any consolation, I think I've stopped growing."

"I certainly hope so, since I've let the hems out of all your father's pants as far as I can." She tied a bow in the string and gave the bundle a pat. "Deliver this to Mrs. Zinna, and don't forget to collect for the week."

"All right."

Wesley tucked the bundle under his arm. The movement revealed an inch of bare, rawboned wrist sticking out past the frayed cuff of his shirt. His mother frowned.

"Oh, dear. While you're gone, I'll see if I can find you a shirt with longer sleeves," she said. "I'd like you to look presentable for our guest."

"So why is this English lawyer coming to see us? Is it just because Uncle Scrooge kicked off?" he asked.

"His name was Septimus and that's completely disrespectful!"

Wesley's shoulders moved up and down in a shrug. "Father disliked him and therefore so will I. Nevertheless, I hope he left us some money."

"Most assuredly, Septimus married and his estate went to his own son." Matilda shrugged. "Perhaps he left your father an heirloom."

"An heirloom?" Wesley wrinkled his nose. "I hope it's something we can sell or trade for food." He headed for the door.

"Be sure to stop by Lombardi's on the way home to buy a tin of biscuits."

He snickered. "You mean cookies, don't you? Whatever you want to call them, we can't afford it."

"I'll just have to economize somehow. Mr. Oakhurst will expect a certain level of gentility."

Wesley surveyed the apartment. "Then he's coming to the wrong place."

His mother bit her lip and tears welled up in her eyes. "I'm doing the best I can."

Shame washed over Wesley and he hung his head. "I'm sorry, Mother. Look, the other day I ran into George Halverson, the supervisor at Palmer's Dock. He was impressed with the muscle I've put on from slinging bags of rice and flour at Lombardi's and told me I could start working for him on Monday if I wanted to."

Matilda's eyes narrowed. "No, you won't!"

He made a sound of frustration. "It would only be temporary until I begin my teaching job this fall. It pays far better than delivering groceries for Lombardi's and you wouldn't have to take in laundry anymore. Maybe we could even move to a better apartment."

"How could you even *think* of working at Palmer's Dock after what happened to your father there? I forbid it."

Wesley scowled. "Fine, but you deserve better than this." He twirled the bundle in the air. "I'll be back with the cookies."

"Don't dawdle. Mr. Oakhurst's last telegram said he'd arrive by two o'clock."

At the door, Wesley grabbed a cloth cap from a hook and slipped it over his thick brown curls. "I hope this lawyer fellow has a solid gold candle snuffer with him and not the family Bible."

"Oh, Wesley!"

Unrepentant, he left the flat and mounted the short flight of stairs from the garden apartment to the sidewalk. The coal delivery cart was rolling past, and Wesley waved to the driver. "*Ciao*, Gino. *Come stai?*"

"*Non mi posso lamentare*, Wes."

Wesley grinned. "*Buono! Arrivederci.*"

After the cart passed, Wesley crossed the street, careful to avoid the fresh trail of manure left by Gino's team of horses. Mrs. Zinna's flat was a few blocks over, in Bensonhurst. As he walked through the neighborhood, he noticed a group of Irish boys—former friends—clustered on the sidewalk, playing jackstones. Wesley groaned inwardly. Today of all days, he couldn't afford a fight. Unfortunately, he'd already been spotted.

"Whatcha got there, Wes?" A stocky redhead stood with his arms akimbo. "More dirty knickers for your mummy?"

"I'd love to exchange insults with you, Liam, but I'm busy," Wesley retorted.

As Wesley turned a corner, he glanced back. *Blast!* The Irish had abandoned their game and were tailing him. He quickened his pace, and sped over to the next street, where a gang of Italian boys was playing kick the can.

Wesley nodded to one of his old classmates. "*Ciao*, Sergio."

Sergio grinned. "*Ciao*."

When Wesley's pursuers spotted the Italians, they dropped back into an alley. Wesley laughed and strolled unmolested the rest of the way to Mrs. Zinna's apartment building. He dropped off his bundle and collected money for the past week, but when he stepped onto the street a few minutes later, the Irish were waiting for him.

"Thought you'd give us the slip, eh?" Liam said. "Where's your silver spoon, pretty boy?"

Wesley's hackles rose, and he assumed a cocky swagger. "How's that sister of yours, Liam? I hear she's lonely for me."

"Shut your filthy mouth about my sister! Why would Colleen be lonely for the likes of wee Lord Fauntleroy?" sneered Liam. He knocked Wesley's cap off his head and into the gutter.

Wesley's knuckles showed white. "Don't *ever* call me that again." He decked Liam with a wide right hook and turned to face the others.

One down, four to go.

⁓

THE CAB ROLLED to a halt outside a rundown building on a dirty street. Mr. Oakhurst consulted his pocket watch. "It's already ten minutes past two o'clock! I had no idea it would take so long to get from Manhattan to Brooklyn."

"This *can't* be the correct address," Belle peered at the residence, aghast.

"I'm afraid it is."

Belle stepped from the cab onto the sidewalk while her father asked the driver to wait. When Mr. Oakhurst moved toward the apartment building entrance, she caught his arm.

"I believe it's down there, Papa." She gestured toward a descending stone staircase.

He peered at the number plate affixed to the wall. "I think you're right."

Mr. Oakhurst followed his daughter down the steps. Before he could knock at the door, however, a woman opened it. Her worn black cotton gown hung off her rail-thin frame, and her hands were reddened and chapped.

"Good afternoon. You must be Mr. Oakhurst," she said.

The woman's unadorned dress, severe hairstyle, and work-worn hands were those of a housekeeper. Mr. Oakhurst handed her his business card. "Mr. Oakhurst and Miss Oakhurst are here to see Lord Frederic Parker. Is he at home, madam?"

A faint blush stained the woman's cheeks. "I'm Lady Frederic, but I'm known as Mrs. Parker here. Please come in."

Belle's eyes widened, despite her effort to mask her surprise. She curtsied nevertheless and stepped into the stifling hot apartment. The odor of detergent and starch assailed her nostrils and perspiration prickled at the back of her neck.

"Please be seated," the woman said. "Would you care for some tea?"

Belle couldn't think of anything she wanted less than a cup of hot tea. "No, Lady Frederic," she murmured. "Thank you."

Similarly, her father shook his head. "Forgive me, but could you tell me when your husband will return? I've come a long way to discuss a matter of urgent business with him."

Lady Frederic sank onto a rickety chair. "I couldn't afford to send a cable overseas, Mr. Oakhurst. I'm afraid I have bad news."

She handed the attorney an official-looking piece of paper. As he read it, a gasp escaped his lips. "This is a death certificate!"

"Yes, my husband was killed in an accident several years ago."

"How very dreadful for you!" Belle exclaimed.

Mr. Oakhurst shook his head. "I'm so sorry, Lady Frederic." He returned the certificate to her with a frown.

"Thank you." The woman averted her eyes. "His loss has been quite difficult to bear."

"I understand. I lost my wife—Belle's mother—going on five years now."

A wave of sympathy crossed her face. "What a tragedy."

"Yes, it was. Lady Frederic, I came to inform your husband of his late brother's wish to reconcile, but Lord Frederic's death changes everything. Since Septimus Parker died without children, your husband was in line to become the eleventh Duke of Mansbury. With no other male heirs, however, the title may become extinct."

The front door burst open and a policeman yanked a bareheaded, bloodstained young man into view. His nose was bloodied, his left eye was purplish, and his lip was split open. Lady Frederic shot to her feet in horror.

"Wesley! What happened, Officer Hannigan?"

The policeman frowned. "Yer son's been fightin', Mrs. Parker."

Lady Frederic threw her hands up in exasperation. "Not again!"

The young man squirmed away from Officer Hannigan's grip. "The Irish started it!"

"Aye, and that's the only reason I didn't book ye with the

rest o' the lot." The policeman gave Wesley's mother a nod. "There were witnesses who said the other lads were followin' him."

She sighed. "Thank you for bringing him home, Officer."

Officer Hannigan wagged his finger at Wesley. "You're too old to be acting like a brawlin' child, for pity's sake. Stay out of trouble!"

He shrugged. "I'll try."

After the policeman left, Wesley Parker seemed to finally notice the newcomers. He smacked the part of his forehead still unmarked by bruises and muttered, "And after all that, I forgot the stupid cookies!" He flopped onto a stool.

His mother slid him a level glance before giving Belle and her father a fixed smile. "Mr. Oakhurst and Miss Oakhurst, allow me to introduce you to my son Wesley—the eleventh Duke of Mansbury."

CHAPTER 2
THE INHERITANCE

Wesley gaped first at the visitors and then at his mother. "You're joking."

"Not in the least," Mr. Oakhurst said.

The solicitor explained at length about letters patent, hereditary titles, and the dukedom known as Mansbury. To Wesley, the legal language was incomprehensible. Even though his mother brought him a wet cloth to clean his face, his injuries had begun to sting, ache, and throb—in that order—and he couldn't concentrate. Worse, Mr. Oakhurst's daughter was staring at him with ill-disguised disgust—or was it revulsion? Why on earth was *she* here? There she sat, in all her ladylike perfection, while he resembled Sunday's raw pot roast. In addition, he'd rolled through the gutters during the scuffle and he smelled like Monday's chamber pot. Even his cap was missing, having been lost during the fight.

Finally Mr. Oakhurst paused and Wesley managed to get a word in.

"Sir, forgive me for being blunt, but I was born in a country where everyone is equal. I don't want any sort of title and I've no intention of leaving America. If you'll excuse me, I'm going to wash up."

He slid off his stool, moved over to the washbasin around the corner, and shrugged off his tattered coat. It had been tight across the chest even before the fight, and the seams were now split open at the back of his shoulders. As gingerly as possible, Wesley washed his battered face and cut knuckles with soap and water. A glance in the cracked mirror hanging on the wall gave him no satisfaction; he looked as bad as he felt.

Miss Oakhurst suddenly appeared in the mirror's reflection. "Are you daft?"

"What?" To his dismay, a drip of water hung from the tip of Wesley's nose. "No."

"Perhaps you got a knock on the head, then? My father and I have come a long way to deliver good tidings and this is your response? That silly speech you just gave left your mama in tears. Perhaps *you* don't care about titles or England, but obviously *she* does."

Wesley dragged his sleeve across his face and turned around. "Ever since my father died I've had no peace. The obituary mentioned his brother the duke, and I've been mercilessly mocked and teased since then until I don't want to hear another word about it! I don't aspire to be a member of the aristocracy whatsoever."

Miss Oakhurst's gaze was unwavering. "You ought to be proud of what you are, Mr. Parker. Although from my perspective, you're well on the path to becoming a delinquent."

Wesley's eyes narrowed. "You don't know a thing about me. And anyway, why should you care?"

Miss Oakhurst's hat seemed to be quivering with righteous indignation. "I don't care about you personally. Your mama, on the other hand, is a great lady and should be treated as such.

Forgive me for saying so, but you really ought to apologize to her and accept your heritage with gratitude and humility."

Annoyance straightened his spine. "Forgive me for saying so, but you really ought not be so stuck up!"

He peered past the young woman and into the apartment, where his mother was indeed clutching a handkerchief to her eyes. A stab of regret made him wince. Although he resented this strange girl lecturing him in such an arrogant fashion, he couldn't argue with her sentiments. His mother *did* deserve better.

Wesley jammed his hands in his pockets, brushed past Miss Oakhurst, and cleared his throat. "Forgive me, Mother. I spoke without thinking just now. If it would please you, I'll accept the title. I think it's what Father would have wanted."

When his mother's smile shone through her tears, it almost made up for the insufferable look of triumph on Miss Oakhurst's face. To escape her smirk, he grabbed a workman's jacket and headed for the door.

"I'll get the cookies and be back soon."

∽

As soon as the visitors left, his mother picked up her skirts and twirled around the flat in glee. Finally, she sank into a chair, out of breath.

"I can't *wait* to go back to England!"

His mother was so happy that Wesley couldn't suppress a smile. "When are we leaving?"

"I asked Mr. Oakhurst to book us on the next available steamship to Liverpool. Until then, we're to move to the Fifth Avenue Hotel in Manhattan. Heaven knows I don't want to stay here a moment longer than I must."

Wesley gaped. "The Fifth Avenue Hotel, did you say?" He

dug into his pocket to produce the few coins remaining after his purchase of cookies. "I don't think this is enough to pay for our stay."

"Mr. Oakhurst gave me plenty of money to settle our bills here, and he's arranged a line of credit at the hotel. Get out our trunks and help me pack. A cab is coming to fetch us tomorrow morning."

"All right, but afterward I have to go tell Mr. and Mrs. Lombardi they need to hire another delivery boy. I'll also have to resign my teaching position, but I suppose I can always write the school a letter."

While Wesley dragged dusty old trunks out of a closet, Matilda began gathering up her meager belongings. As he contemplated making the crossing alongside the Oakhursts, his shoulders drifted upward.

"Look, can't we take a later ship to England?" He gave his mother a pleading glance. "Mr. Oakhurst is all right, but his daughter's a bossy prig."

Matilda folded her arms. "I hope her priggishness rubs off on you, Wesley. If you're to move in English society, you must learn how to behave."

He lifted his chin. "I know how to behave well enough."

"Perhaps you behave well enough for this neighborhood, but because you were born in America, many people in England will expect you to be uncouth."

Wesley shrugged and examined his grubby fingernails. "Well, I *am* uncouth."

"No, you're not! Make an effort to get along, Wesley. Providence has finally seen fit to smile on us, and I intend to take advantage of the opportunity."

The Oakhurst's cab drove onto the Brooklyn Bridge on its way toward Manhattan. Belle stared out the window, nursing hurt feelings. *I can't believe Wesley Parker called me stuck up! That was abominably rude.*

Her father gave her a sidelong glance. "Well, what do you think about the new Duke of Mansbury?"

Her snort was admittedly unladylike. "He behaves more like a stable boy than a duke, and he smells worse than the back end of a horse."

Mr. Oakhurst gaped. "Annabelle, that's uncharitable."

"Perhaps, but it's accurate, nevertheless."

"Wesley Parker is a young man who has had to make his own way since his father died. After he's suitably attired, I think your opinion of him will improve."

"His bruises and cuts will heal, and perhaps you can buy him some decent clothes, but nothing will mask his dreadful American accent or brutish manners." Belle shrugged. "Errol dislikes Americans and I'm not so sure I don't agree with him."

"You find American accents dreadful?" Mr. Oakhurst laughed. "In my opinion, they are charming."

"The novelty will soon wear thin as far as Wesley Parker is concerned unless you can install a veneer of civility to go with his American articulation."

"An excellent suggestion, Annabelle. I'll rely on you to assist him."

Belle gasped. "*What?*"

"You can teach him the rules of gentlemanly behavior and help him practice his social graces. In addition, he must learn to dance. Since you're a dance instructor at Monsieur Caron's studio, you're the perfect candidate."

She rolled her eyes. "I'm certain Monsieur Caron would welcome another pupil."

"There may be little opportunity for extensive lessons,

Annabelle. As soon as His Grace takes up residence at Caisteal Park, he'll receive invitations to balls and parties. Perhaps the Duchess will even host a reception herself. The new Duke of Mansbury must be ready."

Belle struggled to stem her resentment by focusing on the magnificent view of the East River. A myriad of picturesque sailing ships, cargo vessels, and ferries traveled up and down the waterway, leaving white froth in their wakes. She vowed to be more like them, cheerful in her disposition and focused on the destination ahead, shouldn't she? Belle glanced back at the receding Brooklyn shoreline with a sigh of resignation. If she and Wesley Parker were to be thrown together, she would try to make the best of it...for her father's sake.

∽

From behind the privacy curtain that walled off his sleeping area from the rest of the apartment, Wesley fumbled with the buttons on his waistcoat. He knew the garments didn't exactly fit; he was taller than his father had been and broader through the shoulders. Nevertheless, clad in the black cutaway jacket, brocade waistcoat, and striped trousers, he stood straighter than before...until he nearly banged his head on a pipe.

"The cab will be here shortly," Matilda called out. "Come out, Wesley, and let me have a look at you."

He pushed the curtain aside. His mother didn't say anything for a few moments, and he began to think the worst.

"I almost had your father buried in that suit," she said finally. "I'm very glad now that I didn't. You look a proper gentleman, Wesley, apart from the bruising."

He tugged down the sleeves of the jacket in a fruitless attempt to cover his bare wrists.

"I feel like I'm dressing up for a stage performance."

His mother gave him a misty smile. "You'll have to have an entirely new wardrobe tailored for you, of course, but I couldn't have you walk into the Fifth Avenue Hotel dressed like a dock workman." She gestured toward the top hat resting on the kitchen table. "I've dusted your father's hat off. It's a bit shabby, but it'll have to do until you purchase another one."

He frowned. "I don't want to wear a topper! Men wear derby hats these days."

Matilda's expression reflected resolve. "I'm not going to argue with you, Wesley. You'll wear it."

Wesley ran his finger across the brim of the hat. "My friends and I used to make fun of gentlemen who wore toppers." A grin at the memory caused him to wince from the pain of his split lip. "Ouch."

"Serves you right. No more fisticuffs, young man."

"I don't—" he broke off when he realized any argument was pointless. "Yes, Mother."

Matilda busied herself gathering up her frayed gloves and a somewhat moth-eaten reticule. Wesley suddenly noticed her hair was arranged in a more elaborate style than usual, and her face had lost its strained expression. She'd set aside her mourning black and had donned an old, sky blue dress with flounces and slightly yellowed lace. The skirt was quite wide, and Wesley was baffled.

"How do you hold it out?" he asked, gesticulating with his hands.

His mother gave him a cool glance. "A gentleman doesn't concern himself with what's underneath a lady's gown. For your information, however, it's called a crinoline." She cast a critical eye at her reflection in the looking glass. "Crinolines are hopelessly out of fashion, of course, but I've nothing else to wear."

"You look splendid and quite...pretty."

"That's very kind, Wesley."

Her smile cheered him up considerably. "See here, if we can afford it, you shall have all new clothes. I can make do with Father's things for a while."

Matilda laughed. "Weren't you listening when Mr. Oakhurst was explaining your inheritance?"

"Not really. I was in too much pain."

"Well, we needn't concern ourselves about money any longer."

He looked at her askance. "After being poor, I can't imagine ever taking money for granted."

A knock at the door just then heralded the arrival of the cab.

Wesley bent down to grasp the leather handle on the largest trunk. "If you'll answer the door, I'll take care of our things."

"Set it down." His mother put a firm hand on his shoulder. "A gentleman doesn't handle his own luggage."

Astonished, Wesley gaped. "Our trunks won't move themselves!"

"Let the driver do it. That's how he earns gratuities."

Wesley lowered the trunk to the floor, admitted the cab driver, and reluctantly stood aside while the man carried their luggage out. *Gentlemen aren't permitted to do a great many things. So far, being a gentleman doesn't sound fun.*

"I'm going upstairs to relinquish the key to Mrs. Thackeray." Matilda gave the apartment one final glance. "I'm not sorry to leave this place. Your father was never happy here, and neither was I."

Although Wesley hated the apartment too, a surge of nostalgia gripped him. Now that he was facing an uncertain future, the small dwelling suddenly represented a safe harbor. For good or for ill, he was about to say farewell to the last place he'd seen his father alive. He tried to keep his feelings hidden, but his mother must have sensed his turmoil.

She slipped a soothing hand around his elbow. "Staying here won't bring your father back. If his spirit is anywhere, we'll find it at Caisteal Park."

Wesley waited on the sidewalk while his mother went to the landlady's apartment to drop off the key. August heat caused beads of perspiration to form on Wesley's upper lip and he doffed his hat to blot the moisture on his brow. When his mother reappeared, he helped his into the cab and sat next to her while the driver loaded the last of their trunks,

Down the street, Liam was tossing a battered baseball in the air and catching it on the way down with one hand. A familiar cloth cap was set on his head at a jaunty angle.

As the cab drove past, Wesley leaned out the window. "Hey, Liam!"

Dawning recognition in Liam's eyes caused his jaw to drop.

Wesley touched the brim of his topper. "Give my best to Colleen, why don't you?"

With a satisfied grin, Wesley settled back in his seat. *Perhaps being a gentleman has its compensations after all.*

∼

IN THE RARIFIED atmosphere of the handsomely appointed Fifth Avenue Hotel lobby, Mr. Oakhurst and Belle waited for Wesley and his mother to arrive. The floor was covered with a highly polished white marble that echoed the extensive use of marble on the hotel's exterior. Round columns stretched from floor to ceiling, and a flower stand in one corner did a brisk business. Glossy green potted plants softened every corner, and the hotel fairly thrummed with excitement and privilege.

Belle watched the vertical railway doors open and close

nearby. People disappeared into the little movable parlor en route to one of the five floors above her head. She nudged her father to get his attention. "That's truly a marvelous invention. I wrote about it in my letter to Errol last night."

Mr. Oakhurst tore his attention away from the hotel entrance long enough to glance at the vertical lift. "Did you know this hotel was constructed with the first passenger elevator? Originally it was a vertical screw railway, but I believe it's since given way to a more modern rope mechanism."

"Quite clever."

"Indeed, the widespread use of elevators will enable buildings to be taller than we can ever imagine."

Belle shook her head in amazement. "You'd think structures would topple over after a certain height."

"I certainly hope they don't! Ah, I see the young duke and the duchess have arrived. Will you meet them while I alert the manager?" Mr. Oakhurst strode toward the front desk.

Belle gave Wesley an appraising glance as the hotel doorman ushered the Parkers into the lobby. Despite the fact his clothes were in need of a good tailor, the cutaway jacket, vest, and trousers were an improvement over his former disarray. Furthermore, his shiny top hat suited him well. His shoes were abysmal, however, his lip and eye were still swollen, and his hair was indifferently combed. Nevertheless, if one didn't examine him too closely, Wesley Parker resembled a gentleman. His mother's appearance was more relaxed and cheerful than the day before, although her gown was exceedingly dated.

Belle approached. "It's a pleasure to see you again, Lady Frederic…er, I mean, Your Grace." She dipped into a curtsy.

The duchess smiled. "Good morning, Miss Oakhurst."

Belle's curtsy to Wesley was more perfunctory. "Hello, Your Grace."

He stared. "My *what?*"

"Your Grace. It's how you're addressed by those social classes lower than the gentry. Otherwise, you'll be addressed as Duke, or sir. Family and very close friends are another matter."

His eyebrows drew together. "See here, that's nonsense!"

Mr. Oakhurst returned with the hotel manager in tow and sketched a shallow bow to the duchess. "Good morning, Your Grace." He turned to Wesley. "And good morning to you as well, Your Grace."

Belle tried not to smirk at her father's use of Wesley's title.

Mr. Oakhurst gestured toward the man at his side. "Allow me to introduce you to Mr. Darling."

The manager beamed. "Welcome to the Fifth Avenue Hotel." He nodded at Wesley. "Come with me, sir, to sign the register."

As Wesley penned his name in the book at the front desk, Belle felt a slight tug of sympathy at his obvious discomfort. *He's so out of place, I could almost feel sorry for him.*

While the duke was thus occupied, bellboys collected the Parkers' worn trunks. Shortly thereafter, when the manager returned with Wesley, he insisted on showing the Parkers to their suite personally. As Mr. Darling, the duchess, and Mr. Oakhurst headed toward the elevator, Wesley and Belle fell into step just behind.

"I wasn't sure if I should sign the register as Wesley Parker or the Duke of Mansbury," Wesley whispered. "I finally settled on Wesley Parker, the Duke of Mansbury, but it dribbled out into the margin."

"You may style yourself merely 'Mansbury,' Your Grace," Belle replied.

He frowned. "I don't like being called Your Grace. If you don't call me Wesley, I won't answer you."

"Then our conversation will be quite one-sided," Belle replied. "In English Society, rank is everything. You'll be expected to observe it."

∼

Wesley attempted to behave as if he checked into first-class hotels and rode on sumptuous vertical railways every day. In truth, however, he was in mortal fear of saying or doing the wrong thing. Fortunately, Mr. Darling filled the slow steady ride to the top floor with his vivacious conversation.

"The Prince of Wales stayed with us when he was touring North America."

"I read about that in the newspapers." Matilda's smile was gracious. "How marvelous for your establishment."

"Indeed, the Fifth Avenue Hotel attracts dignitaries and statesmen from all over the globe. We have over four hundred employees to serve our guests, you see. Each bedchamber has a private bath and you'll find a fireplace in every room. Oh, and meals are included during your stay here, except the late supper."

Mr. Oakhurst cleared his throat. "The duke and duchess would like to procure a few items of clothing prior to their voyage. Where would you recommend, sir?"

When Mr. Darling flicked a brief glance at the dusty top hat on Wesley's head, he felt a blush of embarrassment heat his cheekbones.

"The renowned Knox Hat Shop on the ground floor has a marvelous selection of men's hats. You may have noticed it on the left just before you entered the hotel. Also, a fine collection of emporiums, boutiques, and department stores can be found on Ladies' Mile, which encompasses part of Sixth Avenue, Fifth Avenue, and Broadway. I recommend Arnold, Constable and Company, at 115 Fifth Avenue. The store is nicknamed the Palace of Trade, and you may even see the Vanderbilts, the Carnegies, or the Rockefellers shopping there."

Matilda gave Wesley a pointed glance and he knew she wanted him to respond.

"Er…thank you for those suggestions, Mr. Darling." He cast about for something else to add. "We are in your debt."

His mother slid him an approving smile. At length, the upward motion of the moving parlor stopped, the doors opened, and the manager led them down the hallway to a suite of three large rooms overlooking Madison Square Park. Miss Oakhurst immediately ran to the windows to admire the view.

While Matilda inspected the suite, taking everything in with obvious pleasure, Wesley tried not to gape. He'd never seen such luxury before, nor imagined it. The sitting room alone was more spacious than the flat in Brooklyn. Dentil moldings accentuated the high ceiling, and tapestry-patterned paper covered the walls. Impressive wooden valances sat atop the windows, which were framed by elegant, heavy velvet drapes. An enormous oriental rug covered the polished wooden floor, and a fringed horsehair sofa, an ornate coffee table, and two chairs made up a cozy sitting area. Nearer the windows was a substantial rosewood desk, where letters could be written or business conducted. A crystal vase on the fireplace mantle displayed a profusion of fresh flowers and ferns, and a smaller cut-glass bowl on the coffee table held an arrangement of hothouse roses, lilies, and cockscomb. The floral fragrances combined to perfume the air.

A basket of fruit on the coffee table made Wesley's mouth water. Ever since his father died, he'd grown accustomed to eating the bruised, smaller pieces of fruit sold in Lombardi's at a discount. He picked up a fresh red apple, marveling at its size, color, and perfection. It almost looked as if it was made out of wax, but the aroma proved otherwise. As he returned the apple to the basket, he noticed a fancy beribboned box marked *Maillard's*.

Mr. Darling followed his gaze. "Chocolates, compliments of the house, of course. Maillard's is also located on the ground floor of the hotel. President Abraham Lincoln adored their bonbons. In addition to chocolates, you can buy perfectly marvelous chocolate ice cream there."

On the table sat a light green booklet entitled *Visitor's Guide to the City of New York*. Mr. Darling gave it a tap. "There's a great deal of useful information about shops and restaurants inside this pamphlet."

When the bellboys arrived with the luggage, Wesley was struck by how worn and battered the old trunks looked, especially in contrast with the luxurious splendor of the room. While Mr. Darling spoke to Mr. Oakhurst and Matilda about arranging transportation for their shopping excursion, Wesley joined Miss Oakhurst at the window.

A tremendous view greeted him. Metal tracks for horse-drawn trolley cars cut through the granite Belgian block pavement on Fifth Avenue, several floors below. Across the street, a long line of cabs was parked alongside Madison Square Park. The large rectangular park was a very pretty sight with its looping pathways and historic monuments nestled amongst large sycamore, oak, and elm trees.

Wesley blew out a long, slow breath. "I'm completely out of my element."

Miss Oakhurst studied him. "Your clothes are a vast improvement from yesterday."

He inserted a finger in between his collar and his neck in a futile attempt to loosen the fit. "They're my father's things and I feel silly in them."

"You don't look silly. I think your suit is rather handsome, even if it's borrowed."

"Thank you." He paused a moment. "I can tell you don't approve of me."

"It's not my place to approve or disapprove of you." She averted her gaze. "I spoke out of turn yesterday. I should've been more courteous."

"I apologize for my comments as well." Wesley shrugged. "Perhaps we got off to a bad start."

"Definitely so. I agree."

A muscle worked in his jaw. "I could really use a friend, Miss Oakhurst."

She gave him a decisive nod. "All right. As a friend, I must inform you that you need new shoes and a haircut."

Wesley roared with laughter. His mirth was contagious, apparently, because Miss Oakhurst began to giggle. His mother and Mr. Darling glanced over while Mr. Oakhurst beamed. "I'm glad to see you two getting along swimmingly."

CHAPTER 3
FIFTH AVENUE

Wesley turned away from the window. "Mr. Darling, may we have lunch here in our suite?"

He bowed. "I'll send a waiter to take your order."

"Excellent. And after lunch, let me know when our carriage is ready to take us shopping."

"Yes, Your Grace."

Wesley smiled. "Thank you, Mr. Darling. I appreciate your attentiveness."

As the manager left, Wesley noticed the Oakhursts and his mother staring at him, as if in shock.

He drew back, perplexed. "Did I do something wrong?"

"No, dear." Matilda blinked. "I've just never seen you give orders before. Well done."

Wesley shrugged. "Perhaps Miss Oakhurst has lent me her considerable courage."

Unable to resist any longer, he plucked up the apple from the fruit basket and bit into it. As he did so, he savored its abundant juice, firm texture, and sweet taste. He brought the fruit with him as he explored the bedchamber that was to be his for the next few days. The four-poster, king-sized bed was covered with a patterned silk coverlet that coordinated with the curtains. As Mr. Darling had promised, the room possessed a handsome fireplace, framed by carved wooden trim pieces and a mantel. The adjoining bath was sparkling clean and elegant, with a marble pedestal sink, scented shell-shaped soaps, electric lighting, and gold-plated fixtures. Wesley cast a longing glance toward the claw-foot bathtub, but a good long soak would have to wait until evening.

He tossed his apple core into the artfully painted tin wastebasket and washed his face and hands in the lavatory basin. As Wesley dried himself off with one of the fluffy white towels hanging from a rack, he stared at his reflection in the mirror. *In these clothes, I really* do *look a lot like Father.* A sudden pang of loneliness was followed closely by a surge of anger toward his uncle. *My father should be here to enjoy these luxuries. If only Uncle Septimus had made up with him years earlier, my father's death could have been averted.*

His mother's voice carried from the sitting room. "Wesley, a waiter has arrived with luncheon menus."

"I'll be right there," he called out.

Before he rejoined his mother and the Oakhursts in the sitting room, Wesley wiped the frown from his face. Despite his surge of melancholy, he was determined to do nothing to upset his mother.

~

As the cab carried Mr. Oakhurst, Belle, the duchess, and Wesley along Fifth Avenue, Belle marveled at the impressive office buildings and fashionable shops lining both sides of the boulevard. The sidewalks were crowded with well-dressed people either out for a stroll or transacting business. City workers swept the street with push brooms, taking care to avoid the horses trotting past.

Belle exchanged an excited glance with the duchess. "Now I understand what Mr. Darling meant earlier. You can buy anything you want here!"

The pretty woman gave a girlish giggle. "I confess, it feels like Christmas day."

"Don't buy too much, Mother." Wesley snickered. "You might sink the ship."

"Oh, don't tease, Wesley." The duchess glanced at Belle's father. "Mr. Oakhurst, when are we setting sail, and how many days will we be at sea?"

"The concierge has confirmed your first class accommodations on the *SS City of New York* leaving this Saturday at one o'clock. I'd plan for a crossing of six days, Your Grace."

"As quick as that?" Her eyes widened. "When Frederic and I crossed twenty years ago, the voyage took two full weeks. The voyage was extremely unpleasant, rather dull, and it didn't help that I was *enceinte* with Wesley."

"Passenger liners have made great strides in improving crossing speeds," Mr. Oakhurst replied. "I think you'll find the vessels themselves quite comfortable and well-staffed."

A very short while later, they arrived at their destination. The building that housed Arnold, Constable & Co. possessed a beautiful marble façade designed in a Second Empire style of architecture. Many luxury carriages were parked outside, hitched to glossy, well-tended horses. Uniformed drivers loitered in a group on the sidewalk, smoking and chatting as they awaited the return of their employers.

Belle decided Mr. Darling must have sent a message ahead, because almost as soon as they entered the department store, managers and salespeople were there to greet them. A team of well-dressed saleswomen whisked her and the duchess off in one direction, while a set of salesmen escorted Mr. Oakhurst and Wesley toward a broad staircase leading upward. Belle stole a glance at Wesley as he was led off, noticing he wore the same somewhat bewildered expression as he'd had in the hotel lobby. Again, she felt an inexplicable twinge of sympathy. *Papa was quite right to say I've been too hard on him. I wouldn't know how to behave if I were thrown into his circumstances.*

For the duration of the afternoon, Belle and Wesley's mother were treated to a private fashion show. Elegant ladies modeled the finest clothes from Europe, including couture gowns from the house of Worth. Wide-eyed, Belle drank in all the sumptuous fabrics, elaborate trimmings, beautiful embroidery, beading, lace, and ribbons. Her head swam at the vast array of accessories, such as hats, day and evening gloves, parasols, muffs, shoes, hosiery, and all manner of nightgowns and undergarments. One particular pink chiffon parasol made her ache with longing. *Perhaps I can save my pocket money and buy something less expensive when I'm next in London. A dainty parasol would make a marvelous addition to my trousseau.*

Once an entire rack was filled with new purchases, the duchess finally shook her head.

"I must stop buying things, otherwise Wesley will never let me hear the end of it." She lowered her voice and leaned closer to Belle. "It's been so long since I've had anything new to wear, I just can't help myself."

"You may need a few more trunks."

"You are right." The woman giggled. "Fortunately, we're in the right place to buy new luggage."

After the duchess signed the bill of sale, she donned one of her new, elegant walking dresses and left her old gown in the dressing room for the staff to donate to charity. When she appeared, clad in her new finery, she brought Belle a long, thin box.

"My dear Miss Oakhurst, this is for you."

Belle opened the lid and lifted a puffy, shell pink chiffon parasol from its cocoon of tissue paper. "Your Grace, it's ever so beautiful!"

"I saw how you'd admired it."

"You're terribly generous." Belle held the parasol as if it would float away. "Thank you!"

"Not at all. Your advice to me while I was shopping was invaluable and the parasol is my way of saying thank you."

"I'll treasure it."

In the luggage department, the duchess chose an array of handsome tapestry bags, Louis Vuitton leather cases, and travel trunks for herself and Wesley.

"Well, that's enough of that." The duchess wore a happy smile. "Although I've had a marvelous time, I've done quite enough shopping for now."

"I enjoyed myself, Your Grace," Belle said. "With your new gowns, you'll light up any room."

"You're a very sweet girl, Miss Oakhurst."

They descended to the ground floor, where Wesley and Mr. Oakhurst were waiting for them in a sitting area near the elevator. Wesley was wearing a new three-piece suit that fit him beautifully. A floppy bow tie and a black bowler hat gave him a dapper look, and his feet were encased in a pair of shiny leather shoes.

"Hullo, Miss Oakhurst." His slow smile made Belle's mouth to go dry. "Hullo, Mother! If it weren't for the fact you're with Miss Oakhurst, I might not have recognized you. You look absolutely splendid."

"As do you, Wesley." The duchess gave him an approving glance. "I like your suit."

"I'm glad." Wesley's brown eyes focused once more on Belle. "I hope *you* think my suit hits the mark?"

She fumbled for a response. "Oh, um, yes. Of course."

"The people here are quite helpful." Wesley grinned as he tugged on the cuff of his sleeve. "They even tailored this suit while we waited. The rest of my things will be delivered to the hotel."

"As will mine." His mother sighed. "I must admit I'm fatigued."

Mr. Oakhurst gestured toward the door. "The cab is waiting outside."

"If no one objects, I'd like to walk back." Wesley paused. "Would you join me, Miss Oakhurst? It's only four blocks."

Belle knew an unchaperoned walk with him was technically improper, but it wasn't as if they could really be alone in such a public place. "Do you mind, Papa?"

"All right, but don't be overlong, or I'll start to worry."

Mr. Oakhurst escorted the duchess to the cab, and Wesley and Belle continued down the street on foot. Although there was a spring in her step as she strolled along Fifth Avenue, Belle felt a slight twinge of guilt. *I'll most certainly not be including this excursion in my next letter to Errol!*

Fashionable matrons and their gentleman escorts sauntered along the granite and bluestone sidewalk, pausing every so often to look at window displays or greet friends. Many of the women carried umbrellas or parasols to shield them from the sun's rays, although nothing could block the August heat. Belle was pleased, nevertheless, that none of the passersby had a parasol as beautiful as hers. With a sense of pride, she unfurled her parasol and let it rest on one shoulder.

Wesley glanced over. "That's new, isn't it? It's very pretty."

"It was a gift from your mama." Belle smiled. "The duchess is very kind."

"I've not seen my mother this contented in a long while. I daresay she was glad to do it."

Belle cast about for another topic of conversation. "I'm grateful for the chance to see the city up close. Manhattan is so vibrant and new."

"There are parts of the city that are neither."

"Well…it's the same in London, of course. There's tremendous poverty alongside fabulous wealth."

"Are New York and London very similar then?"

"Not really, but they're both very exciting cities. You own a townhouse in Belgravia, did my father tell you?"

"I do?" Wesley paused. "Is Belgravia in London?"

She laughed. "Indeed, it's one of the more fashionable neighborhoods. I don't think your uncle used the townhouse very often because of his health, but I expect it's grand."

"Mother will be thrilled to hear it." A thoughtful expression came over Wesley's face. "I can't get over how different she looks in her new clothes. It's not just her appearance that's changed, however. It's the way she holds herself."

"Oh, yes! Your mama has been quite transformed." Belle gave Wesley a sidelong glance. "She's not the only one who has been changed. As Shakespeare wrote, 'the apparel oft proclaims the man.'"

"That's from *Hamlet*, I believe."

Belle's pace slowed momentarily. "I'm impressed."

"I *do* read, Miss Oakhurst. In fact, that's partly why I fell out of favor with my former friends in Brooklyn. They mistook my interest in learning for snobbery."

"Will you miss Brooklyn?"

"I'll miss baseball. The Brooklyn Bridegrooms may win the World's Championship Series this year, and I won't be around to see it."

"I really don't know anything about baseball, but I'm willing to learn."

"From what my father told me about rounders, baseball is like that."

They walked together in companionable silence for a while.

"If it's not too personal a question, may I inquire how your father died?" she asked finally.

"It's a horrible story. My father had a job teaching literature at New York University, but he wasn't satisfied with his wages. Over my mother's objections, he began to work weekends down at the rail-marine terminal, Palmer's Dock." He swallowed hard. "There was an accident."

Belle felt the blood drain from her face. "I'm so sorry, Wesley."

Unexpectedly, he laughed. "You just used my Christian name. May I use yours?"

"It's...it's Annabelle."

"You don't look like an Annabelle to me." Wesley frowned a moment. "May I call you Belle?"

She smiled. "That's what my mother used to call me."

"Then it's settled. Belle is a very pretty name, and it suits you. It's almost musical."

"Thank you."

"It's my turn." He paused "May I ask about your mother?"

"Her name was Lucinda Heathcliff Oakhurst, and she died about five years ago from a fever. It happened so quickly, I could scarcely believe it. Not a day goes by I don't wish her back."

Belle lingered outside a bookstore, which was situated inside a converted row townhouse. "Do you mind awfully if we go inside? There will be a library on the steamship, of course, but I'd like to buy a book or two just the same. I'm fond of reading."

"I'd enjoy a look around myself. I've never been able to buy anything I wanted before. It's an odd feeling, but very liberating."

Wesley held the shop door open for Belle, waiting as she let down her parasol.

She gave him a glance of approval. "You do know manners."

"More and more every day."

After they went inside, Wesley and Belle parted company.

He pointed with his thumb. "I'll be in the adventure section over there."

"All right." Belle nodded. "I'll let you know when I'm ready to leave."

On her way toward the ladies' corner, Belle noticed a large display of books entitled *Little Lord Fauntleroy* by Frances Hogdson Burnett. The brown cloth covering was stamped in red, black, and gold, and a charming young boy with long wavy curls was pictured under the title. Belle read the display card advertisement describing the plot, then picked up one of the books and went to look for Wesley.

He glanced up at her approach. "You're not done already, are you?"

"No, but have you seen this, Wesley? A little American boy discovers he's the heir to a title. That's a great deal like you."

Far from being delighted, however, he groaned. "Oh, yes, that book is all the rage in America. The last fellow to call me Lord Fauntleroy got his nose bloodied."

Belle grimaced. "Am I in mortal danger then?"

"Not from me."

"Good, since I'd like to read the story." She glanced at the book in his hand. "Jules Verne?"

"What can I say?" Wesley shrugged. "I've lived all my life in Brooklyn and I'm fond of adventure."

"Go to it, then."

Belle headed off to choose several dime novels to go with *Little Lord Fauntleroy*.

Wesley appeared at her elbow. "Are you finished?"

She quickly positioned *Little Lord Fauntleroy* on top of the stack. "I believe so, yes."

"Let me carry those to the register for you."

He reached for her books but she shook her head. "No! No, thanks, I mean. They aren't heavy at all."

Wesley gave her a shrewd glance. "You're blushing."

"I'm not! It's just hot in here."

"Belle Oakhurst, you're not as priggish as you pretend. If you think I can't tell you've got dime novels there, you're wrong. I recognize the bindings."

Belle lifted her chin. "Fond of them yourself, are you?"

"No, my mother was constantly borrowing the things from our landlady." He tilted his head to one side to read the titles of her books. "Although...if you wouldn't mind lending me *A Tale of Two Romances* when you're finished, perhaps we could discuss the finer points of its theme and characterizations."

She gave him a severe glance, but her lips could not repress a smile. "You're teasing me."

"Of course. I'm not going to judge what you read. Why would I?"

"My fiancé disapproves of books like these. I thought you may disapprove as well."

His eyebrows rose. "You're engaged? I didn't notice a ring."

"Errol asked me to marry him just before my father and I left for America, so he didn't have time to purchase one."

Wesley looked at her askance. "Even a Brooklyn boy knows to get a ring before the proposal."

Annoyance traveled down Belle's spine. "It's hardly any of your business."

His expression reflected amusement. "Well, that put me in my place, didn't it?"

She made a sound of disgust. "Now I understand why you get into so many fights. You have a way of baiting people."

"At least I don't tell them what to read."

"Hmph." Although Belle pretended otherwise, she had the distinct feeling Wesley Parker had just got the better of her.

When Belle returned to the hotel suite with Wesley a short time later, she discovered the formerly elegant sitting room was in disarray. Arnold, Constable & Company had already delivered the day's purchases, the duchess was directing where the bags, boxes, and parcels were to be put, and several hotel maids were on hand to hang up the new clothes and press out any wrinkles. Wesley and Belle exchanged an alarmed glance, stepped around the activity, and joined Mr. Oakhurst in the corner.

"Hello, Papa." Belle glanced over her shoulder. "We are in uproar, it seems."

"Yes, and I thought it best to stay out of the way." He greeted them with a smile. "I hope you both enjoyed your walk?"

"Thank you, Papa." She lifted her wrapped bundle. "Wesley and I bought some books."

"Wonderful." Mr. Oakhurst nodded in approval. "Your Grace, it's after five o'clock. Perhaps we can convince your mother to let the hotel employees sort this out while we go down to an early dinner?"

"Let's brook no argument," Wesley replied. "I'm famished."

To Wesley, the Fifth Avenue Hotel dining room was more reminiscent of a palatial ballroom or banquet hall than an intimate place to have a meal. The floor was covered with large black and white marble tiles laid out in a checkerboard pattern, and the fluted half-columns protruding from the walls added architectural interest. Elegant chandeliers hung around the perimeter from the high, paneled ceiling, shedding illumination on long communal dining tables draped with white linen tablecloths. The silken jacquard damask napkins at each place setting featured a central embroidered medallion with *Fifth Avenue Hotel* inscribed thereon.

Because the dining room had just opened for dinner, the Parkers and Oakhursts had a table largely to themselves. Not including dessert, there were seven courses to choose from, with several different kinds of soup, fish, boiled dishes, cold dishes, entrées, roasts, and vegetables. Unused to so much abundant food, Wesley agonized over the menu. Finally, he ordered chowder, an entrée of beef filet with mushrooms, mashed potatoes, and baked tomatoes.

Belle selected roast chicken for her entrée, along with sweet potatoes and stewed tomatoes. Mr. Oakhurst was delighted with his roast beef and potatoes, which looked so delicious that Wesley vowed to order it next time. A glance at his mother confirmed she was enjoying her lamb cutlets.

"You look somewhat restored, Mother," he said. "When Miss Oakhurst and I came in after our walk, you seemed distracted."

She breathed a happy sigh. "That's putting it politely. When I saw all our new things, I began to feel overwhelmed. Truly, I'm not sure how I'll manage the crossing by myself. I hope there will be a steward or stewardess on the ship whom I can call upon."

"There are both, but you don't have to manage alone, Your

Grace," Mr. Oakhurst said. "I've contacted the Mrs. A.E. Johnson Employment Agency on your behalf. If you'd like to interview candidates for a lady's maid, you can begin tomorrow after breakfast."

Delighted, Wesley laughed. "My mother is to have her own maid?"

"The agency also has several highly qualified valets for your consideration, Your Grace," Mr. Oakhurst said.

"A *valet?* Like Passepartout in *Around the World in Eighty Days?*" Wesley snorted. "That's silly."

"You must hire someone to attend to your wardrobe and personal needs," his mother said.

"You're not serious?" Wesley shook his head in dismay. "What if I don't want a valet? I can dress myself, thank you very much!"

Belle looked up from her dessert of vanilla ice cream and peaches. "The proper sort of valet can also advise you in matters of dress, etiquette, and even manners. You should interview the candidates carefully."

"*You* do the interviews then."

"It's not as easy as that," Belle said. "The employment agency will screen the candidates, but you must select the one who is most amiable."

Wesley focused his attention on his dish of custard. *I'm now obliged to hire someone to tie my shoes, am I?* His wardrobe might be made of the finest materials, but his pants still went on one leg after the other and he scarcely needed help with that. Furthermore, a valet sounded suspiciously like a nanny, to his way of thinking.

Being a gentleman is getting worse and worse as I go along.

CHAPTER 4
MR. CAVENDISH

A courier for the employment agency arrived at the Parkers' hotel suite the next morning with two separate folders—one for Wesley's mother and one for him. Each folder presented five different candidates for their consideration. Wesley groaned as he leafed through the valet résumés. The candidates each had a lengthy history of service, both in America and abroad, and a long list of references. Each was willing to travel at a moment's notice, and none had any family to speak of.

Wesley gave his mother a perplexed glance. "How am I supposed to interview these candidates?"

"Ask the valets about themselves. As they speak, observe their demeanor and mannerisms. Personally, I'm looking for someone cheerful."

"Cheerful would be good."

"Yes, and whomever we hire ought not be prone to seasickness."

He grimaced. "That would be helpful."

Wesley answered a knock on the door only to discover a matron with a hairy chin waiting in the hall.

She beamed at him. "Begging your pardon, but the agency sent me to interview for the lady's maid position."

"Oh, hullo." He stepped back. "Won't you come in?"

His mother conducted her interview in the sitting room while Wesley picked up one of his books to read. He had scarcely managed to finish the first page, however, when valet candidates began to arrive. Like clockwork, valets and lady's maids arrived every twenty minutes thereafter. Wesley listened with an air of polite attentiveness as the valets enumerated their qualifications. He asked a few questions but was unable to elicit much more than polite yes or no responses.

When the last candidate finally left, Wesley breathed a sigh of relief. "That's it for me." He picked up the Maillard's box, lifted the lid, and perused the bonbons nestled inside.

His mother was absorbed in reviewing the résumés and her notes. "Did you like anyone in particular?"

He shrugged. "They're all deadly dull, but I'm sure any one of them would do."

Matilda glanced over. "You're hiring a valet, not a companion. I spoke with two maids I liked a great deal. In fact, choosing between them will prove difficult."

"I hope you're not going to hire the first one. I found her hair very disconcerting." He tapped his chin.

"Oh, Wesley!"

He popped a chocolate covered cherry into his mouth just as someone knocked at the door. "Were you expecting anyone else?"

His mother blinked. "Why no. Perhaps it's Mr. Oakhurst."

"Good." He licked his fingers. "It's nearly lunch."

Wesley opened the door to discover a slender, dapper man

standing there, beautifully dressed in a gray frock coat, matching vest, and perfectly creased trousers. He held a crisp white paper in his right hand and a bowler hat in his left. His steel gray hair was impeccably groomed, as was his pointed goatee and waxed mustache, and the silver handle of his walking stick under his arm was shaped like the head of a bulldog. The man was so well turned out that Wesley assumed he was a hotel guest who'd arrived at his suite by mistake.

"May I help you with something, sir?" Wesley asked.

"My name is Mr. Cavendish, if you please." The man's English accent was cultivated and beautifully delivered. "I'm here about the valet position."

Wesley frowned. "The employment agency didn't tell me there was a sixth applicant."

"I'm not from the agency, I'm afraid. I heard about the opening through the grapevine and I thought I would apply in person. May I come in?"

"Well...all right." Wesley let Mr. Cavendish into the suite. "This is my mother, the Duchess of Mansbury, and I'm...well, I'm Wesley Parker."

Mr. Cavendish bowed to Wesley's mother in a regal fashion. "Good morning, Your Grace."

"Good morning." She rose. "Excuse me, Wesley. I'm going to freshen up before lunch."

As she left, Wesley could tell his mother seemed as puzzled by Mr. Cavendish as he was.

He jerked his head toward the desk. "Er...come this way, Mr. Cavendish."

They settled into their chairs and the valet offered Wesley his résumé. It seemed Mr. Cavendish had lengthy service as a valet to a baron in England, a Lord James Overton. Thereafter, he had an equally long history as a valet to a banker in New York.

Wesley peered at him. "Why did you leave England?"

"Despite my remonstrations to the contrary, Lord Overton insisted on dying. Since he'd left me a small sum in his will, I decided to travel around the world. The money ran out when my steamer reached port in New York, but as luck would have it, I met my future employer, Mr. Jenkins, on the voyage."

"Mr. Jenkins didn't die too, did he?"

Mr. Cavendish's mustache twitched. "That would indeed be an unusual coincidence! No, he dismissed me, and I've been seeking employment since."

"Why did he dismiss you?"

"He objected to my drinking."

The twinkle in the man's eyes made Wesley wonder if he was altogether serious...or sober. "How very unreasonable of him."

"Well you know how it is." Mr. Cavendish shrugged. "Some people have no tolerance for vice."

Wesley bit back a smile. "Do you have any other vices you'd like to mention?"

"I'm obsessively neat, a bit of a bookworm, and exceedingly economical. I suspect the latter part is why I never married. Oh, and I'm a sports enthusiast."

"Really? Do you like baseball?"

"It's only the best sport in the world! My only reluctance in taking employment overseas is that I'll miss the World's Championship Series this October."

"That's me as well. What's your team?"

"The Brooklyn Bridegrooms. I think they've got a fair shot of winning this year."

Wesley leaned forward. "Who do you like to start? Terry or Caruthers?"

"Terry by far and away has the most strikeouts."

"Yes, but Caruthers has more wins."

Wesley and Mr. Cavendish talked baseball with enthusiasm for the next few minutes, but a glimpse of the luggage in the corner of the sitting room suddenly reminded Wesley he was supposed to be conducting an interview.

"Oh...by the way, do you get seasick?"

"Not after the first day or so."

Wesley scribbled Mr. Oakhurst's name and room number on the résumé and slid it across the desk. "Mr. Cavendish, may I ask you to take your résumé to my solicitor? He can discuss your salary and terms of employment. You do understand we're sailing this Saturday?"

Mr. Cavendish picked up the résumé. "I'm prepared to leave immediately, Your Grace."

Wesley stood and shook the man's hand. After Mr. Cavendish left, Wesley couldn't suppress a pleased grin. *A seasick valet who likes to drink...why I might not see him the entire voyage. How extremely excellent!*

⁓

Mr. Oakhurst stepped out to visit the steamship ticket office after breakfast, so Belle wrote another letter to Errol. In it, she described her impressions of Manhattan, the Fifth Avenue Hotel, its décor, and the food. The letter was deadly dull, but she'd seen so little of the city she couldn't write anything more diverting. Belle took the letter down to the post office in the lobby and was rewarded with a cable from her fiancé expressing sentiments of undying affection. *It's so thoughtful of him to send me a cable. I'm so fortunate!*

After Belle returned to her room, however, she began to chafe at being cooped up indoors. She hadn't come all the way across the Atlantic to read books or write mundane letters, but neither could she sightsee by herself. Not only would it be improper, but it would also be dangerous to set off in a strange city alone. She picked up the *Visitor's Guide to the City of New York* and began to read the history behind Central Park.

When her father returned to the suite at last, Belle ran to meet him at the door. "Hello, Papa. Did you conduct your business?"

"Yes, indeed. I booked first class passage for the Duke of Mansbury and his mother, as well as passage for one lady's maid and one valet." A mischievous smile crept across his face. "And, I paid out of my own pocket to upgrade the both of us to first class as well."

"Not really!" Belle threw herself into her father's arms. "You're simply the best Papa, *ever*."

"How often will we get to travel with a duke, eh? We may as well enjoy ourselves, and we both can be more useful to the Parkers if we're on the same level with all the other saloon passengers."

Belle bit her lip. "Forgive me if my question is impertinent, but can we afford it?"

"We'll manage."

She twirled around in excitement. "I promise to be exceedingly useful, pleasant, and never say another cross word!"

"I wouldn't have it otherwise. Now as it's getting on toward noon—"

A smart tap on the door interrupted him, mid-sentence. Mr. Oakhurst opened the door to reveal a well-dressed gentleman with a walking stick in hand.

"Excuse me, but I'm looking for Mr. Oakhurst." The man's cultured English accent rolled off his tongue as easily as if he were a member of the royal family.

"You've found him."

The man sketched a bow. "My name is Mr. Cavendish, and I'm to be the Duke of Mansbury's new valet."

As Belle took a bite of pecan chicken salad, she decided to suggest an afternoon outing. Before she could speak, however, her father peered at Wesley across the table.

"Your Grace, are you quite sure you wish to hire this Mr. Cavendish? Since he didn't go through the agency, I may not have ample opportunity to properly check his references."

Wesley plucked a freshly baked roll from the basket near his plate. "I like him. Mr. Cavendish was far more interesting than the other candidates. Besides which, if he doesn't work out, I can always dismiss him."

"A bit difficult to do in the middle of the Atlantic," Mr. Oakhurst said.

"The handle of his walking stick was shaped like a bulldog." Belle giggled. "I liked him too."

"As did I," Matilda said. "Although Mr. Cavendish has a very disconcerting way of filling up the room for a man so slight of stature."

Mr. Oakhurst nodded. "I'll grant you, he's very charming and presented himself well."

"It's settled, then," Wesley said.

"All right, I'll do the best I can to reach his most recent employer." Mr. Oakhurst smiled at Wesley's mother. "Your Grace, have you chosen your lady's maid?"

"Mrs. Gertrude Neal will do quite nicely."

Wesley made a face. "She's not the hairy one, is she?"

The duchess sighed. "No, dear, Mrs. Neal was the third candidate I interviewed. She's a widow who has been supporting herself as a seamstress, lady's maid, and a companion. I thought we had a great deal in common."

"Well, then, for the next few hours I'll be much occupied."

Mr. Oakhurst gave Belle an apologetic glance. "Annabelle, you'll be at loose ends until dinner."

She fought to keep her countenance. "Yes, Papa."

Mr. Oakhurst finished his meal quickly and left. Belle gave the duchess a hopeful glance. "Your Grace, perhaps you'd like to take a walk in Madison Square Park after lunch?"

The older woman shook her head. "I wish I could, but I'm afraid I still have a few letters to write. My friends and family in England will be very interested in my change of circumstance. I can't wait to see them!"

Belle smiled, but her heart sank. *At this rate, all I'll be able to see of New York is my hotel room!* Wesley's mother folded her napkin, laid it at the side of her plate and rose from her chair.

Wesley rose too. "Would you like me to escort you upstairs, Mother?"

"Oh no, dear. I'm going to pop into The American Specialty Company next door to pick up some nice stationery for my letters. Enjoy dessert with Miss Oakhurst, why don't you?"

Wesley resumed his seat after his mother left and sank a fork into a piece of Lafayette cake. Glum, Belle pushed her rice pudding away. "I'm sick of being indoors."

"I'll go for a walk with you." He took a bite of cake.

"Thank you, but without a chaperone it really wouldn't be proper."

Wesley swallowed his cake and reached for a glass of water. "You're joking."

"No, I'm not."

"You didn't mind when we walked back to the hotel together from the department store."

"That's true, and I probably shouldn't have done it. My desire to get some exercise and see the city overcame my sense of propriety."

He looked at her askance. "Nonsense. We're leaving New

York very soon and your father is likely to be busy until then. My mother has an extensive family and absolutely loves to write letters. Unless you and I stick together, we won't be able to do anything worthwhile."

Without Wesley to escort her, it seemed she had few options. "Well…since Papa has worked for your uncle all these many years, I suppose we're practically cousins."

He beamed. "I couldn't have put it better myself. We can visit Madison Square Park this afternoon and Central Park tomorrow. Honestly, you'll be doing me a favor. I've never had any pocket money until now and I'd like to spend it on an outing or two."

She couldn't stop the grin spreading across her face. "All right. I'll go upstairs to write a note to Papa, and I'll meet you in the lobby in ten minutes."

Wesley's eyes twinkled. "Excellent."

∽

In her room, Belle scrawled a note to her father and retrieved her parasol. On the descending elevator, she rode alongside a girl about her age who was dressed in a pretty white gown with a blue sailor suit collar. Blonde corkscrew curls were tied back in a light blue satin bow, and she had the air of being very wealthy and pampered…like a princess. Out of the corner of her eye, Belle noticed the girl staring at her parasol. As they stepped from the elevator, the girl stopped her.

"Excuse me, but I've been admiring your parasol. Wherever did you get it?"

The girl's American familiarity was slightly disconcerting. "Erm…it was at a department store called A. Constable and Company."

"You're English! I adore your accent. Some of my cousins are English but I've never met them. Do you know, I'm—"

A woman standing near the front desk waved. "Louise, come along! The cab is waiting."

"Yes, Mama!" As the young woman turned back to Belle, her curls danced. "My name is Louise, as you could probably guess and that's my mother and elder brother." She pointed at a handsome young man lounging against a pillar. "Perhaps I'll see you again."

Belle curtsied. "Miss Annabelle Oakhurst."

Louise's cornflower blue eyes grew wide and she quickly bobbed up and down in a semblance of a curtsy. "I forgot how you English have such lovely manners. Well, good-bye!" The girl hastened off.

Wesley appeared at Belle's elbow. "Hello. Are you ready to go?"

She stared at him. "Where did you come from?"

"I was lurking over there." Wesley gestured toward a potted palm. "I couldn't help overhear your conversation just now. Perhaps you have a career giving lessons in etiquette?"

Belle wrinkled her nose. "I certainly hope not. That would be awfully dull."

As she entered Madison Square Park a few minutes later, Belle felt like skipping. She contained herself, partly because it would have been undignified to skip in front of Wesley and partly because the summer heat was oppressive. Nevertheless, the beautiful trees and fountains went a long way toward alleviating her discomfort.

The park attracted many residents and employees from the nearby East 26th Street brownstone homes and uniformed nannies with prams negotiated the wide pathways with practiced skill. Businessmen strolled along with walking sticks or umbrellas in hand and newspapers under their arm. Children cavorted on the grass under the watchful eyes of their mothers.

Under the shade of her parasol, Belle paused to admire the park's monuments and sculptures. One large, triangular, granite drinking fountain was cleverly designed to serve humans and horses alike. After she thoroughly explored the park alongside Wesley, they walked around the square itself. On Sixth Avenue, the Eden Musee lured them in for a pleasant hour of admiring a broad array of wax figures. Many world leaders were portrayed, and Belle gasped at the life-like wax representation of Queen Victoria.

"She looks so real, I almost want to curtsy." Belle laughed. "I wonder if Her Majesty knows she's a tourist attraction in England's former colony?"

Wesley grinned. "If she did, I daresay she'd demand a share in the proceeds."

As the afternoon sun dipped toward the west, they stepped into the confection shop known as Maillard's.

Belle breathed in the fragrant chocolate aroma. "Oh my! The smell alone is intoxicating!"

He nodded. "I've sampled the chocolates. Believe me, the taste is intoxicating too."

The store was such a visual feast that Belle didn't know where to look first. One of the soberly attired salesladies explained that the huge colorful painting decorating the ceiling was an allegorical piece painted by a French artist, Charles Louis Müller.

"Should I know who that is?" Wesley whispered to Belle.

She gazed at the angelic ladies and children overhead. "I'm afraid I'm at a loss too, but the painting *is* lovely."

Fancy, beribboned candy boxes in various shapes and colors were arranged on marble-topped counters or tall free-standing glass shelves. There were thousands of different candies to choose from, from chocolate bars to bonbons, vanilla chocolates, and ornamental confections. Wesley chose a box of milk chocolate-covered caramels while Belle picked out a small box of chocolates for Errol and a paper bag of chocolate covered marshmallows.

"To share with Papa." She gave Wesley a wink as she reached into her reticule for money.

He produced his wallet. "I'll buy those for you."

"No, thank you." Her reply was a little sharper than she had intended. "I'm sorry, but it's not proper for you to buy me a gift."

"I've put my foot into it once again?" Wesley shook his head. "You didn't complain when I paid the entrance fee at the wax museum!"

"That was a mutual outing, not a gift."

His brows knit together. "I don't see the difference."

"*I* know the difference, and that's what is important."

They paid for their purchases separately and left the shop.

"I'm never going to remember what's supposedly proper and what isn't," Wesley grumbled.

"There's a gentlemen's guide book to etiquette in my father's library. I'll lend it to you as soon as I return home."

He drew back. "Someone wrote a whole book on etiquette?"

"There are several books on the subject, for both ladies and gentlemen." She favored him with a smile. "Don't despair, Wesley. You're not wholly without manners."

"I suppose by that you mean to say I'm not completely hopeless?"

"Far from it!"

"So we're still planning to visit Central Park tomorrow?"

Belle's smile broadened. "If my father gives his permission, then yes, I'd love to."

CHAPTER 5
CENTRAL PARK

At dinner, Wesley consumed a large bowl of consommé to take the edge off his hunger, but he was looking forward to the roast beef and rice with a side of asparagus and potato salad. Mr. Oakhurst, to his right, dipped his spoon into a fragrant bowl of julienne soup.

"Your Grace, I'm having some difficulty confirming Mr. Cavendish's references," he said. "His most recent employer, Mr. Jenkins, embarked a few days ago on an ocean liner bound for Europe."

Wesley glanced up. "That's bad luck."

"I *did* manage to speak with Mr. Jenkins' housekeeper, a Mrs. Thumb. She confirmed Mr. Cavendish's employment and indicated he was extremely charming, well-liked by the staff, and performed his valet duties in an exemplary fashion. Unfortunately, Mr. Cavendish told Mrs. Thumb he was dismissed due to his fondness for drink."

Wesley shrugged. "Mr. Cavendish told me that during the interview."

Matilda glanced up from her mock turtle soup, wide-eyed. "You knew and hired him anyway?"

"I thought perhaps Mr. Jenkins drove him to it." Wesley chuckled. "I won't be nearly as difficult."

Belle frowned. "Be sensible, Your Grace. Wouldn't it be better to hire a valet whose faculties are unimpaired?"

At her use of his title, Wesley slid Belle a withering glance across the table. "Mr. Cavendish had most of his faculties during our interview, *Miss Oakhurst*, and I could scarcely smell any whiskey at all."

She lifted her chin. "You're joking."

"Of course I am. The fellow was completely sober."

Mr. Oakhurst continued. "At any rate, I *did* manage to exchange cables about Mr. Cavendish with Lord Henry Overton."

"Lord Henry Overton?" Wesley shook his head. "I'm sorry, who was that again?"

"He's the younger brother of Mr. Cavendish's previous employer, Lord James Overton. Although Lord Henry did not recall Mr. Cavendish specifically, he said his brother had been exceedingly arrogant and despicable. It was his opinion that if Mr. Cavendish managed to work for his brother more than a fortnight, he was worth his weight in gold."

Wesley grinned. "There you have it. I was right to hire him, wouldn't you say?"

Belle snickered. "So Lord James Overton was just as horrible as the tenth Duke of Mansbury?"

Mr. Oakhurst lifted one eyebrow. "Annabelle, think about the company you're with."

Her cheeks flushed scarlet as she flicked a guilty glance first at Matilda and then at Wesley. "I beg your pardon. I shouldn't have said that about one of your family members. It was frightfully rude."

Wesley's gaze lingered on Belle, whose creamy complexion was rendered brilliant by her blush. "It's all right, Miss Oakhurst. My father didn't like Uncle Septimus any more than you did."

Belle lowered her gaze to her lap. "Nevertheless, I do apologize. I didn't know what was in the duke's heart, and I shouldn't have said it. I understand he wished to reconcile with his brother, so perhaps he came to regret his previous dealings with him."

"Don't make yourself uneasy, dear." As Matilda reached over to touch Belle's sleeve, her eyes grew misty. "I resented Septimus more than I can express. Had he shared just a small portion of his estate with his brother, Frederic wouldn't have been forced to make his living in America."

Wesley hastened to change the subject. "Mother, did you finish writing your letters?"

She sighed. "No, and if I don't get them written and posted, we may arrive in England before *they* do. I'm going to be quite busy tomorrow."

Belle's expression brightened. "And you, Papa? His Grace and I would like to visit Central Park. Are you free?"

Her father frowned. "I'm afraid not. After I visit the employment agency in the morning to complete our arrangements with Mrs. Neal, I'm heading to the steamship ticket office to reserve our deck chairs. Then I'm lunching with an old friend of mine who teaches international law at Columbia."

Wesley exchanged a glance with Belle. "I suppose we're on our own again."

Her eyes grew mischievous. "We'll just have to make the best of it."

THE NEXT MORNING AFTER BREAKFAST, Wesley's mother returned to her room to finish her letters, Mr. Oakhurst set off for the employment agency, and Wesley hired a cab to take him and Belle through Central Park. They entered the park through Scholars' Gate at Fifth Avenue and East 59th Street and headed north. As they drove along, Belle was effusive about the large bodies of water, the landscaping, and the monuments.

"There's even a riding path around Croton reservoir." She smiled. "It reminds me of Rotten Row in Hyde Park."

Wesley laughed. "Rotten Row, did you say? That sounds dreadful."

"It's not really rotten. Long ago the riding track was called *Route du Roi*, which eventually became known as Rotten Row."

"I expect I'll see it for myself before too long."

After the cab reached the northern end of the park, the drive meandered in a looping pattern until the carriage faced south again.

Belle gasped and pointed at a picturesque folly, barely visible through the trees. "What is that?"

Wesley followed her gaze. "Belvedere Castle. It's an observatory."

"May we see it up close?"

"We can walk there, if you don't mind the exercise. After we make a tour of the park, we'll make our way back."

A few minutes later, Belle spied a flock of black and white sheep grazing on the grassy lawn. "There are sheep in the middle of the city!"

He chuckled. "Yes. That red brick complex with the peaked gables is the Sheepfold."

"How absolutely charming!"

Belle's hazel green eyes were sparkling, and her smile revealed even, white teeth. *She's really very pretty—when she's not scolding me or being a prig.* The pink and white dress she wore had puffy sleeves with small pleats, an elaborate ruffled front, and a high collar with a large bow at the back of the neck. Her curly, nutmeg-colored hair was tucked under a white straw sailor's hat, the brim of which was bound with a wide, pink grosgrain ribbon. The whole effect was one of dainty femininity, and Wesley found himself watching her rather than the scenery. Unfortunately, she noticed his stare.

"Is something wrong?"

"Oh...not at all." Wesley waved to get the driver's attention. "Drop us off at the carriage concourse at Cherry Hill, won't you?"

"Yes, sir."

The carriage circled past the pond, and a short while later, the driver brought the cab to a halt next to Central Park Lake. While Wesley paid the driver, Belle climbed down from the cab and scampered down a path toward the water. Chuckling, he struck off in pursuit. Swans and ducks were clustered near water's edge, hoping for breadcrumbs from passersby. Further out, rowboats scooted across the glassy surface, propelled by young gentlemen attempting to impress their female companions with their athletic prowess.

Belle pointed. "Are we crossing that enchanting bridge?"

"Yes. It's the only way to Belvedere Castle from here."

She danced up the path. "Come on!"

Wesley chuckled as he hastened after her. He'd been at this spot with his parents before, but it had never seemed as magical as it did right now, through Belle's eyes.

∽

At the center of Bow Bridge, Belle and Wesley leaned out over against the cast-iron railing to watch the water rippling on the surface of the lake.

"I'm so glad you brought me here," she said. "Do you suppose those men in the rowboats brought their lady friends here to propose?"

"It's entirely possible. Let's watch to see which boat tips over when the gentleman gets down on one knee."

She laughed. "I admire your sense of humor. Errol is always so dignified."

"Errol...is that your fiancé?"

"Yes. Sir Errol Blankenship. He's a knight."

"Does he have a white horse?"

"What?" She gave him a reproachful glance. "Oh, you're joking with me again."

"A bit." Wesley shrugged. "No offense meant."

"None taken. I may seem serious on the outside, you see, but I like to laugh. As Papa would say, I'm frequently filled with flights of fancy."

"What marvelous alliteration! I solemnly salute your sagacious soliloquy."

"Aha! I pay homage to the haste of your homily."

Wesley doffed his derby hat and bowed from the waist. "I'm decidedly defeated by your deft debate."

"You can't be defeated until we conquer the castle together." Belle made a gesture of invitation. "Lead on!"

They made their way to the castle and climbed to the observation deck with a view of the reservoir and surrounding park. Belle admired the whimsical gray granite structure, composed of many towers and wooden pavilions.

"It's like something from a fairy tale," she said.

Wesley looked at her askance. "Surely you've seen a great many castles in England?"

"A fair few, but none so little and charming. Belvedere seems designed to draw people in, whereas real castles are designed to keep people out."

The small breeze Wesley had enjoyed earlier disappeared and he fanned himself with his derby. "I'm beginning to feel the August heat in earnest. If you'd like, we can go to the Casino for lunch."

"Casino?"

"It's a restaurant," he explained. "We can get refreshments there."

Her expression brightened. "Let's do."

They retraced their steps over Bow Bridge and turned onto a path alongside the lake to the east. The Bethesda Fountain lay ahead, the focal point of the lower terrace. In the middle of the fountain, a bronze, winged angel stood on a pedestal to bless the water flowing down to the large round pool. Children clustered at the edge of the fountain, trailing little fingers in the cool, refreshing water.

"This is a very beautiful setting." Belle smiled. "It looks like a palace."

He chuckled. "I wonder if anyone would notice if I took off my shoes and waded in the pool?"

She bit back a smile. "I wouldn't try it. Rumor has it the palace guards can be quite severe."

"Capital offense, eh? Then I'll just have to settle for a cold drink."

Wesley escorted Belle up the expansive stone steps to the upper terrace, where the concert grounds and mall spread out under a long canopy of trees. Despite the heat, the mall was filled with people from all walks of life, from recent immigrants to American aristocrats.

"This is the place to see and be seen, I think," Belle said.

"Yes. It's like a big democratic festival, isn't it?"

A few feet away, a little girl with long dark hair began to wail. Her parents tried, without success, to soothe her as best they could. Belle couldn't understand their language, but she guessed they were of Italian descent.

"Excuse me a moment, Belle," Wesley said.

He hastened over to the family and began to converse with them in their native tongue. The little girl's tears dried up as he spoke, and the father nodded in understanding.

"*Grazie, giovanotto. Grazie mille.*"

Smiling, the mother took her daughter by the hand and the family made their way down the mall.

Belle stared at Wesley as he returned to her side. "You speak Italian?"

"Only a little. I'm sure I butchered the language something awful, but the little girl wanted to find the carrousel. Her parents were lost and about to give up when I told them where to find it." He grimaced. "At least, I hope that's what I said."

"That was very kind, Wesley. How do you know the language?"

"With so many Italians in Brooklyn, you learn a little of their lingo if you want to get along. I used to be friendly with everybody until I committed an unpardonable sin."

"Which was?"

"The Irish discovered I was related to the English aristocracy. After that, I became an outsider to most everyone except the Italians, who didn't seem to care. To them, I was *paisan*—a friend."

A path from the upper terrace led to a charming stone cottage known as the Central Park Casino. Many expensive carriages were parked out front, on a circular gravel driveway. As Wesley escorted Belle up the few steps to the restaurant entrance, she lowered her voice.

"I take it this is a rather fashionable place?"

He whispered back. "Indeed it is. They'll let *you* in, certainly, but they may bar me at the door."

"Don't worry. I'll vouch for you."

The restaurant wasn't that large, but many diners sat outside on the veranda or under the Wisteria pergola at the western edge of the site. As it had grown very hot outside, Belle chose to sit in the cool restaurant and sip iced lemonade. When the waitress returned to take their food order, Belle ordered a light luncheon of fresh stuffed tomatoes and chicken salad. Wesley, on the other hand, ordered a more substantial meal consisting of tenderloin steak, fried potatoes, spinach, stewed mushrooms, and cucumber salad.

While they waited for their food to be served, Belle glanced around. The foliage from many potted palms gave the place a garden appeal, and despite the resplendent patrons, the establishment had a comfortable atmosphere.

She gave a sigh of contentment. "Thank you for today, Wesley. I feel very fortunate to have visited Central Park with you."

A sense of pleasure took root somewhere in the center of his chest and spread throughout his body. "I've enjoyed myself as well."

"My father informs me that tomorrow after breakfast, Mr. Cavendish and your mother's new lady's maid will report to your suite."

"What for?"

"To pack your trunks. Most of them must be sent to the ship ahead of time."

Wesley's heart sank. "Everything's changing so quickly. It's difficult to believe I'm really leaving America."

She studied him. "It must be disconcerting, I can imagine."

"Please don't misunderstand me, Belle. You mustn't think for a moment that I'm not grateful. I'm fully aware how lucky I am, and I'm not complaining one bit. It's just that I feel a little like the proverbial bull in a china shop."

She nodded. "I sympathize with you, truly I do. Furthermore, I regret being rude when we first met. It was unpardonable."

"Not really. I expect I *did* look like a delinquent." Wesley tapped the fading bruise remaining under one eye. "Still do, as a matter of fact."

"Not so."

He cocked his head. "How do I compare to the society gentlemen in your circle then? Do I pass muster?"

Belle picked up her glass of lemonade. "Erm...I daresay you won't be able to escape the attentions of debutantes all over England, even if you wished to."

He felt his face flush. "I'm sorry, I was referring to my manners."

"Oh, I'm sorry." Belle averted her gaze. "Manners, moving in society, and the rituals of courtship are inextricable, Wesley. Your American birth is...intriguing. I wouldn't worry overmuch how you may compare to anyone else."

In the next moment, she glared at the ceiling fan.

"Are you cold?" Wesley asked. "We can move away from the fan if you like."

Belle stopped scowling. "Oh, er, no, thanks. I was just thinking how much Errol would enjoy it here. I'll be sure to tell him about this restaurant in my next letter."

CHAPTER 6
FOLLY

As Belle and Wesley escaped the summer heat inside the Metropolitan Museum of Art, she couldn't help but compare Wesley to Errol. Where the new duke was enthusiastic, Errol was soulful. Wesley could be playful, but Errol was uniformly decorous. Both men were handsome in different ways, but Errol's perfectly groomed brown hair had never invited her touch. By contrast, she was constantly stifling the urge to push Wesley's tousled curls back from his forehead. For the first time, she was forced to consider whether or not Sir Errol Blankenship might be wanting.

Her feelings of disloyalty weighed heavily upon her mind, but she allowed her enjoyment of the afternoon to take precedence. When the clock struck five, Wesley hailed a cab to drive him and Belle back to their hotel.

With a happy smile, she relaxed against the upholstered carriage seat. "I can't tell you when I've had a more wonderful day."

"Nor I, even though it's as hot as blazes." He mopped his brow with his handkerchief.

"By Monday evening, you may wish the warm temperatures back again. The Atlantic Ocean can be very cold and foggy. At a different time of year, we would even see an iceberg or two."

"Really?" Wesley paused. "Is there much to do on board the ship?"

"Although there is usually some form of entertainment at night, passengers are expected to amuse themselves during the day. Papa brought me a cabin brochure from the Inman Line ticket office. The *City of New York* is quite large, with a library and gentlemen's smoking lounge. The ship is designed to hold over five hundred first class and two hundred second class passengers. It can also carry one thousand in steerage, but we won't have any steerage passengers on the eastbound voyage."

"Did you get seasick on the crossing?"

"No, but many people did." She shuddered. "It was horrible for them, and even the most stalwart traveler can become ill in rough seas. At any rate, the *City of New York* is much larger than the ship my father and I took from Liverpool, so perhaps we'll feel the movement of the ocean less."

"Before the Brooklyn Bridge opened, I used to take the ferry to Manhattan with my father. Neither of us became queasy, but I expect an ocean voyage is different."

"A vast deal different and a great deal longer. Hopefully, the other passengers will prove amiable. If so, we'll arrange a card game or some other entertainment." She paused. "My father thinks you should learn to dance."

"Dance?"

"Perhaps you already know how."

"There are very few fancy parties in the Brooklyn neighborhood where I grew up."

"Every gentleman should know how to dance." Her eyes flickered to his profile. "I can help you learn to waltz or polka, but we'll need more people to form a quadrille or practice a promenade."

He met her gaze. "I hope you won't laugh at me if I prove to have two left feet."

"I expect you'll be a wonderful dancer."

"What makes you think so?"

She flushed with embarrassment. "The movements of your arms and hands are quite graceful."

Wesley cleared his throat. "You're trying to prop up my confidence."

"Not at all, I assure you. But if you'd rather not—"

"No, no, I didn't say that. I'm merely reluctant to make a fool of myself. If you're game, then so am I."

Her shoulders relaxed. "Good. When our voyage gets underway, we'll find a quiet spot to practice…assuming neither of us becomes queasy."

~

As Wesley changed his clothes for dinner that night, he hummed under his breath. The thought of learning to dance with Belle was followed by apprehension…as well as the thrill of anticipation. Despite her encouragement, he felt about as graceful as a newborn colt. He brushed his hair vigorously, in a fruitless attempt to flatten the curl.

When he emerged from his room, he discovered Matilda dressed in a lovely deep purple satin gown.

"You look splendid, Mother."

"Thank you." She focused on his neckwear. "You only *imagine* you don't need a valet. Let me help."

Her skirt rustled as she crossed over to retie his silk four-in-hand. Wesley tried to stand still as she fussed with him.

"Mr. Oakhurst has asked Belle to teach me how to dance. We're going to practice on the ship."

"That's a splendid notion. I must say, the Oakhursts are terribly thoughtful." Matilda finished with his tie and brushed off his lapels. "Now you look perfect." She peered at him. "I hope you aren't becoming too attached to Miss Oakhurst."

Wesley covered his surprise with a bewildered sort of laugh. "Why would you say such a thing? Belle—I mean Miss Oakhurst—and I just met."

His mother's shrewd eyes seemingly missed nothing.

"Oh dear. Wesley, she's a lovely girl and very pretty, but she's engaged to be married."

"I know that. She's mentioned her fiancé several times."

"After we're ensconced at Caisteal Park, you'll likely see each other infrequently, if at all."

"She can't possibly live more than a few miles away."

"Geography isn't the point." Matilda sighed. "Let's not quarrel, dear. Enjoy visiting with Miss Oakhurst. She'll be married soon enough, and after you taste the delights of society, you'll forget her altogether."

Out of respect for his mother, Wesley bit back a sharp retort. He escorted her down to the dining room, where they met the Oakhursts for the evening meal. Belle had changed into a gown of green silk with dainty pink rosettes scattered across the fabric. When she smiled, the sight of her dimples made Wesley's stomach lift. *Forget Belle? Impossible!*

∼

AFTER BREAKFAST THE FOLLOWING MORNING, Mrs. Neal and Mr. Cavendish reported for work. Wesley was amused to see Mr. Cavendish had traded his bulldog walking stick for one with a nifty compass embedded in the handle. As his mother and her new lady's maid discussed which gowns and accessories would be needed on the voyage, Wesley showed his valet the new clothes he'd purchased.

"Very nice." Mr. Cavendish picked up Wesley's old top hat. "But this won't do at all."

"That hat was my father's. I bought a derby instead."

"And a perfectly marvelous hat it is, for New York City. Bowler hats, as they are called in England, are fine for the banking set, but not for a duke. Furthermore, styles in top hats have changed from your father's day. We're going to have to nip down to the hat shop to purchase something more suitable."

Mr. Cavendish reached into the valise he'd brought with him and produced a set of barber's tools in a leather case. "First, however, you must have a haircut."

Wesley peered at the implements, taken aback. "Do you take your scissors everywhere you go?"

"Not usually, but I observed your hair was unkempt when I was here for the interview and therefore came prepared."

The valet brought a chair into the bathroom and bade him take a seat. After he draped a towel around Wesley's shoulders, Mr. Cavendish styled his hair with aplomb. Wesley turned his head to admire his new haircut in the mirror.

"You tamed the curl!"

"Yes, indeed. There's no excuse for you to go around looking like a Teeswater ram."

"Mr. Cavendish, did Mr. Oakhurst warn you that I'm new to all this aristocracy business? I only found out about the title a few days ago."

"He did happen to mention that, Your Grace. I'll do all I can to smooth your transition. And please, call me Cavendish."

Wesley accompanied Cavendish to the Knox Hat Shop on the ground level of the hotel. After the clerk took a measurement of Wesley's head, he produced a black silk top hat with a ribbed band encircling the brim. The crown was very slightly larger than the brim, lending the hat a jaunty look.

"It's the very latest fashion," the clerk explained.

The hat fit perfectly, and Wesley was pleased with the way it sat on his newly cropped hair. "I like it."

"We'll take two," Cavendish told the salesclerk. "If one should meet with an unfortunate accident, we don't want to be caught short."

Wesley decided to wear the hat out of the shop. His derby was packed in the hatbox, along with the spare top hat, and Wesley paid the bill without even wincing at the total. Cavendish carried the package with him as he and Wesley returned to the suite. Matilda was writing a letter at the desk while Mrs. Neal was packing garments nearby as carefully as Easter eggs.

Mrs. Neal spared Cavendish a worried glance. "The porter will be calling at three o'clock, Mr. Cavendish, to pick up the large trunks bound for the steamship. You need to mark which trunks you want in the cabin, and which will be checked into the baggage hold."

Cavendish gave her a stately bow. "Thank you, Mrs. Neal, we'll be ready." He turned to Wesley. "I have this in hand, Your Grace, if there is somewhere else you'd like to be this afternoon. Perhaps you can arrange an outing with Miss Oakhurst?"

Wesley was impressed by the man's shrewdness. "If you insist, Cavendish. I'll go check with her at once." He paused. "And thanks."

Wesley backed out of the room and strode down the hall toward the elevator, eager to show off his new hat to Belle.

Cavendish has proven to be invaluable so far. Perhaps I need a valet after all.

⁓

Belle sat in the sitting room reading *A Tale of Two Romances*, but her mind kept wandering. She glanced at her father, who was sorting through a sheaf of papers at the desk.

"Papa, when you're finished, may we visit the Statue of Liberty? I'd love to see it up close."

"I'm afraid I can't just abandon my duties. What if the Parkers should need me for some last-minute details?"

Belle swallowed her disappointment. "Of course, Papa. I understand."

A knock sounded at the door, and she jumped to her feet. "I'll get it."

Belle opened the door to discover Wesley standing in the hallway. He removed his hat and bowed. "May I come in?"

She beamed. "Certainly."

As he entered the room, Belle got a better look at him. "You've had a haircut!"

"And purchased a new hat." He gave it a flourish. "Cavendish has acquitted himself admirably on both accounts."

Mr. Oakhurst rose. "How may I help you, Your Grace?"

"Since my valet is packing my trunks, I have the rest of the day to myself. Would you and Miss Oakhurst care to do some sight-seeing?"

"What a capital idea, Your Grace!" Belle exclaimed. "Do you suppose your mama would enjoy a visit to the Statue of Liberty?"

"I don't see why not." Wesley smiled. "Mrs. Neal seems to

be on top of things and I think a little fresh air would do my mother a world of good."

Mr. Oakhurst nodded. "I'm at your service, Your Grace."

"In that case, my mother and I will meet you in the lobby shortly." Wesley headed for the door.

Belle did a pirouette and danced toward her room. "I'll get my hat."

∽

From the Battery, the Oakhursts and the Parkers boarded one of the hourly ferries to Bedloe Island. The ferry wasn't particularly full, so they had their pick of seats. Wesley and Belle sat together toward the prow of the vessel, watching the Statue of Liberty grow closer. Every so often, Belle glanced over her shoulder toward her father and the duchess, who were deep in conversation several rows back.

She met Wesley's gaze. "Was it difficult to convince your mother to come today?"

"A little. After Mrs. Neal reassured my mother she would complete her tasks well in advance, however, my mother couldn't refuse."

"Your timing was impeccable. I'd just asked my father if he would accompany me here today, but he declined."

"Why?"

"For him, this isn't a vacation. He works for you, Wesley, and he wanted to make sure your needs were met." She giggled. "Fortunately, your needs have happily coincided with mine."

"I'm very glad. This is my first visit to Bedloe Island."

She drew back. "How can that be?"

"My father had planned to take us after the Statue of Liberty was dedicated, but he died before we could go."

Empathy coursed through her veins. "What a shame."

Almost of their own volition, her gloved fingers reached out. She meant only to give his hand the briefest of squeezes, but he captured her fingers in his and held them fast. Belle locked eyes with Wesley for several seconds before she remembered to breathe.

With an apologetic smile, she withdrew her hand. "I'm sorry, but—"

"Oh, yes, I know. It's not proper," he murmured.

Belle stared straight ahead as she willed her heart to quit racing.

∼

Wesley wished the warmth of Belle's hand would not fade from his fingertips quite so quickly. *I shouldn't have done that. She's engaged, after all. And yet...had she felt nothing, wouldn't she have pulled away more quickly?* Perhaps Belle was too polite—or too concerned for her father's continued employment—to rebuke him openly. *I've put her in an awkward position, haven't I? I should be more guarded and considerate in my behavior toward her.*

He cleared his throat. "Forgive me if I took advantage of your kindness just now. It won't happen again."

A long silence followed his words.

"Thank you, Wesley," she said finally.

Her response was so soft that he nearly missed it. Wesley couldn't bring himself to look at Belle's face, for fear he would see relief in her hazel eyes.

CHAPTER 7
THE SS CITY OF NEW YORK

A trio of seagulls circled overhead as the ferry pulled alongside the dock at Bedloe Island. To Belle's relief, the awkward tension between her and Wesley seemingly dissipated as they joined the short queue to disembark. After they set foot on the dock, they practically raced toward Lady Liberty with coltish glee. Mr. Oakhurst and the duchess followed at a more leisurely pace, reuniting with their offspring in the observation balcony at the top of the pedestal.

"It's a splendid view, but I'm rather keen to climb all the way to the top." Belle gave her her companions a hopeful smile. "Would anyone care to join me?"

"That's quite a climb." Mr. Oakhurst was wide-eyed. "It was one hundred ninety-two steps to this observation deck and there are one hundred sixty-two additional steps to the crown!"

She shrugged. "Then we've already done the hard part."

The duchess sighed. "If only I were filled with your youthful energy! I'm content to wait for you right here."

Mr. Oakhurst chuckled. "And I'm content to keep you company, Your Grace."

"I'm happy to make the climb, Miss Oakhurst," Wesley said.

Belle giggled conspiratorially. "Somehow I knew you would be."

They joined a small group who was assembling to ascend. As four children and two men filtered into the stairwell, Wesley made a sweeping gesture with his arm.

"After you, Belle."

"Oh, no. Unless he's escorting her on his arm, a gentleman always precedes a lady on the stairs when ascending and follows her when descending."

He peered at her. "More rules for gentlemen I've never heard of? This process of civilizing me requires constant vigilance."

"The forging of a magnificent sword always requires heat and a hammer, but I'm certain the results will be worth it." Belle winked. "After you, Wesley."

∽

A sensation of light and warmth filled Wesley's chest as he mounted the narrow metal steps. *Belle just compared me to a magnificent sword, didn't she?* He loped upward at a good clip until reality began to stake a claim on his muscles...and his thoughts. *Best not to read too much into anything. Nevertheless, it must mean Belle has put what happened on the ferry in the past. What a resilient and sweet temperament she has!* He continued to climb more deliberately, pausing every so often to listen for the sound of her footsteps on the stairs. Excited chatter from children echoed within the statue, from higher up on the staircase.

About halfway, he stopped climbing and peeked over the side of the spiral.

"Hullo down there!" he called out.

His voice reverberated against the copper sheeting that formed Lady Liberty's robes. Two spirals below, Belle leaned over the railing and turned her face toward him. With a merry smile, she waved.

"How do you climb so fast?" she replied.

"Why are you so slow?"

"It's these wretched skirts. But fear not, I'm right behind you!"

Her head disappeared and Wesley resumed his upward trek. When he reached the small observation deck a few minutes later, perspiration was rolling down his forehead. The closeness of the quarters forced him to remove his top hat and even then he had to take care not to hit his head. He longed to shrug off his jacket but dared not, lest the dampness from his exertions be revealed. Fortunately, a crisp handkerchief was tucked in his pocket, which he used to mop his brow.

Belle joined him. "Oh, my, that's indeed a prodigious climb…and it's awfully hot in here, isn't it?" She withdrew a lacy swatch of fabric from her reticule and patted the moisture from her upper lip. "I must look a fright."

"I resemble a cat in a rainstorm. You, however, are merely glowing."

"That's a very gallant thing to say, Wesley."

A semi-circle of twenty-five windows beckoned them near. As they found an unoccupied spot, Wesley gasped with pleasure. "What a gorgeous view!"

"I had no idea how high up it would be!" Belle's voice was infused with wonder. "You can see forever from up here."

As the children became bored and began to filter back down the stairs with their fathers, Belle and Wesley were left alone. They moved from window to window, drinking in the view of Manhattan, Brooklyn, and Governor's Island. Sailboats and steamships painted a charming picture as they glided merrily through the sparkling harbor below.

"We must remember to wave at Lady Liberty as we go past tomorrow." Belle's eyes shone with excitement. "Are you looking forward to setting sail?"

"Yes, although the prospect seems a bit unreal. Less than a week ago, I was a poor man from Brooklyn, wondering how I could possibly afford a tin of cookies. Now, I'm traveling first class to England, with a valet no less. My mother, however, is taking all of it in stride."

"I believe my mother and yours would have had much in common. They both gave up a great deal when they married, but did so happily."

He gave Belle a puzzled glance. "What do you mean?"

"Your mother married Lord Frederic Parker, knowing his inheritance was likely to be nothing. In my mother's case, her father was a gentleman of extensive property. When she married, my grandfather cut her off entirely. As a result, I've never met anyone from that side of the family."

Wesley was taken aback. "How unfair!"

She shrugged. "Many people often pay a steep price for going against their family's wishes. It's more common than you may think, actually."

"I can't imagine why they didn't welcome Mr. Oakhurst with open arms. He's reliable, steady, and everything amiable."

"Thank you, Wesley. Had my father been titled or exceedingly rich, my grandparents would have adored him. Even so, don't feel too sorry for Mama. She loved my father unconditionally and was quite happy." Belle smiled. "Shall we go back down?"

"I take it you've no interest in climbing the ladder into the torch?"

Belle laughed. "Until women may wear trousers, I'm afraid not!"

The thought made him smile. "That's not terribly likely, is it?"

"I can't imagine such a scandalous fashion ever catching hold, but if it does I'll be the first to buy a pair."

∽

Morning had long since dawned, but Wesley lay in bed on his stomach. The previous day's exertions had transformed his legs into leaden weights so exquisitely painful he was unable to turn himself over without groaning. The door to his bedchamber opened, and someone entered the room. Moments later, the drapes were pulled back.

"I've ordered breakfast sent to your suite, Your Grace," Cavendish said. "Rise and shine."

Wesley spoke into his pillow. "I can't."

"Why not?"

He managed to turn his head. "I climbed the Statue of Liberty yesterday and I can't move."

"Ah. Well, I didn't come away from my travels without resources."

Cavendish removed his jacket, hung it in the closet, and rolled up his sleeves. Wesley suddenly found the covers whisked from the bed.

"What are you doing?"

"I'm going to give you a massage using ancient techniques I learned in China."

"A *what?*"

"Just relax, Your Grace."

Ten minutes later, Wesley rolled out of bed in shock. "I can move my legs again! Cavendish, you're a marvel!"

"No, I'm a valet. There's a large difference." With a twitch of his waxed mustache, Cavendish rolled his sleeves down and retrieved his jacket. "I believe I hear the breakfast cart arriving. If you'll don your dressing gown, I'll set up the meal in the sitting room."

Wesley gaped as the older man left. *Now I'm certain I need a valet!*

~

MATILDA WAS ALREADY EATING breakfast when Wesley slid into his chair. She wore a dressing gown of flowing floral silk, and her hair was hanging loose about her shoulders.

"Good morning, Wesley." She gave him an apologetic smile. "I hope you don't mind me starting without you, but I like my eggs hot."

"I'm glad you did, Mother."

The extensive number of dishes on the white, linen-draped table included broiled ham, smoked bacon, scrambled eggs, toast, and oatmeal. There were also pots of coffee, chocolate, and piping hot water for either English, green, or Oolong tea.

"With so much for us to do this morning, Cavendish was very thoughtful to order up breakfast." Matilda sipped her tea. "He's quite a find."

"Yes, he is. He's laying out my suit as we speak."

"Mrs. Neal is preparing my traveling gown and drawing my bath. I feel so spoiled, but I'm beginning to wonder what I ever did without her."

"I know what you mean."

As he reached for a piece of toast, Wesley noticed yet another one of Cavendish's walking sticks propped up in the corner. This one was slender, fashioned of a highly polished dark wood, and sported a deep blue cut-glass knob handle. *I wonder how many walking sticks the man has?*

Since there was much to be done, Cavendish didn't allow his master to linger overlong at breakfast. After Wesley bathed, his valet gave him a shave and manicure.

Wesley examined his buffed fingernails, impressed. "I'm not uncouth anymore."

"I daresay you never were, Your Grace."

Wesley met the man's gaze in the mirror. "Tell me, Cavendish, how many walking sticks do you own?"

The valet chuckled. "I've never actually counted them, Your Grace, but I *am* quite the collector."

Wesley read Jules Verne until his mother was ready to go, while Cavendish sat nearby reading a pocket-sized copy of *L'Art de la Guerre.*

Wesley gave the book's title a curious glance. "That's French?"

"Yes. It's *The Art of War* by Chinese military general Sun Tzu."

"I've never heard of him. He wrote a book in French?"

"No, Sun Tzu lived thousands of years ago. This is a translation from Chinese."

Wesley cocked his head. "Why don't you read it in English?"

"Sadly, the English translation does not exist. Since I'm fluent in French, however, it's no hardship."

Wesley returned to his book, puzzled. *The man is extremely learned for a valet. Could there be more to Cavendish than meets the eye?*

∽

Mr. Darling ordered a Concord hotel coach large enough to accommodate the Oakhursts, the Parkers, their servants, and whatever luggage remained. Mr. Darling slipped Wesley his business card while the luggage was being loaded.

"When you return to New York, the Fifth Avenue Hotel will always be at your service," he said. "*Bon voyage.*"

"I couldn't imagine staying anywhere else." Wesley smiled. "We've enjoyed ourselves immensely."

He shook Mr. Darling's hand, entered the coach, and took a seat across from Belle. He immediately noticed dark circles under her eyes.

"Didn't you sleep well, Miss Oakhurst?"

"I confess my love of exercise yesterday exceeded my ability, Your Grace. I was most appreciative of a long hot bath this morning." She sighed. "Even now, I can't move without thinking of those extra one hundred sixty-two steps with rancor."

Wesley laughed. "I understand. If not for Cavendish, I believe I'd still be languishing in bed."

The coach headed west toward the river, and then south to Pier 46, where the *City of New York* nestled against the dock in sleek black breathtaking splendor. The ship was five hundred sixty feet long, sixty-three feet across, and its three evenly spaced smokestacks jutted skyward as if the ocean liner were thumbing its nose at the elements. The clipper bow featured a fantastic carved female figurehead reminiscent of those on vessels long ago. The *City of New York* was also equipped with three auxiliary masts and sails, wholly unnecessary to her ability to maneuver, but beautiful nonetheless.

As porters took their luggage aboard, Wesley lingered on the pier to admire the ship from stem to stern. Mr. Oakhurst and Cavendish flanked him on either side.

"Her top speed is twenty knots, Your Grace," Mr. Oakhurst

said. "She was built in the Thomson Shipyard in Scotland, christened two years ago by Lady Randolph Churchill, and has a British staff and captain at the helm."

"I'm looking forward to making the ship's acquaintance," Wesley said.

"May she act like a lady all the way to Liverpool," Cavendish added in his rich, deep voice. "Afterward, she can let down her hair and cavort like a hoyden."

Wesley and Mr. Oakhurst shared a laugh.

"She can indeed, Cavendish," Wesley replied.

Boarding the *City of New York* proved challenging due to the throngs of people on deck. The Parkers separated from the Oakhursts at the saloon deck entrance, as each family was shown to their accommodations. A uniformed steward named Finnegan led the Parkers to the promenade deck, where they were obliged to weave through an exuberant crowd. Wesley was jostled to and fro and nearly lost his hat.

"Pardon me, Mr. Finnegan," he said. "I thought the ship only held about two thousand passengers and crew? There are far more than that onboard."

"Most of these people are friends and family who've come to see the passengers off," explained the steward. "They'll disembark when the captain sounds the warning bell."

A slight tightening of his throat made Wesley swallow hard. No one would be there to wish him or his mother *bon voyage*. He wondered if anyone from the neighborhood would really miss him at all.

Mr. Finnegan first showed Matilda and Mrs. Neal to their deck cabin, and then led Wesley and Cavendish to a nearby deck cabin of their own. Inside were a sitting room and an attached bedroom, with a private lavatory and bath. The suite was richly decorated, not unlike the one at the Fifth Avenue Hotel—but without the hanging chandelier. The windows, covered with fringed drapery, looked out over the ocean.

"Why, it's a little house!" Wesley exclaimed.

Cavendish glanced out the window. "With a very big view."

"This sitting room converts to a sleeping chamber for your valet, Your Grace," Mr. Finnegan said. "Mr. Oakhurst felt you and your mother would be more comfortable with your servants close at hand." He gestured toward a green glass bottle nestled in an ice bucket on the table. "May I open this champagne for you?"

Wesley had never tasted champagne but he did not wish to appear unsophisticated.

"Absolutely, yes. That would be very helpful."

While the steward wrestled with the champagne cork, Cavendish began to unpack Wesley's brand new trunks. Wesley suddenly noticed a second set of very fine luggage in the corner. The chests and trunks were Mediterranean blue leather, with black bumpers and brass locks, braces, and rivets.

"I'm sorry, Mr. Finnegan, but I believe this luggage must belong to someone else." Wesley gestured toward the stack. "I don't recognize it at all."

Cavendish paused from his duties. "I beg your pardon, Your Grace, but those are mine. I had them forwarded to the ship yesterday."

"Oh, of course," Wesley said.

The pop of the cork distracted Wesley from the luggage. Mr. Finnegan poured him a glass of the clear bubbly liquid, and Wesley took a sip. Although the champagne tasted like grapes, the bubbles tickled his nose.

Mr. Finnegan checked his pocket watch. "We're to set sail at one o'clock sharp, a little over an hour from now. Since we've no steerage passengers heading east, we're sailing light. I'll make the rounds shortly with the passenger list."

"Passenger list?" Wesley echoed. "Whatever for?"

"It makes a nice souvenir of the voyage." The steward leaned forward as if to impart a confidence. "And the list helps passengers decide with whom to acquaint themselves and whom to avoid."

"Aha."

"If there's anything I can help you with, please let me know."

Wesley slipped the man a gold coin. "Just make sure my mother has whatever she needs."

The steward beamed. "Yes, Your Grace. I'd be delighted."

CHAPTER 8
PRIDE & PRETENSE

After Belle's father was shown to his cabin on the saloon deck, a steward escorted her to her cabin on the upper deck. The corridors were crowded with excited passengers, young and old, trying to find their rooms. Belle's cabin was located in the interior, which meant it had no view, and she would have to share the bathroom at the end of the hall. Nevertheless, the cabin was private, considerably larger than the one she'd occupied on her last crossing, and nicely decorated in floral patterns that were soothing to the eye. There was also a small washbasin for her to use that cleverly folded away.

The steward lingered by the door. "Whenever you'd like a bath, you'll need to reserve a time with Mrs. Bartlett, the stewardess for this section. Dinner is at six o'clock, on saloon deck. Promenade deck is where you'll find the library and ladies' drawing room. I do hope you enjoy the voyage."

Belle gave the man a small tip and he departed. After she checked to make sure her trunks were all there and tested her bed to see if it was comfortable, there was little else to do but unpack. She opened her largest trunk and hung up her gowns in the closet. The task didn't take long, so she decided she might as well join the throngs on deck. Although she didn't know anybody, the festive atmosphere outside was better than the solitude of her cabin.

When she emerged from her room, the sounds of a row reached her ears. Down the hall, a well-dressed American matron was arguing with the harried stewardess.

"I'm telling you, Mrs. Bartlett, my daughter needs a deck cabin or suite with a private bath!"

A pretty young girl was leaning against the wall nearby, with her arms folded across her chest. At the woman's words, the girl sighed impatiently and trained her gaze on the ceiling. Belle suddenly recognized her from their brief meeting in the Fifth Avenue Hotel lobby. *That's Louise!*

"Madam, all the deck cabins and suites are occupied. I wish I could help, but my hands are tied," Mrs. Bartlett said.

"Oh, Mama, the room is perfectly *fine*," Louise interjected. "If you're so concerned about a private bath, I'll be happy to switch with *you*. Otherwise, I'd like to go outside now!"

"You're not to go walking by yourself amongst the rabble, Louise! Wait until after the warning bell, when they leave."

Louise caught sight of Belle. "Why, hullo! Isn't this a wonderful coincidence?" She laced her arm through Belle's. "Mama, this is my dear friend, Miss Oakwood! I may have mentioned how she and I met at the hotel? We'll chaperone one another on deck."

Before her mother could object, Louise hustled Belle around the corner and up the stairs. "Golly, I hope you didn't mind me using our acquaintance to get away, but my mother is like a dog with a bone sometimes. She'll argue with that stewardess until the ship is mid-ocean."

"I hope not," Belle said. "But my name is Oak*hurst*."

"Oh, sorry. I'm awfully bad with names. You don't have to stay with me if you don't want to. I may be able to find my brother, Stephen."

"No, let's stay together." Belle smiled. "It's nice to have a friend."

∽

Wesley's feeling of loneliness that had begun earlier surged after the steward left. He sank into an upholstered chair, drained the rest of his champagne, and stared into the glass. It crossed his mind to seek out Belle, but he didn't know her cabin number. Even if he had, she would probably consider a visit to her room to be *improper*. A tap on the door startled him from his reverie. He rose to answer it, but Cavendish got there first.

"Good afternoon, Your Grace."

"Is my son here?" Without waiting for a reply, Matilda stuck her head inside the room and beckoned to Wesley. "Come outside, dear. Friends have come to see you off."

"What?"

Puzzled, Wesley emerged from his cabin. He was shocked to see Mrs. Zinna, Gino, Mrs. Lombardi, Mrs. Thackeray, Sergio, and even Officer Hannigan. Elated, Wesley shook hands and exchanged hugs with each of them.

"I'm so glad to see you but how did you come to be here?" he asked finally.

His mother laughed. "What letters do you think I've been writing these past few days? Some were to England, but the rest were to our Brooklyn friends."

"There are a lot of folks in the neighborhood who couldn't come to see you off, but they sent their best wishes," Mrs. Zinna said.

Mrs. Lombardi took Wesley's face in her hands. "We're going to miss you and your mama. You're *buono gente*, eh?" She let go, giving his cheek a final slap.

"*Grazie*, Mrs. Lombardi," Wesley said. "You and Mr. Lombardi are good people too."

Officer Hannigan, who was wearing his street clothes, gave Wesley a playful cuff on the jaw. "Stay out of trouble lad, you hear?"

"I'll do my best, Officer. Thanks for all those occasions you could've arrested me but took me home instead."

The policeman waved away his thanks. "Your father always had a kind word for me, Wesley. Maybe it was my way of returning the favor."

"When I realized I had a future duke living in my apartment building all this while, I could *die!*" Mrs. Thackeray said. "I'm so proud of you, Wesley."

"*Per viaggiare in sicurezza.*" Sergio pressed a Saint Christopher's medal into Wesley's hand. "For safe travel."

The medal was hung on a ribbon, to be worn around the neck. Wesley slipped it over his head and patted it as it rested on his chest.

"*Grazie, amico mio.*" He suddenly found tears stinging the backs of his eyelids. "Thank you for coming, all of you. It really means a lot to me."

~

BELLE AND LOUISE made their way to the promenade deck. Passengers and their guests crowded the walking track which was situated underneath a series of lifeboat girders. On the other side of a brass railing, next to the deck cabins, were lounge chairs reserved for the first class passengers.

"My brother is here somewhere…or more likely in the bar

having a drink." Louise waved her hand in the air. "He graduated from Harvard with honors, so Papa decided to send him on a European tour as a reward. At the last minute, Mama and I decided to go too. Poor Mama is miffed because some crusty old duke got the last two deck cabins. Even though we're still in first class, Stephen and I had to go a bit lower."

Belle winced. "As it so happens, I'm traveling with a duke. The Duke of Mansbury is neither crusty nor old, but he and his mother may indeed have booked the last two deck cabins. I hope you won't hold it against him for long."

Louise's eyes went wide. "Is he young and handsome? My mother would like nothing better than for me to marry an English aristocrat."

"Well, I—"

"Are *you* an aristocrat? Oh, tell me that you are! With your manners and looks you absolutely *must* be. Mama will love it that we've made friends."

Louise's pretty face was almost childlike in its earnestness, and Belle found she wished to please her.

"Er...my grandfather on my mother's side is a baronet as a matter of fact."

It was completely outlandish for Belle to pretend an intimate acquaintance with her grandfather, who was no more a baronet than he was a giraffe. In addition, baronets were only slightly above the knighthood in terms of rank and considered commoners when compared to the peerage. Even so, she suspected Louise wouldn't know the difference. *Americans are hopelessly ignorant about titles anyway*, she reasoned. *It's a harmless deception, after all, only meant to last for the duration of the voyage. When we land in Liverpool, Louise and I will part company, and she'll forget everything I've told her.*

"I knew it!" Louise exclaimed. "Should I address you as Lady or something like that?"

"No...not yet, at least. I'm engaged to a knight and once we are married, I'll be Lady Blankenship. Presently, however, I'm just Miss Annabelle Oakhurst."

"You're engaged, then? You must tell me all about him."

"Certainly, but there's plenty of time. Shall we find my friend, the duke?"

"Oh yes, please!"

Belle forged a path through the throngs. She finally found Wesley and his mother, but they were talking and laughing with a small crowd of people who had evidently come to see them off.

"I think we should wait a bit to go over," Belle said. "They're visiting with friends at the moment."

"Is *that* the duke...the one in the top hat?" Louise squeaked. "My heavens, I'm smitten already!"

A handsome young man came up behind Louise, wearing a blue blazer with brass buttons, a striped shirt with a bow tie, and a jaunty straw boater. Unlike the fashion of the day, he was clean-shaven. The lack of mustache and whiskers drew attention to his high cheekbones and rugged jaw.

"Louise, you have that scheming look about you." He gave his sister a fond glance. "Should I be worried?"

She wheeled around, curls flying. "Stephen! Did Mama send you to follow me?"

"Somebody has to make sure you stay on the straight and narrow." Stephen's slow, lazy smile at Belle made her spine straighten. "If I'm not around, I'm afraid the task will fall to you, Miss..."

"Oakwood," Louise supplied.

"Oak*hurst*," Belle said.

"Yes, that's right. I'm just impossible with names." Louise rolled her eyes. "Annabelle, this is my brother, Mr. Van Eyck. Stephen, this is my new friend, Miss Oakhurst."

"Delighted to make your acquaintance, Miss Oakhurst." Stephen sketched a bow.

Belle curtsied. "Thank you. Your sister and I met in the elevator of the Fifth Avenue Hotel the other day."

"Really? Between the two of us, Louise has always had the better luck."

Stephen's straight blond hair shone in the sunshine like a halo. Although he had the appearance of an angel, the gleam in his eye was anything but seraphic. Heat rushed to Belle's face and she averted her gaze.

"Annabelle is engaged to a knight, Stephen," Louise said.

"Engaged?" Stephen's mouth turned down in a charming pout. "My heart is broken."

"And her grandfather is a baronet," Louise added, to Belle's dismay.

"How very English," Stephen said. "Have you been presented at court, Miss Oakhurst?"

Belle seemed to be unable to veer from the course she'd set for herself. "Er...yes, my grandfather sponsored me this past season." The lie was so smooth, she could almost believe it.

The sudden noise of a clanging bell made her flinch. Stewards could be heard calling out, "All ashore who are going ashore!"

"We're about to shove off." Stephen grinned. "This is rather exciting."

As Wesley's guests filed past on their way off the ship, Belle took Louise's arm. "Are you ready to meet my friend now?"

"Yes, please." Louise shot her brother a level glance. "Stephen, you're about to meet a duke, so behave."

He made a face. "I'll behave if he does."

Belle caught Wesley's eye and beckoned. He hastened over with a broad smile. "Did you see that, Miss Oakhurst? My friends came all the way from Brooklyn to say good-bye. I didn't think they would."

"That was very kind of them, Your Grace." Belle noticed the medal glinting around his neck. "Is that a Saint Christopher's medal? I didn't realize you were Catholic."

"I'm not, but I suppose a good luck medal can't hurt, can it?"

"I suppose not." She glanced at the Van Eycks. "Allow me to introduce two new acquaintances of mine, Miss Louise van Eyck and her brother Mr. Stephen van Eyck. Miss Van Eyck and Mr. Van Eyck, I present the Duke of Mansbury."

Wesley bowed to Louise and stuck out his hand to Stephen. "Let's not bother with my title, shall we? The name is Wesley Parker. I'm pleased to meet you both."

Stephen had a mild look of surprise on his face as he shook Wesley's hand. "You're American."

"Born and bred. The title is newly inherited, and I'm not used to it. Miss Oakhurst has been very helpful in acclimating me."

Stephen turned his blue eyes in Belle's direction. "Is that so? Since I'm to rub elbows with the English in the near future, perhaps you can advise me how best to fit in."

"I'd be delighted," Belle said.

Wesley's smile slipped slightly. "Say, would anyone like some champagne? I've an open bottle in my sitting room that I can't possibly finish by myself."

Louise jumped up and down. "I *adore* champagne."

As they headed into the deck cabin, Wesley fell into step with Louise's brother. "Who do you like for the World's Championship Series, Mr. Van Eyck?"

"Call me Stephen. I'm from Philly, but I admit the Bridegrooms are the team to beat, no question."

While Wesley and Stephen conversed about baseball and

sports, Cavendish poured champagne and handed around the glasses.

Louise cleared her throat. "I propose a toast. To new friends."

"To new friends," Wesley, Belle, and Stephen echoed.

The steward appeared in the open doorway with a stack of papers in the crook of his arm. "Excuse me if I'm interrupting, but I have the passenger list." Mr. Finnegan handed one to each person in the room, including Cavendish.

"Hot off the press, it seems," Louise said, reacting to the warmth of the paper.

"Yes, we have our own print shop on board. The ship's newspaper is called the *City of New York Gazette*. If you have any news or bits of gossip, please let your steward or stewardess know." Mr. Finnegan headed for the door. "Oh, and we're weighing anchor in fifteen minutes."

As the steward left, Stephen and Louise poured over the passenger lists with avid interest.

Louise bit her lip. "I wish I knew who all these people are."

"That's part of the fun, not knowing right off." Belle shrugged. "It's like a treasure hunt."

"The deck chairs are marked with names, so that makes it easier," Stephen said.

"They've been marked?" Louise stared at her brother. "How perceptive of you to notice that."

Stephen's deep masculine laugh filled the cabin. "Don't act so astonished."

Mrs. Van Eyck peeked through the open doorway with a passenger list clutched in her hand. "Louise and Stephen, what are you two doing in here? I've been looking for you everywhere. Fortunately, I heard your voices just now."

Uninvited, the woman swept into the sitting room. Wesley got to his feet, but she ignored him and rounded on Cavendish instead. "I must say, Duke, it was horribly rude of you to take two entire deck cabins and discommode my children."

Cavendish gave her a gracious smile as he bowed. "Madam, your charm is exceeded only by your beauty. We're mortified if we've caused you any inconvenience whatsoever."

A blush crept over Mrs. Van Eyck's cheekbones, and she seemed unable to speak.

Louise giggled. "Mama, you've made a mistake." She gestured to Wesley. "*This* is the Duke of Mansbury. Wesley, this is my mother, Mrs. Van Eyck."

Wesley bowed. "It's an honor."

Mrs. Van Eyck stared first at Wesley and then at Cavendish. "If *he's* the Duke of Mansbury, then who are you?"

"Bartholomew Xavier Cavendish, at your service."

"Oh." Mrs. Van Eyck edged toward the door. "Well...come along, children. We must wave good-bye to New York as we set sail."

Stephen and Louise stood and followed their mother from the cabin.

"We'll talk later," Louise called over her shoulder.

Belle and Wesley exchanged an amused glance with Cavendish.

"You handled that well, Cavendish," Wesley said.

"Thank you, sir."

Belle rose from her chair. "Shall we also wave good-bye to New York?"

"Yes, let's," Wesley replied. "It seems the thing to do."

CHAPTER 9
KNOCKED FLAT

Wesley escorted Belle out to the deck, where they joined Matilda, Mr. Oakhurst, and their fellow passengers at the dockside railing. As the *City of New York* weighed anchor and slipped from its berth in the North River, Wesley and his mother waved at their friends and neighbors who were cheering from the pier. Although the Oakhursts couldn't have known anyone in the crowd, they waved, too. After the huge ocean liner sailed down the river, into Upper Bay and past Liberty Island, the excitement dissipated, and passengers began to disperse.

Wesley crossed to the far side of the ship as it skirted Brooklyn on its way to Lower Bay. The cheerful sunshine that had heralded their departure had disappeared, blocked by dark clouds rolling in. Erratic gusts of wind threatened to blow his hat over the side of the railing, so he removed it and held it in his hand. As the ship cleared Rockaway Peninsula, the ship's bell tolled the half-hour.

Belle joined him. "It looks like stormy weather ahead, but I overheard one of the stewards saying the tide is in our favor. As soon as we're on the other side of the Sandy Hook lighthouse, it will be full steam ahead."

"That's good news."

"Are you terribly sad to be leaving New York?"

He glanced at Belle, whose pretty features were etched with concern. "Not really. Since my father died, I can't think of a happy memory...until this past week."

"I take that as a compliment." She smiled. "You didn't have a sweetheart in Brooklyn, did you?"

"Er...I was rather fond of Liam Kennedy's younger sister for a while, but after he turned against me, so did she."

"Oh, dear. Since you're now a duke, I expect Miss Kennedy will never let her brother forget you, will she?"

Wesley laughed. "You may be right. She has a redhead's temper, so it could be some time before Liam receives a kind word from her."

"That notion should lighten your mood! Listen, I'm going to my cabin to freshen up and I'll see you at the captain's *bon voyage* reception."

"I'll look forward to it."

Wesley watched Belle walk away. A gust of wind lifted the hem of her skirt, revealing her slender ankles. He rather enjoyed the spectacle until he noticed Stephen van Eyck watching her as well.

∽

IN HER CABIN, Belle removed her hat, unpinned her windblown hair, and brushed it vigorously. She twisted her tresses into a loose coil and secured it with hairpins. After she added a tortoiseshell comb decorated with moonstones, she examined the effect in the mirror. Unbidden, a question popped into her mind. *Does Wesley think I'm pretty?* It was doubtful, if his taste ran to temperamental, red-headed Irish girls. Belle frowned at her reflection. Her complexion and straight teeth were praiseworthy, she'd been told, but she had a pair of dreaded dimples to deal with. Stephen van Eyck had flirted with her, but Belle couldn't help but think he would flirt with any lady under the age of forty. Oddly enough, Wesley Parker wasn't a flirt, and had never mentioned her looks, but when she was with him, Belle felt prettier than she ever had before.

The roll of the Atlantic Ocean made itself known as she left her cabin and ascended the stairs to the saloon deck. The soreness in her muscles made it difficult to move effortlessly, so she kept a firm grip on the handrail. As she made her way down the corridor, the sound of music and laughter from the reception floated into the hallway. An unaccustomed wave of shyness slowed her pace and self-doubt began to seep into her consciousness. Her father may have paid to upgrade their tickets, but that didn't mean she necessarily fit into first class.

For some strange reason, however, Cavendish flashed into her mind. He was a mere valet, but his carriage and demeanor bespoke a far grander heritage. *If Cavendish can manage to pull off a regal attitude, then so will I.* Belle lifted her head and sailed into the dining hall as if she were a princess.

Captain Howe stood just inside the wide glass doors, greeting his first class passengers with affable charm. Although her legs screamed in protest, Belle managed a creditable curtsy. Unfortunately, the ship chose that exact moment to pitch to the side. Her muscles were unable to compensate for the sudden movement, and she tumbled over. A gasp of horror went up throughout the hall, accompanied by several titters. Embarrassed, Belle wanted to die on the spot. She contemplated crawling under a table, but Stephen van Eyck rushed forward, dropped to one knee, and offered Belle his hand.

"I must say, Miss Oakhurst, that was quite an entrance. Will you allow me to assist you?"

"Thank you, Mr. Van Eyck," she managed.

Her face flaming, Belle took his hand and got to her feet. The surrounding onlookers burst into applause, which made her embarrassment worse.

"Are you injured, miss?" Captain Howe asked.

She shook her head. "Only my pride, Captain."

The ship pitched again but Stephen's firm grip allowed her to stay upright this time.

The captain gave her a rueful smile. "I'm afraid we may be in for some rough seas."

"I'll try to make the best of it, sir," she said.

As Stephen escorted her into the reception, everyone seemed to be staring at her. *So much for feigning a regal attitude.*

Wesley hastened over. "Are you all right, Miss Oakhurst?"

"I'm humiliated, but beyond that I'm perfectly fine." Belle took a deep breath and let it out. "I blame the Statue of Liberty."

Wesley laughed. "I comprehend you perfectly."

"What was that, Miss Oakhurst?" Stephen's eyebrows drew together. "Did I hear you correctly?"

She managed to smile. "Wesley and I climbed to her crown yesterday and I, for one, am a bit worse for wear."

Louise approached, her eyes shining. "Annabelle, that was brilliant! Everybody is talking about you, and how gallant my brother was just now."

"You mean they are laughing at me." Belle bit her lip.

"Perhaps some were, at first. But now ladies will be falling over at the slightest wave, hoping for rescue."

"I didn't do it on purpose. It was all very bad timing." Belle glanced around. "Is my father here?"

"Not yet, nor my mother," Wesley replied. "I'm sure they'll both be along directly."

As her composure returned, Belle was finally able to take in her surroundings. The magnificent, spacious two-story saloon had a barrel ceiling of stained-glass skylights. Two rows of long tables stretched from one side of the room to the other, flanked by upholstered mahogany swivel chairs attached to the floor. In between the long tables was a wide carpet runner. Smaller alcoves, complete with ocean view portholes, lined either side of the hall. The alcoves were fitted with smaller tables for family or group dining. Altogether, three hundred diners could be accommodated at once. Dark, gleaming woodwork defined the lower half of the dining room. Up above, the woodwork had been painted ivory to give a light, soaring look to the hall. Directly over the spot where Belle had fallen, on the second story, was a small glassed-in bay window where the drawing room looked out over the saloon.

"This is very elegant." Belle gazed at the turquoise, amethyst, and topaz colors in the stained-glass ceiling. "Except for the movement of the ocean, I might have imagined this was a five-star hotel."

Arrangements of food had been set up on the sideboards bracketing the doorway. Waiters were circulating with trays of drinks, as well as pots of coffee and tea.

Belle's stomach gurgled with hunger. "Shall we get something to eat?"

"Make yourself comfortable, Miss Oakhurst, and I'll fix you a plate," Stephen said.

"How kind of you," she replied.

A muscle quivered in Wesley's jaw. "I'd be happy to oblige, Miss Van Eyck."

"What a treat." Louise beamed. "Thank you ever so much."

Wesley and Stephen departed for the sideboards. As Belle

and Louise headed toward an unoccupied booth, Mrs. Van Eyck crossed their path.

"I hope you are uninjured, dear?" Mrs. Van Eyck asked. "You took quite a tumble."

"Yes, thank you. I'm recovered now," Belle said.

"Mama, this is Miss Annabelle Oakhurst." Louise gestured toward Belle. "She's the one I was telling you about."

Mrs. Van Eyck gave Belle an appraising glance. "Oh, yes. Louise informs me your grandfather is a baronet. I'd like to hear more about him at some point."

Belle forced a smile to her lips. "I-I look forward to chatting with you, Mrs. Van Eyck."

"Excellent. Please excuse me."

Mrs. Van Eyck joined a group of ladies at a table nearby, and Belle and Louise settled into a more private alcove.

"Mama has noticed Stephen likes you." Louise's expression was apologetic. "Prepare to be vetted."

Belle was taken aback. "I should hope your brother likes me well enough, but only as a friendly acquaintance."

"Stephen didn't offer to get me food and he's my elder brother!"

"He's all politeness, I'm sure."

"I don't think that's it."

∼

WESLEY AND STEPHEN finished loading two plates of food apiece and turned away from the buffet table.

Stephen frowned. "The ladies are not where we left them."

Wesley spied Belle, waving from an alcove. "This way."

As they crossed the saloon, the ship's movement caused them both to stagger like drunken sailors. When they arrived at the booth, Stephen put a plate in front of Belle and sat across the table from her with a plate of his own.

"This is lovely, thank you Mr. Van Eyck." Belle picked up a scone and broke it in half.

Wesley lowered a plate to the table in front of Louise. "I didn't know what you liked, Miss Van Eyck, so there's a little bit of everything."

"Thank you, Wesley." She gave him a pretty smile.

He responded with a smile of his own. "My pleasure."

"The storm has picked up, I think." Stephen draped a napkin across his lap. "I could barely keep my footing a few moments ago." He folded a piece of lemon cake into his mouth.

Wesley felt the ship crest a swell and slide down the other side. "I expect the waves will soon confine many people to their cabins, fighting seasickness."

Belle shrugged. "I feel fine so far."

"Me too." Louise helped herself to a triangular sandwich with visible layers of mustard and delicate, thinly sliced pink ham. "In fact, I'm starving."

After a waiter stopped by their table with glasses of ice water, a woman suddenly hurried past with a handkerchief pressed to her lips. She rushed from the room, followed by a worried-looking gentleman.

"The lady's complexion was quite green, I must say," Wesley murmured. "Is that our first casualty of the night?"

Stephen chuckled. "Probably not the last."

"We all may find ourselves knocked flat before it's through." Wesley nibbled on a crustless minced roast beef sandwich.

"Let's hope for the best." Belle glanced over her shoulder.

Wesley cocked his head. "Is something wrong?"

"I'm concerned about my father." She peered at the clock on the wall. "He should have been here by now."

"You're right," Wesley said. "That goes for my mother, too."

He beckoned to a waiter. "I'm the Duke of Mansbury, Wesley Parker. May I ask someone to inquire after Mr. Oakhurst and my mother?"

"Right away, Your Grace."

The waiter managed to hasten from the room despite the rising and falling floor.

Stephen cleared his throat. "I would be happy to check on your father personally, Miss Oakhurst, if you give me his cabin number."

"That won't be necessary, Mr. Van Eyck," Belle said. "But it's very thoughtful of you."

"One might say it was *unusually* thoughtful of you, Stephen," Louise said drily.

Mrs. Van Eyck hastened past the table just then, with her hand over her mouth.

Louise grimaced. "Oh dear. It looks very much like Mama's ill. I should go help, but I'm not sure what I could do for her."

"Make sure the stewardess brings her some bark tea," Belle said. "It eases the nausea."

"Right. Bark tea." Casting a furtive look around, Louise grabbed a sandwich from her plate and hurried off.

Belle sighed. "Well, that's bad luck, isn't it?"

The waiter returned and bowed to Wesley. "Excuse me, sir. Her Grace and Mr. Oakhurst have both succumbed to *mal de mer*."

"Oh, no." Belle frowned. "And after my father did so well on our last voyage too! I should make sure he's drinking bark tea as well. Excuse me, gentlemen."

She left her plate largely untouched and followed Louise from the saloon. Wesley and Stephen exchanged a rueful smile and a shrug before devouring every last crumb of food on the table.

Wesley folded his napkin and tucked it under a plate. "Well...what should we do now?"

Stephen shrugged. "There's always the smoking room."

"I don't smoke, do you?"

Stephen sat back in his chair with a frown. "No, not at all."

"We could play cards...or cribbage."

"Cribbage?" Stephen snickered. "How exciting."

"Fine." Wesley gave him a pained glance. "I'm out of ideas."

"There are probably games in the library?"

"It's better than watching people fall ill from *mal de mer*." Wesley grinned. "Let's go have a look."

Nestled between the first and second smokestack on the ship, the walnut-paneled library on the promenade deck was oddly shaped. On one wall, hundreds of brightly bound books filled elegantly finished cases built to curve around the smokestacks. On the opposite side of the room, a cozy semi-circular ottoman invited long hours of repose. Overhead, rain thrummed steadily against a stained-glass octagonal skylight. Bracketing the skylight were two wooden pillars intersecting square writing tables. There, passengers could sit and read, or choose one of the other upholstered, skirted chairs available for the task.

When Stephen and Wesley entered the carpeted library, it was unoccupied. They spent a few minutes admiring the gold-lettered books, the paneled ceiling, and the stained-glass windows upon which quotations of maritime poetry had been inscribed.

Stephen gaped. "I want a library like this when I grow up."

Wesley chuckled. "There are worse aspirations."

Board games of all sorts could be found in the cabinets

underneath the bookshelves. They played several lively games of checkers, punctuated by occasional epithets such as "foul fiend!" and "scoundrel!" At one point, the seas became so rough that the checkers slid from the board and slid to the floor. The game was ruined, so Stephen sat back with his hands laced behind his head.

"Tell me, Wesley, do you have plans for when you get to Europe?"

"I really haven't had time to make any. When my lawyer feels up to it, I'll broach the subject with him."

"Your lawyer?"

"Miss Oakhurst's father."

Comprehension dawned on Stephen's face. "Oh, so *that's* why she's traveling with you. I thought perhaps you and the Oakhursts were old family friends."

"I haven't known her long, but Miss Oakhurst and I have become friends. I suppose my first task is to settle into my estate, and then I'll decide what to do with myself. Before I found out about the inheritance, I was to begin a teaching job in the fall. I think now, however, I'll turn my hand to writing a book."

"Why don't you come to London? Louise and I will be in town a great deal. There are bound to be parties and such. You and I could knock about together."

"Two American gentlemen in London—it would be fun, wouldn't it? I'm informed I have a townhouse there."

"That's perfect then!"

"Only…I must ask what your intentions are toward Miss Oakhurst. You know she's engaged to a knight, don't you?"

Stephen threw his head back and laughed. "Engaged isn't married, Wesley." His lips curved in a smirk. "You like her a great deal, don't you?"

Wesley brushed aside the inquiry. "Miss Oakhurst has

made it clear she's spoken for. Besides which, she recently compared me to a delinquent."

Stephen lifted an eyebrow. "It could be she prefers delinquents to knights."

"I doubt that. I'm probably not good enough for her, if truth be told."

"But you're rich *and* you are a duke!"

"A title means nothing."

"Not to you or me, but to the English it counts for a great deal. You could possess two horns and a pointed tail, but if you're a duke, the girls come flocking."

"Are you suggesting I have two horns and a pointed tail?"

Stephen snickered. "I hadn't noticed one way or the other."

At that, Wesley laughed. In fact, he found he was enjoying himself tremendously. *Stephen van Eyck isn't bad company at all…as long as he keeps his distance from Belle.*

Stephen scooped up some checkers and deposited them onto the board. "Shall we have one last game before we dress for dinner?"

Wesley nodded. "Yes, but I claim the red checkers this time."

"A fitting color for an American devil."

∽

Wesley returned to his cabin, fully expecting to find Cavendish drunk or flat on his back with nausea. Instead, he discovered the man wielding a pair of long whalebone needles and a skein of woolen yarn.

Wesley blinked. "You're *knitting!*"

"Ah, yes. I learned to knit years ago from a seaman when we sailed 'round the Cape of Good Hope. I've enough yarn for a scarf and a sleeping cap, I believe." Cavendish put down his needles and stood. "I've laid out a fresh change of clothes, Your Grace. As you are to dine at the captain's table this evening, I thought white tie would be appropriate."

"What makes you think I'm dining with the captain?"

Cavendish picked up an envelope. "His personal invitation was delivered about an hour ago."

"Oh." Wesley peered at him. "How is it you're so hale?"

"Knitting has a soothing effect."

CHAPTER 10
FRIENDS & RIVALS

Mr. Oakhurst's stomach seemed to settle after he drank his tea, but he begged off dinner.

"It would be better for all concerned if I stayed here, my dear. I'm not altogether certain I could hold anything down and I wouldn't want to embarrass myself."

As if to underscore the accuracy of his statement, the ship rose and fell on the crest of a wave. Mr. Oakhurst groaned and lowered himself gingerly onto his bed.

"Run along, Annabelle. I'm glad one of us is still fit. Have you any information on the Parkers?"

"The duchess took to her cabin earlier this afternoon. When I last saw him, Wesley was fine."

"Perhaps the young are more resilient. Please turn the light off when you leave."

With one last sympathetic glance over her shoulder, Belle left her father's cabin and headed to dinner. Soothing music greeted her as she entered the saloon. She'd dressed in a dinner gown with a sapphire and black striped bodice and a plain sapphire skirt. The arms were long and fitted, with puffs at the top of the sleeves, and the neckline formed a gentle curve across her décolleté. The hall was only two-thirds full, which was not surprising considering the seasickness that had befallen so many passengers. Waiters flitted throughout the room as they brought drinks and dispensed menus with practiced alacrity.

Belle hesitated in the doorway. She scanned the crowd, searching for Wesley, but didn't find him. She'd resigned herself to sitting at one of the long tables, alone, when she spotted Louise and Stephen waving at her from an alcove. As she approached, Belle noticed three other young people at their table in addition to the Van Eycks. The eldest was a fellow not more than twenty years old, and the two girls were slightly younger.

The gentlemen stood as Belle approached.

Stephen gave her an admiring glance. "Good evening, Miss Oakhurst."

"Good evening, Mr. Van Eyck." Belle slid into a chair next to Louise.

Louise smiled. "If you're looking for Wesley, he's seated at the captain's table up front."

"Oh?" Belle tried to cover her disappointment. "Of course he would be. I hope Mrs. Van Eyck is feeling better?"

"Mama is as well as can be expected," Louise said. "She conveys her thanks for suggesting the bark tea."

"Apple bark tea proved invaluable to many of the passengers on my last voyage, but the seas were not quite so rough then." Belle glanced at the trio of strangers. "Will you introduce me to your friends?"

"Yes, of course." Louise cleared her throat. "Miss Oakhurst, may I present Miss Stacy Egermand, Miss Eva Egermand, and Mr. Carl Stanger from Chicago."

Carl's self-effacing grin reminded Belle of Wesley. "Actually, it's Stenger and Egermann."

Louise threw her hands up in defeat. "I'm so sorry!"

"No reason to apologize, Miss Van Eyck." Carl's eyes sparkled with good humor. "It's a pleasure to make your acquaintance, Miss Oakhurst."

Belle liked him right away. "Thank you."

Stacy gave Belle an appraising look. "Miss Van Eyck informs me that your grandfather is a baronet."

Belle made a non-committal response. *I can't seem to free myself from my web of deceit!*

"What's it like to be related to a baronet?" Eva asked.

A slight fog of panic descended over Belle. "I-I am not sure how best to answer that."

Fortunately, the waiter arrived to pass out menus, and further conversation was suspended. Belle accepted her menu and pretended to be absorbed by it.

Louise leaned over to whisper. "Mr. Stenger and the Egermann sisters are part of a large and very wealthy brewing family. The matriarch, Mrs. Anna Stenger, is sitting at the captain's table too."

Belle lowered her voice as well. "Your new friends seem very amiable."

"Yes, they are. We entered the dining room together by chance, and Stacy invited Stephen and me to join her family for dinner."

Belle laughed. "If we had one more boy, we could form a square."

"What?"

"I was just thinking out loud. I promised to teach Wesley to dance during the voyage. We can work out the waltz and polka together, but for the group dances we must have four couples."

Eva caught Belle's eye. "I couldn't help but overhear, Miss Oakhurst. Did you say something about a dance?"

"Oh...I was just telling Louise that between all of us at this table and the Duke of Mansbury, we nearly have enough for a square," Belle said.

"We're only shy one gentleman," Carl said.

"This is marvelous!" Stacy's eyes sparkled with enthusiasm. "We've been invited to all sorts of parties and balls during our European tour and we desperately need to practice."

Eva rolled her eyes. "The three of us are rusty at that sort of thing, especially Carl."

"The fault for that is entirely mine." Carl's expression turned sheepish. "I ducked out of dance class every chance I got. Mother was vexed with me, but I didn't think I'd ever really need to dance."

"There's a piano in the drawing room. We can practice there," Louise said.

"I can certainly use the practice," Stephen said. "Surely we can find one other gentleman who'd like to join in?"

Belle was seized by an idea. "Perhaps we should form a dance club?"

Stacy clapped her hands in delight. "I was wondering what we were going to do for fun on this voyage. I don't know much about cards after all."

Conversation for the rest of the meal revolved around drafting a pianist, which dances they were to learn, when practices could be scheduled, and who could serve as the extra gentleman.

"Let's do pick someone good-looking," Eva said.

"That's silly." Stacy looked at her sister askance. "What does it matter what the fellow looks like so long as he can dance?"

Carl shrugged. "There's always Horatio."

Stacy groaned and Eva closed her eyes.

"Who is Horatio?" Belle asked.

"He's my cousin." Carl lifted his chin. "And he's a fine lad."

"Horatio is our younger brother." Stacy exchanged a pained glance with Eva.

"He's fourteen and an insufferable blatherskite," Eva added.

"That's unfair, Eva," Carl said. "Horatio can't help that he's smarter than everyone else. And I must point out that he attends dance class without fail. He'd be an asset to our endeavor."

"Where is he now?" Belle asked.

Stacy snickered. "He annoyed us on the train from Chicago, so we banished him to the children's dining hall for the duration of the voyage."

"*We* did no such thing, Stacy." Carl frowned. "That was you and Eva. I say we let him out of purgatory and allow him to join the group."

Stacy, Eva, and Carl began to argue again. Belle was secretly pleased; as long as those three bickered, they didn't have time to ask her anything about her grandfather.

∽

As FLATTERING as it was for Wesley to be invited to the captain's table that evening, he was apprehensive. With his limited experiences, what could he possibly add to the general conversation? He vowed to say as little as possible but shortly after Captain Howe introduced him, however, he became the center of attention.

"An American duke? How terribly interesting," Mrs. Stenger remarked. "You must meet my youngest son, Carl, my nieces Stacy and Eva, and my nephew Horatio. We're touring Europe together."

He gave her a gracious nod. "I look forward to it, ma'am."

The remainder of the dinner was quite congenial, particularly when one of the English gentlemen, Mr. Francis Ley, broached the topic of sports.

"Tell me, Your Grace, have you any enthusiasm for baseball?"

A smile sprang to Wesley's lips. "Yes, Mr. Ley. Sadly, I'm going to miss the World's Championship Series this year."

"That's unfortunate. There's a pitcher for the Cleveland Spiders who recently pitched a three-hit shutout in his major league debut—"

"Cyclone Young!" Wesley exclaimed. "They say he destroys stadium fences with his fastball."

"That's the very one! I'm a fanatic for baseball, personally." Mr. Ley smoothed his thick white mustache with a thumb and forefinger while giving Wesley an appraising glance. "You may be interested to learn that I'm building sports grounds for workers at my foundry in Derby. The central feature is a baseball stadium."

Wesley cocked his head. "I didn't realize anyone played baseball in England."

"It's not widespread as of yet, but perhaps between the two of us we can change that. You're quite welcome to attend a ballgame when you are next in Derby. Indeed, we'll have you throw out the first pitch."

Wesley beamed. "Why thank you, Mr. Ley. That's very hospitable of you."

When dessert was finished, the guests began to filter away from the table. Mr. Ley shook Wesley's hand. "It was a pleasure talking to you, Your Grace. Say, would you fancy a game of chess?"

"I'd be delighted! I know for a fact there's a set in the library."

"I'll meet you there in ten minutes."

∽

After dinner, Belle lingered in the saloon, alone, to wait for Wesley. He finally left the captain's table, spotted her, and hastened over.

"I just had the most splendid meal." He chuckled. "Everyone I met at dinner was very amiable, and, thanks to you, my manners drew compliments."

"I'm so glad, Wesley. Mr. Van Eyck, Louise and I made friends too, and they're waiting for us in the drawing room. We've formed a dance club!"

"I can't go just now. I promised to play chess with Mr. Ley. We've a lot in common, he and I."

His face shone with eager anticipation. Belle covered her disappointment with a smile. "Oh...that sounds wonderful, Wesley."

"You don't mind?"

"Not at all. I'll just go on ahead then. Perhaps you can join us later?"

"Absolutely."

Wesley left the saloon without a backward glance. Crestfallen, Belle made her way to the drawing room. The skylights overhead were dark and the windows that afforded an ocean view during the day were at night covered by sliding mirrored panels that lent the room a festive atmosphere. Red velvet ottomans lined the walls, and a pretty bay window looked out over the saloon.

Stacy was playing a waltz at the upright piano angled in one corner. In the center of the spacious, carpeted room, Eva and a tall, slender lad were moving awkwardly together in a semblance of dancing.

Carl joined Belle. "That's my cousin, Horatio."

As the music ended, Horatio made a sound of impatience. "Eva, I feel like I'm pulling you around like a sack of potatoes! Keep your weight over your toes and remember to rise and fall."

Louise noticed Belle. "Hang on, where's Wesley?"

"He had a prior engagement, as it turns out, but perhaps he'll join us later." Belle moved toward the piano. "That's a lovely piece of music. I've never heard it before."

Stacy beamed. "It's *The Emperor Waltz* by Johann Strauss, published just last year. My music teacher had me play it in a recital this past spring."

"You play it beautifully...and from memory, too!"

Stephen sauntered over. "Since Miss Oakhurst has arrived, let her and Horatio show us how the waltz is supposed to look."

Eva sighed. "Miss Oakhurst, allow me to present my brother, Mr. Horatio Egermann. Horatio, this is Miss Oakhurst."

As Horatio approached Belle and bowed, his burnished blond hair fell over his brow like a forelock. "If indeed you know how to waltz, please relieve my suffering and consent to dance with me, Miss Oakhurst."

Behind Horatio's back, Eva stuck out her tongue.

Belle bit back a smile as she curtsied. "Thank you, sir."

The lad led Belle to the center of the floor, and Stacy began to play *The Emperor Waltz* from the beginning. Belle soon discovered the young man was an accomplished dancer. They moved around the room, careful to avoid colliding with ottomans or onlookers. Horatio's icy expression thawed, replaced by one of genuine enjoyment. When the last note faded, he bowed once more.

"That truly *was* a pleasure, Miss Oakhurst."

She curtsied. "Thank you, Mr. Egermann."

Carl stepped forward to clap his nephew on the back. "You really were paying attention in dance class, weren't you? Well done."

Stephen held his hand out to Belle. "It's my turn."

Stacy selected *Tales from the Vienna Woods* from the sheet music available, and began to play. Whereas Belle's dance with Horatio had been light and innocent, Stephen's demeanor was entirely different. The intimate way he looked at her as they danced brought a blush to her cheeks wholly unrelated to the physical exertions of the waltz.

Once the dance ended, Carl folded his arms across his chest. "I can hardly compete with *that*."

Louise looked at her brother askance. "I distinctly recall you saying you were out of practice."

Stephen shrugged. "Dancing with Miss Oakhurst must have inspired me."

His smoldering glance left Belle flustered. "You're a dreadful tease, Mr. Van Eyck." She crossed over to the piano. "Let me play for a bit. I think I can manage something simple."

Before Stephen led Stacy to the dance floor, he leaned down to whisper in Belle's ear.

"I was perfectly serious, as you are well aware."

A delicious shiver went down her spine, but Belle feigned indifference. Her attention focused on the keyboard as she warmed up her fingers with a few chords.

∼

Mr. Ley moved his bishop and sat back. "Checkmate, sir."

Wesley stared at the chessboard but there was no escape to be found. Finally, he conceded defeat and shook his opponent's hand.

"Well played, Mr. Ley. I'm fairly certain I've never been beaten so quickly before, nor so soundly."

"It was a good match, Wesley. The turning point came, however, when you left your queen unprotected. You allowed my bishop to distract you."

"I admit that was a stupid move. I'll be more careful in the future."

Mr. Ley stood. "I take my leave, but I enjoyed the evening immensely. Perhaps you can find some young people with whom to pass a pleasant interlude until bedtime?"

"I shall. Good night, Mr. Ley."

As Mr. Ley left, Wesley swept the chess pieces into their wooden box, folded up the board, and replaced the set in the cabinet. He left the library and traveled the short distance to the drawing room, peeking through the glass door at the activity inside. Stephen and Belle were dancing together—a waltz, he presumed. Stephen's hand was resting on her upper back in a familiar fashion. In return, she was smiling at him in what could only be described as a flirtatious manner. A surge of jealousy mixed with a sudden sense of chagrin. *I'm a fool! I could've been here with Belle, but instead I was trounced at chess!*

Stephen and Belle dipped and turned with athletic grace, seemingly with no thought for anyone else but each other. *I can't dance with Belle like that. Blast Stephen!* Wesley opened the door and slipped inside.

"There you are, Wesley!" Louise exclaimed.

The piano music stopped, and all eyes turned toward him. Belle and Stephen froze for a moment before splitting apart.

"Hullo," Wesley said, suddenly tongue-tied. "Sorry I'm late."

"Better late than not at all," Stephen said. "Unfortunately, we just danced the last dance."

After Belle performed the introductions, she glanced around the room. "Well...shall we discuss when and where we're to meet next?"

"We were unusually fortunate to have the drawing room to ourselves this evening," Stacy said. "I doubt we'd be that lucky again."

"I've been thinking. Since there are no steerage passengers, couldn't we get permission to use their exercise deck in the afternoons?" Stephen asked. "We could meet at half past two o'clock."

Eva's expression brightened. "What a wonderful idea! I'm sure there will be a piano on that deck we could use."

Stacy frowned. "I wish we had a pianist that wasn't one of us. We'll never have a complete square at this rate."

"We could always advertise in the ship newspaper, asking for volunteers," Wesley said. "I'll broach the matter with my steward."

Belle slid him a smile. "That would be wonderful."

Horatio stifled a yawn. "Good night, then."

Carl Stenger and the Egermann sisters left with Horatio, but Stephen, Wesley, Belle, and Louise lingered.

"Miss Oakhurst, may I escort you to your cabin?" Stephen asked.

"Er...thank you, Mr. Van Eyck," Belle said.

Wesley gritted his teeth. *Never leave your queen unprotected!* "I'll go too. I'm curious to learn which cabin is yours, Miss Oakhurst."

Louise sniffed. "My cabin is just down the hall from hers, should anyone wonder."

CHAPTER 11
CHOPPY SEAS

When Wesley returned to his cabin, he remembered to ask Cavendish whether or not he'd eaten dinner.

"Thank you, Your Grace, I have. There's a separate sitting for servants and the food was most excellent."

"Good."

Wesley slumped into a chair, morose. Cavendish paused his knitting needles long enough to peer at him. "I can't help but notice something seems amiss."

"My friends have formed a dance club, and I don't know how to dance. Stephen van Eyck was dancing with Miss Oakhurst just now, like he was born to it."

"Nobody is born knowing how to dance. It's a learned skill."

Wesley sprang to his feet and began to pace. "I understand, but I'm going to look stupid. For him to show me up is intolerable."

"If you'll permit me, I can give you pointers."

Wesley's footsteps paused. "You know how to dance?"

"In my day, the polka was all the rage, along with the redowa, mazurka, schottische, and galop, among others. At present, I believe the emphasis is on the waltz and two-step, but you never know when a polka, quadrille, or promenade will be required, especially in the highest society."

"I take that as a *yes*. Cavendish, you're a lifesaver!" He paused. "Can you teach me to waltz tonight?"

"I can teach you the basics. After that, you'll have to practice with a female partner—preferably a graceful one."

"There's a practice tomorrow afternoon at half past two, assuming we can get permission for the space. That reminds me, I must write a note about it to Mr. Finnegan. We're also putting an advertisement for an accompanist in the ship's newspaper."

"I'd be happy to oblige in that regard too, if you'll release me from my valet duties during those hours."

Wesley peered at him. "You play the piano? Cavendish, is there anything you can't do?"

"I'd rather not bore you with a lengthy list."

Wesley dashed off a note to the steward, asking for permission to use the steerage exercise deck and a piano.

"I'll take that to Mr. Finnegan's cabin, Your Grace," Cavendish said. "When I return, we can get started."

∼

HER BERTH WAS COMFORTABLE, warm, and snug, but so much had transpired that day that Belle was too restless to sleep. She'd met a great many wealthy American friends with illustrious pedigrees. Her warm acceptance among them had been intoxicating, and the girls had even progressed to calling each other by their Christian names. Carl, Horatio, and Stephen had sought her out as a desirable dance partner—and what fun she'd had!

Admittedly, Carl Stenger was in dire need of practice, but he was willing to work hard. Horatio had been a very able dancer, but he paled in comparison to Stephen. Never before had she had such a capable partner! Errol disliked dancing, and although she'd partnered many sweaty young men at Monsieur Caron's Dance Academy, few had a sense of grace or timing. In Stephen's arms, she'd felt as if she could fly. She giggled at the memory of him whispering in her ear. The fellow was certainly high-spirited and impudent.

The only moment of the evening she did not reflect upon with satisfaction was the wounded expression on Wesley's face when he saw her dancing with Stephen. A spray of briny seawater couldn't have dampened her mood more effectively. Neither was she pleased to notice the previously congenial relationship between Stephen and Wesley turn cool. Even as the two men had accompanied her and Louise to their cabins, they'd exchanged subtle barbs the entire time. What on earth could've turned them against one another? She was engaged, after all, and could scarcely be expected to form an attachment to either of them.

Confused and discomfited, Belle turned over in bed yet again. Errol had discouraged her from traveling to America, and perhaps she should not have left his side. She considered all the reasons she'd fallen in love with him. Her eyes flew open in a moment of panic; she was in love with him, wasn't she? Yes, yes, of course she was...she adored his handsome face, noble brow, and melodious voice, especially when he read to her from *Fordyce's Sermons*. Errol had such a romantic, long-suffering air, and she'd fallen for him almost immediately. In fact, he'd taken all the ladies of Mansbury by storm when he arrived in town.

Many of Belle's friends sighed when the dashing Sir Errol strolled by in church and gazed at him with longing when he rode past in a smart gig pulled by his high-stepping mare, Isolde. Maureen Crane, the mayor's daughter, had set her sights on him right away, but her hopes withered when Errol had quickly singled Belle out as the object of his affection.

A week from now, when she and Errol were together again, all her doubts would be laid to rest. Far away from idle flirtations with a good-looking Philadelphia heir, and the amiable company of a certain handsome American duke, she would plan her wedding—and a glorious wedding it would be! Thus persuaded, Belle allowed the ship to rock her to sleep.

~

Dawn broke over the clear North Atlantic skies with an inspired beauty that would stir the imagination of even the most hard-hearted curmudgeon. Wesley emerged from his cabin and was immediately drawn to the railing by the view of the distant Nova Scotia shoreline. A myriad of fishing vessels dotted the coastal waters, and a pod of humpback whales cavorted in the glassy waters not too far from the steamship. One of the enormous creatures breached the surface and displayed its belly, as if to invite Wesley's admiration.

The steward came to stand by Wesley's side. "A prettier view is not to be had, Your Grace. I never tire of it."

"Good morning, Mr. Finnegan. It's a magnificent day."

"That it is."

"Has my mother arisen, do you know?"

"Aye. In fact, she just went down to breakfast."

Wesley's eyebrows rose. "Oh? She must be feeling better."

"Yes, sir. By the way, your request to use the steerage exercise deck has been granted. It's being set up for you as we speak."

"Please tell the captain I'm terribly grateful."

As Wesley strode along the deserted promenade deck, he felt so ebullient that he couldn't help practicing his newly learned waltz steps. When he came around full circle, an invisible sylph in his arms, he suddenly realized a well-dressed, elderly couple had paused to watch. Red-faced, Wesley stopped and dropped his arms to his sides.

"Sorry. I was just, you know, practicing," he mumbled. "Morning exercise, sea air, and all that."

The gentleman exchanged an amused glance with his wife. "Don't let us stop you, lad. We were once young, too."

∽

Passengers were beginning to trickle into the saloon when Wesley arrived. Matilda was sitting alone at one of the smaller tables, reading a copy of the ship's newspaper, *City of New York Gazette*.

He slid into a chair across from her. "Morning, Mother. How are you feeling today?"

"Well enough to eat a little toast, thank you." She tapped the paper. "You're the subject of curiosity."

"What do you mean?"

Matilda read the story aloud. "'A certain saloon passenger, whose story bears a passing resemblance to that of *Little Lord Fauntleroy*, has excited much conversation regarding his romantic fancy. Which shipboard maiden will he favor? *City of New York* scuttlebutt says it's too soon to tell'."

Wesley made a sound of disgust. "Who would want to read that tripe?"

She gave him a sidelong glance. "Don't be so stodgy!

There's little else to do on these voyages besides gossip. It helps distract people from seasickness and boredom."

"You say that now, but wait until *you're* the subject of a silly story."

His mother giggled. "I'll be rather disappointed if I'm not."

"Well, I'm happy to report I've something better to do than gossip. My friends and I have formed a dance club and we're to practice in the afternoons."

Matilda regarded her son with admiration. "That's very enterprising, Wesley."

"It's Miss Oakhurst's idea, really."

"She's a clever girl."

"Mr. Oakhurst was seasick yesterday too." Wesley scanned the room. "Have you seen him or Miss Oakhurst this morning?"

"I haven't, I'm afraid," she murmured, her attention wholly on her newspaper. "Perhaps we'll see them at the church service later on."

Wesley ordered food from a waiter. A few minutes later, Louise entered the saloon. He waved, and she hastened over with a broad smile on her pretty face.

He rose as she approached. "Good morning, Miss Van Eyck. Have breakfast with us, if you like."

"Oh, yes, thank you. I was afraid I'd have to eat alone." She slid into a chair. "I think my mother and brother must still be sleeping."

"Mother, this is Miss Van Eyck." Wesley took his seat once more. "Miss Van Eyck, allow me to introduce you to my mother, the Duchess of Mansbury."

Louise beamed. "I'm ever so delighted to meet you. Did Wesley happen to mention our dance club?"

"He did indeed, and I think it's an excellent notion."

"We've received permission to use the steerage deck and a piano," Wesley said. "And my valet has agreed to play for us."

Matilda stared at him, wide-eyed. "Cavendish plays the piano too? The man continues to amaze me."

The waiter brought Wesley's orange juice. While Louise ordered breakfast, an idea began to form in Wesley's mind. Wouldn't it be wonderful to surprise Belle with his newfound dance skills? *I daresay I want her to be impressed...more so than she was with Stephen van Eyck.*

After the waiter left, Wesley gave Louise a pleading glance. "Miss Van Eyck, my experience in the waltz is minimal at best. Our dance club meets at two thirty, so could you arrive a half-hour early to practice with me? That way I wouldn't feel so much the oaf when others are watching."

She brightened. "I'd like nothing better."

Wesley felt his shoulders relax. "Good. I hope I won't tread on your toes."

"You could scarcely be worse than poor Mr. Stenger was last night." Louise grimaced. "He'd never waltzed before and all of us felt quite sorry for him."

Wesley kept his countenance but inside he quailed. *Please let me be better than Carl Stenger! The last thing I want is Belle's pity.*

Matilda folded her newspaper and left it on the table. "If you'll both excuse me, I'm going to get a little fresh air before church. It's glorious weather out."

After Wesley's mother left, Louise pulled the *Gazette* toward her and began to read it avidly.

"Oh no, not you too!" Wesley exclaimed.

"Oh come now," Louise said. "Aren't you the least bit curious what's in it?"

"I've already been told."

BELLE DONNED A DEMURE, high-collar dress suitable for church. The fabric had a dark green background with a lush, pretty pattern of ripe peaches. The sleeves were gathered into puffs at the top but gave way to feminine apricot lace from the elbow to the wrist. A double row of matching lace around the hem gave the plain skirt movement when she walked. The gown was one of Errol's favorites.

After she left her cabin, she went to her father's cabin. Mr. Oakhurst answered her knock at his door, already dressed and looking far more energetic than he had the previous evening.

"Good morning, Papa! Do you feel like eating a little breakfast?"

"Tea and crumpets would not go amiss."

As they entered the saloon, Mr. Oakhurst paused to admire the arched, stained-glass ceiling. Daylight illuminated the colors of the glass beautifully.

"My heavens but that ceiling is incredible!"

Belle smiled. "Indeed it is. And at night, it's lit by hundreds of incandescent lights from within, like starlight."

As she glanced around the room, Belle spotted Wesley in a booth with Louise. The two sat practically shoulder to shoulder, pouring over a newspaper together. A pang of jealousy made Belle nearly bite her tongue. *It's none of your business, and you've no right to be jealous!* She averted her eyes and steered her father toward the opposite side of the saloon, choosing an unoccupied alcove table where her father could look out the porthole window. As her father glanced over the menu, Belle leaned over slightly until she had a view of Wesley's table. Immediately she wished she hadn't. He was laughing at something Louise had said, and they appeared to be terribly cozy.

As Belle sat back in her seat, Stephen van Eyck and his mother approached.

"Good morning, Miss Oakhurst." Stephen beamed. "Do you mind if my mother and I join you?"

Belle hoped the dismay she felt regarding the arrival of Mrs. Van Eyck was not reflected on her countenance. "That would be delightful."

Mr. Oakhurst stood as Belle introduced Mrs. Van Eyck and Stephen to him. Stephen's mother seemed none too steady as she lowered herself into a chair.

Belle bit her lip. "How are you feeling, Mrs. Van Eyck?"

"I'm not yet recovered from the rough seas of yesterday." The woman gulped. "And the ship's bell rang every half hour to keep me awake. Perhaps a deck cabin was not such a good idea after all."

As Mrs. Van Eyck and Mr. Oakhurst began to converse about seasickness and its various remedies, Belle couldn't help but notice Stephen looked quite handsome in his high collar and red Ascot tie. He caught her staring, and she quickly lowered her gaze to the floral arrangement in the center of the table.

"I think Louise must be here," he said. "Did you happen to see her?"

"No," Belle lied. "But then, my father and I only just arrived."

As the meal progressed, she became increasingly apprehensive. She pretended to attend to Stephen's stories about Philadelphia life, but her attention was actually focused on Mrs. Van Eyck. *Please don't let her broach the subject of my grandfather, especially in front of Papa!*

Mrs. Van Eyck ate sparingly and then excused herself to return to her cabin. At the same time, Mr. Oakhurst also left to take a walk on the promenade deck. With the danger of exposure past, Belle stopped twisting the napkin in her lap and let her hands rest on the table instead.

Stephen demeanor turned flirtatious. "Miss Oakhurst, please allow me to tell you how pretty you look this morning."

"Oh...thank you."

Without warning, he covered her hand with his. Before she could react, he'd gripped it so firmly she could not pull away without creating a scene.

"We've only just met, but I'm quite taken with you. After last night, I've begun to hope you feel the same way."

Her eyes widened. "Mr. Van Eyck, I implore you to release me this instant!"

Too late, Belle saw Louise and Wesley making their way to the table. Louise's expression was one of delight, but Wesley's eyes were narrowed with displeasure. Belle's face flamed hot.

"I hope we're not interrupting." Ice caressed Wesley's every syllable.

Stephen loosened his grip, and Belle's hand quickly returned to her lap.

"In point of fact—" Stephen began.

"No." Belle cut him off. "You're not interrupting at all. Please join us. Um...have you had breakfast?"

"We just finished," Louise said.

She slid into a chair, but Wesley remained standing.

"We were waiting for you for the longest time, Annabelle," Louise continued. "Finally, I glanced across the room and there you were!"

"Papa and your mother just left." Belle knew she had done nothing wrong but she felt guilty nevertheless. "We breakfasted with them."

"I didn't see you here, Louise. I thought perhaps you'd fallen overboard." Stephen gave Belle a little wink.

Louise scoffed. "I'd never give you the satisfaction of being an only child."

Belle glanced up at Wesley. "Would you care to sit with us for a while?"

"Thank you, no." His words were clipped. "I'm going for a stroll before the Sunday service."

As he turned on his heel and strode from the room, Belle stifled the impulse to run after him. Louise prattled on about arrangements for the dance club. When Carl, Eva, Stacy, and Horatio entered the saloon with Mrs. Stenger, Belle seized on an excuse to leave.

"The Stengers and Egermanns are here." She rose. "Could you let them know the time and place of our dance club meeting? I must speak to my father about something, but I'll see you at the church service later on."

Belle left the saloon and mounted the stairs to the promenade deck. Although she didn't see Wesley, she noticed Mrs. Van Eyck sitting in a deck chair several yards off, seemingly dozing and draped in a blanket. Belle tried to tiptoe past but Mrs. Van Eyck opened her eyes at that exact moment.

"Oh, Miss Oakhurst, why don't we have our chat now? I'd love to hear all about your grandfather, the baronet."

∼

WESLEY STRODE along the promenade deck without taking in the view. So Stephen van Eyck had wormed his way into Belle's favor with his slick Philadelphia manners? Couldn't she see he was an insincere dandy? Wesley's pride was further wounded by the fact she'd allowed Stephen to hold her hand. This, after Belle had taken *him* to task for the very same thing! Belle Oakhurst was engaged, for mercy's sake, and even Wesley knew Stephen's behavior was inappropriate. Evidently the girl's judgment was flawed, and her character was not as stellar as she'd let on. It was fortunate he'd discovered the truth before he'd grown too attached. Stephen had done him a good turn, really. He ought to feel relieved…but he wasn't.

Hoping to confide his woes to Cavendish, Wesley returned to the cabin. The sitting room was empty, however, since his valet had apparently gone to breakfast. Wesley slumped in a chair, wondering how he should best manage the remainder of the voyage. Only one course seemed clear; he should keep his distance from Belle as much as possible. Sadly, in the middle of the Atlantic Ocean, that would be easier said than done.

CHAPTER 12
MISSTEPS

Anyone not stricken with seasickness crowded the saloon for Sunday service. Belle and her father came early to find an alcove seat and the Parkers arrived shortly thereafter. Although Wesley could not have failed to see Belle wave to him, he escorted his mother between the long tables and sat up front. The snub was so obvious, even Mr. Oakhurst noticed.

"You and His Grace haven't quarreled, have you?"

Belle frowned. "We've had a small misunderstanding."

His father's expression was serious. "We owe most of our livelihood to him and can't afford to give offense. Should he discharge me for any reason whatsoever, it will be a black mark on my record."

Mr. Oakhurst's tone was not sharp but Belle was mortified. "Yes, sir. I mean to rectify matters as soon as possible."

"See that you do, Annabelle."

She frowned as she fixed her gaze on the ocean view. The voyage had not gone well for her so far and it had only been one day! Not only had she lied about her grandfather but her idle flirtation with Stephen had led to a dreadful misunderstanding. Since she'd held herself out as a paragon of virtue, Wesley must be terribly disappointed.

Her father interrupted her reverie. "Monsieur Caron is exceedingly generous to permit you time away from teaching."

"Er...yes, Papa."

"I'm grateful you have steady employment with him. I know it isn't fashionable for women to work but should anything jeopardize your engagement with Sir Errol or my income, you'll at least be able to support yourself."

Belle peered at him. "Nothing will jeopardize either, Papa. The misunderstanding with Wesley will pass, and when I return to Mansbury I'll plan my wedding. I'll be married before Christmas, come what may, so please set your mind at ease."

Carl, Eva, Stacy, Horatio, and Mrs. Stenger joined Belle and her father at their table and Stephen and Louise arrived a few moments later. Belle ignored Stephen's impassioned glances as best she could.

"Mama is outside, snoring in her deck chair," Louise whispered. "She had such a bad night, I thought it best not to disturb her."

"She's still a bit peaked, so I daresay the fresh air may do her good," Belle replied.

Her conversation with Mrs. Van Eyck earlier had, unfortunately, resulted in a repetition of the fabrication regarding her grandfather. *I should have just confessed the truth, but if my friends discover I lied to them, they'll shun me. Papa will notice, and ask me why...and then I'll be completely undone. I'm cornered!*

Louise glanced around. "Where's Wesley?"

Belle was ready with a response. "The Parkers are sitting at the front of the hall. It was crowded when Papa and I arrived, so we were obliged to sit back here."

She felt her father's eyes on her but she refused to meet his gaze. *It's amazing how easily the lies fall from my lips these days... and just before a church service, no less! The more I practice at dissembling, the better I become.*

No clergyman was aboard to deliver a homily, so the service was quite short. The pipe organ played the hymn *Eternal Father, Strong to Save*. Captain Howe said a few words, read Psalm 107, and led everyone in a recitation of the Lord's Prayer. One of the ship's engineers brought out his Scotsman's bagpipes and finished the service with a touching rendition of *Amazing Grace*. Afterward, passengers scattered, bent on distracting themselves for a few hours until lunch.

Belle's attempt to speak with Wesley came to naught. She lingered at the saloon doorway, hoping to catch him on the way out. But either he eluded her in the crush or he'd escorted his mother out of the saloon by the back door. She debated with herself a short while about calling on him in his cabin. Although it was improper for her to do so, she would have no rest until she'd smoothed over their quarrel.

Just as she set foot on the staircase leading to the promenade deck, Louise's voice rang out. "There you are, Annabelle! If you're not otherwise engaged, Eva, Stacy, and I would love to learn whist."

Although Belle's heart was heavy, she allowed herself to be coaxed into the drawing room. She would see Wesley at lunch, after all, and he couldn't avoid her then.

∼

Wesley was determined to occupy the hours until lunch with Jules Verne. In other circumstances, he would have preferred to bring his book outside and relax in his deck chair. At the moment, however, he was in a dour mood and disinclined to chat with his fellow passengers about inconsequentialities.

Cavendish returned from his breakfast. His attire was as dapper as ever, and he was sporting a turned rosewood walking stick.

Wesley glanced up from his book. "That's a handsome walking stick. I haven't seen that one before."

"Thank you, Your Grace. It has a rather clever feature." Cavendish flipped open the rounded silver top to reveal a timepiece.

"Very nice, but the time is wrong," Wesley observed.

"That depends on your perspective. It's been set to Greenwich Mean Time ever since that was established in 1884."

Wesley frowned. "Did you do that because you're homesick?"

"Perhaps a trifle. I confess I'll be happy to set foot upon my native soil once more." He paused. "If you don't require my services at present, I would like to take my exercise."

"Please do. It's a wonderful day for it."

"Indeed, it is."

A knock sounded on the door, and Cavendish opened it to reveal an older man. "Is His Grace available?"

"Mr. Ley!" Wesley put his book down and got to his feet. "Please come in."

Mr. Ley stepped into the cabin, all the while peering at the manservant. Cavendish bowed and left, closing the door behind him.

"That man is your valet?" Mr. Ley asked.

"Yes, he is." Wesley cocked his head. "Is something wrong?"

"I can't place him, but he seems familiar to me." The gentleman shook his head, as if to clear it. "Well, no matter. I wondered if I could impose upon you. You see, I need an opponent for shovelboard."

"I'd be happy to oblige, but I've never played."

"The rules are easy enough to learn. Come along, lad. The day is too fine to be cooped up inside, and we'll by no means be assured of such good weather going forward."

They played shovelboard in the sunshine until noon, when Wesley invited Mr. Ley to join him and his mother for lunch. Due to the lovely weather and calm seas, his fellow passengers turned out for the midday meal in droves. Inwardly, Wesley congratulated himself on the way events were unfolding. He genuinely enjoyed Mr. Ley's company, and the man's presence provided him with a ready excuse to avoid Belle. And yet, even as he dined, Wesley could not stop his eyes from scanning the saloon in the hope of catching a glimpse of her. His heart gave a little leap when he saw Belle framed in the doorway along with Louise, Eva, and Stacy, but his gaze immediately dropped to his bowl.

His mother gave him a curious glance. "Is the oxtail soup not to your taste?"

"Not at all. It's quite delicious. Why do you ask?"

"You were frowning at it most severely just now."

Wesley forced a chuckle to his lips. "I can't think why."

∽

Belle and her friends sat at the end of a long table, next to a widows' tour group from Ohio. Belle had noticed the group of five ladies walking on the promenade deck the day before. The wind had blown their black widows' weeds about, giving the group the appearance of a murder of crows.

"It seems as if our principal activity onboard the ship is to while away the hours between meals," Louise joked.

"Oh, I don't know about that," Eva said. "I've been learning loads, although I definitely need more practice at whist."

"With five more days at sea, you'll have the opportunity. I

need more practice at dancing." Stacy wriggled in her seat. "I can't wait for this afternoon. We're to have a real accompanist and everything!"

"Have you learned anything new on this voyage, Annabelle?" Louise asked. "Perhaps we can teach you about something American."

Belle's thoughts focused on Wesley's love of sports. "Have you ever been to a baseball game?"

The girls erupted into excitement, with an overlapping conversation about what they liked best about baseball.

"For me, it all comes down to the ball park food." Louise wore a dreamy expression. "I love salted peanuts, roasted in the shell."

"Horatio likes to collect baseball trade cards," Stacy said. "He's got a whole scrapbook full of them."

Eva giggled. "Our dear younger brother harbors a secret desire to be a professional ball player, I'm absolutely certain."

"But what are the rules of the game?" Belle asked.

The question set off another firestorm of responses. By the time her chicken pie entrée had arrived, Belle felt she might have a rudimentary grasp of the American sport. *Now when Wesley talks about baseball, I won't feel so left out—if indeed he ever speaks to me again. I'll make things right between us—I must!*

At length, the conversation turned from baseball to bicycles. Eva was longing to buy one, but Stacy thought they were unladylike. Lost in a reverie, Belle fell silent.

"What do you think, Annabelle?" asked Louise.

Belle glanced over. "Er...I'm sorry. What was the question?"

"Should women take up bicycling?" Eva asked.

"My fiancé disapproves of ladies with bicycles, but I see no harm in it," Belle said. "In fact, I believe the exercise would be quite beneficial."

"Ha!" Eva gave her sister a smug smile. "I told you so."

The spirited debate that ensued took Belle's mind off her troubles for a little while.

∽

A FEW MINUTES before two in the afternoon, Wesley and Cavendish arrived at the steerage exercise area to make sure everything was in order for the dance club meeting. The large space, about three hundred square feet, was accessible by a separate staircase from the saloon deck and was shielded from the sun by canvas tarps strung overhead. The few chairs left on the deck had been pushed to one side, and an upright piano was angled in the corner.

Cavendish sorted through the sheet music stored in the bench, sat down at the instrument and warmed up his fingers with a few scales.

"My previous employer allowed me to use his piano, which was a very fine instrument indeed. Nevertheless, I may be a little out of practice."

He shifted from scales to a haunting melody.

"Tchaikovsky," he said, in response to Wesley's quizzical glance. "*Romeo and Juliet, Love Theme*. But perhaps that doesn't set the proper mood."

His fingers danced along the keyboard. The notes of Chopin's *Minute Waltz* cascaded from the piano like milky white cream poured from a silver pitcher. As he was finishing the piece, Louise descended the stairs.

"How very pretty," she said. "I wish I could play the piano half so well."

Although Wesley was vexed with Belle, he still did not want to look idiotic on the dance floor. "Are you ready to help me practice, Miss Van Eyck?"

"As ready as I can be."

Cavendish arranged a piece of sheet music on the music rack. "Shall we start with *Voices of Spring*, Your Grace?"

Although Wesley was unfamiliar with the song, he pretended otherwise. "Certainly." As he faced Louise, however, Wesley's throat suddenly went dry and his palms became moist. "Er...what do I do first?"

"You bow to the young lady..." Cavendish prompted.

"Oh, that's right." Wesley took a deep, ragged breath and bowed to Louise. "May I have this dance?"

She giggled as she offered him her hand. "Yes, thank you."

So far, so good, Wesley thought.

~

AFTER LUNCH, Belle excused herself to change out of her Sunday dress and into a gown suitable for dancing. Although the dress was not ostentatious, Belle thought the lines made the most of her slender waist. In addition, the gold trim on the olive fabric brought out the gold in her eyes. As she arranged her hair, she debated about what to say to Wesley. Despite her best efforts, the words kept crumbling on her tongue like a sandcastle at high tide.

Fifteen minutes after two o'clock, she slipped on her gloves, left her cabin, and climbed to the promenade deck. Be it proper or not, she hoped to find Wesley in his cabin and ask him for a word in private. A few minutes alone should suffice to clear the air, and they would still be able to attend the dance club meeting at the scheduled hour.

Her knock at his door went unanswered, unfortunately, but the duchess was reclining in a deck chair nearby, reading a penny dreadful.

Belle gave her an apologetic glance. "Excuse me for interrupting, Your Grace, but do you happen to know where Wesley has gone?"

"Oh, you'll find Wesley at the dance club meeting, Miss Oakhurst. He's been gone for at least fifteen minutes."

"Thank you."

Belle descended to the saloon deck and hastened toward the stern of the ship. As she approached the stairs leading to the steerage exercise deck, music and laughter became audible. *Am I late, or did the meeting start early?* Midway down the staircase, she stopped abruptly and gripped the railing with both hands. Wesley and Louise were waltzing together down below, alone. The air in Belle's lungs seemed to leave her body all at once and her knees threatened to buckle. *He asked Louise to teach him how to dance, not me.* Moisture pricked the backs of her eyelids, and she retraced her footsteps before she could be seen.

Belle kept her composure until she reached her cabin, and even then she wouldn't allow more than a few tears to fall. In fact, she *couldn't* give in to the wall of hurt that threatened to consume her. The time of the dance club meeting was quickly approaching. If she could not control herself, the ravages of sorrow would be written on her face, laid bare for everyone to see. *Perhaps I can send a note to the group with the stewardess, begging off due to seasickness.* No, that wouldn't do; one of her friends might come to check on her, and she wouldn't be able to blame swollen eyes and a red nose on *mal de mer*.

She blotted her face with a towel moistened by the water from her washbasin. *Why do I care if he prefers to learn from Louise?* Could it be hurt pride that was upsetting her so…or was it something deeper? *I must cover my feelings with poise and smiles; otherwise I'll disgrace my father and myself. This afternoon I'll be the consummate actress, playing the part of a carefree young woman*. It would be a lie, of course, but she was used to lying by now.

∽

AT HALF PAST TWO O'CLOCK, the dance club members began to assemble. As Wesley waited for everyone to arrive, he tried to ignore the nervous pit in his stomach. *How can I be anticipating Belle's appearance and dreading it at once?* Eva, Stacy, Carl, and Horatio ran down the stairs like a quartet of eager puppies. When Wesley didn't see Belle among them, he suddenly realized he was holding his breath. Stephen and Mrs. Van Eyck appeared next, far more sedately.

Wesley bowed. "Good afternoon, Mrs. Van Eyck. Are you to be a part of our little club?"

"I decided to attend as a chaperone." The woman lifted her chin. "With all due respect to your valet."

It was clear from the slightly mistrustful expression on Mrs. Van Eyck's face that she still didn't know how to deal with Cavendish. With his usual aplomb, the valet took her attitude in stride and even found her a chair.

Belle sailed into the meeting a few minutes late, as effervescent as a spring day. "Hello! I'm *so* sorry if I've kept anyone waiting." She glanced around the deck. "What a wonderful space we have to practice."

"Yes, it truly is," Louise said.

Despite his vow not to stare at Belle, Wesley realized he was doing exactly that.

"How shall we get started?" Stephen asked.

Belle cleared her throat. "If nobody objects, may I suggest some simple rules? We change partners at the end of every waltz, and no gentleman can dance with the same lady until he has first danced with all."

"I like that rule." Carl chuckled. "That way, nobody can avoid dancing with me."

"You give yourself too little credit, Mr. Stenger," Belle said. "It's been a pleasure watching you improve."

"In that case, Miss Oakhurst, may I claim you for the first dance?" Carl asked.

"I'd be delighted."

As Wesley waltzed with Stacy for the first dance, his confidence grew. The movements, if not yet rote, were at least familiar. He was grateful his feet seemed to know what to do, because Belle's presence was very distracting. With a mighty effort, he wrenched his attention away from her and back to his own partner.

When the last chords of the music faded, the next rotation brought Belle face to face with Wesley. She curtsied in response to his bow, and they jockeyed slightly to achieve the proper hold. *Please don't let him feel me trembling!* Cavendish played a few bars as an introduction and Wesley flinched—as if he was unsure whether or not to move.

"Wait," Belle whispered. "Ready...*now*."

Exactly on the beat, Wesley stepped out and Belle followed. They made one complete rotation, and then another. His careful and studied movements were common for a beginner, but his instincts, grace, and timing were admirable. *I knew Wesley would be a good dancer.* A burst of pride brought a brief smile to her lips, followed closely by the surge of emotions she'd kept at bay. To her horror, her eyes grew moist and her throat tightened. She focused on the space over his right shoulder and for the remainder of the waltz she worked the multiplication table in her head to avoid thinking about anything else. At the end, she stepped back and curtsied.

"Well done, Wesley," she murmured.

"I nearly blundered at the start, didn't I?"

"An understandable mistake for anyone unfamiliar with the music."

Belle rotated into Horatio's arms. Her inner turmoil eased as she waltzed with him, until Wesley danced past with Louise. His playful smile and easy manner with Louise drove a sliver of ice through Belle's heart.

Eighteen times eighteen is three hundred twenty-four.

CHAPTER 13
OPINIONS

After an hour of playing music, Cavendish took a break. Stacy sat at the piano, played a few chords, and then launched into a familiar tune.

Eva laughed and wrinkled her nose. "Oh, Stacy, not *Chopsticks*!"

"Why not?" Stacy tossed her head. "It's a waltz, after all."

"Indeed it is." Cavendish strode over to Mrs. Van Eyck and bowed. "Madam, may I have this dance?"

Louise clapped her hands, jumping up and down with glee. "Oh, yes, Mama! I'd dearly love to see you waltz."

Mrs. Van Eyck blushed, but rose from her chair. "I don't mind if I do."

Amongst delighted chatter, the younger people stepped aside and allowed Cavendish to lead Mrs. Van Eyck to the center of the floor. As Stacy played the *Chopsticks* waltz again, Belle drifted to the back. While all eyes were on Cavendish and Mrs. Van Eyck, Stephen came to stand next to Belle.

"I'd like to offer my apology, Miss Oakhurst. I believe I may have offended you this morning," he murmured.

"Indeed, Mr. Van Eyck, you imposed on me."

He pouted. "Do you dislike me that much?"

"I don't dislike you at all. It's just that my affections are engaged elsewhere."

"I hope you don't mean *Wesley*," he scoffed. "Clearly he's besotted with my sister."

Her annoyance boiled over. "I was speaking of my fiancé, sir!"

Her voice was louder than she intended. Several heads turned in their direction, and Belle felt Wesley's gaze rest upon her for a few moments. Stephen waited to speak until everyone was once again focused on the waltzing couple.

"You should know, Miss Oakhurst, I'm not easily discouraged."

Belle stared at him in astonishment. "You don't lack for nerve!"

He gave her an impudent grin. "That's what renders me so appealing."

The waltz ended. Amidst applause, Cavendish bowed to Mrs. Van Eyck and escorted her off the dance floor.

"That was beautiful, Mama!" Louise exclaimed.

The woman's hands fluttered. "Thank you, my dear. I was fond of dancing when I was your age."

"Do let's have an encore, Cavendish," Carl said.

"Yes, please, Cavendish," Louise begged. "Dance with one of us."

The dapper man gave each of the young ladies a mischievous look in turn, until his gaze fell upon Belle. He gave her a sweeping, courtly bow.

"Miss Oakhurst, will you do me the honor?"

She curtsied. "Why thank you, sir."

As Cavendish and Belle danced a graceful, fast-paced waltz with dazzling changes of direction.

Stephen gave Wesley a sidelong glance. "I think we've been eclipsed, Wesley."

"Perhaps *you* have," Wesley murmured. "I'm not even in the same solar system."

Mrs. Van Eyck sidled over. "That man is no common valet, Your Grace."

"He's an uncommon valet, ma'am," Wesley said. "I count myself fortunate to have him in my employ."

The dancers were breathing hard when the waltz ended, and the group clapped with enthusiasm.

Cavendish sketched a bow. "Miss Oakhurst, thank you for indulging an old man."

"You're still in your prime, Mr. Cavendish, and quite energetic," Belle said. "In fact, I could barely keep up with you."

"But you *did* keep up with him, Miss Oakhurst," Mrs. Van Eyck said. "Where did you learn to dance?"

"From Monsieur Caron, the dance master in Mansbury. He teaches the sons and daughters of the local gentry," Belle said.

"You must have been one of his best pupils."

"Thank you." Belle smiled. "I assist Monsieur Caron in his studio."

"That explains why you're so accomplished," Louise said.

Belle murmured something about writing a letter to Errol and took her leave. Everyone else dispersed, and as the August sun raced toward the western horizon, Cavendish and Wesley made their way back toward their cabin.

"Miss Oakhurst was extremely dispirited this afternoon," Cavendish said.

Wesley peered at him. "What are you talking about? She was almost more exuberant than I've ever seen her!"

"A brave attempt to mask her feelings. I admire her intestinal fortitude. She has, as they say, *grit*."

"I don't know what you are talking about." Wesley shook his head. "She quarreled with Stephen van Eyck while you were waltzing with his mother. Perhaps that was it."

"Actually, I believe her upset stemmed from your practice with Miss Van Eyck."

Wesley frowned. "How could she possibly know about that?"

"I saw the hem of Miss Oakhurst's skirt on the stairs several minutes before practice was to begin," Cavendish said. "The gold trim was unmistakable. When I saw her next, her smile was quite forced."

"Why would my practice with Miss Van Eyck disturb Belle?"

"Didn't you mention Miss Oakhurst had offered to teach you?"

Wesley stared at him, bewildered. *Is he suggesting I hurt Belle's feelings somehow?*

"Thank you, Cavendish," he said finally. "You can go into the cabin if you like. I'm going to stay on deck for a little while."

When he was alone, Wesley wandered toward the ship's railing. The boat had skirted Nova Scotia all day, and the shoreline was still in sight. Icy winds from the north chased the blood from Wesley's fingers, and he was obliged to stuff his hands into the pockets of his frock coat to keep them warm. He inhaled a lungful of salty air and blew it out slowly. The notion that he'd hurt Belle bothered him. *Maybe Cavendish is wrong. Of course, the man hasn't been wrong about anything else. Is it possible I overreacted this morning because I was jealous of Stephen?*

Cavendish appeared at his elbow. "Excuse me, sir, but it's

awfully chilly." The valet had brought Wesley his overcoat and was holding it ready.

"Thank you, Cavendish, but I'm going inside."

The valet folded the coat over his arm and stepped back. "After you, Your Grace."

"Oh, I'm not going to the cabin. I'm going to speak with Belle."

Cavendish's mustache twitched. "Very wise course of action, sir."

∽

I can't deny it any longer…I've allowed my feelings for Wesley Parker to erode my regard for Errol. Tears slipped from underneath Belle's lids as she lay on her bed, full of misery and regret. *Better that I should have stayed home and never met the Eleventh Duke of Mansbury!* She remembered the first glimpse she'd had of him back in Brooklyn. With his bare head, cuts, bruises, and rawboned wrists sticking out of a threadbare, bloodstained shirt, Wesley Parker had resembled a disreputable street urchin. How had the young American managed to matter to her so very much in such a short period of time? Perhaps it was because beneath the tough exterior, his vulnerability had touched her heart in ways she could not have anticipated. And now that he didn't seem to need her anymore, it hurt like blazes.

A tap on the door made her flinch. "Belle, may I have a word?"

Wesley!

She sat up. "Um…just a moment."

Belle made hasty use of her handkerchief, and splashed water on her face. A quick glance in the mirror confirmed her suspicions; there was no way to hide the fact she'd been crying.

I need an excuse! She grabbed one of the novels stacked on the table and went to open the door.

Wesley peered at her. "Are you all right?"

Belle waved her book in the air. "Forgive me, but I just read the saddest passage. My emotions got the better of me."

He glanced at the book. "*Little Lord Fauntleroy.* Is it that sad?"

She had not checked the title before grabbing the book, and Belle felt her cheeks glowing with embarrassment.

"Well...the young lad is forced to separate from his mother for the first time in his life and it's, er...tragic." Her chin lifted at Wesley's skeptical expression. "Was there something you wanted?"

"I...um, couldn't help but notice Stephen annoying you at practice today. Do you want me to thrash him?"

A crooked smile twisted her lips. "A thrashing won't be necessary, thank you. I reprimanded him for taking liberties this morning at the breakfast table and I'm sure that will put an end to it."

"Stephen is a very charming fellow."

Belle shrugged. "Mr. Van Eyck seeks to recommend himself to every girl he encounters, but not every girl he encounters finds him worthy of serious consideration. I know I don't."

Wesley's eyebrows rose. "I see. Well, if he should impose on you again, let me know and *I'll* put an end to it."

"You're very kind."

He frowned. "Um...thank you again for saving me from a misstep during our waltz. Cavendish worked very hard teaching me last night, but we didn't have any music then."

"*Cavendish* taught you?" Belle was astonished.

"Yes, it was quite a sight." Wesley chuckled at the memory. "He and I looked very silly, I'm sure."

"But Louise—"

"I asked Louise to practice with me before the dance club. In truth, I was terrified of making a fool of myself in front of you, and I very nearly did, anyway."

His gaze dropped to the plush carpet beneath his shoes.

Belle reached out for his hand. "You could never make a fool of yourself as far as I'm concerned, Wesley."

Wesley stared at her hand a moment before lifting it ever so slowly to his lips for a whisper-light kiss.

Belle gulped. "I look forward to dancing with you again tomorrow."

A fierce light shone in his eyes. "Definitely."

Smiling, she stepped back into her cabin and shut the door. A giddy feeling sent delicious shivers down her spine. Then, as she came to her senses, she smacked herself in the forehead with the palm of her hand. *Why am I giving Wesley encouragement? I've promised Errol Blankenship that I will be his bride. If I'm labeled a jilt, it will ruin my father's career just as surely as if I'd eloped with the milkman. I must be losing my mind!*

And yet...the touch of Wesley's lips on her hand had affected her more deeply than any physical sensation Errol had ever aroused. *What am I to do?*

∽

THE FINE WEATHER HELD OVERNIGHT, and the *City of New York* steamed past the Newfoundland coast the following day. Pods of dolphins appeared on both sides of the ship, gamboling in its wake.

After a good night's sleep, Belle convinced herself she'd been overwrought the previous day, and that she was merely experiencing premarital jitters. As soon as she was reunited with Errol, she was certain her feelings for him would reassert themselves. In the meantime, she vowed to behave toward Wesley and Stephen in a circumspect manner.

In the *Gazette*, a mention of the dance club apparently engendered much interest and speculation because when Belle arrived for practice that afternoon, she discovered the entire widows' group perched on chairs to one side, like a shadow.

The group's leader, Mrs. Hamm, gave her an apologetic smile. "We thought perhaps the dance club could use chaperones."

"We're delighted to have you," Belle said.

Nevertheless, she thought the widows' presence inexplicable until Cavendish trotted down the stairs. Upon his arrival, the widows tittered and patted their hair. The valet, who wore a magnificent waistcoat embroidered with silver thread, paused to give them a theatrical bow before seating himself behind the piano. The ladies glanced at one another and sighed with pleasure.

Belle took Wesley aside. "I think Mrs. Van Eyck must be extolling Cavendish's virtues."

He chuckled. "Don't tell the widows he also knits. He'll receive five ardent declarations of love before nightfall."

During practice, Stephen behaved in such a gentlemanly fashion that Belle's guarded manner toward him thawed slightly. As for Wesley, he managed to incorporate more style into his waltz.

During the midpoint break, Mrs. Hamm sat down at the piano to play *The Blue Danube Waltz*. Cavendish smiled at the remaining quartet of widows seated on the sidelines. "Could I persuade one of you ladies to dance with me?"

Four ladies rose. After a little awkwardness, the eldest widow prevailed and allowed Cavendish to escort her to the floor.

Belle shot Wesley a pointed look and murmured. "He cannot dance with them all at one time."

After a startled moment of dawning comprehension, he crossed over to a widow and asked her to dance. Annoyed at having been outdone, Stephen promptly persuaded one of the remaining ladies to join him on the floor. A subtle pinch from Stacy sent Horatio to rescue the last widow. Unaccountably cheerful, Carl leaned against the wall to watch.

Belle joined Eva on the sidelines. "Mr. Stenger appears happy there are no more widows."

Eva stifled a laugh. "The widows are most certainly relieved there's only one Carl."

Louise hastened over. "Wesley was so gallant just now. He set a good example for the other gentlemen."

Belle nodded. "I agree, his behavior does him credit."

"My brother suspects Wesley is partial to me," Louise murmured. "After all, he did ask me to practice with him yesterday before the meeting. What's your opinion?"

A worm at the end of a hook could not have squirmed more. How was she to respond? Belle owed her allegiance to Errol, so if Wesley and Louise truly were developing an attachment, she ought not frustrate the relationship.

"Wesley has certainly been very cordial toward you." Belle cast about for something else to say. "Any girl lucky enough to secure his good opinion will be quite fortunate, I think."

Louise studied her a moment. "After the meeting, let's talk about your fiancé."

∽

IN THE SECOND half of the practice, the group began to learn the six parts of the quadrille. Mrs. Hamm kindly assisted on the piano so Cavendish and Belle could demonstrate the figures.

Louise squealed when she nearly collided with her brother during a complicated maneuver.

"How will I ever remember the order of figures and which way to turn?" Louise exclaimed.

"Repetition, Miss Van Eyck," Cavendish said.

"And if that fails, you can always feign an injury and decline to dance," Stephen said.

Louise gasped. "What a clever idea!"

After the dance club was adjourned, the widows clustered around Cavendish to ask his opinions on music.

Wesley chuckled. "If you'll excuse me, I'm off to a late afternoon game of shovelboard with Mr. Ley."

"I'm a fair shovelboard player myself," Stephen said. "Carl, let's you and I challenge Wesley and Mr. Ley to a game or two. Horatio, you can take bets should anyone wish to place a wager."

Horatio's eyes widened. "Er, I'm too young to gamble. Thanks for the invitation all the same."

He loped up the stairs, followed by Wesley, Stephen, and Carl. The girls ascended to the saloon deck, where they discussed what to do until dinner. Eva planned to read a few pages of *Wuthering Heights*, while Stacy was obliged to write a letter.

"I promised Mama to write something in a letter each day about the voyage," she said. "I'll post it once we arrive in Liverpool."

"By the way, are we playing cards tonight?" Eva asked.

"Yes, after dinner," Belle said.

"We'll see you later then," Stacy said.

As the two sisters headed off, Louise laced her arm through Belle's. "Now let's go for a walk on the promenade deck. I want to hear about Sir Errol."

CHAPTER 14
DISTRESS CALL

With the shoreline of Newfoundland in the distance, Belle and Louise strolled alongside the railing.

Louise gave Belle a sidelong glance. "Well?"

"Sir Errol Blankenship and I met at a large party in May," Belle said. "He was newly arrived in town and all the girls were mad for him. Fortunately, he asked to be introduced to me."

"Yes, but what do you like about the man?"

Belle frowned. "Errol is very cultured, refined, and learned. He's quite extraordinarily handsome, too."

"What color are his eyes?"

"Hmm, I hadn't thought about it before. They're gray, I believe." She paused to consider the matter. "Yes, I'm sure of it...his eyes are a bluish gray color."

"Like Wesley's?"

"Oh, no, Wesley's eyes are brown...a lovely, warm brown, like those of a fawn."

Louise cocked her head. "Let's play a little game. What would you say Wesley's best qualities are?"

Belle laughed. "I thought you wanted to talk about Errol! Let's see...Wesley is tremendously funny, adventuresome, kind, and generous. He can also be very sweet, too, and thoughtful."

"That's what I was afraid of," Louise said.

"What's wrong?"

"You're in love with him."

"Of course I'm in love with him! Errol and I are engaged."

"Not Errol, you goose. Wesley."

Belle's spine straightened. "That isn't true. It can't be."

"Of course it is. I asked you to describe Errol and you gave quite the most dispassionate details. Then, when you spoke of Wesley, your entire face glowed."

"Louise, no. No, I simply *can't* be in love with him."

"How difficult is it to tell Errol you've changed your mind?"

"Since I've given my word, it's impossible. Wesley and I are friends and that's the end of it. Please, let's don't speak of this again."

"As you wish, Annabelle, but it doesn't change the facts. You're in love with Wesley Parker, and I suspect he's in love with you."

~

WESLEY AND MR. LEY won their first shovelboard game with Stephen and Carl, but lost the second. Stephen took every opportunity to crow about the victory. His poor sportsmanship set Wesley's teeth on edge, but since the dinner hour was drawing near, there was no opportunity for a tie breaking game.

When Wesley entered his cabin to dress, his valet was nowhere to be found. Just as he was laying out a fresh change of clothes for himself, Cavendish burst into the cabin.

"Forgive my tardiness, sir. The widows were most persistent."

Wesley chuckled. "You're a great favorite with the ladies, Cavendish. I wonder that you never married."

A red flush stained Cavendish's cheekbones. "I was engaged many years ago, but bungled things terribly. Thereafter I vowed to remain a bachelor."

"What happened to the lady, if I may ask?"

"With her considerable beauty and charm, I believe Miss Christianson must have married." The valet's usually cheerful energy became muted. "May I suggest we turn our attention to the task at hand? The dinner hour rapidly approaches."

WESLEY and his mother were again seated at the captain's table that evening, but Captain Howe was absent. In his stead was a uniformed crewman whose wiry red hair, ginger whiskers, and accent revealed his Scottish heritage.

"Captain Howe sends his regrets, but he will be much occupied on the bridge for the next twelve hours." The Scotsman gave a decisive nod. "My name is Mr. Duncan, the Chief Officer."

Mr. Ley's eyebrows drew together. "We've calm seas and splendid weather. Is anything wrong with the ship itself?"

"Not in the least. We've entered the Grand Banks."

Mr. Ley frowned. "The Grand Banks is a fisherman's paradise, from what I've heard."

"Yes, but after the Grand Banks we'll be passing through the most treacherous waters in the Atlantic." Mr. Duncan paused for dramatic effect. "*Iceberg Alley.*"

Mrs. Stenger blanched. "Iceberg Alley?"

"Aye. Pieces o' ice break off the glaciers on the west coast of

Greenland and drift south with the current into shipping lanes. It can be tricky to navigate through an ice field safely."

"I'd like to see an iceberg," Wesley said. "They must be magnificent."

"Icebergs can be so astonishing and strange, I've oft wondered if God and the devil don't take turns carving 'em." Mr. Duncan's expression became rapt. "I've seen mountains o' ice as tall as the smokestacks on this ship, and so varied in shape, no two look alike."

"You make them sound beautiful," Wesley said.

"Beautiful, aye, but wicked dangerous. What shows on the surface is but a wee part o' the mass, and therein lies the rub." The chief officer stabbed a finger in the air. "Many a ship has skirted by an innocent-looking lump o' ice, while the devil peels back her keel under water with his savage, wicked claws."

Wesley's mother gulped. "Mr. Duncan, all this talk of icebergs is making me uneasy."

"You need not be concerned overmuch, Your Grace. Most likely 'tis too late in the season for any real danger from ice."

She relaxed. "That's a relief."

"Of course, nothing is for certain except uncertainty." Mr. Duncan folded his hands. "And as Mr. Ley pointed out, there are many fishing vessels to be found in the Grand Banks. At almost twenty knots, the *City of New York* can't be turned as if she were a mare. If one o' these vessels should happen to cross our bow on a foggy night...well, I need say no more."

Matilda exchanged an alarmed glance with Mrs. Stenger. Both women flagged down the waiter at the same time.

"Please bring me another glass of white wine," Matilda said.

"I'll have one too," Mrs. Stenger said. "If we're to collide with icebergs and fishing boats, a few glasses of wine will numb the terror quite nicely."

Wesley hid his mirth behind a napkin.

Mr. Ley cleared his throat. "A glass of wine all around wouldn't go amiss." He paused. "Actually, make mine a scotch."

∽

After dinner, Mr. Ley begged off chess to retire to his cabin.

"I'm afraid scotch and chess don't mix." He gave Wesley a wry grin. "I shall retain my dignity and play again another day—assuming the ship is not struck by a parade of horribles in the night."

Wesley chuckled. "I attended a Horribles Parade in Brooklyn last July Fourth. Although there were a great many floats, none of them were icebergs."

Mr. Ley laughed so hard at Wesley's joke that tears squeezed from the corners of his eyes. "Very good, my boy. Either that was very witty or I've had far too much to drink."

Still laughing, the older man ambled off.

Stephen appeared at Wesley's elbow. "For a moment I thought the fellow was having a fit. What did you say to him?"

"Just a joke about an iceberg."

"Hmm. It must've been a good one."

Louise bounded over. "Annabelle taught us to play whist. Would either of you like to play?"

Stephen pulled a face. "You know I don't know how to play whist."

"As for me, the only card game I know is solitaire." Wesley shrugged.

When Belle arrived shortly thereafter with the Egermann

siblings and Carl Stenger, Wesley had a sudden flash of inspiration.

"I have an idea. Why doesn't Miss Oakhurst teach Carl, Horatio, and me how to play whist while you ladies teach Stephen?"

Stacy brightened. "What an excellent notion. You can be my partner, Mr. Van Eyck."

Outmaneuvered, Stephen could only smile. "I'd be honored, Miss Egermann."

The group trooped upstairs to the library, where Wesley spent a very pleasant evening learning the game of whist. Every so often, Stephen shot him a baleful look from across the room, which Wesley answered with a delighted grin.

~

THE NEXT TWO days passed without incident, although occasional sightings of what Mr. Finnegan called *bergy bits* brought passengers running to the promenade deck rail for a glimpse. The elephant-sized lumps of ice were floating in the ocean like gigantic hailstones, but never came close enough to the ship to pose any danger. Clear, warm weather was the rule, and the seas remained calm enough that only a very few sensitive individuals were plagued with continued seasickness.

Never before had Belle been in such amiable company. Pleasant and diverting shipboard activities presented themselves at every turn, and she was getting along with everyone famously. Most importantly, she and Wesley had settled into a comfortable relationship, with nary a disagreeable moment. True to her word, Louise had not said anything more about Belle's feelings, and Belle had managed to occupy herself so thoroughly she didn't have time to dwell on them. Although she couldn't pretend her contentment would last forever, she was determined to enjoy it as long as possible.

The dance club continued to make progress on the quadrille, practicing it so frequently that even Carl became familiar with the parts and movements. At the end of the meeting on Wednesday afternoon, Belle had a suggestion.

"Since we are arriving in Liverpool Saturday, we really have only two days left for dance club meetings. Would anyone like to learn the polka tomorrow?"

Eva and Stacy let out little exclamations of excitement.

"Yes, please!" Louise's curls bobbed up and down with the movement of her body. "What fun!"

"I'd love to learn the polka," Wesley said.

"Nothing would please me more," Stephen said.

Carl rolled his eyes. "I'll probably be just as good at the polka as I am with the waltz."

"And you, Mr. Egermann?" Belle asked.

"I already know how to dance the polka," Horatio replied.

Stacy and Eva groaned and exchanged a glance.

Wesley glanced at their pianist. "Cavendish, do you know any polka tunes?"

"A fair few, sir." The valet played several spritely stanzas of Dvorak's *Polka in E major*.

Belle smiled. "It's settled, then. Tomorrow, we polka."

                              ∾

THAT EVENING, the saloon passengers were invited to a concert in the second class dining hall. The D'Oyly Carte Opera Company was returning to England after a tour in the United States, and they were to present an evening of music from *The Pirates of Penzance*, complete with props and costumes. The news had created a general sense of excitement among the saloon passengers; Wesley was looking forward to it as well.

After dinner, he escorted his mother downstairs for the performance. The dining hall in second class had no soaring dome or ceiling, but it was large, comfortable and well-appointed nonetheless. The concert proved so popular that Wesley and many other gentlemen were obliged to give up their seats to ladies and move to the back. He found himself standing next to Stephen, where the air between them crackled with ill-disguised static.

As the concert commenced, Wesley admired the Major General's patter and chuckled throughout *I am a Pirate King*. Thereafter, a pretty soprano began to sing *Poor Wand'ring One*, and as she sang, the girl strolled among the passengers and continued on to the back of the room. After her song was finished, the ingénue gave Wesley a kiss on the cheek. The room burst into applause.

Flustered, Wesley could scarcely listen to the company's fine rendition of *How Beautifully Blue the Sky*. When the singers paused to change props, Stephen leaned over to needle him. "You really *are* an American devil, aren't you?"

"What are you talking about?"

"Your lady friend, the soprano."

Wesley peered at him. "She's *not* my lady friend, Stephen. I never saw her before in my life."

"Right you are. She just picked you out of a whole room of people at random?"

"As a matter of fact, yes." Wesley fumed at Stephen's insinuation. "Furthermore, people would more easily expect a string of lady friends from you, not me."

"I should thrash you for that."

Wesley shot him an angry glance. "I wouldn't want you to muss your hair."

Stephen balled his fists. "See here—"

Just then, Mr. Duncan brushed past on his way to the front of the dining hall. "Excuse me, everyone! Can I have your attention?"

The chatter stopped.

"Sorry to interrupt," Mr. Duncan said. "About an hour ago, we came across a steamer in distress."

The dining hall was immediately filled with a frightened din, which the chief officer tried to calm. "The *City of New York* is in no danger, I assure you! But our assistance has been requested, and Captain Howe is obliged to render aid. Does anyone here speak Italian?"

Wesley glanced around, assuming someone fluent would respond. Nobody did, so he cleared his throat. "Mr. Duncan, I speak a very little Italian. How can I help?"

"Come with me, Your Grace. And to everyone else, please forgive the interruption. Continue with the concert, if you like."

Mr. Duncan escorted Wesley from the room, trailed closely by Stephen.

"What's the situation?" Wesley asked as they mounted the stairs.

"I'm not entirely sure myself, Your Grace. A half hour ago, five crewmen rowed a longboat over from the *Apollo*, requesting our help. After they conferred with the captain, he sent me to find someone who speaks Italian. That's all I know."

When Wesley emerged on deck, he saw the *Apollo* crewmen wearing cork jackets underneath Macintosh coats, huddled in conversation with Captain Howe.

"Captain, His Grace speaks Italian," Mr. Duncan said.

Wesley hastened to clarify. "Only a little...a few words here and there. I'm not sure if I'm of any use at all."

"Son, we've canvassed everyone on the ship and you're the

best we've got." Captain Howe's expression was strained. "The SS *Apollo* was en route to New York when she suffered an engine explosion. She's hulled and taking on water. Captain Yarborough needs his passengers and crew to evacuate the ship as quickly as possible."

Wesley was mystified. "That's horrible but what can I do?"

"The saloon passengers apparently understand the situation full well, but the steerage passengers are another matter. They're Italian emigrants, speak not a word of English, and are terrified out of their wits."

"The *Apollo* doesn't have anybody on board who speaks Italian?"

Captain Howe shook his head. "The interpreter was killed in the blast."

Wesley grimaced. "All right. I'm happy to help in any way I can."

"Excellent. The *Apollo* crew will row you to their vessel, where you must convince the Italians to evacuate the ship... women and children first."

Several passengers had followed Wesley from the concert and formed a crowd of curious onlookers.

Matilda pushed her way through in time to hear Captain Howe's request. "No! A tiny rowboat in the Atlantic Ocean isn't safe! Captain, you're asking too much."

Wesley gripped his mother by the arms. "If I don't go, people will die."

Matilda's eyes shone with emotion. "I won't have you risk your life, Wesley. You're all I have left."

"Mother, I wouldn't be any kind of a man if I don't help."

"Your Grace, he'll wear a cork jacket and carry a life buoy." Captain Howe nodded. "And the longboat is quite seaworthy."

Stephen shouldered past Mr. Duncan. "I'll go too."

Wesley looked at him askance. "You don't speak Italian."

"I studied Latin. How different can it be?" Stephen's teeth gleamed in the lamplight. "Besides, if there are ladies to cajole, I'm just the person to do it."

Wesley groaned. "Now I've heard everything.".

At that point, Cavendish stepped forward. "I volunteer as well."

Captain Howe held up his hand. "Mr. Van Eyck may be of some use. But as much as I laud your offer, Mr. Cavendish, this is no fit task for aught but the very young."

Wesley exchanged a glance with Stephen. "When do we get started, Captain?"

"There's no time to lose, lad."

As cork jackets and life buoys were brought around, Mrs. Van Eyck arrived, and began to remonstrate with her son. Wesley suddenly noticed Belle standing nearby, her hazel eyes wide with fear. Before he could say anything, she threw herself into his arms. As they embraced, he could feel her trembling uncontrollably.

His arms tightened around her body. "You're cold."

"No, I'm frightened."

Wesley nuzzled her hair with his cheek. "It's going to be all right, you know."

"Just the same, I won't rest until you return, safe and sound." Belle kissed him on the cheek. "That's a promise."

While Wesley shrugged on his cork jacket, Stephen took Belle's hand. "I could very well perish out there."

She nodded. "Yes, I—"

Without warning, Stephen pulled her into a kiss. Wesley had to restrain himself from dragging him back by the collar like a cur.

"That's enough, Stephen," he said, tight-lipped. "It's time to go."

Stephen released Belle, with obvious reluctance. "Thank you, Miss Oakhurst. Now I can die a happy man."

Mr. Duncan dropped a cork jacket over Stephen's head, helped him tie it around his waist, and thrust a life buoy into his hand.

"You're all set, lads. Good luck to you."

Wesley and Stephen approached the winch that would lower them down the side of the ocean liner and into the waiting longboat.

Wesley shot Stephen a level glance. "You'll pay dearly for that."

Far from being cowed, the man chuckled. "Come now, Wesley. You're just angry you didn't think of it first."

∼

ALTHOUGH BELLE WAS HORRIBLY EMBARRASSED about Stephen's kiss, she was too frightened for him and Wesley to do much of anything except stifle a rebuke. *Just when I thought he was acting like a gentleman!* As the two young men disappeared over the side of the ship, Louise hugged Belle and sobbed. Over Louise's shoulder, she caught Mrs. Van Eyck's eye. Belle's face flooded with heat when she realized Stephen's mother must have seen the kiss. *Blast Stephen! He's put me in a horrible position!* Instantly she regretted the thought. It sounded too much like a curse, and although she was furious with Stephen, she didn't want anything to happen to him. Belle said a quick silent prayer for Wesley's safe return…and slipped in a grudging word for Stephen as well.

Afterward, she pulled Louise toward the railing. "Let's watch them as long as possible."

The bedraggled *Apollo* crew had already taken their places in the longboat by the time Wesley and Stephen were winched down. Once the two were seated forward in the prow, the longboat's oars were lowered into the water.

As the boat moved off, Mr. Duncan came to stand next to Belle and Louise. "Those are two brave lads. 'Tis lucky we're in the Grand Banks and not the Flemish Cap."

Belle studied him. "Why is that, sir?"

"The ocean current moves in a clockwise direction in the Flemish Cap and we'd be further separated from the *Apollo* for certain." He paused. "Of course, nothing is for certain except uncertainty."

Belle gulped. As she watched the longboat increase its distance from the *City of New York*, she knew one thing at least was certain—Wesley Parker and Stephen van Eyck had just placed themselves in mortal danger and she'd never been so afraid for anyone in her life.

CHAPTER 15
OPTIMISM

Waves lapped up against the side of the wooden longboat, spraying frigid saltwater onto the men inside. The heat left Wesley's body so quickly, he longed to row with the crew to stay warm. Stephen, who was sitting on the bench next to him, must have felt the same way because he nudged Wesley with an elbow and pointed to a pair of long oars at their feet.

Wesley nodded. "Let's do it."

They turned around until they were facing the *City of New York*, lunged for the oars, fitted them into the oarlocks, and began to row in concert with the crew. As the blood flowed into his muscles, Wesley's misery was only slightly alleviated. Nevertheless, the exercise took his mind off the fact he was in a small boat in the midst of a vast, pitiless ocean. The unrelieved blackness that stretched out on all sides made Wesley feel small and insignificant. He gritted his teeth against the maelstrom of fear that threatened to paralyze his thoughts and fixed his gaze on the rapidly retreating *City of New York* instead.

The *Apollo* was at a far greater distance than she'd looked from the deck of the huge ocean liner. Worse, the waves of the Atlantic slowed the longboat's progress. The better part of an hour passed before they reached their destination. By then, Wesley was at once clammy with sweat and chilled to the core. His fingers were seemingly frozen to the oar's handles, but he peeled them free to climb the rope ladder onto the three-masted, single-screw ship. His muscles were so logy that his progress was slow. When he finally set foot on deck, a blanket was thrown over his shoulders and a mug of hot coffee was thrust into his hands. Stephen staggered on board a few moments later and was similarly greeted.

The ship's captain emerged from the bridge. "Welcome aboard. My name is Captain Yarborough."

To Wesley's humiliation, his teeth were chattering uncontrollably. "W-Wesley P-Parker, Duke of Mansbury."

Stephen fared little better. "S-Stephen V-Van Eyck."

The captain ushered them below deck and into the first class dining hall, where the acrid smell of smoke from the boiler room explosion immediately assailed Wesley's nostrils and stung his eyes. The room, filled with almost one hundred fifty well-dressed people, was perhaps one-third the size of the saloon on the *City of New York*. Passengers, their faces twisted with fear, rushed forward to pepper the new arrivals with questions and demands for help. Wesley noticed one bejeweled lady held a barking Yorkshire terrier.

"Quiet!" Captain Yarborough waited for the din to cease before turning toward Wesley. "Do you have a message for us, Your Grace?"

Wesley took a deep breath and tried to slow the shivers racking his body. "Captain Howe of the *City of New York* is prepared to offer his assistance."

His statement was met with a cacophony of reactions—cries of relief, more questions, and shrill demands. Wesley exchanged an exasperated glance with Stephen, who lost his temper.

"Stay calm and be *quiet!*" he bellowed.

To Wesley's mild surprise, the crowd fell silent. Even the dog stopped barking.

"Thank you," Wesley said, as much to Stephen as to anyone else. "Captain, we've room on the *City of New York* for your passengers and crew, but evacuation will be nearly impossible unless you decrease the distance between our vessels."

"It will be done."

The captain rattled off orders to his Chief Officer, who sped from the room to comply.

"Captain Howe requests the first evacuees be women and children," Wesley said.

A look of aggravation crossed Yarborough's face. "Yes, of course, but my steerage passengers are the difficulty. In fact, they are presently under guard lest they overrun the ship in panic. I can't seem to make them understand."

"Take me to them," Wesley said.

"You speak Italian?"

"A little. I just hope it's enough to help."

Wesley and Stephen shed their blankets, Mackintosh jackets, and cork vests. As Captain Yarborough escorted them from the saloon, Wesley noticed piles of luggage stacked near the entrance.

He glanced at the captain. "There's no possible way to transfer those things to the ship."

"I understand full well," Yarborough replied. "The passengers were instructed to take only what they could carry, but they won't listen to reason. That's why I opened the weapons locker to my men, just in case things turn ugly."

The captain led Wesley and Stephen past the bridge and down a staircase to the deck below. When compared to the

City of New York, the *Apollo* was very compact. The ceilings were lower, the passageways and staircases narrower, and the finishes were far less luxurious. If Wesley had not first seen the *City of New York*, however, he would have thought the *Apollo* a handsome sort of ship. Mahogany panels lined the walls, highly polished brass fixtures reflected light from electric sconces, and tasteful artwork was on display.

Stephen peered at the lights. "You still have electricity? How is that possible?"

"We lost our engine in the explosion, but the generator remains intact—for now. The *Apollo* is sinking, and the generator may soon be swamped."

Wesley grimaced. "How long do we have?"

"An hour, if the sea stays calm and our luck holds. After that, we'll have to make do with kerosene lanterns."

Near the bottom of the steps, two crewmen with pistols stood at attention as the captain approached.

"Fall in behind and have your weapons ready," Yarborough ordered.

"Aye, aye, Captain."

Hazy thick smoke lingered in the air at this level, making it difficult to draw breath. Wesley's shoes squished as he stepped from the carpeted stairs into the wet passageway, and raised voices became audible.

Stephen winced. "Sounds like one big argument going on."

The three of them, flanked by the armed crewmen, ducked through the doorway into a dining hall. Around fifty Italians were inside, sitting on long wooden benches with their legs drawn up, or on the dining table itself. Several older children floated paper boats in the briny seawater while the younger ones cried in their mother's arms. As soon as the passengers saw Captain Yarborough, the shouting began in earnest. One tall swarthy man approached, spewing Italian curse words Wesley recognized but would never repeat. The crewmen brandished their weapons, but Wesley stepped forward and held up his hands.

"My name is Wesley," he shouted. "*Ascoltare!*"

The din paused and the painful process of trying to communicate began. Mocking laughter greeted Wesley's attempts to speak Italian, and he felt his face flush red. Just when he was about to give up in despair, a young child pointed at Wesley's chest.

"*È San Cristoforo!*"

Wesley glanced down. His shirt had torn open when he removed his cork vest, revealing the Saint Christopher medal Sergio had given him. *Thank you, Sergio!* A sense of relief flowed through Wesley as he lifted the medal from around his neck and held it up for everyone to see.

"*Si, è San Cristoforo*," he said. "Please listen. *Per favore ascoltare.*"

Wesley slipped the medal over the child's head and began to speak again. With the hostility defused, the passengers tried to understand him this time. The swarthy man finally tapped his barrel chest.

"*Mi chiamano* Matteo. *Vuoi che venga con te alla barca grande?*"

Wesley could only make out a few words, but they were the important ones.

"*Si,* Matteo, *alla barca grande,*" he repeated, nodding in an exaggerated fashion. "To the big boat. Ladies and children first. *Donne e bambini prima.*"

At that point, the women began to protest while the men tried to make them see reason. Wesley glanced at the captain. "They understand now, I think. How soon before you can drop lifeboats into the water?"

"The *Apollo* has been turning the whole while we've been down here. I'll go topside to check on her progress."

After Yarborough left, Wesley sagged against the wall, emotionally and physically spent. He couldn't help notice Stephen's smirk.

"You've something to say?"

Stephen shrugged. "Yeah. That wasn't too bad, Wesley. Well done, actually."

Wesley peered at him. "You know, I'd like you far better if you left Miss Oakhurst alone."

In response, Stephen laughed. "On that, we must agree to disagree."

∼

Captain Yarborough managed to halve the distance between the *Apollo* and the *City of New York* before ordering the first of the lifeboats lowered into the water. Wesley and Stephen tried to coax the steerage woman and children from the dining hall, but they cried and clung to their husbands and fathers. Finally Matteo raised his voice over the din. His words crackled with authority, and the women reluctantly picked up worn carpetbags, took children by the hand, and followed Wesley and Stephen on deck.

Overhead, clouds had blotted out the moon and stars, and the ocean swells had doubled in size. Wesley did not have to be an expert sailor to recognize the increased danger. The crew of the *Apollo* busied themselves guiding women and children passengers into lifeboats, and a short while later the first of the boats pushed off for the *City of New York*. It rose up on the crest of a huge swell and then disappeared on the other side. As the second lifeboat prepared to depart, a fracas ensued. The woman holding her dog was bristling with indignation as she bent the captain's ear with a shrill English accent.

"Captain Yarborough, I simply *refuse* to ride with steerage!"

Stephen and Wesley exchanged a disgusted glance.

"Madam, you've no choice—" Yarborough began.

"Here." Stephen marched over. "Let me help."

The woman gasped when he plucked the dog from her arms and handed the squirming animal down the side of the ship, into the waiting arms of a crewman. Although she was beside herself, she hastened to follow her pet into the lifeboat. She repeated, "Well, I never!" the entire way, but at last the boat shoved off.

"Thank you, lad," Yarborough said, patting Stephen on the shoulder. "I was about to throw the beast into the drink."

"Which beast?" Stephen muttered.

The captain shouted orders to his crew to move faster. After the women and children were loaded, a shoving match broke out amongst the men over their place in line. Since many of the crew were engaged in either rowing lifeboats or trying to keep the *Apollo* from drifting, Wesley and Stephen stepped in to sort things out. Wesley took a blow to the jaw for his efforts, but the third and fourth lifeboats finally began inching across the writhing ocean to safety. By then, the *Apollo* was sitting decidedly lower in the water, and the larger waves were sending spray onto the deck. The electrical lights on board began to flicker and the remaining crew lit kerosene lamps.

"Lads, time is running short. I want you on the next boat," Yarborough said.

Stephen grinned and gave him a salute. "Aye, aye, Captain."

∼

The crew and passengers on the *City of New York* formed a human chain to receive refugees from the *Apollo*. Belle and Louise handed out blankets to cold, wet, and terrified women and children before stewards led the refugees to their quarters in steerage. Most of the new arrivals were emotionally numb and compliant, but one dreadful woman with a dog in her arms demanded to see Captain Howe. He emerged from the bridge and listened patiently as she reeled off a list of requirements: she would have a deck cabin, chopped chicken liver for her pet, and the ship must turn around and head to New York as soon as may be.

"I'm sorry, madam, what may I call you?" the captain asked.

"Mrs. Stilton of Gosling Manor, Gloucester. My dog's name is Princess."

Captain Howe beckoned to a waiting steward.

"Mr. Kelly, please escort Mrs. Stilton and Princess to the finest accommodations we have—in steerage."

"What!" Mrs. Stilton exclaimed, trembling in outrage. "I never!"

"You're welcome to take your meals in the saloon, Mrs. Stilton, but all our first and second class rooms and cabins are full. Furthermore, I plan to arrive in Liverpool only a half-day behind schedule. Welcome aboard."

Captain Howe bowed, turned on his heel, and returned to the bridge. Belle and Louise exchanged an amused glance, which Mrs. Stilton unfortunately noticed. She singled Belle out for her wrath.

"Having a joke at my expense are we?" she snapped. "You'll regret it, I'm sure."

Belle curtsied. "I beg your pardon."

Mrs. Stilton strode off with Mr. Kelly, her nose in the air.

Louise stared after her, aghast. "What was *that* all about?"

Belle sighed. "Adversity can bring out the best or worst in people. Obviously, Mrs. Stilton falls into the latter category."

~

WESLEY HASTENED toward the *Apollo* saloon, relishing the idea of spending a few moments someplace warm. Stephen rubbed his hands together and stuck them under his armpits.

"Playing the hero is chilly work, I must say," he said.

"Agreed." Wesley rubbed his bruised jaw. "And occasionally painful."

"When I get back to the *City of New York*, I'd like a sandwich and a tot of brandy. Not necessarily in that order."

The lights sputtered, but stayed lit.

"I'm glad we're getting on the next boat," Wesley muttered. "I believe the ship is sinking sooner rather than later."

Apprehension showed in Stephen's eyes. "Right you are."

They burst into the saloon, past the pile of abandoned luggage, and then dashed toward the cork vests and Mackintosh jackets they'd left on the table. Wesley suddenly noticed a well-dressed man kneeling in front of an open trunk.

"You should be on deck, sir," Wesley called out. "The last of the lifeboats are loading now."

As the man straightened, he slipped a handful of jewelry into his pocket with a furtive motion. "Thanks, kid. Much obliged."

The man's American accent had a Western twang. Wesley glanced at the luggage; many of the trunks were open and their contents strewn onto the floor.

Stephen frowned. "It looks an awful lot like you're stealing valuables that don't belong to you."

The fellow's eyes narrowed. "That's none of your business, is it? Besides, it's all going into Davy Jones's locker anyway."

Stephen lifted his chin. "Nevertheless, I'm going to notify the captain."

Before Stephen could take more than a few steps, a second man stepped out from behind the door and swung a cane at Stephen's head like a club.

"Watch out!" Wesley yelled.

The corner of the cane struck Stephen's temple with a sickening thud and he dropped to the ground, out cold. Wesley launched himself toward Stephen's assailant. Before the man could pull back the cane for another strike, Wesley knocked him flat. The first thief leaped over the luggage and shoved Wesley backward. The two exchanged several blows, but Wesley finally hit the fellow hard enough to send him flying over the long dining table. He rushed to Stephen's aid, but then something heavy came crashing down on his head and the lights went out.

∽

BLACKNESS AND A THROBBING headache greeted Wesley when he opened his eyes. *Am I blind?* He sat up, reached out his hands into the darkness...and encountered a body.

"Stephen, is that you?" Wesley shook him and was rewarded with a groan. "Wake up!"

"Where are we?"

"I don't know." Wesley struggled to his feet. In the process, he kicked over what sounded like a metal bucket. "Blast!"

"Don't make any more noise!" Stephen exclaimed. "My head hurts like the devil and it's making me queasy. I may get sick."

"Please don't. We're in a closet."

"A what?" Stephen repeated, confused. "Why are we in a closet?"

"Those two thieves must have dragged us in here after they knocked us unconscious."

"How long have we been out?" Stephen sat up quickly, banging into a shelf. "Ow!"

"I don't know, but we have to get to the lifeboat."

Wesley fumbled around until he found the door. Unfortunately, there was no knob and the panel would not yield to pressure.

"Damnation, we're locked in!"

He pounded on the door, and shouted, but there was no answer. Stephen joined him, but still nobody came.

"We're making a horrible racket! Why doesn't anyone come?" he asked finally.

Wesley made a sound of frustration. "Nobody can hear us. They're all on deck."

"There's nothing for it, then. We'll have to break the door down."

Wesley and Stephen used their shoulders as battering rams. After several painful blows, the hinges began to give way. At last the door crashed to the ground and they emerged from the closet into more darkness.

"I suppose the generator finally went out," Stephen said. "More bad luck."

Wesley peered across the room, where he discerned a glow. "I see some light."

"I see it, too."

The ship rolled to the one side just then, lying almost flat in the water. Stephen was thrown into Wesley and they both ended up on the floor. Nearby, the sound of breaking glass was followed closely by the strong odor of alcohol. The ship finally righted itself, accompanied by a cacophony of ominous creaks. Wesley and Stephen got to their feet.

"Do you smell that? We must still be in the saloon," Stephen said. "And if the ship experiences another roll like the one we just had, it will sink for certain."

Wesley could hear the tension in Stephen's voice.

"We'll be on the *City of New York* before that happens," he replied.

Wesley crept forward in the dark until he encountered one of the swivel chairs anchored next to the dining table. As he felt his way across the room, Wesley felt compelled to make conversation...if only to fill the silence.

"Terrible waste of fine scotch, from the smell of it," he called out.

"An utter tragedy, separate and beyond the loss of the ship," Stephen replied from the opposite side of the table.

"I must tell you, I've never been stuffed into a closet before."

"Nor have I. An ignominious end to a heroic escapade," Stephen replied. "But it'll be the worse for the rascals who put us there, when we get hold of them."

"Indeed. I take umbrage at being savagely attacked and left for dead, don't you?"

"Umbrage of the highest sort," Stephen agreed. "Umbrage supreme, I think."

They left the saloon and tore up the stairs to the deck of the ship. When they emerged into the open air, Wesley and Stephen stood there agape. Light from the kerosene lamps revealed the deck was clear of people, the *Apollo* had been abandoned completely, and they were on their own. Wesley repeated a few Italian curse words out loud.

"This explains why nobody came to help," Stephen said.

Although panic had seized him by the throat, Wesley

forced himself to stay calm. "We can lower a lifeboat into the water and row to the *City of New York*. Between the two of us, we're strong enough to manage."

"Right."

Wesley and Stephen each grabbed a kerosene lamp off its hook and went in search of a lifeboat. Unfortunately, a quick examination of the *Apollo* revealed all the longboats had been deployed.

Stephen stared at Wesley, stricken. "We're dead men."

"Look, there has to be *something* buoyant we can use as a raft," Wesley said, desperate. "Perhaps we can lash a few doors together and float until a ship passes by and picks us up."

"The *City of New York* is long gone, Wesley. Just how long do you think we'd last in that water? For heaven's sake, I nearly froze to death in the longboat as it was!"

"They'll notice we're missing and come back for us."

"Surely everyone but the crew has turned in by now. By morning, the *City of New York* will be a hundred miles from here and we'll have drowned."

"Belle won't have gone to bed," Wesley said. "She's waiting for us."

"Quit being so damned...hopeful!" Stephen snapped. "We're done for. Even if they wanted to look for us, we've no generator. Without lights, we might as well be invisible!"

"The *Apollo* might not sink after all," Wesley said. "It seems like the waves have diminished."

A huge wave broke over the side of the ship at that moment and sprayed both men with frigid sea foam.

As Stephen dried his face with his sleeve, a crooked grin crept across his lips. "You're right, Wesley. The ocean has grown calm and the ship won't sink. It's also possible a dirigible airship flown by leprechauns will pass overhead and pluck us off the *Apollo*. Anything could happen."

For some strange reason, Wesley grinned back. "That's the spirit. You never know, perhaps an iceberg will happen by. We could jump on and ride it all the way to South America."

"Or a pod of whales might offer to give us a lift to Greenland."

Wesley and Stephen dissolved into hysterical laughter.

"Let's...let's go find those cork jackets and put them on," Wesley said finally.

Stephen looked at him, askance. "More optimism?"

"No." Wesley swallowed hard. "It's just that should anyone come searching for us, they'll have a better chance of finding our bodies if they're afloat. I'm thinking of my mother."

Stephen averted his eyes. "Yes. Agreed."

"And while we're in the saloon, perhaps we can find an unbroken bottle of scotch to keep us warm."

Stephen slapped Wesley on the back. "Now *that's* a reason to be optimistic."

CHAPTER 16
GOING AWAY PARTY

From the moment Wesley and Stephen departed the *City of New York*, Belle kept a vigil. Similarly, Cavendish paced up and down the promenade like a caged badger. Mr. Oakhurst pleaded with his daughter to go inside to get warm or to turn in for the night, but she refused. "No, Papa. I need to make certain Wesley is safe. Stephen van Eyck too. I can sleep all day tomorrow."

Defeated, her father brought up a heavy coat from her cabin and made her put it on. Louise helped with refugees as long as she could, but finally wilted with the lateness of the hour. She settled into a deck chair near the staging area.

"Annabelle, you must wake me as soon as Stephen and Wesley return." Louise yawned. "Promise me you will."

Belle nodded. "Of course."

The increasingly choppy waves fomented a general resurgence of *mal de mer*. Many stalwart passengers helping to receive the *Apollo* refugees were obliged to retire in misery. Carl, Horatio, Stacy, and Eva lent their assistance until Mrs. Stenger sent them to bed. Mrs. Van Eyck and the duchess sat in deck chairs, wrapped in coats and blankets. They stole catnaps here and there, waking up with each new batch of refugees. After midnight, however, neither woman could keep her eyes open.

The fourth longboat disgorged its passengers, and Belle noted a few men among the mix. *They've evacuated all the women and children now, so Wesley and Stephen should be on the next boat.* But the next three boats arrived without them and she began to be impatient. *Why hasn't the captain of the* Apollo *sent them on? Surely he doesn't need their help any longer, does he?*

Belle caught the arm of a newly arrived *Apollo* crewman as he crossed toward a rolling cart laden with fresh coffee, hot cider, and chocolate.

"Excuse me, sir, but how many lifeboats does the Apollo have?"

"Eight, miss, and each one full to bursting."

She released him. "Thank you."

Moments later, Mr. Oakhurst draped a blanket around Belle's shoulders. She gave him a grateful smile. "Thank you, Papa."

"The saloon is serving light refreshments until the last soul has been rescued." He jerked his head toward the deck house. "Go downstairs and get something to eat."

She shook her head. "There's only one more lifeboat to be accounted for, Papa. I can wait until then."

Mr. Oakhurst stared out over the water. "I understand how you feel. I can't rest until they are safe either."

Belle glanced toward Cavendish, who was slumped on a deck chair with his head in his hands. The man's ordinarily pristine attire was rumpled and his hair awry.

"We're not the only worried ones, it seems," she said.

"I think His Grace will be touched when he hears of his valet's loyalty."

A sudden surge of moisture blurred Belle's vision. "Wesley Parker has the uncanny ability to make people care about him, Papa, whether they want to or not."

"Are you speaking of your personal feelings?"

She was glad her blush could be explained by the blustery wind. "I-I only meant he'll make a good duke. His servants and tenants will find him a vast deal more amiable than his predecessor."

"Hmm. True." Mr. Oakhurst paused. "I've developed a high regard for the lad myself."

Just then the last longboat appeared, emerging from the increasingly heavy fog that had formed after the storm passed. Belle roused Louise, and then returned to the railing to watch for Wesley and Stephen. Louise, bleary, crossed over to her mother and the duchess to shake them awake.

As the longboat came alongside the *City of New York*, Belle peered down at the passengers. Despite the darkness and distance, she picked out the captain of the *Apollo* by his hat and uniform. She saw neither Wesley nor Stephen at first, so she moved closer for a better view and scanned each man one by one. *This can't be right.* As a tall swarthy Italian was hauled up from the lifeboat, Belle checked the faces again…and then a third time. Her heart stopped and she clutched her father's sleeve.

"Papa, he's not there! I've looked, and Wesley's not there! Stephen van Eyck isn't there either. What has happened?"

Belle's knees buckled, but her father caught her around the waist and led her to a deckchair.

"Are you sure, Annabelle? Perhaps he came aboard before and you didn't notice with all the confusion?"

Tears streamed down her face, but Belle didn't bother to wipe them away. "Ask Cavendish! Do you think he would be out here if Wesley had returned?"

The valet had nodded off, but he came awake at the sound of his name. He blinked and looked around. "What?"

"He's not here, Cavendish," Belle cried in anguish. "The last lifeboat has come and Wesley isn't on it!"

The duchess, Mrs. Van Eyck, and Louise overheard and stared at Belle in utter shock. White-faced, Cavendish rushed to the railing to see for himself. At that moment, the captain of the *Apollo* stepped from the winch onto the deck. His waiting crew gave him a salute, but Belle didn't bother with formalities. She sprang from the deckchair and launched herself into his path.

"Where are Wesley Parker and Stephen van Eyck, the gentlemen who came to help you?" she demanded.

The captain was bewildered. "I sent them back after the fourth boat, miss. They must be here. Have you checked in their cabins?"

"You left them behind!" Belle's voice rose in volume until it was almost a scream. "They helped you and you left them to *die*."

∼

WESLEY HELD up a kerosene lamp to illuminate the wreckage in the bar. "Aha." He wrapped his fingers around a bottle of amber liquid and held it up for Stephen to see. "This scotch is older than we are."

"Bring it."

Stephen slipped a bottle of champagne in one pocket of his Mackintosh jacket and a couple of drinking glasses in the other. "I hate to drink on an empty stomach, even one covered with cork." He patted the vest tied around his middle. "Let's find the galley. There has to be something to eat on this boat."

"I hope the galley is on this deck because the one below is probably flooded."

Fortunately, the galley was adjacent to the saloon and accessible through a sliding door. Broken crockery crunched under Wesley's feet as he surveyed the contents of the icebox.

"Mutton, cold chicken, or sliced roast beef?" he called over his shoulder.

"Roast beef," Stephen replied from the pantry. "I've got bread for sandwiches, and cake too."

They piled their provisions onto a rolling cart.

"Where shall we have our going away party?" Stephen asked.

"The bridge," Wesley said. "Except for the masts, it's the highest point on the ship."

The *Apollo* creaked and groaned as Stephen pushed the cart from the galley and through the saloon. He held the lamps while Wesley balanced the food on a large serving tray and carried it up to the deck. The sea was calm by then, but a thick eerie fog was stealing across the water like steam.

"It looks like we've sailed into a tea kettle," Stephen said.

Wesley shivered. "If only it were that warm."

Inside the bridge, Stephen hung the kerosene lamps from hooks on the ceiling and emptied the coal scuttle into the pot-bellied stove. Wesley arranged the feast on a map table and pulled up a pair of tall stools. Stephen produced the glasses and champagne from his pockets. As he set the bottle on the table, he frowned. "Oh, blast, I forgot a corkscrew."

Wesley held up the required instrument. "I brought one from the galley."

Stephen grinned. "We make a good team."

"I was just thinking that myself." Wesley poured a quantity of scotch in the glasses and handed one to Stephen for a toast. "Here's to going away."

"And away we go." Stephen drained the scotch and shuddered. "Ugh! I suppose it's an acquired taste."

They devoured a sandwich apiece, ate half the cake, and then settled down to drink. After a while, Wesley wasn't sure if the swaying on the bridge was from the ship, or the strong spirits.

"I should apologize to you, Stephen. It's my fault you're in this mess." He gestured with his glass. "In hindsight, giving away my Saint Christopher's medal was ill-considered."

Stephen shook his head. "No, I invited myself along, don't you remember? Serves me right for trying to impress a girl. Guess I'll never do *that* again."

They shared a laugh, but the merriment was cut short when the ship rolled to its starboard side. Wesley steadied the bottles to keep them from tipping over and Stephen picked up the glasses. Wesley held his breath as he waited to see if the *Apollo* would straighten. To his relief, the ship came upright once more, albeit listing slightly. He let out his breath slowly and glanced at Stephen, whose face was ashen.

"I admit, I'm not quite ready to die." Stephen's voice cracked slightly. The silence that followed his remark was filled with unspoken emotion. His hands shook uncontrollably as he set down the glasses and reached for the scotch. "At least not until I've finished this bottle."

Belle's face flashed into Wesley's mind, like a beacon. *I'm not going to leave her like this!*

He shot to his feet. "We're not going to die. I won't have it."

"What do you propose?"

"I'm going to climb the masts and hang lit kerosene lanterns as high as I can. If anyone is out there, maybe they'll see the light and come to our aid."

"You'll slip and fall, Wesley!"

"Perhaps that will be a mercy."

Stephen stood and brushed cake crumbs from his clothes. "All right, I'll help. If we're going to die, we may as well go down swinging."

At the base of the mainmast, Wesley tied the end of a rope around his waist.

"When I reach the uppermost yardarm, tie the lamp handle to the rope and I'll haul it up," he said.

Stephen squinted at the mast. "It's awfully far."

"I don't want to think about it."

Before he changed his mind, Wesley began to climb the rigging. If it had been broad daylight, he might not have been brave enough to make a climb thirty feet high. As it was, the nighttime fog gave him the sensation of being wrapped in a silken cocoon. When he reached the yardarm, he gave the rope a tug. Stephen tugged back; Wesley pulled up the kerosene lamp and used a shorter length of rope to tie the lamp in place. He climbed down and then repeated the process with the foremast and the mizzenmast. The three lamps hanging high overhead sent a distinct glow that pierced the misty fog.

When he reached the deck for the third and final time, Stephen gave him a look of admiration. "You have nerves of steel, Wesley."

"Not really. It's just that I can't see past ten feet due to the fog."

"While you were up there, I thought of something else. We could take turns ringing the ship's big brass bell hanging next to the bridge."

Wesley stared at him, dumbfounded. "That's brilliant."

"It was the fog that made me think of it."

Stephen took the first turn, ringing the bell vigorously, as if he were on his way to a fire. When his arm grew tired, Wesley took over. Then they switched off again, all the while pretending not to notice the water lapping over the deck. Stephen had just begun to use his left arm on the clapper rope when Wesley flinched. "Stop! I hear something!"

Stephen quieted the bell with his hands. "All I hear is ringing in my head."

"Shh!"

Wesley ran to the railing and listened. A very faint "Ahoy there!" reached his ears. He turned toward Stephen, chortling with glee.

"Did you hear that? Someone's out there! Keep ringing!"

As Stephen rang the bell for all he was worth, Wesley cupped his hands around his mouth and shouted. "Hullo! We're here! Hullo!"

The fog prevented him from seeing any boats on the water. *If I can't see them, maybe they can't see us!* Wesley tore into the bridge, grabbed the empty coal scuttle and bottle of scotch, and brought them both onto the open deck. After he shrugged off his Mackintosh coat, he untied his cork jacket, threw it in the tall metal scuttle, and doused it with scotch.

"What are you doing?" Stephen yelled. "Have you gone mad?"

"No, I'm desperate."

He tossed a burning kerosene lamp into the scuttle and stepped back. A whooshing sound accompanied a surging gust of flame, which shot over eight feet into the air. Wesley was forced to drop to the deck and crawl away to escape the billowing conflagration. Stephen gaped but did not stop ringing the bell. Wesley snatched his Mackintosh jacket from the wet deck and sloshed through water toward Stephen. They watched in dismay as burning embers rose into the air toward the sails hanging from the foremast.

Wesley gulped as he watched the flames. "I just set the *Apollo* on fire."

Seawater lapped at their feet and Stephen stopped ringing the bell. "Doesn't matter. The ship is sinking anyway."

"Climb the rigging," Wesley said. "I'll keep the bell going as long as I can before I join you."

"I'm staying, not you. You don't have your cork jacket anymore."

"That was my decision and you shouldn't have to pay for it. Get going."

"Don't be stupid!"

"I'm not stupid, I'm practical."

"I'm *not* going without you!"

Just then, the lower foremast sail caught fire. The intense heat drove Wesley and Stephen back from the bridge.

"Have it your way, Stephen," Wesley said. "We'll both go."

He led the way toward the stern of the ship, where rigging spread out on either side of the mizzenmast. Stephen took one side and Wesley took the other. Halfway up, however, the *Apollo* rolled for the last time. With a splintering crack, the mizzenmast broke at its base and fell with a slow arc into the frigid Atlantic.

Wesley's ankle became entangled in the rope rigging, and he was submerged. The shock of the cold water nearly stopped his heart, but something inside wouldn't let him give up. He managed to free himself from the rigging and swim to the surface. His breathing was fast and deep, as if he could not get enough oxygen, and the strength was ebbing from his limbs. *I'm so sorry, Belle, but I'm not going to make it after all. I wish we could've had more time together.*

Suddenly he felt something tugging on his coat, and an arm went around his chest.

"I'll hold onto you as long as I can," Stephen rasped.

"Thanks," Wesley managed.

In the water nearby, the *Apollo* was ablaze and sinking fast. A fuzzy, sleepy sensation began to dull Wesley's senses. The next thing he knew, a wooden wall was sliding past his face. Confused, he reached out a hand to push it away. Something grabbed his elbow and he panicked. His feeble struggles came to nothing, but he kept fighting—with whom or against what he could not say.

"Stop struggling, Wesley!" Stephen said.

"*Dannazione!*" a deep voice cursed. "*Smettere di lottare ragazzo!*"

"Wesley, let us help you," Cavendish said.

Unable to respond, he felt his body being pulled out of the water. He rolled into the boat, barely conscious. In the next moment, a rough blanket covered him.

"Stephen," he muttered.

"We've got him, lad," Mr. Oakhurst said. "We've got you both."

CHAPTER 17
AFTERMATH

Belle burst into tears of relief when the *Apollo* longboat pulled alongside the *City of New York*, carrying its rescue crew of Mr. Oakhurst, a large Italian man, Cavendish, and Captain Yarborough, plus two additional passengers—Wesley and Stephen. The duchess, Mrs. Van Eyck, and Louise also began to cry with deep shuddering sobs. None of them would rest until the ship's surgeon confirmed Wesley and Stephen would survive their ordeal. They'd both been brought aboard nearly unconscious, with blue-tinged skin and bloodless fingernails that had made Belle gasp with dismay.

Finally, Mr. Oakhurst sent Belle to her cabin. She gave him a hug before she left.

"Thank you for saving him, Papa," she said. "Thank you."

Exhausted, Belle could barely manage to remove her clothes before collapsing into her berth. Although her mind would not truly be at ease until she'd spoken with Wesley, her body had its own agenda and she fell asleep immediately.

The hot air balloon soared over the Atlantic, its red, white, and blue colors reminiscent of the American flag. Wesley grinned as he leaned over the edge of the basket to admire the pod of purple whales keeping pace in the waves below.

"I told you we'd be rescued, Stephen!" he called out.

"You were right, Wesley. I promise to be much more optimistic next time!" Stephen replied.

Wesley pointed as a land mass became visible on the horizon. "Land, ho!"

"Do you suppose it's South America?" Stephen asked.

"I couldn't say, but I hope it's someplace warm."

As the balloon flew over solid land, it gained altitude so quickly that Wesley and Stephen were thrown to the bottom of the basket.

"What's happening?" Stephen exclaimed.

"This can't be good!" Wesley cried.

Cavendish appeared out of thin air, completely green and sitting cross-legged. "It's all part of the tour, Your Grace. We're after the pot of gold, don't you know."

"Cavendish? When did you become a leprechaun?"

Wesley and Stephen struggled to stand just as the balloon crossed over the mouth of an open, active volcano. The heat of the lava was so intense that Wesley could feel it on his bare skin. Colors on the balloon began to melt and drip on his face like hot wax. He opened his mouth to speak, but in the next moment the balloon had burst and he was screaming, falling to his death...

Wesley woke with a startled gasp. When he realized he'd been dreaming, his racing heart slowed. Several moments of confusion followed as he tried to figure out where he was and how he'd gotten there. His memories swirled like the flakes in his mother's prized French snow globe; he focused on the rosewood-paneled ceiling and allowed his thoughts to settle.

I'm not dead.

He sat up just as Cavendish appeared in the doorway of his

bedroom. The valet had dark circles under his eyes, as if he hadn't slept.

"Good morning, Your Grace. How are you feeling?"

Events from last night finally slid into place.

Wesley gulped as he formulated a question. "Stephen van Eyck? Did...did he make it?"

"Indeed he did, although he's a bit worse for wear. You were both quite lucky to have survived your ordeal. I'm going to send for the ship's surgeon to check you over and then I'll order a light breakfast for you."

"I have to speak with Captain Yarborough and Captain Howe. There are two refugees onboard who should be arrested and charged with attempted murder."

"Yes, sir." Cavendish averted his eyes a moment, overcome with emotion. "I'm glad you're alive, lad."

Wesley cleared his throat as he fought his own surge of emotion. "Cavendish...I seem to remember you were in the rescue boat last night. Thank you for coming after me."

"I couldn't have faced Miss Oakhurst otherwise. The instant the last lifeboat arrived without you, she raised the alarm."

"Somehow, I knew she would."

After the valet left, Wesley fell back onto his pillow, realizing far too late he had a painful raised knot on the back of his head the size of Manhattan. *Blast!* Further sleep was impossible, so he rose and headed for the bathroom. His ankle immediately gave him trouble, and he concluded he had injured it when the mast fell.

Eager to wash the sticky saltwater from his hair and skin, he drew a bath. The fresh warm water enveloped him in a warm cocoon. *This feels heavenly!* He lingered longer than was necessary, but he emerged and had begun to dress himself when Cavendish reappeared.

"The surgeon is on his way and the ships' captains will be along directly." The valet peered at Wesley's face. "What the devil did you do to yourself?"

A glance in the mirror revealed Wesley's eyebrows, eyelashes, and bits of his hair were singed at the ends.

"I needed to attract your attention last night, so I took my cork vest off and set it ablaze," Wesley said. "The resulting fireball must have come closer than I thought."

Cavendish sighed. "Between almost burning to death and then nearly drowning, you had a very difficult evening."

Wesley shuddered. "That I did."

~

Anxiety was written on Matilda's face as she watched the ship's surgeon examine Wesley. "How is he, Dr. Vane?"

"Except for a sprained ankle, he's fit enough."

"Oh, thank goodness!" she exclaimed.

Dr. Vane gave Wesley a severe look. "Nevertheless, Your Grace, you've had a shock to your system, so it's bed rest today and no visitors. If you feel up to it, you may attend dinner in the saloon tonight…but no gallivanting about afterward."

No sooner had Dr. Vane departed than Mr. Finnegan arrived with a breakfast tray. Matilda shooed Cavendish off to his own breakfast while she waited on Wesley. Although Wesley appreciated her ministrations, after a short while her solicitousness became grating. When she tried to salt his scrambled eggs for him, he stayed her hand.

"Mother, please don't fuss! You heard Dr. Vane say I'm fine. My ankle is tender, my muscles are stiff, and I'm singed here and there, but I can feed myself."

Her eyes filled with tears. "When I realize how close I came to losing you, I can't bear it."

"Well…" He cast about for some small service she could perform. "Could you spoon some apricot preserves onto my plate for me?"

She brightened. "Why, of course!"

Wesley could have handled the jar of preserves perfectly well by himself, but his mother's piece of mind was worth the sacrifice of a little personal dignity.

"We seem to have good weather and calm seas today," he said.

"It's beautiful outside. The captain has the engines running at full speed, trying to make up for the delay. Nevertheless, we'll arrive in Liverpool late Saturday instead of Friday night or Saturday morning."

"I wonder how the *City of New York* plans to feed all the newcomers?"

"I was curious about that myself, so I asked Mr. Finnegan. He said due to seasickness, people hadn't eaten as much as was originally planned. If they curtail the late night meal, the provisions on board should be more than enough to last the voyage. In any case, Captain Howe is putting the refugees off at Queenstown. Representatives from the shipping line will be there to deal with them."

"I'm sorry, where is Queenstown?"

"Really, Wesley, you need to brush up on your geography! Queenstown is a port city on the southern coast of Ireland, in County Cork."

"Oh. Right."

Captain Yarborough arrived with Captain Howe shortly thereafter, and Wesley described the altercation that had taken place in the saloon of the *Apollo*.

"The man who attacked Stephen had a full black mustache. The other one was a tall, well-dressed American with fair hair and a Western accent," Wesley concluded.

Captain Yarborough's eyes narrowed. "The fair-haired one is named Mr. Randolph, and his friend is Mr. Fife. They're both Americans. I suspected them of being cardsharps almost the moment they came aboard my ship."

"Cardsharps?" Wesley echoed.

"Professional gamblers who are adept at cheating," Captain Howe said. "They travel on steamships in teams, pretending not to know one other, whilst duping unsuspecting marks into high-stake card games."

"Cardsharps are the scourge of the Atlantic," Captain Yarborough added. "Now, it seems, these particular cardsharps have branched out into attempted murder."

Wesley held up the swollen knuckles of his right hand. "You'll find bruises on their faces roughly the size of my fist."

The two sea captains chuckled appreciatively.

"Good lad," Captain Howe said. "We'll arrest Randolph and Fife without delay. You'll need to identify them as your assailants, of course, but they'll be kept under guard until we reach port."

Matilda bristled. "The sooner they're locked up, the better."

"Agreed." Wesley stood. "In fact, I'll be happy to identify them right now."

His mother gasped. "But Dr. Vane ordered you to rest!"

Captain Yarborough held up his hand. "Best to follow doctor's orders, Your Grace. Besides which, I haven't seen Randolph or Fife since they left the *Apollo*. By now, they've probably heard of your rescue and may be hiding."

"I'll have my crew search the ship from stem to stern." Captain Howe's expression was grim. "If they're aboard, we'll find them."

Belle awoke just before noon, dressed hurriedly, and rushed to her father's cabin. He answered her knock, moving a little slower than usual after the night's exertions.

"Have you seen Wesley, Papa? Is there any word?"

Mr. Oakhurst shook his head. "I've not seen him, but I did speak with the ship's surgeon. His Grace is awake and resting quietly, but he's not to have visitors for the time being."

Belle swallowed her disappointment. "And Mr. Van Eyck?"

"His mother assured me he's as well as can be expected. He, too, has been ordered to rest in his cabin, although Mrs. Van Eyck has had difficulty keeping the young fellow quiet."

"I can very well imagine. And are you feeling fit?"

Mr. Oakhurst stretched out his biceps and shoulder muscles. "I'm afraid I'm not as young as I used to be, but I'll be fine. By the way, we've been invited to dine at the captain's table tonight."

"Whatever for?" Belle blinked. "You and I are hardly luminaries."

"It's mere conjecture on my part, but I suspect it has something to do with our having assisted in the rescue last night."

"You did far more than I. I merely sounded the alarm."

"When we came across Wesley, he was literally moments away from sliding underneath the water forever. If you had not sounded the alarm when you did, he would not have survived."

Belle's throat contracted with emotion, but she forced a smile to her lips. "Have you eaten lunch, Papa?"

"I had a very late breakfast, but I'll sit with you, if you like. It's a beautiful day."

"That's not necessary. It's probably a good thing if you rest, too."

She kissed her father on the cheek and headed for the saloon. When she entered the dining hall, Louise waved and called out her name. Belle joined her at a table with Carl, Stacy, Eva, and Horatio, who were just ordering their lunch.

"We were worried you would sleep the whole day away!" Louise exclaimed.

"I nearly did. May I inquire after your brother?" Belle asked.

"He's talking non-stop. Oh, there's so much to tell you and I don't know where to begin. There was a horrible reason he and Wesley got left behind on the *Apollo*!"

Louise went on to detail everything she'd learned from Stephen, beginning with the moment he'd left the *City of New York*. She paused for breath only long enough to let Belle order lunch, or to eat a bite of lobster salad every so often. Belle found herself hanging on Louise's every word, as did everyone else at the table. When Louise described how Stephen and Wesley had been attacked and locked in the closet, Belle was aghast.

"Who are these criminals? Have they been arrested?"

"I don't know," Louise said. "I certainly hope so." She glanced over her shoulder, as if the men might be standing right behind her.

"Go on, Louise." Eva was wide-eyed. "What happened next?"

"I can't stand the suspense!" Stacy exclaimed.

Louise resumed telling the story with great relish, culminating with the moment Wesley and Stephen were rescued.

"And so Stephen says if it hadn't been for Wesley he would have given up hope," Louise concluded in a dramatic fashion. "He owes Wesley his life."

"But it sounds like your brother saved Wesley's life too, at the very end." Belle felt a rush of gratitude toward Stephen, despite the very public kiss he'd pressed on her last night. Perhaps he was not as shallow as she had imagined.

Carl sat back in his seat. "I think that's the most remarkable tale I've ever heard."

Horatio nodded. "In some cultures, Wesley and Stephen would now be considered blood brothers."

Carl chuckled. "Yes...like in an adventure novel."

"But in this case, it's all a true story!" Eva said.

"I can't believe we missed the excitement." Stacy pouted. "Mama made us go to bed."

"Oh, you should have seen Annabelle after the last lifeboat arrived without Wesley and my brother," Louise said. "Mama and I were useless, but she was a firebrand."

"That's a gross exaggeration, Louise—" Belle began.

But Louise brushed off her protest. "You're a heroine. If you hadn't insisted you could see lights through the fog, no rescue would have been mounted until morning."

A shiver shook Belle's frame. "I can scarcely think about it. In fact, I'm looking forward to dry land more and more."

"As am I," Stacy said. "The last few days of our voyage won't be nearly as diverting without the dance club."

"That's true, but even if Wesley and Stephen were fit enough to continue, we no longer have a place to meet," Eva pointed out.

"That's right. The steerage deck is now occupied with the refugees and crew from the *Apollo*," Horatio said.

"Did you know one of the first class passengers from the *Apollo* has a pup?" Carl asked.

"Oh, yes! She tried to bring the animal to breakfast this morning, but the staff wouldn't allow it in the saloon," Stacy said.

Louise lowered her voice. "That woman is odious. Her name is Mrs. Stilton, and she's attached herself to Mama, probably hoping she'll give up her deck cabin!"

"That's not likely," Belle said.

"I read in the *Gazette* there's to be a clothing drive this afternoon for the refugees," Eva said. "They came away from the *Apollo* with very little."

"I have an ugly yellow skirt to donate," Stacy said.

Eva peered at her. "That's ungenerous of you."

"Just because *I* think it's ugly doesn't mean anyone else will," Stacy retorted.

"I know the skirt," Eva said. "You're right, it's quite ugly."

Stacy sniffed. "If you're going to be like *that*, I'll donate a pair of gloves too. I've outgrown them anyway."

"Mama and I worked at a clothing drive in Philadelphia once," Louise said. "Volunteers are always needed to sort things and hand them out in an orderly fashion."

"This afternoon we'll be the volunteer club, then," Horatio said. "Perhaps it won't be as much fun as dancing, but a clothing drive will give us something useful to do."

"I'm pretty sure I've a few things to donate," Carl said.

"Let's all canvass our wardrobes for donations and meet back here at two o'clock," Belle suggested. *Perhaps keeping busy will help divert my thoughts from Wesley. I can't wait to see him!*

∼

IN HER CABIN, Belle examined her clothes, gown by gown. Her wardrobe wasn't so extensive she could easily donate any of it without sacrifice, but she knew the people who'd fled the *Apollo* had come away with less. With some regret, she selected her peach-pattern dress. *I hope its new owner will make good use of it, and enjoy the dress as much as I have.*

She set the dress aside and sat down to write Wesley a note on ship stationery:

Dear Wesley,

Louise related a little of your ordeal to me, as recounted by her brother. I understand there was much heroism and bravery on your part, and that in all ways you behaved admirably. I'm so terribly thankful your life was spared and that you'll live to see your dukedom! Although I'm told you can't have visitors yet, I hope this letter finds you resting comfortably.

Yours truly,

Belle

P.S. My father and I are to dine at the captain's table this evening! I hope you are able to join us.

As she left for the clothing drive carrying her dress over one arm, she stopped by the stewardess's cabin and gave her the letter to deliver. For some reason, her small communication with Wesley made her feel more cheerful. Belle hastened to the saloon with a lighter heart.

CHAPTER 18
EN GARDE

As the day wore on, Wesley began to chafe at his confinement. Sunlight shone through the portals, calling him out to soak in its warming rays. Cavendish had at last assumed the role of nanny, unfortunately, and dissuaded him from doing anything more strenuous than reading. When Mr. Finnegan delivered Wesley's luncheon tray around one o'clock, he also brought with him a stack of letters.

Wesley stared at the pile. "What's all this?"

"Well wishes and sentiments of that nature, I imagine," Mr. Finnegan replied.

"Really?"

"Your shipmates have not forgotten you, Your Grace." The steward left.

Wesley glanced through the stack; there was a note from Mr. Ley, an invitation to dine that evening from Captain Howe, and several messages from fellow passengers with whom Wesley had an acquaintance. He was most pleased to discover a letter from Belle, and he read it with a smile on his face.

Afterward, he beckoned to Cavendish. "I'd like to answer this one right away."

"Very good, sir."

The valet brought stationery and a Waterman fountain pen to the table so Wesley could write his reply:

Dear Belle,

Dr. Vane has been cruel to forbid me visitors, but he informs me I may go to dinner tonight despite a sprained ankle. I look forward to seeing you then, but you must promise not to laugh at my singed hair. Along with my supposed bravery and heroism, I engaged in a great deal of poorly conceived idiocy.

Sincerely,

Wesley

P.S. I'm in your father's debt, as he was among the rescue party. I can't express how grateful I am.

P.P.S. Most especially, I owe you my heartfelt thanks. If not for your vigilance, Stephen and I would have perished.

He sealed the note in an envelope, wrote Belle's name on the front, and asked Cavendish to give it to the steward to deliver.

Before Wesley tucked into his solitary lunch of roast beef, new potatoes, and asparagus, he re-read the letter Belle had sent to him. Smiling, he slid it into the breast pocket of his jacket for safekeeping. She had kept a vigil for him last night, which pleased him to no end. Had Belle done so out of friendship...or something deeper?

Mr. Duncan had been assigned to spearhead the relief effort, along with the Chief Officer of the *Apollo*, Mr. Wilmington. Belle was impressed at the generous quantity of clothes and toiletry items donated by *City of New York* passengers. She and her fellow volunteers sorted the offerings into categories and further divided the clothes as to size. Just as they'd finished sorting the last few things, the ship's barber entered the saloon, carrying a basket filled with combs and shaving supplies.

"Mr. Duncan, you should know that whilst I was assembling these relief supplies, some things were stolen from the lot," he said.

"Are you certain you didn't miscount?" Mr. Duncan asked.

The barber shook his head. "I laid out shaving soap, brushes, and razors, ten sets in all. Only nine remained when I returned with the combs."

Mr. Duncan sighed. "How unfortunate. I'll tell the captain."

As the barber left, Mr. Wilmington gathered the volunteers together. "Well, everyone…are we ready for distribution?"

"I think so." Louise pointed. "We've put gentlemen's clothes on the right hand table. Ladies' and children's things are on the left."

"How are we to proceed?" Belle asked.

"Mr. Duncan and I will go to the steerage deck and send passengers up alphabetically, in groups." He brandished an Italian phrase book. "I found this in the ship's library, so I can make myself understood."

When the first group of refugees appeared several minutes later, Mrs. Stilton was amongst them. Belle was taken aback. "There must have been some sort of revolt below deck," she whispered to Louise. "I'm pretty sure 'Stilton' does not belong in A through F."

"How right you are," Louise replied, low. "And she looks as if she's been sucking on a lemon."

Mrs. Stilton's expression was indeed rather sour as she glanced over the clothes laid out on the table. "Insupportable," she muttered. "Cast-offs and rags."

Nevertheless, she moved quickly alongside the table to have first pick of everything available. To Belle's dismay, the woman selected the peach-pattern dress she'd donated. The woman also snatched up a very pretty petticoat of the highest quality, and Stacy's gloves. With her nose in the air, Mrs. Stilton departed, sweeping past a trio of Italian ladies staring at the table of donated finery in awe. Despite her irritation, Belle ignored Mrs. Stilton and helped the ladies as best she could by encouraging them to pick up the dresses or to feel the fabrics. Finally they chose some things and left, well pleased.

"*Grazie. Grazie mille*," they repeated.

Carl and Horatio were on hand to assist the men, and Belle, Stacy, Eva, and Louise worked with the women and children.

"You know, this is rather fun," Belle whispered to Louise. "Most everyone is thankful just to have a change of clothes."

"I agree. It makes me feel a little humble, really," Louise replied.

Shortly after the distribution began, Belle caught sight of the tall swarthy man who'd helped rescue Wesley and Stephen the night before.

"Mr. Matteo, isn't it?"

He glanced over and a smile of recognition lit his face. "*Buon pomeriggio, signorina.*"

Although Belle hadn't a clue what the man had just said, she desperately wanted to convey her gratitude for his help.

"Um...*mille grazie.*" She bit her lip. "Or is it *grazie mille*? Wait."

Belle called Mr. Wilmington over. "I want to thank Mr. Matteo here for rescuing Wesley Parker last night. Can you help me?"

"Er..." The Chief Officer began to leaf through his phrase book.

"Wesley?" repeated Matteo.

"Yes, Wesley," Belle said.

"*Come è Wesley?*" Matteo glanced around, as if looking for Wesley.

Belle glanced at Mr. Wilmington, but he was still leafing through his phrasebook with a befuddled expression.

"Wesley is resting," Belle said. She folded her hands together and laid her head down on them as she pantomimed sleep.

"Ah," Matteo said. "*Buono.*"

"Yes. Well, I just wanted to say *grazie mille* again."

She knew she was butchering the pronunciation, but Matteo suppressed a grin and waved off her thanks.

"*Non è niente.*"

He gave her a little bow and went back to looking for clothes, just as Mr. Wilmington found what he was looking for on the page.

"Ah, here we are...*Grazie* is the word you're looking for," he said. "That means thanks."

"Thank you, Mr. Wilmington," Belle said. "You've been a great help."

Flushed with success, Mr. Wilmington wandered off. At the end of the afternoon, most everything had been distributed, and the two Chief Officers thanked the volunteers.

"Well done, everyone," Mr. Duncan said.

Mr. Wilmington nodded. "We couldn't have done it without you."

"Captain Howe wants to convey his gratitude in a more practical manner." Mr. Duncan beamed. "Beginning tomorrow, the captain will allow you to use the saloon for your dance practice, from two to four o'clock."

"Oh, joy!" Eva said, clapping her hands.

"The volunteer club becomes the dance club once again!" Louise said.

"That's absolutely splendid," Carl said. "Please convey our thanks to Captain Howe."

Mr. Duncan nodded. "He's quite happy to oblige."

Belle touched his sleeve. "Pardon me for asking, but have you arrested the two men responsible for attacking the Duke of Mansbury and Mr. Van Eyck?"

Mr. Duncan and Mr. Wilmington exchanged a sober glance.

"No, miss. We've scoured the *City of New York,* but they've not turned up," Mr. Wilmington said. "We're beginning to think they may have jumped ship."

Horatio looked at him askance. "Straight into the Atlantic?"

Mr. Wilmington shrugged. "The *Apollo* longboats were set adrift after the refugees were brought on board. Perhaps Mr. Fife and Mr. Randolph decided to take their chances with one of them, hoping to be picked up by a passing ship."

"Of course, the only thing that's for certain is uncertainty," Mr. Duncan said. "There are a lot of places to hide in an ocean liner this size. I don't recommend you young people go poking into any dark corners."

Louise shuddered. "We wouldn't dream of it."

∼

As Wesley dressed for dinner, he was surprised by how much he was looking forward to leaving his deck cabin—and seeing Belle.

Cavendish gave him an appraising glance. "You are favoring your right extremity a great deal. Is your sprain worse?"

"It's quite tender, actually."

"Good."

Wesley's eyebrows rose. "*Good?*"

"Your injury provides the perfect excuse for you to borrow one of my walking sticks."

"That's a very generous offer...but why do I need an excuse?"

"I made some discreet inquiries this afternoon. The two men who assaulted you are still at large. The theory is that they fled the ship in one of *Apollo*'s lifeboats, but I don't believe that's true."

"No?"

"No, unless one assumes these men are unintelligent as well as predatory. I believe they're hiding, waiting for the chance to silence the primary witness to their crimes."

"Hold on, I'm not the only witness. Stephen van Eyck saw them too."

"He's far less of a threat. According to your account, Mr. Van Eyck never saw the man who hit him. Furthermore, he only saw the other gentleman for a few moments. I'm willing to wager both men have altered their appearances by now. Therefore, Mr. Van Eyck may not be able to identify them at all. Neither can you, if you are dead."

Startled, Wesley could only gape. Cavendish crossed over to his luggage, unlatched the clasp on the longest trunk, and threw open the lid. An assortment of walking sticks was revealed, resting inside custom-made trays.

"You may have noticed most of my walking sticks serve more than one function. Sometimes, they can be quite deadly."

The valet lifted out two trays in succession and set them aside. In the third tray, at the bottom of the trunk, he selected a polished black walking stick with a heavy silver handle in the shape of a snake.

"If you're confronted with danger, simply insert your thumb in the snake's mouth and press down on its tongue to release the catch. Then you may slide the blade free from the wooden sheath, like so."

Cavendish released the catch, unsheathed the sword, and traced a pattern in the air with an impressive swishing noise. "*En garde!*"

He lunged forward in a graceful fencing stance, withdrew, and then returned the sword to its sheath. "My blue glass-topped walking stick also contains a sword, but I believe it's too short for you. This one should do nicely."

The valet presented the walking stick to Wesley, who peered at him. "Who *are* you really, Cavendish?"

The man bowed. "I'm your humble servant, sir...and *you* are late for dinner."

∼

Strains of Chaminade's *Scarf Dance* flowed through the crowded dining hall from the pipe organ set in the elevated orchestra niche. Belle and her father were seated at the captain's table with Captain Howe, Captain Yarborough, Mrs. Van Eyck, Louise, and Wesley's mother. Three empty places remained, and Belle kept glancing at the saloon entrance and twisting the napkin in her lap. She'd worn her best dinner gown, which was white with a black velvet bodice. Her puffy off-the-shoulder white sleeves were trimmed with tiny black velvet bows, and black bows were scattered across the fabric of her white skirt at regular intervals. The hem ended with a length of frilled chiffon that billowed as she walked. Although Errol had pronounced the neckline to be a trifle risqué, the gown was one of her favorites and she thought it was becoming.

Waiters had begun to take orders when Stephen finally appeared in the doorway. Instead of coming inside the saloon, however, he was looking the other way—as if waiting for someone. Moments later, Wesley limped into view with a walking stick in hand. Both men wore dark cutaway suits with white vests and bow ties. Belle thought they were devastatingly handsome. With a broad grin on his face, Stephen shook Wesley's hand and said something that made him laugh.

When they entered the saloon, a ripple of applause ensued. The *Gazette* had printed Louise's account of the entire adventure, as told to her by her brother, and apparently there were few who had not read it. As the two young men made their way toward the captain's table, Stephen beamed at the attention but a dull flush darkened Wesley's cheekbones. Belle felt a tug of pride. *Wesley Parker is a man content to do good deeds without fanfare from anyone.* She joined in the applause, feeling at once like a silly schoolgirl in the throes of her first infatuation.

Stephen slid into the chair between his mother and Louise, and Wesley took the empty seat next to Belle. As he did so, he handed off his walking stick to the waiter for safekeeping.

"Good evening." She glanced at Wesley's hair. "If you hadn't mentioned your singed ends in your letter, Your Grace, I don't think I would have noticed."

He laughed. "If I didn't know you were scrupulously honest, Miss Oakhurst, I'd say you were telling a little white lie."

Stephen gave Belle a wink. "It's too late for dissembling, Miss Oakhurst. I've already abused him about his appearance."

Belle winced at the black and blue bruise visible on Stephen's temple. "I'm afraid neither of you emerged from your adventure unscathed."

"It's good to see you lads up and about." Captain Howe signaled to the waiter. "Let's have some champagne."

"Captain, it's good to be here." Wesley glanced around the table. "I've many of you to thank for that."

"As do I," Stephen said. "I thank *you*, Wesley, most particularly." He paused. "There was one moment on the *Apollo* when I truly thought we were done for. Do you remember that? We were on the bridge, when the ship nearly rolled over."

A haunted expression flickered in Wesley's eyes, and Belle suppressed the urge to take his hand.

Stephen's expression was uncharacteristically sober. "I was at my lowest just then, but Wesley said, 'I won't have it.' And he proceeded to fight like the devil to make sure we survived."

"We fought alongside one another." Wesley nodded. "And you hung onto me, at the end."

Stephen shrugged. "Only because I hate it when you show me up."

Everyone laughed. Stephen picked up the flute of champagne that had been set before him. "I raise a glass to Wesley Parker, the best of men and one of the bravest."

Belle's heart nearly burst with pride as she drank the toast. In the next moment, however, a new arrival made her nearly spit it out. The gentlemen rose.

"Forgive me for being late." Mrs. Stilton was clad in Belle's peach-pattern dress, and her ample flesh strained the seams. "Rather than wear this hideous garment, I almost chose to take dinner in my cabin."

Belle felt the blood rush to her face, and she lowered her gaze to the napkin in her lap.

"But then I remembered I *have* no cabin; I'm in steerage." Mrs. Stilton leveled a hard glance at Captain Howe.

The dreadful woman seated herself next to Captain Yarborough, who went around the table, making introductions.

Mrs. Stilton gave Wesley a simpering smile. "I have no idea last night that you were a duke, Your Grace. You and your friend are both heroes."

A ghost of a smile lifted the corners of Wesley's lips. "I

think your dress is uncommonly pretty, Mrs. Stilton. How did you come to be in possession of it?"

"It's a cast-off. All my worldly possessions sank with the *Apollo*, I'm afraid."

"Not all." Stephen's expression was emotionless. "You still have your dog."

Belle bit her lip, trying not to laugh.

Mrs. Van Eyck shot her son a quelling glance. "Mrs. Stilton has been through a terrible ordeal."

"*I* think the dress is very pretty, too." Louise's words were accusatory. "In fact, it was Annabelle's."

Mrs. Stilton flushed a mottled red. "In that case, I thank you, my dear Miss Oakhurst," she said with a tight smile. "I'm sure it looked far better on you."

Because she didn't know how to respond politely, Belle said nothing.

"My daughter has always had a generous nature," Mr. Oakhurst said.

"I've noticed that myself, even on short acquaintance," Wesley said.

Belle's distress at Mrs. Stilton's insult eased. *What are the comments of one sour woman when compared to the praise of friends and family!*

"Indeed, Miss Oakhurst's tireless efforts on behalf of the refugees drew the admiration of all who witnessed them," Captain Howe said. "Miss Van Eyck was remarkable as well."

Captain Yarborough lifted his glass. "On behalf of the Mount Olympus Shipping Company, the passengers of the SS *Apollo*, and its entire crew, I thank you all."

Mrs. Stilton's audible sigh indicated her boredom.

CHAPTER 19
UNDONE

After Mrs. Stilton consumed several glasses of champagne and a quantity of artichoke appetizers, she seemed to mellow.

"I apologize for my temper." She glanced around the table with a flirtatious smile. "I'm usually not so disagreeable, but after the boiler blew up on the *Apollo* I thought Princess and I would perish. Fortunately we did not, but I left my jewelry case behind on the ship. It contained many fine pieces given to me by my late husband, and they were all I had to remember him by." Her smile disappeared and she touched her napkin to the corners of her eyes.

"Oh, dear." Mrs. Van Eyck frowned. "I would be upset, too."

"Thank you, Mrs. Van Eyck. I *do* appreciate Captain Howe has done for me...and Miss Oakhurst." Mrs. Stilton added that last part grudgingly.

"I was merely doing my duty, madam," Captain Howe said.

"It was my pleasure," Belle murmured, more out of obligation than sentiment.

"Tell me, Mrs. Stilton, what is your business in America?" Mr. Oakhurst asked.

"My son left England to make his fortune in the New World. I'm to visit him in San Francisco," she replied.

I wonder if he'll be happy to see her when she finally arrives? Belle thought. *Poor man.*

As the meal progressed, Mrs. Stilton interrogated Captain Yarborough on how the Olympus Shipping Company planned to make up her financial losses and what she could expect in terms of completing her voyage. Since Belle yearned to hear from Wesley and Stephen, not Mrs. Stilton, her resentment deepened. When the dreadful woman paused to take a sip of wine, Belle seized the opportunity to change the subject.

"Your Grace, I encountered your Italian friend this afternoon...Mr. Matteo. I tried to thank him for his part in your rescue. Given the language barrier, I hope he understood."

"Ah, yes, Matteo. He was very helpful with his countrymen on the *Apollo* when I was explaining the need to evacuate," Wesley said.

"Wesley had a little help from Providence in that regard," Stephen said. "If not for his Saint Christopher's medal, I don't think the Italians would have listened to him."

Wesley chuckled. "I must write my friend, Sergio, in Brooklyn and thank him again for that medal."

Mrs. Stilton fixed Wesley with her gaze. "I find your situation extremely interesting, Your Grace. Mrs. Van Eyck informs me you are an American who came into your title recently?"

"Yes, my late uncle, Septimus Parker, was the tenth Duke of Mansbury," Wesley said.

The duchess added, "My husband was Septimus's younger brother, and predeceased him several years ago."

"Annabelle's grandfather is a baronet," Louise blurted out. "Perhaps she'll inherit the baronetcy from him someday."

Belle's heart began to hammer, and she felt her father's eyes upon her.

"The title of baronet is not inheritable by females, my dear," Mrs. Stilton said.

"Ugh! I'll never understand this business of titles," Louise said. "How do English people keep it all straight?"

"It's not always easy to do so, I grant you. Some people count on the ignorance of others to puff themselves up as nobility when they are not," Mrs. Stilton said. "If you make enough inquiries, the truth will out, sooner or later."

Belle forced a laugh. "Your Grace, 'The truth will out' is a quote from Shakespeare. Can you guess which play—"

"Miss Oakhurst, may I ask the name of your grandfather, the baronet?" Mrs. Stilton interrupted.

"Hamish Heathcliff from Gloucester," she replied faintly.

"Hamish Heathcliff! Imagine that!" Mrs. Stilton exclaimed. "Why, I have lunch with his wife Maude at least once a month. How is dear *Mr.* Heathcliff?"

This awful woman knows my grandfather? The blood left Belle's body, and the ship shifted...or so she thought until she realized a wave of dizziness had tilted her world.

"I believe he's in excellent health, Mrs. Stilton," she managed.

"It's very strange Maude Heathcliff never happened to mention her husband is a baronet," Mrs. Stilton continued. "In all the years I've known her, she also never mentioned Mr. Heathcliff had a granddaughter. Of course, Maude is his second wife, so perhaps there are some family secrets to which she's not privy?"

Mr. Oakhurst cleared his throat. "I believe there has been some misunderstanding. Due to a family rift, I'm afraid my daughter has never had the pleasure of her grandfather's acquaintance. Furthermore, my father-in-law is not in possession of a title, as far as I know."

An expression of confusion passed over Mrs. Van Eyck's face. "I'm sorry, Miss Oakhurst, but I thought Sir Hamish had arranged to have you presented you at court last year. Didn't you tell me that, Louise?"

A cold, clammy hand reached down Belle's throat and squeezed the breath from her lungs.

"Oh, Mama, you know how I get everything wrong." Louise expression was strained. "I simply made a mistake."

Into the ensuing, fragile silence, only Mrs. Stilton dared to wade.

"You see, Your Grace, how a few probing questions can serve to unearth a handful of worms?" she said with cloying sweetness. "Furthermore, in terms of the nobility, a baronetcy is nothing at all. If I were to tell such a falsehood, I would have chosen a viscount, at least."

Everyone at the table stared fixedly at Belle. She felt as if she were Hester Prynne in *The Scarlet Letter*...but the scarlet letter burning on her chest was the letter L—for liar. *Now I must mount the scaffold in disgrace.*

"No, Louise, you didn't get it wrong. I misled you and I apologize." Belle couldn't bring herself to gauge Wesley's reaction, but the shock on Louise's face brought tears to her eyes. She stood. "Forgive me, but I've developed a sudden headache. Please enjoy your evening."

Belle left the captain's table and walked the entire length of the saloon with her head held high. Passengers were engaged in conversation or in eating, so few took much notice of her departure. *Would that my path be a gauntlet to expiate my sins!* As she passed beyond the double doors, she mounted the stairs to the promenade deck. *I can't bear to be shut away in my cabin just now. Let the canopy of stars be witness to my shame.*

The last lingering rays of sunlight had faded when Belle emerged on deck, and the aurora borealis was rippling and glowing, as if a cosmic fire were about to spill over the northern horizon. A kaleidoscope of luminous turquoise and lilac lights streaked and pulsed in a magical display that would ordinarily have lifted her spirits. At the moment, however, she could barely see the beautiful phenomenon through the tears filling her eyes.

Mrs. Stilton's sweet triumph was Belle's complete and utter humiliation. First and foremost, her lies had publicly embarrassed her father. Further, she'd likely lost the affection of her new friends, since even the remaining members of the dance club would soon hear of her exposure. Worst of all, however, was losing Wesley's respect in a way that would haunt her forever. She gripped the railing with both hands, as if the steel could somehow lend her its strength. *I can't bear this!*

∽

When Belle stood and took her leave, Wesley struggled to his feet in concert with the other men at the table. Mr. Oakhurst immediately folded his napkin and set it next to his plate. "Pardon me. I must see to my daughter."

As Mr. Oakhurst left, Wesley flagged down the waiter. "Please bring me my walking stick right away."

"I've lost my appetite, I'm afraid." Stephen shot Mrs. Stilton a withering glance as he got to his feet. "Excuse me."

Mrs. Van Eyck caught Stephen's hand. "Don't go chasing after the girl!"

"Oh, yes, Stephen, please do," Louise pleaded. "Tell her I don't care if her grandfather is a baronet or a bricklayer."

"She doesn't deserve your sympathy!" Mrs. Van Eyck exclaimed.

"That's so," Mrs. Stilton said. "Mendacity is an unforgivable quality in a young woman."

"'Let he who is without sin, cast the first stone,'" Captain Howe murmured.

Captain Yarborough nodded his agreement. "Hear, hear."

Stephen frowned at Mrs. Van Eyck. "Mother, Miss Oakhurst was instrumental in saving my life...or don't you care?"

"I might add, who among us hasn't said something silly from time to time?" Matilda said. "I really don't see that Miss Oakhurst's assertions were so very terrible."

Louise lifted her chin. "Neither do I."

Helpless without his walking stick, Wesley nodded to Stephen. "Go find her. I'll follow as soon as I can."

Stephen hastened off, choosing to take a side route instead of the central aisle which was largely blocked by servers. As soon as the waiter returned with his walking stick, Wesley joined the pursuit. Unfortunately, his limp slowed his pace. He and Mr. Oakhurst were delayed by the crush of servers juggling trays of food, whereas Stephen disappeared from the saloon long before Wesley and Mr. Oakhurst managed to reach the exit. Neither Stephen nor Belle were visible by then and Wesley punched the air in frustration.

"There are a thousand places Belle could've gone!" A muscle worked in his jaw. "I'll search the promenade deck."

"I'll check her room." Mr. Oakhurst darted off toward the descending staircase.

One painful step at a time, Wesley mounted the stairs to the uppermost level. He would look in the nearby drawing room first, and then inside the library. If he had no luck, he'd circle the promenade deck. Belle's distress had affected him deeply. *I must find her!*

~

THE LIGHTS in the nighttime sky seemingly gamboled for her amusement, but Belle was oblivious. *I'm completely undone and there's no escape. I must endure two more days on this ship, with nowhere to hide. Then I travel by train to Mansbury with my father, Wesley, and the duchess. Oh, how they must despise me as a liar!*

"Miss Oakhurst."

Startled, Belle wheeled around to discover Stephen van Eyck had followed her.

"Mrs. Stilton is a dreadful person." His expression reflected sympathy. "Please don't think about her any further."

"She *is* dreadful, but it doesn't change the fact that I lied to you...and everyone else."

"Are you in the habit of lying?"

"No, not ordinarily. I just wanted so badly to impress Louise."

"Ha! Louise has been trying all this time to impress you."

Although Belle knew Stephen was telling a joke, she didn't see any humor in it.

He sighed. "What if I confessed I've grossly exaggerated my sporting abilities to garner favor with girls? Would that shock you?"

Despite herself, Belle finally smiled.

"I can see you think me quite capable of it." Stephen chuckled as he pulled Belle into a comforting embrace. "Actually, the fact you aren't perfect makes me like you all the more. We're quite suited to one another."

As Belle clung to him, a sense of affection and gratitude

warmed her heart. Steven Van Eyck may be a little vain and shallow, but he'd saved Wesley's life.

"You're very kind, Mr. Van Eyck."

She lifted her face to give him a smile, and suddenly his lips captured hers in a tender kiss.

∽

PHYSICALLY SICKENED, Wesley stared at Belle and Stephen as they embraced—his relief at finding her replaced by searing jealousy and despair. She'd misled Louise about her grandfather, and apparently she'd lied to *him* about her feelings for Stephen van Eyck. The throbbing pain in his ankle was nothing compared to the wound in his heart. *What a naïve fool I've been! Belle is less trustworthy than a fox!*

The empty passageway between deck cabins provided a temporary refuge while Wesley tried to collect himself. *I must speak with Mr. Oakhurst to let him know where Belle is...and then I believe I'll pay a lengthy visit to the bar.* He headed inside, so distracted by his own misery that he paid no attention to the two waiters coming toward him. Instead of stepping to one side, they blocked his path.

"I beg your pardon," Wesley said, annoyed. "May I pass?"

In the next moment, he was staring at the barrel of a revolver. Although the man holding the weapon was presently clean-shaven, Wesley knew him right away. His companion had shaved off his black mustache, but Wesley recognized him too.

"Randolph and Fife," he said.

Randolph laughed. "Smith & Wesson is all you need to know."

∽

Belle pulled away from Stephen. "Please don't misunderstand, Mr. Van Eyck. That kiss was for Wesley."

Stephen scratched his head. "I've the greatest of respect for the duke, but don't expect me to pass it on."

"What I mean is, you rendered him a great service and you have my gratitude."

"But not your affection?"

"I *do* feel some affection for you, but as I told you earlier, my heart is much engaged elsewhere."

A frown passed over Stephen's handsome visage. "Are you quite sure? You wouldn't want to leave a window open just a crack?"

"I'm quite sure of *my* feelings, Mr. Van Eyck, but not of his." Belle averted her eyes.

"Then it's Wesley, after all."

"It doesn't matter. After tonight it's a hopeless case."

∽

Randolph gestured toward the door with his weapon. "Get outside and keep quiet."

Wesley felt for the catch on his walking stick with his thumb. "I'm afraid I can't walk very well," he said, to play for time.

Fife produced a Derringer and trained it at Wesley's chest. "I could shoot you where you stand, if you like."

Cavendish lurched into view with an unsteady gait, whereupon Randolph and Fife quickly pocketed their weapons. The valet's normally perfect hair was mussed, his shirt had been pulled free from his trousers, and even his waxed mustache drooped on one side. When he caught sight of Wesley, he planted his blue glass knobbed walking stick in the carpet and struggled to stand upright.

"If it isn't His Grace." Cavendish's words were slurred. "I thought you'd be at dinner." He swayed too far to one side, and staggered into Randolph. "Oops, sorry my good man."

Cavendish is feigning drunkenness! Wesley thought. *He was stone cold sober less than an hour ago.* Nevertheless, Wesley narrowed his eyes as if he were angry. "Cavendish, you've been drinking."

"Just a little tipple to go along with the baseball game." Cavendish giggled and gave Wesley an exaggerated wink.

"A double header?" Wesley asked.

"Batter up," Cavendish replied. "And you'd best look sharp."

Before Randolph and Fife realized what was happening, Wesley slid his blade free from its sheath and held the tip to Fife's throat. "Keep your hands where I can see them."

At the same time, Cavendish whipped his own sword out and brought the sharp edge down across Randolph's forearm. The man screamed as he went down on one knee, clutching his wound.

His hands up, Fife backed away from the point of Wesley's blade.

"Stay where you are!" Wesley ordered.

Wesley moved to follow, but his ankle caused him to lose his balance. Fife grabbed his Derringer and a small caliber bullet embedded itself in an oil painting inches away from Wesley's head. Cavendish bounded over and ran Fife through with his blade. Randolph, bleeding from a slashed arm, managed to pull the revolver from his pocket with his left hand. As he trained the weapon on Wesley, Mr. Oakhurst appeared.

"Watch out, lad!"

Mr. Oakhurst pushed Wesley to the ground just as a gunshot echoed throughout the corridor. When Wesley looked back, Cavendish had stabbed Randolph with his sword and the man had crumpled to the ground.

"Are you hit, Cavendish?" Wesley exclaimed.

The valet, grim-faced, shook his head. "No." He wiped his blade on Randolph's jacket. "And you?"

"I think I'm fine," Wesley said. "Mr. Oakhurst, you just saved my life again."

"I'm glad," Mr. Oakhurst murmured. "But I'm afraid—"

He leaned against the wall and then slid down into a sitting position. Cavendish's eyebrows drew together as he jumped over Randolph's body and went to Mr. Oakhurst's aid. Wesley scrambled to his feet...and stared with horror at the rapidly spreading red stain on Mr. Oakhurst's pristine white vest.

"Get Dr. Vane," Cavendish said.

Panic rooted Wesley's feet to the ground.

"*Move*, Wesley!" Cavendish commanded. "There's no time to spare!"

Despite his sprained ankle, Wesley began to run.

CHAPTER 20
POLKA

Wesley kept a tense vigil with Belle, Stephen, and Cavendish outside the surgeon's office, which was converted into an emergency operating room. In the wee hours of the morning, Dr. Vane finally shooed them away.

"Mr. Oakhurst is stable. I'll send word, Miss Oakhurst, if there's any change for the worse."

A bleary-eyed Cavendish headed to the deck cabin while Wesley and Stephen escorted Belle to her room.

"I shan't sleep a wink," she said.

"Please try," Wesley said.

"It won't do your father any good if you make yourself ill," Stephen added.

Although she nodded in agreement, Wesley knew Belle was in for a difficult night. After her door closed, Wesley and Stephen doubled back toward Stephen's cabin.

"I feel responsible for Mr. Oakhurst's injuries," Wesley murmured.

"Nobody could possibly blame you, Wesley. Miss Oakhurst doesn't, does she?"

"She's too distressed at the moment to be assigning blame, but she may yet come to that conclusion."

"I doubt it. I hate to admit this, but her regard for you is insurmountable. I gave it my best shot, but so far she finds me resistible."

Wesley cast a dark glance in Stephen's direction. "You needn't spare my feelings. I saw the two of you kissing earlier."

"You saw that, did you? Don't take this the wrong way, but Miss Oakhurst said that kiss was for you. Seems she was grateful I saved your neck. Gave me second thoughts about having done so, I must admit."

A ray of hope shot through Wesley, warming him more thoroughly than a bottle of twenty-five-year-old scotch.

Stephen laughed. "Don't be so cheerful, Wesley. Miss Oakhurst may yet change her mind. You've made headway, admittedly, but you still have her pesky fiancé to contend with."

Wesley's smile slipped. "They've not been engaged very long. When Sir Errol is presented with the situation, surely he will step aside."

"Perhaps so, if he is any sort of gentleman." Stephen's expression hardened. "It may be callous of me to say it, but I'm not sorry Fife and Randolph are dead."

"Neither am I." Wesley averted his gaze. "If that makes me a bad person, so be it."

∽

EVERY CREAK WESLEY heard that night woke him from a fitful sleep. In the morning, the dark smudges underneath his eyes revealed his exhaustion. He dressed quietly, so as not to disturb his snoring valet, grabbed his walking stick, and slipped out to his mother's cabin. She was not quite ready to go to breakfast, so Wesley sank into a chair in her sitting room to wait. The next thing he knew, Matilda was shaking him awake.

When they entered the saloon several minutes later, heads swiveled in their direction, and there was an audible pause in the general conversation.

Wesley glanced at his mother. "Everyone has heard about the events last night, evidently."

She lowered her voice. "I'm beginning to dislike being the center of attention."

"Believe me, so am I."

Although Wesley had anticipated Belle wouldn't be at breakfast, he was surprised how keenly he felt her absence. Furthermore, so frequently did passersby interrupt with questions and inquiries about the attack, Wesley couldn't enjoy his food. He appreciated their concern, but he would've liked to finish his eggs before they went cold. He finally glanced down at the congealed mess on his plate and tossed his napkin on the table.

"I'm done."

"Oh, dear. Perhaps we should've taken breakfast in your cabin."

"I would have, but I didn't want to bother Cavendish. After what he did for me last night, I thought he should be able to sleep in."

"The man deserves a raise."

The Stengers and Egermanns arrived just then, and clustered around his table with yet more questions.

Matilda intervened. "Wesley, why don't you go check on Mr. Oakhurst? I'll fill your friends in for you."

Wesley gave his mother a grateful nod, excused himself,

and limped from the saloon. When he reached Dr. Vane's office, he discovered Mr. Oakhurst was awake and propped up in bed. His right arm was in a sling, his chest was heavily bandaged, and his complexion was waxy white.

"Good morning, Mr. Oakhurst." Wesley sank into a chair. "How are you feeling?"

"As if I've been stomped on the chest by a bull elephant, thanks." His smile was weak. "Dr. Vane informs me, however, I was lucky. Since the bullet missed my lungs and vital organs, it could've been far worse."

"I'm so relieved. Mr. Oakhurst, you pushed me out of harm's way last night, and I can't help but feel responsible for your injuries. If there's ever anything I can do for you, don't hesitate to ask."

"I'd say I was just doing my job, but that wouldn't be the entire truth. Annabelle and I have both grown quite fond of you."

At that, Wesley's throat closed up, and he had to clear it several times before he could speak. "Thank you, sir. I almost look upon you...well, as a father." He paused, trying to choose his words carefully. "If your daughter wasn't already engaged, I would be in mind to pursue her."

"If you're asking for my blessing in that regard, you have it, but you're fighting an uphill battle, I'm afraid."

"You approve of her fiancé?"

"Not at all. The whole point of bringing Annabelle on this trip was to separate her from the man."

"Is she that much in love with him?"

"I suspect her affection for Errol has waned considerably. In fact, I guarantee as much."

"In that case, I'll convince her to end the engagement as soon as possible."

"It won't be easy. Despite that nonsense last night

regarding her grandfather, Annabelle ordinarily has a high regard for keeping her word."

"I'll do everything in my power as a gentleman to sway her opinion."

"Best of luck, Your Grace. Just between us, I hope you succeed."

Dr. Vane strode into the room just then, carrying a tray with tea and toast. "No visitors at present." He glowered. "Not even you, Your Grace."

Wesley raised his hands in a conciliatory gesture. "I'm leaving." He gave Mr. Oakhurst one last smile. "I'll let Annabelle know you are doing better."

Dr. Vane set down his tray and pointed to the door. "Out."

⁓

Wesley slipped past the stewardess's cabin to knock on Belle's cabin door. Almost before he could put his hand down, she jerked the door open. Her red-rimmed eyes were wide and fearful. "Is it Papa?"

"He's all right," Wesley said. "I just spoke with him."

The frightened expression on her face eased slightly.

"The surgeon doesn't believe any vital organs were damaged," Wesley said.

Barefooted, Belle started forward into the empty corridor. "I must see him."

Wesley caught her around the waist. "Not yet. Your father is resting comfortably and Dr. Vane does not want him disturbed. In fact, he tossed me out of the room."

Her muscles tensed, as if she wanted to argue.

"You don't want to make things worse, do you?" Wesley asked.

Slowly, Belle shook her head from side to side. "Of course not."

Wesley helped her return to her darkened cabin, where she collapsed onto the bed like a rag doll. Worried, he snapped on the light and sat down next to her. Belle's hair had fallen from its careful arrangement, but hairpins were still entangled in the long brown strands. As gently as possible, Wesley took the pins out and put them on the dressing table.

Belle's hand crept into his. "Thank you."

He shivered with pleasure at her smooth, warm skin. "Are you hungry? It's past breakfast, but I can order something sent to your cabin."

She shook her head.

He sighed. "How about a cup of tea?"

"Nothing."

"Have you slept at all?" he asked.

"I've been too frightened." Her voice sounded hoarse and raspy. "First I nearly lost you, and then my father. I can't take much more." Her eyelids drooped.

"The danger is past and you've nothing else to fear." Wesley stroked her hair. "Perhaps you can rest now?"

"Stay with me until I fall asleep?"

He smiled. "I can do that."

Under his ministrations, Belle managed to close her eyes. Wesley waited by her side until her hand relaxed in his. Even when her breathing became deep and regular, he didn't leave right away, for fear of waking her. As the pulse on her neck fluttered, Wesley couldn't imagine feeling more protective of anyone or anything. He watched her sleep for a little while longer, marveling at the angles of her face and sweet curve of her lips. *She's like an exquisite orchid or a Calla lily...and I'm just a Yankee from Brooklyn.*

A sigh escaped Belle's lips. Wesley released her hand,

turned off the light, and checked the corridor outside to make sure it was still empty. Unobserved, he left Belle's cabin and closed the door as quietly as possible. *Sleep well, my love.*

∼

CAVENDISH LOOKED up from his knitting as Wesley entered the deck cabin. Exhaustion was written on the valet's face, but he gave his employer a smile nevertheless.

"Thank you for allowing me to sleep this morning," he said. "I'm quite grateful."

"We were all up late, worrying, but it seems Mr. Oakhurst has pulled through." Wesley passed a weary hand over his eyes. "I remember how I felt after my father's accident. I was stunned and scared out of my wits, but at least I had my mother. Belle has no one except for a grandfather who has never shown any interest in her."

"Fortunately, Miss Oakhurst has very good friends."

"I'm trying to do what I can." Wesley studied Cavendish for a moment. "I never thanked you properly for intervening last night. That makes twice you've saved my life."

"You're quite welcome, Your Grace. I trust there won't be any need for a third occasion?"

"Let's hope not."

Cavendish resumed his knitting while Wesley settled into a chair and put his ankle up on a footrest. With the steady click of knitting needles in the background, Wesley closed his eyes and drifted off to sleep.

∼

A SOUND STARTLED BELLE AWAKE, and she instinctively reached for Wesley. With a sense of disappointment, she realized he'd gone. *Did I only dream he was here?* When a knock sounded on the door again, fear clutched her heart. *Papa!* She wrenched the door open to find Louise, Eva, and Stacy waiting in the corridor.

Belle gripped the door in relief. "I thought you were Dr. Vane with bad news."

Louise gave her an appraising look. "The only bad news is your appearance."

"We're here to help," Eva added.

The three girls filed into Belle's cabin.

"First off, I'm taking you down the hall to the bath." Louise's demeanor brooked no opposition. "You'll feel a lot better afterward."

"While you're bathing, we'll tidy your room and lay out something fresh for you to wear," Eva said.

"We've also ordered lunch sent down. You're going to eat, Annabelle." Stacy's tone was firm. "You simply must."

Tears leaked from Belle's eyes. "Thank you for taking care of me."

Louise tossed her head. "Nonsense! What are friends for but to help one another?"

A half hour later, Belle was bathed, dressed, and in a much better humor. As Stacy promised, lunch was delivered to the cabin. While Louise, Eva, and Stacy ate and chatted about inconsequentialities, Belle managed to eat a few bites of chicken cutlets. Although she didn't participate in the conversation overmuch, she appreciated the sense of normalcy the small talk imparted.

"Thank you," she said finally. "You are being so kind and I can't figure out why—especially after I misled you so."

"We *like* you, Annabelle, that's why." Eva said.

"There is no better reason to be kind." Her sister nodded.

"Besides which, if it hadn't been for you and Louise, Eva and I would have died of boredom."

"And I know why you mentioned your grandfather." Louise lowered her gaze to her lap. "It was because I was carrying on and on about titles and nobility, like an idiotic goose. You probably thought it would hush me up."

"You can't shield me from my transgression as easily as that, Louise," Belle said. "But I thank you for the effort." She gave her friend a hug.

"Before we forget, let's exchange addresses," Eva said.

Belle passed around sheets of the ship's stationery.

"Mama, Stephen, and I are staying at the Savoy Hotel while we're in London." Louise scribbled her home address. "Do you know it, Annabelle?"

"I haven't visited the Savoy, but I hear it's a splendid hotel," Belle said. "It was built by Richard D'Oyly Carte and opened just last year."

Louise's eyebrows rose. "The Gilbert and Sullivan man?"

"The very same. I hope you will write to me," Belle said.

"I hope I can do better than write," Louise said. "I'd love to come visit you."

"Stacy and I will come too, if we can find a way to slip out from under Mama's nose," Eva said.

"Wouldn't that be splendid? Although someone will have to show me where Mansbury is on a map," Stacy said.

Belle's eyes filled with tears. "I'll miss the three of you very much."

She embraced Louise, Eva, and Stacy in turn, and then her smile turned mischievous. "I wonder...should we have one last meeting of the dance club this afternoon? I promised to teach you the polka after all."

Louise squealed with delight. "I was hoping you'd feel like going on with it. Are you sure?"

"Absolutely. It will take my mind off my troubles and the captain did offer us the saloon. We can't insult him by refusing, can we?"

～

"There's nothing like a foundering ship, attempted murder, and near drowning to take the fun out of traveling." Stephen buttered a warm, crusty roll at lunch. "Half so eventful a voyage would have suited me."

Wesley laughed. "I would have preferred it to have been positively dull. May all our future journeys be ordinary."

"Mother, Louise, and will be met in Liverpool tomorrow afternoon by our British cousins," Stephen said. "I'll have a great many stories to tell them on our way to London."

"I believe we'll spend the night in Liverpool so Mr. Oakhurst can rest. Then we'll travel directly to my estate the following morning," Wesley said.

"I was perfectly serious before, about meeting you in London. You'll look into it, won't you?" Stephen asked.

"Yes, of course...but I'd also like to have you stay at Caisteal Park."

Louise slid into the chair next to her brother. "I'm glad I caught you both. The dance club is on for this afternoon! Annabelle has agreed to teach us the polka."

Wesley was taken aback. "She has? How did you manage that?"

Louise giggled. "With a liberal dose of kindness and a serving of chicken cutlets."

Wesley frowned. "I can't dance with my sprained ankle."

"Not to worry, old boy." Stephen smirked. "I can partner Miss Oakhurst on your behalf."

Wesley gave him a level look. "Thanks. I knew I could count on you."

───

ANY REMINDERS of the midday meal had been removed by the time the club assembled in the saloon. Although Wesley couldn't participate physically, he watched and listened as Belle demonstrated the basic polka steps. Cavendish seated himself at the organ situated in the orchestra niche, and when he began to play the *Tritsch-Tratsch Polka* by Johann Strauss, the lively tune set Wesley's uninjured foot tapping. Since the dance club was one gentleman short, each lady sat out at least one polka. When it was Belle's turn, she slid into the seat next to Wesley. Her eyes were bright and her skin was flushed from the exercise.

"It's very good to see you cheerful again," Wesley said.

"I was completely undone this morning. Thank you being so lovely to me. When I awoke, I thought it must have been a dream." She watched the dancers for a few moments, a misty smile on her lips. "I'm going to miss this."

"So will I. I've been thinking…does Caisteal Park have bedrooms enough for all our friends?"

"With plenty to spare."

"I'd like to invite everyone to Mansbury for a week or two."

"Oh, Wesley, that would be so much fun!" Her smile slipped slightly. "It would give everyone a chance to meet Errol."

Although Wesley had the overwhelming urge to take Belle's hand and ask her to break the engagement, he didn't think it was the time or place or to discuss intimate matters.

"Indeed it would." His response was as gallant as possible. "There's a ballroom at Caisteal Park, I trust?"

"An enormous one, with a grand piano. In all the years your uncle was in residence, I doubt the ballroom was ever used."

"That will soon change."

After the last dance, Wesley gathered his friends together to tell them about the house party. He was gratified when his announcement was met with excitement and glee.

"I'll have my mother send formal invitations, of course, but it will be three weeks from Saturday, and you're welcome to stay as long as you like. I understand the house is very grand, and I'd enjoy your company."

"Caisteal Park almost a palace," Belle said. "In fact, the word *caisteal* is Gaelic for castle."

"I hope Mama hasn't already made plans," Eva said.

"If she has, she can change them," Stacy retorted. "I'm going to Wesley's house party."

"I agree," Carl said. "How often do we get invited to a house party in the English countryside?"

"By a duke, no less," Horatio added.

"I'll inform Mama that Stephen and I are going," Louise said. "I don't care what she has to say about it."

"Mrs. Van Eyck is welcome, too," Wesley said. "Mrs. Stenger as well."

"There are more than enough rooms for everyone," Belle said.

Wesley glanced at Stephen. "What say you?"

He chuckled. "You couldn't keep me away."

∼

AFTER THE DANCE club meeting was adjourned, Belle made her way to Dr. Vane's office, only to find her father asleep. Her eyes widened at her father's unhealthy pallor, and she backed out into the corridor to speak with the ship's surgeon.

"Is my father supposed to be so pale, Dr. Vane?"

"He lost a great deal of blood, and I gave him laudanum to help him sleep. Don't worry overmuch, Miss Oakhurst. I've attended lectures by Joseph Lister himself on the best ways to prevent infection." The doctor's smile was sincere.

Belle managed to take a deep breath. "May I speak with him later?"

"I daresay he'll be awake soon. Why don't you fetch a change of clothes for him, lass? He'll need something to wear when he leaves the ship tomorrow—and he's not to carry anything at all until his wound closes completely."

"I'll see to it, Dr. Vane."

Heartened by the doctor's prognosis, Belle hastened to her father's cabin to gather together a change of clothes and any toiletries he would need. Her father was awake when she arrived, fortunately, and she was pleased a trifle more color had returned to his face.

"Hello, Papa!"

She gave him a kiss on the cheek before setting his things on a nearby table.

"I've caused a bit of trouble, haven't I?" he replied, glancing down at his bandages.

"You are brave, heroic, and no trouble whatsoever." Belle turned serious. "I owe you an apology, Papa. I shouldn't have made up a story about Grandpapa. I embarrassed you at dinner last night and I'm very sorry."

"You didn't embarrass me, Belle, but telling a falsehood is never a good thing. Therefore, I owe you an apology as well."

"What do you mean?"

"I let you believe your grandfather didn't want to see you." A muscle worked in his jaw. "That isn't true. It was my choice to keep you from him."

Belle was taken aback. "Why?"

"Hurt pride at the way he treated me, partly. The other reason was pure selfishness. Hamish Heathcliff is a very wealthy man, and he could have given you a great many things I couldn't. I was afraid of losing you to his influence."

"Oh, my dearest Papa, don't apologize. I've wanted for nothing and you could never lose me."

"Thank you, Annabelle, but I'm heartily ashamed of my behavior."

"As far as I'm concerned, you can do no wrong."

Belle poured her father a glass of water from the pitcher nearby, fluffed his pillow, and straightened his blankets. "Now, I don't want you to worry about a thing except for getting better."

A sharp sense of remorse accompanied Belle as she left to dress for dinner. It was *she* who was in the wrong, not her father. Her lie had caused him pain in a way she hadn't anticipated and uncovered old resentments best left buried in the past. *I've failed in my duties as a good daughter, and Mama would be so disappointed in me. I mustn't fail him again—no matter what the cost.*

∽

AFTER DINNER, Belle retired to the ladies' sitting room for a game of whist with Louise, Eva, and Stacy. Stephen challenged Carl and Horatio to a cards-in-the-hat contest, and Mr. Ley claimed Wesley for a final game of chess. The match went on far longer than any of their previous games. Three times Wesley managed to check Mr. Ley's king, but the older man still won.

He clapped Wesley on the shoulder. "Well played, sir. You're becoming a formidable opponent, I must say. In the few matches we've had, you've learned to protect your queen. The instinct for knowing when to attack will develop with practice."

Wesley sat back with a crooked grin. "Does that apply to courtship as well?"

Mr. Ley roared with laughter. "In my opinion, it's far easier to secure a victory in chess than in love."

"But far less rewarding," Wesley said.

"Truer words were never spoken."

Mr. Ley produced his calling card and gave it to Wesley. "I'd be happy to propose you for membership to my gentlemen's club in London."

Wesley glanced at the card, the back of which was inscribed with *The Adventurer's Club*.

"Let me know when you'll be in town next, and you can have a look around," Mr. Ley said. "It's not as traditional or fancy as the Carlton Club or White's, but it's a nice place to put your feet up and have a drink."

Genuine pleasure lit Wesley's face. "That's very kind, sir, and I'd be delighted to meet your friends. I do hope you'll come for a visit at Caisteal Park. In fact, I'm hosting a ball in about three weeks."

Mr. Ley beamed. "I'll await your invitation."

CHAPTER 21
SIR ERROL

Saturday morning found the *City of New York* only a rainbow's width away from the port city of Queenstown, Ireland. After a very brief stop during which the *Apollo* passengers and crew were to disembark, the ship was to sail north through St. George's Channel, around the Isle of Anglesey, and then due east toward the mouth of the River Mersey, England.

Only a slight tenderness remained when Wesley tested his ankle that morning, so he returned his borrowed walking stick to Cavendish.

"I think you may safely pack this away."

"Are you sure, Your Grace?" The valet replied. "You never know what rascals you may encounter amongst the kippers."

Wesley laughed. "If I should come across any such rascals, I'll dispatch them with my fork."

After he left his cabin, he paused at the railing to admire the approaching Ireland coastline. Dubbed Emerald Isle in the poem *When Erin First Rose* by William Drennan, the island was an astonishing green, with rolling low hills and majestic, craggy cliffs seemingly carved out by the teeth of an enormous giant. Although Wesley remembered the poem, the words hadn't really resonated with him until now.

"*'The em'rald of Europe, it sparkled and shone, in the ring of the world the most precious stone,'*" he quoted.

His mother emerged from her cabin. "Good morning." She joined him at the railing. "What a marvelous view."

"Good morning, Mother." He nodded toward the coastline. "Nothing could be quite as beautiful as one's first glimpse of Ireland."

"Nor so sad as one's last." She sighed. "I thought I'd never see it again. How peculiar are the twists and turns of life."

"I wish Father could've been here."

Matilda squeezed his arm. "I think he must be watching over you, like a guardian angel."

At that, Wesley's heart lifted. "I hope so." He made a gesture of invitation. "Shall we go to breakfast?"

When they entered the saloon, the atmosphere was thick with excitement and anticipation.

"I sense everyone is eager for the journey to be over." Matilda nodded toward a table. "There's Miss Oakhurst."

As Wesley and his mother drew near, Belle glanced up from the *Gazette*.

"Good morning!" She set her paper aside. "Please join me for breakfast."

"Thank you, my dear," Matilda said.

Wesley took the chair next to Belle. She was wearing the same pink and white dress he'd seen on their outing in Central Park and looked very pretty.

"The coast of Ireland is in view, Miss Oakhurst. Did you happen to see it?"

Her expression brightened. "Yes I did and it's incredibly gorgeous."

Wesley wished he could grasp her hand. "Are you ready to disembark?"

"I've yet to pack my father's things." She gave him a rueful smile. "I'm going to be very busy today."

"How is Mr. Oakhurst this morning?" Wesley's mother asked.

"He's doing splendidly, but the doctor has forbidden him from lifting anything," Belle shook her head. "I dread the idea he must be moved at all, but it can't be helped."

"After Cavendish returns from his breakfast, I'll send him to your father's cabin to help you pack, Miss Oakhurst," Wesley said. "The efficient soul has already finished with my things."

"I would welcome Cavendish's assistance, Your Grace. Thank you."

"Mrs. Neal shall be very busy packing today too," Matilda said. "It's a good thing we aren't disembarking at Queenstown or we'd never be ready in time."

"You're in the *Gazette* this morning, Your Grace." Belle pushed the paper over to Wesley's mother. "Did you know?"

Matilda's eyes grew wide. "What?" She picked up the paper and began scanning the headlines.

"It seems you were spotted talking with Captain Howe on the bridge." Belle gave Wesley a wink.

Matilda's eyes darted back and forth as she read, and her nostrils flared in annoyance. After she finished, she folded the paper up into quarters and placed it back on the table with a sharp tap.

"How despicable! I'm most assuredly *not* smitten with our dear captain. I was merely asking him a question about nautical charts."

Her cheeks had flushed a bright scarlet, and Wesley stifled a grin. "Well, Mother, you said you'd be disappointed unless you were featured in the *Gazette*. What do you think now?"

"I don't wish to speak of it further." With her dignity drawn around her like a cloak, Matilda beckoned to a waiter to take her breakfast order.

∽

THE *CITY of New York* weighed anchor in Cork Harbor, Ireland, and a tender was dispatched from shore. As Captain Yarborough, his crew, and the refugees waited on deck for the tender to arrive, Wesley searched for Matteo. Over the big man's protests, Wesley pressed a gold coin into his hand.

"*Un regalo per fortuna.*" Wesley nodded. "A gift for luck."

An Olympus Shipping Company representative and an Italian interpreter came aboard when the tender arrived. The representative explained that the passengers were to lodge at a hotel in Queenstown until another New York-bound ship could be readied. As the interpreter repeated the information in Italian, Mrs. Stilton brushed past with Princess in her arms.

"I'm staying on board this ship. I *insist* on disembarking in Liverpool!"

Captain Yarborough plucked the dog from her. "*You* may stay, madam, but the dog goes."

With the quivering Princess under his arm, Yarborough headed for the tender without a backward glance. Mrs. Stilton trembled with outrage for a moment before she followed. The remaining passengers laughed and burst into applause.

For Wesley, the rest of the day passed in a flurry of activity. He had many people on board to thank and to bid good-bye. Fond farewells were exchanged with Mr. Ley, the Egermanns, the Van Eycks, and the Stengers. As the ship sailed into the

River Mersey and approached Liverpool, however, it was only Belle's company he craved.

They stood on deck together, admiring the sailing ships and cargo vessels moored to the many interconnected and enclosed granite-rimmed docks. Warehouses lined the river, and Wesley was agog at the miles of bustling commerce.

He shook his head in amazement. "I understood Liverpool was a port, but I had no idea how truly vast it would be."

"That's because the Mersey is so deep that far larger ships can be accommodated. Also, the rail system in and out of Liverpool is extensive."

Wesley glanced over at Belle, whose eyes were sparkling with infectious enthusiasm and pride for her country. She'd been away from home for over a month, and had nearly lost her father in the process of bringing the eleventh Duke of Mansbury back to England.

A wave of gratitude swept over him. "Thank you."

She blinked. "For what?"

"You were expecting to find a sophisticated aristocrat in America and instead you got me—with my rough edges and all. Thank you for your help and friendship. I don't think I could do this without you."

Belle leaned toward him. "You aren't what I expected, Wesley, but you've far surpassed anything I could've imagined."

Her lips curved into a sweet smile, and if there hadn't been so many people around, Wesley would have kissed her. The moment passed, however, and the *City of New York* drew alongside its landing stage. When the ocean liner dropped anchor, a loud cheer arose from the passengers on deck.

"Welcome to England, Wesley Parker, Duke of Mansbury," Belle said over the din.

Before any of the passengers were allowed to disembark,

however, two Liverpool policemen came aboard to investigate the shooting. They interviewed Wesley, Cavendish, Mr. Oakhurst, Captain Howe, and Dr. Vane. Apparently satisfied with the answers they received, the officers gave permission for the disembarkation to proceed. Passengers and their luggage began to stream down the gangplank like a giddy parade.

Mr. Oakhurst was furnished with an elaborately carved, three-wheeled invalid chair, and a crewman pushed him all the way to the cab. Although Mr. Oakhurst was assisted into a waiting vehicle as gently as possible, a wince of pain flitted across his features every so often. Wesley helped his mother and Belle into the cab, gave directions to Cavendish and Mrs. Neal as to the luggage, and climbed in himself.

Wesley peered at Belle's father. "I hope you're not too uncomfortable, Mr. Oakhurst."

The man was pale. "Nothing that a nice cup of tea won't cure."

As the cab lurched forward, its wheels rattled against the rough pavement. Belle bit her lip with worry, but her father gave her a reassuring smile.

"I'm fine, dear. Really."

Matilda glanced at the bandages supporting Mr. Oakhurst's right arm. "Does that sling help at all?"

"Surprisingly, it does," he said. "Dr. Vane lectured me most severely about keeping the arm still."

Belle frowned. "I wish you could sleep in your own bed tonight, Papa."

"And miss the turtle soup at the Adelphi? I think not."

"Turtle soup?" Wesley wrinkled his nose. "Is that good?"

"Their turtle soup is world famous," Belle replied.

"The hotel keeps turtle tanks underground and they make quite a business of soup," Mr. Oakhurst said.

"If you say it's good, I'll have to try some," Wesley said. "Turtle soup sounds very English." To his alarm, Matilda brought a handkerchief to her mother. "Mother, what's wrong?"

She gave him a teary smile. "I just realized...I'm home."

⁓

THE JOURNEY by rail from Liverpool to Mansbury the following day took many hours and required several transfers. By the time the Oakhursts, the Parkers, and their two servants arrived at the small Mansbury train station, Mr. Oakhurst was visibly exhausted and quite pale. Wesley immediately engaged one of the waiting cabs to transport Belle, Mr. Oakhurst, and their luggage home.

After Mr. Oakhurst was settled in the cab, Wesley turned to Belle. "This is good-bye for now."

"I hope you find Caisteal Park to your liking," she said.

"I'm sure that I will. I'll visit you tomorrow, to see how you and your father are getting on."

"With everything attendant to settling in, you may not be able to spare the time."

"I'll make the time, I promise."

He helped her into the carriage and as the vehicle drove off, Wesley felt almost a physical pain.

Cavendish approached. "A cab is waiting for you and your mother, Your Grace. Mrs. Neal and I will be along with the luggage directly."

"Thank you, Cavendish."

"In Liverpool, Mr. Oakhurst asked me to send the staff a telegram to announce your impending arrival. You are expected."

"Excellent."

Wesley joined his mother inside the vehicle, which then drove through town on its way to Caisteal Park.

He peered through the window. "So this is where Father grew up? I can't picture it somehow."

"Frederic adored Mansbury. When Septimus refused to share his inheritance, he felt he must leave altogether. It was simply too painful for him to stay any longer."

She went on to tell Wesley a little about the town; Mansbury was a charming and prosperous place, founded centuries ago on either side of a narrow, meandering stream. Picturesque stone bridges served to unite the two halves of the town, and barefooted children could often be found playing at the water's edge. Main Street was no Fifth Avenue, but its numerous, ivy-covered shops did a brisk trade in everything from bread to yarn. Clustered around the town, tidy farms raised sheep, goats, or cultivated grapes.

"In fact, Caisteal Park has its own vineyard and winery," Matilda said.

Wesley's eyebrows rose. "I'm a vintner too?"

"The winery was your father's favorite part of the estate."

Ancient, stately oak trees towered over the long driveway to Wesley's new home. His jaw dropped at his first glimpse of the four-story house, modeled after a French Renaissance chateau. The gabled gray slate roof, tinted green by the oxidized copper trim, set off the warm ochre of the stone beautifully. On the front lawn, a round reflecting pool accented the lengthy expanse of emerald grass. Beyond the house, Wesley spied rolling hills covered with rows of grapevines. To one side, a huge manicured garden beckoned his eye with a dazzling display of brightly colored flowers.

He shook his head in amazement. "I didn't envision Caisteal Park being this grand."

"Yes, it's an absolutely magnificent property," Matilda said.

"I visited here several times while your father and I were courting, and it hasn't changed a bit."

As the cab pulled up to the entranceway, an elderly woman and a formally attired butler emerged from the house.

"Oh my heavens, that woman is Mrs. Blount!" his mother whispered. "I would've thought she'd be retired by now. She was the housekeeper when Frederic's papa was alive."

As Wesley alit from the cab, he suddenly felt awkward. *What am I supposed to say?* He cleared his throat.

"Hello. I'm the Duke of Mansbury, and this is my mother, the Duchess."

The smartly attired man bowed. "Welcome to Caisteal Park. I'm Ulrick, the Head Butler."

Mrs. Blount curtsied. "Welcome home, Your Grace." She smiled at Wesley's mother. "And it's lovely to see you again, Your Grace."

"It's wonderful to be back, Mrs. Blount," Matilda said.

Under the watchful eyes of the fearsome gargoyles protruding from the building, the large staff assembled in the courtyard to meet the new duke and his mother. After the first few introductions, however, Wesley gave up trying to remember everyone's name. *I'll have to ask Mrs. Blount for a list!*

After Ulrick dismissed the staff to return to their duties, Mrs. Blount gave Wesley and his mother a very brief tour of the house. As Wesley wandered through the numerous rooms and corridors that made up his new home, he was increasingly impressed with the complicated tapestries, polished woodwork, and elegantly carved limestone pillars he saw at every turn.

"Mrs. Blount, how many rooms are there?" he asked.

"Near two hundred rooms, not including broom closets and the like. There are also fifty fireplaces and two separate kitchens and dining rooms."

His eyebrows drew together. "Why two separate kitchens and dining rooms?"

"One for the family and one for the staff, Your Grace."

The tour ended up in the library, where Mrs. Blount showed Wesley and Matilda the portrait of the Ninth Duke of Mansbury posing with his sons Septimus and Frederic. Wesley's eyes lingered on his father's image for a few minutes before settling on his uncle's visage.

"So that was old Ebenezer Scrooge?" Wesley murmured. "I wonder if his mortal chains weigh a great deal?"

"Wesley!" his mother exclaimed.

Fortunately, the housekeeper was slightly hard of hearing. "Beg pardon, sir?"

"Never mind, Mrs. Blount." Wesley asked. A growling noise emanated from underneath his waistcoat. "Er...when is the dinner hour?"

"The former master always had his dinner at seven o'clock."

He bit back a groan. "I'm not sure I can wait until then."

"I can send tea trays to your rooms now, if you like?"

"That sounds wonderful, Mrs. Blount," Matilda said. "Let's meet tomorrow about menus and household matters. I'm too exhausted to think right now."

"Cavendish and Mrs. Neal will be arriving with our luggage at any moment, if they aren't already here," Wesley said. "If you could make them both welcome, I'd appreciate it."

The housekeeper nodded. "Yes, Your Grace."

Wesley and Matilda followed the housekeeper up the winding grand staircase leading to the uppermost floors. As he climbed, Wesley admired the fanciful iron chandelier hanging in the entry hall, featuring twenty-six gaslights. Although the house was a marvel of magnificence, a queer feeling of loneliness suddenly descended over him. *It's easy to feel small and isolated in a place this size,* he thought. *Perhaps that's why Septimus Parker became so cross.*

Mrs. Blount showed Matilda to her beautiful suite of rooms first, and then escorted Wesley to his, which was in an entirely separate wing of the house.

"I'd like to extend my condolences on the loss of your father." The housekeeper gave him a misty smile. "Frederic Parker was always the kind one in the family. Perhaps it's not right to say so, but he was always my favorite."

"Thank you, Mrs. Blount. I certainly wish he were here."

The elderly woman pushed the double doors to his suite wide open. "I'll send a maid up with your tea directly." She bustled off down the hall.

Wesley explored his luxurious rooms with a sense of wonderment, but despite all the elegance and beauty, something was lacking. *What's missing here at Caisteal Park is the presence of Belle Oakhurst.*

∼

ORDINARILY, Belle would have been thrilled to see the two-story gray stone cottage and orchard she called home, but she was too concerned with her father's well-being to think about much else. After she made sure he was resting comfortably in his room with a cup of tea, she went into the library to sort through the raft of correspondence that had arrived in the last month. There were several official-looking letters for her father, several bills to be paid, a few invitations to answer, and a letter from her aunt, Mrs. Meg Mills. Belle opened her aunt's letter first; in it, Aunt Meg invited her to London to shop for her trousseau. Belle frowned, suddenly forlorn. How much happier would the occasion be if she were to marry Wesley! Instead, the idea of marriage to

Errol was beginning to feel like she was knotting rope for a noose.

The doorbell rang, and Belle groaned. *Can't I be left alone for just a few minutes?*

The housekeeper appeared in the doorway shortly thereafter. "Sir Errol, miss."

Belle's heart sank. "Show him into the drawing room, please, Mrs. Beveridge, and bring tea."

She took a few minutes to compose herself before making her way to the drawing room. Errol was posed next to the fireplace in a fetching manner. He wore his smartest jacket, a ruffled front shirt, and cream-colored pants that tucked into fine leather boots. His wavy brown locks were brushed back off his face, and he had never appeared more romantic. Belle felt her shoulders relax. *You see? Now that he's here you'll fall in love with him all over again.*

Errol smiled as she entered the room. "Annabelle!"

"How kind of you to call, Errol. We've only just arrived home."

"You're more beautiful than I remember." He took both her hands in his and bestowed a lingering kiss on her cheek. "Travel agrees with you."

"I've just ordered tea. I hope you'll stay?"

"Certainly. From your letters, I rather expected you back yesterday afternoon."

"We were delayed. Oh, Errol, so much has happened!"

Mrs. Beveridge rolled in a cart which held a pot of tea, two cups and saucers, lemon, sugar, a platter of sliced cake, and a tray of small sandwiches.

"Thank you, Mrs. Beveridge." Belle nodded. "I'll pour, but be so kind as to take some sandwiches to my father."

"Yes, miss."

As Belle poured two cups of steaming, amber liquid and

began to narrate events from when the *City of New York* weighed anchor in the North River until it reached Liverpool, leaving out those details which would only lead to awkward questions.

"Your poor father." Errol shook his head. "I imagine he'll need a great deal of rest over the next week or so. We'll do our best to make him happy, won't we?"

"I'm determined he should focus all his energy on getting well."

"In your first letter from America, you described Wesley Parker as little more than a street urchin." Errol gave her a reproachful glance. "You shouldn't have rushed to judgment, especially since the young duke has revealed himself as a remarkable sort of person."

A feeling of relief flowed through Belle. *It will make things so much nicer if Errol and Wesley become friendly.*

"You're quite right, and I'm ashamed of what I wrote." She beamed. "I'm sure you'll like His Grace very much. He's only a few years younger than you are, so you should have many of the same interests."

Errol's liquid gray eyes seemed to caress her face. "I'm quite certain we do. I'll call on him tomorrow."

"That would be most kind." Pleased, Belle poured Errol more tea, and added two lumps of sugar. "Now, tell me what you've been doing since I've been away."

In response, Errol rose from his chair, came to sit next to Belle on the narrow love seat, and took her hand in his. "I've missed you so very much, Annabelle."

"I can't think why. I wrote you faithfully."

He leaned in and gave her a gentle kiss. His lips moved from her mouth, across her cheek, and down her neck with increasing passion.

Belle twisted away. "Errol, this is improper!"

"Is it improper for a man so much in love to express his feelings to his fiancée? Annabelle, I'm going to apply for a license from the clergyman tomorrow. It's time to set a date for the wedding."

Belle was taken aback. "But...we've no wedding ring."

Errol fished a ring out of his vest pocket. "Will this suit you, my love?"

The gold ring featured an enormous round cut diamond, with smaller diamonds clustered all around like the petals of a clear, sparkling flower.

"It's beautiful," she said, quite truthfully.

He slipped it onto Belle's finger and resumed his caresses. She closed her eyes and found with a great deal of effort she was able to imagine Wesley's arms around her and his lips stirring her emotions. So complete was her fantasy, that when Errol whispered her name, she was brought to her senses with a shock.

Flushed and embarrassed, she pushed him back. "I'm sorry, Errol, but I—"

"My ardor increases every moment. Don't make me wait, my love. Let's marry as soon as may be."

"I can't marry you!"

In the shocked silence that followed, Belle jumped to her feet, pulled the ring off her finger, and set it down next to Errol's teacup.

"Forgive me, but my travels have given me a different perspective. To accept your proposal was a hasty, youthful mistake, and done without malice. Although I continue to hold you in the highest regard, I find I can't marry you."

Errol's face was impassive as he rose and straightened his clothes.

"Oh, I think you'll find you can."

Belle peered at him, confused. "Did you not hear me? My feelings forbid it."

"Do your feelings forbid a breach of promise lawsuit?"

If Errol had slapped her full across the face, she couldn't have been more shocked. "You wouldn't!"

"Such a lawsuit would cause quite a scandal and cost your father a great deal of money he doesn't have. You see, while you were gone, I was rather curious how a country lawyer of modest means could afford to bring his daughter with him to America. I discovered he took out a mortgage on this house."

Her eyes narrowed. "That's a dreadful falsehood."

"I performed a search on the property, and the mortgage showed up as a cloud on the title. Your father is in debt, Annabelle, and is therefore ill-equipped to pay a legal judgment which would surely accrue in my favor."

Belle backed away as Errol drew closer, until the wall prevented any further retreat. He insinuated his body full against hers.

"As I was saying, I'll apply for the marriage license tomorrow." His lips hovered next to her ear, tickling the hair on her neck with his hot breath. "Three weeks should give you enough time to buy a wedding gown and plan the wedding breakfast. Do we understand one another?"

Trembling, Belle barely managed a nod. His eyes traced a path from her mouth to her décolleté and back again.

"Good. Welcome home."

Errol picked up his hat and riding crop. A slight smirk tugged at his lips as he departed, leaving the ring behind.

CHAPTER 22
CAISTEAL PARK

The clatter of horse hooves on the driveway faded, but Belle stood frozen like a statue. A sudden lightheadedness threatened to overwhelm her, and she ran from the house as if pursued by the hounds of hell. The orchard became her refuge, and she wandered through the trees, gasping for air.

What had happened to change Errol? Before she left Mansbury, he'd been attentive, courtly, and tender; a touch of his hand on hers and a chaste kiss or two was all they'd ever exchanged. Now the man was demanding, pitiless, and almost cruel in his disregard for her feelings. He seemed serious about the lawsuit. Certainly his male beauty and romantic air made him a sympathetic witness, but could he prove his case for breach of promise? Her heart sank as she recalled all the letters she'd written to him during her travels. The first one especially had expressed her eagerness to become his bride and was the perfect evidence. The tone of her letters must have altered thereafter, alarming Errol enough to seek leverage against her—but why? A gentleman would just let her go.

Her thoughts focused on Errol's assertion that her father was in debt. Could such a thing be true? Belle immediately returned to the house and went directly into the library, where her father kept his desk. She didn't have to search long; the bank documents she sought were inside the first drawer she opened. Her father had indeed borrowed the funds to purchase her passage to America and back, and the house was pledged as collateral. *Dear, sweet, generous Papa! You've always indulged me far too much, and I've taken it for granted.* She remembered what he'd told her about her grandfather and his money; had the ticket been her father's way of trying to compensate? Belle returned the papers to the drawer, slid it closed, and pressed her fingertips against her throbbing temples. *What am I to do?*

The late afternoon sun slanted through the library windows, illuminating swirling dust motes and casting shadows across the floor. Belle tried to find a way out of her dilemma, but as the sun dipped toward the horizon, the shadows lengthened, and her options dwindled. Almost trancelike, she stared at nothing until Mrs. Beveridge came into view with Errol's ring in her hand.

"I beg your pardon, Miss Oakhurst, but I found this in the drawing room and thought it must be yours."

Belle snapped out of her reverie and took the ring with a sense of dread. "Thank you, Mrs. Beveridge."

I can't tell Papa what has happened, and I can't break the engagement. I'm trapped.

~

After breakfast the following morning, Matilda met with Mrs. Blount to discuss menus and housekeeping matters while Wesley went off to explore. One of his first destinations was the carriage house, where the coachman, Bartleby, showed him several carriages at his disposal.

The amiable man nodded. "If there's ever anywhere you'd like to go, Your Grace, just send word."

"I'm going to pay a call after lunch, but I'm exploring Caisteal Park on foot this morning."

"Would you like a horse, Your Grace? The estate is quite extensive, and you can cover more ground that way."

"Thanks, but I really ought to take riding lessons first." He chuckled. "Otherwise, I'll break my neck and annoy the horse."

Wesley left the carriage house and strolled through a series of exquisite, soothing gardens. He walked upon a carpet of green velvet so lovely he had to touch it with his fingers to make sure the surface was real. On either side of the path were banks of flowers, interspersed with large tufts of grasses, ferns, and plants of all shapes and textures. Further along, large, towering hedges formed natural walls.

In the flower garden, Wesley sat inside a gazebo and watched bees flit from bloom to bloom. From his vantage point, the view of the glorious estate was breathtaking. It was as if he were sitting in the center of a jewel box, surrounded by a crown of colored gemstones. The cloudless sapphire sky glowed overhead, the emerald hills stretched as far as he could see, and explosions of citrine, opal, ruby, and lapis lazuli-colored blossoms dotted the garden. Caisteal Park was truly far more magnificent than he'd anticipated, and he still couldn't quite believe it was his. A warm breeze sent a gust of intoxicating perfume his way, and he wished Belle were there to enjoy the moment with him.

AT LUNCH, his mother was effervescent. "I received an answer to one of my letters this morning. My sister Constance and her husband Tom have agreed to visit next month from Bristol, and they'll be bringing your three cousins. Isn't that exciting?"

"It will be wonderful to meet actual relatives."

"I'm going to order calling cards, so we can begin visiting the more prominent families in the neighborhood." She paused. "Mr. Oakhurst's advice would have been so useful in that regard, but I hate to bother him while he's recovering. Perhaps we may rely on his daughter's observations?"

"Miss Oakhurst will have to give us an approved list. It wouldn't do to cultivate the lowly, would it?"

Matilda gave him a reproving glance. "Jest if you like, but we must put our best foot forward."

"I'll leave it in your capable hands, Mother, so long as you handle the details of my house party. There's to be a ball the first night, and the rest is up to you. The names and addresses of my friends are on the desk in the study."

"A ball is the perfect occasion to invite the local nobility and gentry," Matilda said.

"Whatever you like, but written invitations should be sent as soon as possible."

"Actually, I'm quite looking forward to hosting a house party." Her eyes sparkled. "It should be a great deal of fun."

∼

CAVENDISH HELPED WESLEY don a fresh shirt, waistcoat, and jacket for his visit to the Oakhurst residence. Wesley told his valet about his conversation with the coachman.

"Apparently to be a gentleman, I must learn to ride."

Cavendish nodded. "It is somewhat expected, Your Grace."

Wesley frowned. "I don't suppose you could teach me?"

"Certainly, although the proper attire is a prerequisite. We'll have to purchase a riding habit and boots for you."

"I wonder if Uncle Septimus had riding clothes I could use in the meantime? See to it, would you?"

Wesley flinched as a deep chime sounded. "What's that?"

"The doorbell." Cavendish brushed Wesley's jacket to remove any speck of dust. "A visitor has come to call."

"Blast! I'm on my way to see Miss Oakhurst. Do you think anyone would notice if I slipped out the back?"

"Shall we find out who it is first?"

Wesley made a sound of frustration. "I suppose so."

Cavendish disappeared for a few minutes. When he returned, he had a calling card on a silver salver.

"Who is it?" Wesley asked, reaching for the card.

"Sir Errol Blankenship."

Wesley's hand froze, mid-air. "You're not serious?"

"I can show you the back staircase, if you like."

"That won't be necessary." A grin spread across Wesley's face. "I wouldn't miss this for the world." With one final glance in the mirror to check his appearance, he strode from the room.

∽

As Wesley approached the drawing room, he heard his mother's voice. "Truly, we're quite lost without Mr. Oakhurst's guiding hand, Sir Errol, but we have every confidence he'll rebound. In the meantime, Miss Oakhurst has been most accommodating."

"My fiancée is very useful sort of person," a man replied. "I think that's why I'm attracted to her."

Annoyance ran down Wesley's spine at the note of superiority in Errol's voice, and he took a moment to square his shoulders. When he entered the drawing room, the visitor rose.

"Wesley, this is Sir Errol Blankenship," Matilda said. "Sir

Errol, allow me to introduce my son Wesley Parker, the Duke of Mansbury."

Wesley and Errol bowed to one another.

"Welcome to Mansbury, Your Grace," Errol said.

"Thank you." Wesley nodded. "It's a pleasure to meet you at last. Miss Oakhurst has spoken of you often."

As the two men sized each other up, the temperature in the room plummeted. Errol was beautiful to the point of being effeminate, down to the ruffles on his shirt and way he dressed his hair. Wesley hated him on sight. *The stupid lout wouldn't have lasted two minutes in Brooklyn.*

"I must say, you are a vast deal different than Annabelle described in her letters," Errol said. "Far younger and far less... dangerous."

"First impressions can be misleading." Wesley paused. "Miss Oakhurst and I had a rather colorful introduction, but I believe her opinion of me improved greatly afterward."

"Hmm." Errol smirked. "Perhaps I'll give a party to welcome you to the neighborhood. Do you ride?"

"Not yet."

"Shoot grouse or pheasant?"

"I wouldn't dream of it."

Errol made a dismissive sound. "What *do* you do?"

"I'm rather good with fisticuffs," Wesley snapped.

They locked eyes.

Matilda cleared her throat. "Miss Oakhurst has been teaching my son to waltz, Sir Errol. Perhaps a dance would be in order?"

"Ah, yes." Errol lifted an eyebrow. "Annabelle teaches dancing at the local dance studio. She could probably teach a pig to fly."

His insult was so obvious, Wesley began to laugh. After a

moment, Errol joined in. A bewildered smile crept onto Matilda's lips.

"A dance it is, then." Errol's mirth faded. "I'll have to schedule it for a date following my wedding, however. Annabelle and I are to be married in three weeks."

Wesley couldn't stifle his exclamation. "What?"

"Yes, we set the date yesterday afternoon," Errol said. "You're both invited, of course. It would be an honor to have a duke and a duchess attend the ceremony."

A wave of nausea roiled Wesley's stomach. *It isn't possible!*

"Oh, dear." Matilda frowned. "Wesley has already scheduled a house party for that weekend. What a terrible shame to miss the wedding!"

Errol sighed. "I'm devastated at the thought."

Matilda brightened. "I have an idea! Would you consider having your wedding breakfast here? Amongst Wesley's guests are many of Miss Oakhurst's acquaintances."

"That's terribly kind of you, Your Grace. Annabelle will be thrilled at the idea, I know. There's no finer estate in the county."

After bowing to Wesley one last time, Errol took his leave. Matilda waited to speak until she heard the front door close.

"What in blazes is wrong with you, Wesley?" she exclaimed. "I feared for a few moments you and Sir Errol would come to blows!"

"Errol Blankenship is an arrogant, preening, supercilious *popinjay*, and I'm going to make sure he never marries Miss Oakhurst!"

Wesley stormed from the drawing room, ignoring his mother's expression of shock.

∽

Wesley's coachman drove him to Belle's house in an open-air carriage pulled by a dappled gray gelding called Kelpie. The afternoon heat was not nearly as oppressive as it had been in New York, and the air was remarkably fresh and free of soot. The bleating of sheep grazing in a field off to one side would ordinarily have made Wesley chuckle, but he was too irked to pay it any attention.

The Oakhurst's house came into view, neat and cheerful. Thick ivy creepers clung to the walls, giving the cottage the appearance of having sprung from the earth. A horse was tied to the hitching post out front, but Wesley was too distracted to take much notice of it. Almost before the carriage had come to a stop, Wesley jumped down.

"Wait here for me, please."

The housekeeper answered his knock.

"The Duke of Mansbury, to see Miss Oakhurst." A muscle worked in Wesley's jaw. "I'm sorry, but I haven't any calling cards yet."

The woman bobbed up and down in a flustered curtsy. "Please wait here, Your Grace."

Wesley was left on the doorstep, staring at the red door and its grape cluster knocker made of iron. At length, the door opened again, and the housekeeper ushered him inside. He followed her to the drawing room, where she announced him before hastening off to her duties.

To his shock, and great displeasure, Errol stood behind Belle's wingtip chair, leaning against it in a possessive fashion. Although the man seemed very well pleased with himself, Belle's expression was strained.

She stood as Wesley entered the room. "How kind of you to call, Your Grace." Belle curtsied.

"Thank you, Miss Oakhurst."

Wesley placed his hat upon a table and sat down in a chair directly opposite Belle.

Sir Errol neither sat nor moved. "What a pleasure to see you again so soon, Your Grace." His lip was curled.

"Likewise," Wesley shot back.

"Errol was just telling me of your invitation to host our wedding breakfast at Caisteal Park." Belle's smile seemed forced. "I'm overwhelmed at your generosity, and I can't tell you how much it adds to my happiness."

Despite Belle's words, Wesley could discern no happiness within her whatsoever.

"Miss Oakhurst, my mother and I hold you in the highest esteem." Wesley paused. "How is Mr. Oakhurst?"

For the first time since he'd arrived, a natural smile crossed Belle's lips. "He's beginning to rail against staying in bed, so he must be improving."

"Good." A flood of words were on the tip of Wesley's tongue, but Errol's presence served to check them. "Er...my mother would like your opinion on a few matters, Miss Oakhurst. Would you be free for lunch tomorrow?"

She averted her gaze. "I'm afraid not, Your Grace. I'm traveling to London to buy my wedding gown and trousseau."

"Will you be away long?"

"Perhaps a week. I'm uncertain."

An involuntary movement of Belle's hand drew his attention to the distinctive ornament on her finger. The sight of her wearing an engagement ring hit him in the gut, and he swallowed hard.

"What an unusual ring." He peered at the bauble more closely. "I've never seen anything quite like it."

"It's a family heirloom." Errol smirked. "My father was heavily invested in diamond mines before he died."

Wesley cocked his head. "And your mother? Are we to have the pleasure of meeting her at your wedding?"

Errol waved his hand in a dismissive fashion. "Unfortunately, my mother travels a great deal and it's difficult to reach her.".

The man seemed to be in no hurry to leave, and Wesley was certainly in no mood to linger in his company. He rose and collected his hat. "I must be going. Please give your father my best regards, Miss Oakhurst, and let him know I'll check on him while you're away." He bowed. "Good day to you both."

Belle stood. "Your Grace, please wait a moment. I-I promised to lend you a book, and I must keep my word."

The delicate scent of roses hit Wesley's nostrils as Belle passed by.

"A book?" Errol echoed, after she left. "I didn't realize Americans could read."

"There are an educated few to be found amongst the savages," Wesley replied.

"Surely not."

"You should travel more, Sir Errol. It would broaden your horizons."

As the two men glared at one another, Belle entered the room carrying a leather-bound volume. "This is the book we discussed, Your Grace. Consider it a gift."

Errol reached out a hand. "May I?"

As Belle gave Errol the book, Wesley was puzzled at the flicker of fear that crossed her face. Errol examined the title and burst into mocking laughter.

"Etiquette? Why, that's *perfect*. Well done, Annabelle."

Wesley felt his face flush with embarrassment, accompanied by a flash of irritation. *How could she give me a book on etiquette in front of Errol? If she meant to humiliate me, she's succeeded quite well.*

"I'll return for the book after Sir Errol has finished reading it." Wesley gave the knight a level glance. "He seems terribly amused by the subject matter and would no doubt find it instructive."

Wesley's annoyance was ill-disguised, but he didn't care. He turned on his heel, and left without a backward glance. Just as he was climbing into his carriage, the front door burst open and Belle darted out. "Wait!"

With the book in one hand and her skirt in the other, she ran to him. Tears were glistening in her lashes, but he was so angry he glanced away.

"Wesley, please take the book," she pleaded. "There's information in it which may be interesting to you in the future."

Although a sharp retort was on the tip of his tongue, Wesley could hardly say what was on his mind with the coachman watching. With a feeling of distaste, he accepted the volume.

"Thank you, Miss Oakhurst. I'm sure it will prove most edifying. Drive on, Bartleby."

Belle stepped back as the carriage rolled down the drive. Wesley thought for a moment he heard a sob escape her lips, but when he looked back, her face had become a mask. *Goodbye, Miss Oakhurst. Perhaps you and Errol deserve one another.*

When he returned to Caisteal Park, Wesley stormed into his manor and mounted the stairs two steps at a time. After he reached his room, he wanted to hurl the etiquette book across the floor but contented himself with dropping it into a drawer where he didn't have to ever look at the thing again. Why had Belle chosen to embarrass him in front of Errol? Even more baffling was why she was marrying the man in the first place. Could she be so blinded by his dazzling appearance that she was willing to overlook Errol's self-centered, narrow-minded meanness?

He was reminded of the way Stephen van Eyck had rubbed him the wrong way for a short while. The fellow had seemed superficial, but like an iceberg, he'd proven to have a great deal of depth under the surface. Errol, on the other hand, was as insubstantial as a bergy bit and twice as dangerous.

Morose, Wesley stared through the leaded glass pane window at the vast garden outside. How was he supposed to snatch Belle from the jaws of an unwanted marriage—particularly when he wasn't entirely certain she wanted to be rescued. He'd been intending to woo Belle, to tell her of his feelings, and beg her to break her engagement. If Errol hadn't been there, would she have listened? If he were to be honest about it, she'd given Wesley no incontrovertible indication that she returned his affection—just a few tender moments which he had interpreted in his favor.

Frustrated beyond measure, Wesley went in search of Cavendish, to ask for a riding lesson. Perhaps if he were thrown off his horse a time or two, the concussion would knock Belle Oakhurst from his head.

Nothing, however, will ever remove her from my heart.

∾

BELLE WAS SO angry as she packed for her trip to London that she wanted to slam the lid of her trunk down on her hand. She settled for hurling the box of chocolates she'd intended as a gift for Errol against the wall. The afternoon hadn't gone like she'd planned. In anticipation of Wesley's visit, she'd composed a letter and slipped it inside *Etiquette for Gentlemen* precisely because she knew he wouldn't look at it right away. In fact, she'd counted on him not opening the book for months, or perhaps even years, at which time the sentiments she'd expressed might bring Wesley peace.

The inopportune arrival of Errol, along with his news about a wedding breakfast at Caisteal Park, had upset her so badly she couldn't think straight. Then, when Wesley came to call, Errol's cold manner had driven him away almost immediately. In a panic, she'd run off like a complete ninny to retrieve the book from the library. It would have been easy for her to tuck the letter inside a volume of Shakespeare instead and just as logical. Why in heaven's name hadn't she kept a cool head and done so? She'd embarrassed Wesley with the etiquette book and made him the butt of Errol's scorn. From the look of resentment on Wesley's face as he left, he would never forgive her. In all likelihood, *Etiquette for Gentlemen* would find its way into the fireplace, and her letter would be burned, unread. Belle sank to the carpet and wept.

Maybe it's better this way.

CHAPTER 23
WEDDING JITTERS

As Belle stood before the full-length mirror clad in an ecru wedding gown of uncommon beauty, Aunt Meg clasped her hands together and exclaimed with delight. The gown's taffeta underdress was covered with a sumptuous layer of gathered chiffon which billowed out behind in a glorious waterfall of fabric. The rounded neckline was edged in a flounce of delicate wired lace, and on one shoulder a spray of tiny wax lilacs added texture and feminine appeal. Chiffon formed dainty puffed sleeves.

"My dear, I've never seen a more lovely bride." Her aunt beamed. "What do you think?"

Belle turned to examine her reflection in the floor-length mirror. "Truly, it's everything I ever dreamed of in a wedding dress, Aunt."

The older woman beckoned to the seamstress. "I wonder, should we take in a little around the waist?"

"The waistline can only be adjusted by pulling in the laces, Mrs. Mills, but if we tighten them much more, we'll have unsightly bunching in the fabric," the seamstress replied.

Aunt Meg frowned. "Annabelle, dear, if you lose any more weight, the dress won't fit. You're to eat extra bread with lunch and dinner...and I encourage you to have dessert, too."

"Yes, Aunt Meg." Belle sighed. "I'll try."

"Now that the matter of wedding clothes is settled, we can go shopping for your bridal nightdress."

Panic at the image of her bridal night with Errol caused Belle to blanch and her eyes to widen. "Must we? I can't bear the thought!"

Her aunt turned to the seamstress. "Will you excuse us?"

The woman nodded. "Certainly. I'll be out front."

After the seamstress disappeared from the dressing room, Aunt Meg lowered her voice.

"It was the same with me, dear," she confided. "As repulsive as the whole procedure is, you end up with a baby in the end. Just have several glasses of wine at the wedding breakfast, and you won't mind so very much what happens after."

Tears welled up in Belle's eyes. Her aunt would be very much shocked if she knew how much she secretly longed to share Wesley Parker's bed in a night of wedded bliss. *With Errol, however, an entire bottle of wine will be necessary to render me insensible!* As Belle's tears began to flow down her face, Aunt Meg gasped.

"Oh, no! Tilt your head back, Annabelle, before you cry on the dress!"

Aunt Meg ran to the curtain which separated the dressing area from the shop. "Mrs. Lemon, you're needed!"

With the seamstress's help, a sobbing Belle was quickly freed from the wedding gown before any damage was done. Clad only in her chemise and petticoat, Belle sat on a three-legged stool and cried.

Aunt Meg knelt beside her and stroked her hand. "The

secret is to get with child as soon as possible and then your husband will let you alone."

Belle sobbed harder. She could hardly imagine Wesley abandoning her bed, whether she was *enceinte* or not. "How *horrible*."

Aunt Meg misunderstood. "I know, but try not to think about it anymore. Let's get you dressed, dear, and go out to an early lunch, hmm? Perhaps a few glasses of champagne will calm your nerves."

∽

SADDLE-SORE, Wesley soaked in a large, claw-footed bathtub filled with hot water and bath salts. Afterward, he donned his breeches gingerly. Cavendish's lips twitched underneath his mustache as he assisted Wesley with a shirt and waistcoat.

"You *will* grow accustomed to the saddle, Your Grace. It takes time."

Wesley groaned. "This gentleman business is tougher than it looks."

"You're doing splendidly, but why don't you take a break from lessons today? You've been working hard for three straight days, and there's no need to become an expert equestrian immediately."

"I *shall* take a break from lessons, but that doesn't mean I won't ride this afternoon. I promised to check in on Mr. Oakhurst while Belle is away, so I'll take Kelpie. Tomorrow, however, we'll go twice as long with lessons. Next week, I'd like to try some jumps."

The valet shook his head. "Not on Kelpie, you won't. I'm informed he's skittish when it comes to jumps."

"That's too bad. I've become fond of him, but I'll have the groom pick another horse for jumping, then."

Cavendish peered at him. "You can ride to the Malagasy Protectorate and back, but it won't lessen your feelings for Miss Oakhurst one iota. I speak from personal experience."

Wesley sat to pull on his boots. "I have to do *something* to keep occupied, or I'll lose my mind."

"Have you thought about the best way to win her back?"

"That's *all* I can think about, but when Belle humiliated me in front of Errol, she made her choice clear."

Wesley despised the note of anguish in his voice.

Cavendish frowned. "Such callous behavior doesn't sound like Miss Oakhurst."

Wesley noticed the loathsome book of etiquette was lying on top of the bureau. "So you found that, did you?" He made a dismissive gesture toward the offending tome. "Belle insisted on giving me that book, as if I were some sort of American rube in need of remedial education. Errol enjoyed himself tremendously at my expense."

Cavendish folded his arms across his chest and regarded Wesley with something approaching disdain. "Are you quite finished feeling sorry for yourself?"

Wesley drew back "I'm not feeling sorry for myself and why would you say such a thing?"

"You haven't slept for days, you barely eat, and you've ridden until you can't sit down. Your self-pity is blinding you, lad."

Wesley gave him a level glance. "That's uncalled for."

"I disagree. Besides which, the next time someone gives you a gift, you may want to look at it before hiding it away."

"What are you talking about?"

Cavendish picked up *Etiquette for Gentlemen* and pressed it into his hands. "This."

Wesley peered at him, confused.

The valet made a sound of impatience. "Leaf through the pages."

When Wesley opened the leatherbound volume, he discovered a sealed envelope wedged somewhere near the center. He shot Cavendish a startled glance. "It's addressed to me, in Belle's handwriting. You knew about this?"

"I was organizing your drawer while you were taking your morning bath and discovered the letter."

Wesley opened the envelope and brought the letter inside over to the window seat. As he read the words written on the page, the muscles in his throat tightened so much the pain radiated into his clenched jaw.

Dear Wesley,

When you read this, my wedding will be long past. Please understand, I married my fiancé to protect my family. Since you and I are never to be together except as distant acquaintances, I feel free to confess a most passionate admiration and respect for you, without regard to whether my feelings are returned. You're undoubtedly the bravest and most thoughtful gentleman I've ever met. Nevertheless, I made a promise that must be kept or dire consequences would have ensued. I don't expect you to acknowledge this letter in any way, nor should you attempt to interfere with my marriage. Just know that I'll always care for you. No, it's more than that, Wesley. I'll always love you.

~ B.

Poignant despair was laced with pure elation. *Does a majestic eagle feel the same way as I do now—joy while he soars on the wind, just before a hunter's arrow pierces his heart? She loves me. Belle Oakhurst loves me, but she's to marry Errol.*

Wesley read the letter over again. When taken together, two phrases in particular gave him pause. '*I married my fiancé to protect my family.*' The only member of her family she could be protecting would be her father. Why would Mr. Oakhurst need protection, and from whom? *'I made a promise that must be kept or dire consequences would have ensued.'* The promise Belle was referring to must be when she agreed to marry Errol, but if she did not keep that pledge, what calamitous outcome would follow? *I must find some way to help her out of this mess. She never gave up on me when I was stranded on the* Apollo *and I won't let her down now!*

He glanced at his valet. "More is going on with Belle than meets the eye. Errol has some sort of hold on her which she won't reveal."

"Hmm." Cavendish stroked his mustache and goatee. "There *is* something odd about that man, admittedly."

"You don't have to tell *me!* The preening, vainglorious Errol seems bent on emulating Lord Byron."

"I've been asking discreet questions in the servant's quarters regarding the fellow. Nobody seems to know much about him, except that he moved to Mansbury from London this spring. Usually, servants know everything about everyone."

"It wouldn't surprise me to learn he was birthed from a reptile egg."

Cavendish chuckled. "It can often be said that a man without a past is a man with something to hide."

Wesley nodded in agreement, but in the back of his mind he wondered if the same logic could apply to his valet. Although he trusted the man implicitly, his past was nothing if not murky. What was he hiding and why? With more pressing matters to attend to, however, Wesley pushed his curiosity about Cavendish to the side.

"I'll visit Mr. Oakhurst right after breakfast," Wesley said. "It may be ill-mannered to call on him so early in the day, but I don't think he'll mind. He doesn't like Errol much more than I do."

The housekeeper showed Wesley into the library, where Mr. Oakhurst was sitting behind a desk wearing a dressing gown. When Wesley appeared, the solicitor made as if to stand.

Wesley held up a quelling hand. "No, please don't get up. You're fine as you are." He sat in a chair facing the desk.

"Thank you, Your Grace." Mr. Oakhurst relaxed. "Pardon my attire, but it's devilishly tricky to manage dressing myself with only one hand."

Wesley eyed the sling around Mr. Oakhurst's neck and arm. "Forgive my interference, sir, but shouldn't you be in bed?"

Belle's father laughed. "That's debatable, but since my daughter has gone off to London, I need answer to no one."

"I suppose not." Wesley smiled. "Have you heard from Belle?"

"She's coming home tonight." Mr. Oakhurst sighed. "My sister wrote to say Annabelle is suffering from a severe case of premarital jitters."

"It's more than that, sir. Belle left a communication for me, which I happened to read just today. Although she didn't say so openly in the letter, I believe she isn't entering into this marriage of her own free will. She claims to be protecting you from Errol."

"Protecting me, eh?" Mr. Oakhurst stared out the window with a thoughtful expression on his face. "Since Lucy died, I've done everything in my power to take care of Annabelle, but I often wonder at times if it hasn't been the other way around."

"I wouldn't press the matter if it weren't of the utmost importance, Mr. Oakhurst. Can you speculate what Errol may be threatening?"

He frowned. "I cannot."

"What do you know of him?"

"Not enough, I warrant, although I *was* acquainted with his father several years ago. Mr. Richard Blankenship was a respectable gentleman who made vast sums of money investing in South African diamond mines."

"Perhaps we could contact Richard Blankenship to ask a few subtle questions about his son?"

"Unfortunately, the poor man perished of malaria shortly after losing much of his fortune. His wife, Nora Delacroix, was a retired stage actress who has since remarried. Errol seldom speaks of her, and I gather he doesn't approve of his mother's new husband."

Wesley gave him a puzzled glance. "I find it curious that Errol would move to Mansbury and immediately attach himself to Annabelle. She's exceptionally beautiful, of course, but a man like him strikes me as the sort who would rather marry for money."

"Your grasp of the fellow's character is discerning, and I've wondered the same thing. I did make him aware that Annabelle's dowry is modest, but he wasn't dissuaded. It's all very puzzling."

"It's maddening."

Mr. Oakhurst's frown deepened. "My sister's letter has me quite worried about Annabelle's frame of mind."

Wesley leaned forward. "I'll do anything to help, Mr. Oakhurst. Anything at all."

"My relationship with her grandfather, Mr. Heathcliff, has been strained, to put it mildly. I thought if I mended fences it would cheer her greatly."

Wesley nodded. "Annabelle had some harsh words for her grandfather at one time, but I detected a certain wistfulness when she spoke of him. It definitely would help lift her from her doldrums if he showed interest in her."

"To that end, I sent Mr. Heathcliff a letter inviting him to the wedding but I've not heard back. It's possible he may be harboring some rather understandable ill will." Mr. Oakhurst peered at him. "Would you be willing to travel to Gloucester, to speak with him on my behalf?"

The notion eased Wesley's frustration. "I'd be delighted to be of service, and if Mr. Heathcliff can return with me to Caisteal Park, so much the better. I'll have you and Annabelle over for dinner and we'll surprise her."

"Excellent. I knew I could count on you."

Mr. Oakhurst took his arm out of its sling long enough to scratch something on a piece of paper. "You'll find Mr. Heathcliff at this address. Will you do me one additional service?"

"You need only ask."

"Before Annabelle and I embarked on our journey to America, I took out a small mortgage on this house. I thought it would be wise to have extra funds along, in case of an emergency. Since I didn't spend anything out of the ordinary, I can repay the note of indebtedness immediately."

Mr. Oakhurst produced a leather envelope full of cash and a letter to the bank manager, written in spidery handwriting.

"It's a good thing I didn't perish from my wound, or no one would have known this money was secreted underneath the false bottom of my trunk." Mr. Oakhurst laughed. "Would you take it to the bank and bring the cancelled note back with you? I'd be exceedingly grateful."

Elated to be embarking on a course of action at last, Wesley gathered up the leather envelope, letter, and Mr. Heathcliff's address. "I'll return from the bank within the hour, and then Cavendish and I will take a train to Gloucester this afternoon."

"Where shall I say you've gone, should Annabelle inquire?"

Wesley pondered the question. "If she asks, tell her I went to town. Just don't mention which one."

CHAPTER 24
MR. HAMISH HEATHCLIFF

Mr. Heathcliff's country estate, called Brimstone Manor, was located about ten miles from the Gloucester rail station. Built of gray Cotswold stone, the structure was constructed in an open-ended E shape, with a steeply pitched brown stone tiled roof. The grounds were extensive, with a mix of open fields, stands of trees, and gardens. As Wesley and Cavendish emerged from the cab onto the courtyard, Wesley gave the house an appraising glance.

"It's rather Medieval-looking," Wesley observed.

"Sixteenth-century Elizabethan architecture, I believe," Cavendish said.

Wesley nodded. "Whatever it is, I like it."

Cavendish asked the driver to wait. Wesley's boots crunched in the light gravel as he made his way to the door. The cast-iron door knocker was fashioned in the head of a lion, and Wesley laughed.

"Is something funny?" Cavendish asked.

Still chuckling, Wesley pointed at the door knocker. "It's just so Dickensian."

The valet rolled his eyes. "You Americans are quite easily amused."

Cavendish lifted the iron ring and let it drop. After a short wait, a butler opened the door. "Welcome home, sir—" The man's eyes widened as he realized his mistake. "Oh, pardon me, gentlemen. I thought you were the master. May I help you?"

"I'm the Duke of Mansbury, and this is Mr. Cavendish," Wesley replied. "We're here to see Mr. Heathcliff."

"I'm expecting him back from London any moment. Would you care to wait?"

"Thank you, yes," Wesley said.

The butler ushered Wesley and Cavendish inside and showed them into the drawing room. "My name is Trask. Please ring if you require anything."

He bowed and left. Cavendish took a seat on one of the elaborately carved sofas and entertained himself by admiring the many intricate and colorful tapestries hung on the walls. Wesley focused immediately on the enormous oil painting hung over the large marble fireplace. The beautiful woman depicted therein bore a striking and uncanny resemblance to Belle.

He pointed. "That must be Belle's grandmother!"

Cavendish tore his gaze away from a ten-foot long tapestry, and peered at the painting instead. "My heavens, the likeness is remarkable."

The woman's hand was resting on the back of a chair, and a pretty little girl wearing dark ringlets was sitting at her feet.

"The child must be Miss Oakhurst's mother," Cavendish mused.

"I wish I could've met them both." Wesley glanced around the room. "No painting of the current Mrs. Heathcliff?"

"That must annoy her exceedingly."

A commotion in the entry hall heralded the arrival of Mr. Heathcliff. After a brief, muffled conversation in the corridor, the man himself entered the drawing room. His imposing presence preceded him; steel gray hair encased his head like a warrior's helmet, and intelligent blue eyes sized Wesley up as if he were a battle to be fought.

"I don't believe I've had the pleasure," Mr. Heathcliff said.

Wesley bowed. "My name is Wesley Parker, the Duke of Mansbury. Please allow me to introduce Mr. Cavendish."

Cavendish bowed graciously. "At your service, sir."

Mr. Heathcliff returned their bows, but his gaze immediately focused on Wesley. "You're that American chap I read about in the newspapers."

Taken aback, Wesley hesitated. "I-I didn't realize I was in the papers."

"You're in quite a few articles, as a matter of fact. Your heroics on the voyage to England were impressive, as were those of your valet. My son-in-law acted heroically as well. Apparently, Oakhurst got himself shot while foiling an attack on you?"

"Yes, sir, but he's at home recovering."

"Seldom have I ever approved of my son-in-law, but his behavior on that occasion was admirable." Mr. Heathcliff gave him a curious glance. "To what do I owe the honor of your visit?"

"Your granddaughter is getting married very soon, and Mr. Oakhurst sent you a letter inviting you to the wedding." Wesley nearly choked on the words, but he pushed forward. "He hopes you'll attend for Annabelle's sake. Since you've sent no reply, I came to plead his case."

Mr. Heathcliff cocked his head. "I never saw any such letter." Mr. Heathcliff rang for Trask, who appeared in the doorway. "Bring me any correspondence that arrived in my absence."

"Right away, sir." The butler disappeared.

A sardonic smile crept onto Mr. Heathcliff's lips. "My wife ought to have forwarded my letters to me while I was in town, but she takes every opportunity to thwart me."

Wesley was unsure how to respond. "I'm sorry to hear it."

"As am I." The older man shrugged. "Mrs. Heathcliff and I became estranged over her son Dickie, who is a scoundrel, a rake, and a thief. If he should cross my path, I'll have him arrested, despite his mother's remonstrations to the contrary."

"Your wife isn't at home then, I take it?" Wesley asked.

"No, we're never in residence at the same time anymore. She left for Italy yesterday, per my instructions." Mr. Heathcliff folded his arms across his chest and looked at Wesley, askance. "So on the occasion of Annabelle's wedding, Lionel Oakhurst will finally allow me to meet my granddaughter?"

Wesley and Cavendish exchanged a confused glance.

"I don't understand," Wesley said. "Forgive me, but I thought your disinterest stemmed from your disapproval of Mr. Oakhurst...not the other way around."

"My disinterest?" An expression of sadness added ten years to Mr. Heathcliff's age. "In marrying Oakhurst, Lucy disobeyed my wishes, yes, but after my granddaughter was born my opinion softened. By then, however, my son-in-law resented my attitude too thoroughly to allow me to have a normal relationship with either Lucy or Annabelle. To be perfectly honest, I don't blame him."

Trask entered the drawing room with a bundle of envelopes, presented them to his employer, and left. Mr.

Heathcliff sorted through the stack until he found Mr. Oakhurst's letter. He slit the envelope open, and scanned its contents. To Wesley's bewilderment, Mr. Heathcliff's eyes widened, his face flushed, and his hands began to tremble.

"*Great Scott!*" His thundering imprecation filled the room.

Trask burst into the room at a run. "Is anything amiss, sir?"

"Have Benson pack a trunk for me with fresh clothes," he exclaimed. "I'm leaving for Mansbury first thing tomorrow morning."

∽

THE COOK HAD PREPARED Belle's favorite chicken pie for dinner, but she only ate a bite or two before pushing her plate away.

Mr. Oakhurst gave his daughter a worried glance. "My sister mentioned you weren't eating well, and I can see for myself you've lost weight. Can't you finish your meal?"

To please her father, Belle picked up her fork. "Yes, Papa." A few bites later, however, she could eat no more and pushed her plate away. "Aunt Meg served a sumptuous breakfast this morning. I believe it must have filled me up."

"I'm sure it would have, if you'd eaten any of it," her father murmured.

Belle pretended not to have heard him. "Shopping is very exhausting work. I had no idea."

"Meg wrote that you'd purchased very little for your trousseau."

"Perhaps not, but we did visit a great many shops. Whatever I need can be found here in Mansbury, and it will help the local economy besides." Belle smiled as she examined her father's visage. "You look a vast deal improved, Papa. I'm very glad to see it."

"I'm healing rapidly. I find I'm able to dispense with the arm sling for short periods of time and already I've managed to do a little work."

"You're doing amazingly well, Papa. Did you know your name is in the London newspapers?"

"What?"

"Yes, I brought some of the articles home with me. In the events surrounding the *Apollo* and the aftermath of its foundering, you, Mr. Van Eyck, and His Grace are painted as heroes. Even Cavendish received a glowing mention."

An expression of distaste crossed Mr. Oakhurst's face. "I would have preferred to have been left out of it."

"Why? You *were* a hero, and you should be honored as such. Perhaps the publicity will help attract clients to your practice."

"Believe me, I have all the work I can manage dealing with the young duke's business affairs." Mr. Oakhurst took a sip of water. "I'm feeling so much better, I may take the carriage to Caisteal Park tomorrow afternoon with some documents for His Grace to sign."

Although it would be a form of exquisite torture, Belle was longing to see Wesley—even if from afar.

She frowned. "Would you mind awfully if I accompanied you? His Grace might like to see the newspaper articles."

"Wesley isn't at home at present. He went to town for a day or two."

Belle tried to hide her disappointment. "Oh. Perhaps I'll call upon Her Grace, then. When last we spoke, Wesley mentioned that she wished to speak with me."

"If you finish all of your dinner tonight, breakfast tomorrow, and lunch thereafter, I welcome your company."

Belle gasped. "That's not fair!"

"Nevertheless, those are my terms."

With a rebellious and unladylike snort, Belle picked up her fork again and stabbed a bite of chicken pie.

Mr. Oakhurst beamed. "That's more like it."

∼

"Your Grace, I invite you to spend the night at Brimstone Manor. We'll take a train to Mansbury first thing tomorrow morning," Mr. Heathcliff said.

"Thank you for your hospitality," Wesley managed.

Mr. Heathcliff rang the bell for his butler, who arrived promptly. "Trask, have our guests' luggage brought in and dismiss the cab. His Grace and his manservant will be staying with us tonight."

"Very good, sir."

"And find suitable quarters for the duke's valet," Mr. Heathcliff said.

Trask nodded. "Yes, sir."

Wesley sensed Mr. Heathcliff wished to speak to him in private. "Cavendish, could you check on my luggage?"

"Yes, Your Grace." Cavendish bowed and followed the butler from the room.

Once Mr. Heathcliff and Wesley were alone, the older man sighed. "I won't keep you in suspense a moment longer. Sir Errol Richard Blankenship, Annabelle's fiancé, is my stepson, Dickie. He has the face of an angel, but a bigger devil was never born."

Wesley gasped in shock and his jaw fell open. "You're joking!"

"Amongst his other crimes, which include despoiling several young maids in my employ, he stole the ring you see portrayed in my first wife's painting. I couldn't prove it, but all circumstances pointed to him as the culprit."

"Belle is wearing that ring at this very moment," Wesley said. "I've seen it."

"That's my proof, I'm afraid." Mr. Heathcliff shook his head, sadly. "I'm sorry she fell in love with Dickie, but I will not permit the marriage to take place."

Hope ignited in the center of Wesley's chest. "She's not in love with him any more. Perhaps she was a little at first but she has since changed her mind."

"Her change of heart coincided with her acquaintance with you, I imagine." Mr. Heathcliff gave Wesley an appraising glance. "Why didn't she throw him over?"

"Although Belle wouldn't be specific, she indicated a sense of obligation. In addition, Errol has threatened her father in some fashion."

"Dickie is despicable enough for that." Mr. Heathcliff nodded. "The man is a predator and he had Annabelle in his sights."

"Are you suggesting Sir Errol came to Mansbury to prey upon her?" Wesley frowned. "I can't understand why, Mr. Heathcliff, unless it was to revenge himself upon you."

"For money, of course," Mr. Heathcliff said. "Upon my death, my wife will receive a modest stipend. The bulk of my estate, however, will go to Annabelle. Dickie knew of my estrangement from Lionel and so thought himself safe from discovery."

"I said from the beginning Errol had the eyes of a snake." A muscle worked in Wesley's jaw. "When I get my hands on the lout, I'm going to thrash him."

"Mind that you don't kill the man entirely." Mr. Heathcliff smirked. "I mean to have him arrested so he can rot in jail."

"If Sir Errol has any warning of his impending arrest, he'll flee," Wesley said.

"Agreed," Mr. Heathcliff said. "We must go about this carefully."

"Excuse me for asking, but how did you know Mr. Cavendish was my valet?"

"From the newspaper articles, Your Grace."

"The newspapers have it slightly wrong, Mr. Heathcliff. Although Cavendish has graciously consented to act as my valet, I consider him a very good friend."

SINCE HER FATHER didn't yet have the use of both arms, Belle took the reins for their drive to Caisteal Park. As she drove the gig onto the estate's long driveway, a sigh of pleasure escaped her lips. Afternoon sunlight filtered through the canopy of oaks overhead, painting dappled shadows on the ground below. The ivy and ferns snaking up the tree trunks resembled ruffles and lace.

"I do love this estate," she said. "It's so very beautiful."

"You didn't think so when Septimus Parker lived here," Mr. Oakhurst said. "Your improved opinion must have something to do with Caisteal Park's new owner."

"There's truth in that." Her smile was sad. "My admiration can now be freely bestowed."

"Annabelle…I don't wish to see you married to a man you don't love."

"Papa, let's not discuss anything disagreeable today. I'm determined to be of good cheer."

Her father chuckled. "Be of good cheer, then, child. I forbid you to marry Sir Errol and that's final."

Belle blanched. "You can't do that!"

"I should have done it sooner, but I've not been thinking properly. I believe the gunshot wound addled my brain."

"I *must* marry Errol, Papa." She gulped. "I must marry him or he has promised to sue."

"Let him sue." Mr. Oakhurst gave her a sidelong glance. "I'm a solicitor, after all."

"But we can't pay the damages!"

"The damages, if any, would be minor. I can easily pay, and it would be worth it to see you happy."

"You can't pay damages and service the mortgage, Papa! You'll be ruined, and it will be all my fault."

"How do you know about the mortgage?" Mr. Oakhurst regarded his daughter in astonishment. "Besides which, that debt has been repaid already."

"What?"

"The loan was temporary, to make sure we had emergency funds for our trip. Is *that* what Errol has been holding over your head? How dastardly of him!"

Speechless, Belle stared first at her father, and then straight ahead. *Can this be true? It must be, since my father wouldn't lie about such a thing.* Her hands trembled on the reins. *I don't have to marry Errol after all?* As the gig emerged from underneath the trees, the sunlight hit her full force. Tears of relief gathered at the corners of her eyes and streamed down toward her chin. Her father gently took the reins from her and brought the horse to a halt in front of the house.

"Set the break, child," he said.

Barely able to see what she was doing, Belle complied. Mr. Oakhurst embraced his daughter as best he could and patted her back soothingly.

"Thank you for trying to take care of me, Annabelle. You're a wonderful daughter." He kissed her on the cheek. "And if I had two good arms, I would show Errol exactly what I think of him. As it is, I think I'll leave that to Wesley when he returns."

Belle laughed through her tears. "Oh, Papa!"

A footman emerged from the residence to assist Belle and her father down from the gig. Before they entered the house, Belle peeled off her glove and removed Errol's ring from her finger.

"Keep this in your pocket for me, Papa. I can't bear to touch it a moment longer."

CHAPTER 25
BEST LAID PLANS

As Wesley's cab arrived at Caisteal Park from the Mansbury train station, his heart swelled with pride. Glistening in the late afternoon sun, the house and its immediate grounds had never looked better.

Mr. Heathcliff nodded his approval. "You've an exquisite property here, Your Grace. I'm duly impressed."

"Thank you, Mr. Heathcliff. I can still scarcely believe my good fortune." Wesley spied an unfamiliar horse and gig tied to a hitching post nearby. "I think I have a visitor."

"Why don't I have a look around the grounds and stretch my legs for a few moments before coming inside?" Mr. Heathcliff suggested. "That way, you may greet your visitor properly."

"Take your time, sir. Cavendish, will you show Mr. Heathcliff to the garden?"

"It would be a pleasure." The valet smiled. "It's a fine day for a walk, I must say."

Wesley headed toward the house as Cavendish and Mr. Heathcliff moved off toward the flower garden.

Ulrick greeted him at the door. "I hope you had a good trip, Your Grace."

"Yes, it was quite successful. Could you please prepare a room for my guest, Mr. Heathcliff, and have our bags brought in from the cab?"

"Right away, sir."

"Who has come to call?"

"The Oakhursts, sir. They are in the drawing room with Her Grace."

Wesley gave him an exuberant smile. "*Thank you*, Ulrick! You have no idea how happy you've made me."

"You're welcome, sir," he managed.

Wesley bounded down the hall and burst into the drawing room.

"Oh, hello, Wesley," his mother said. "I didn't expect your return so soon."

When Belle caught sight of him, she rose and took a half-step forward. The soft, sweet expression on her face made him want to turn a handspring. Instead, he removed his hat, tossed it onto the nearest table with a flick of his wrist, and strode toward her like a man possessed.

"Belle." He opened his arms and she threw herself into his embrace. As his arms encircled her, Wesley closed his eyes for a few precious moments and surrendered to the indescribable sensations her body invoked within him. "My beautiful Belle. I'm never going to let you go."

"You don't have to," she murmured. "My father has forbidden me to marry Errol."

Wesley was so overwhelmed with emotion, he didn't hear Belle at first. "You don't have to marry Errol and I've brought someone with me to prove it."

As their words finally sank in, Wesley and Belle pulled back slightly and stared at one another in confusion.

"Wait..." He shook his head. "Your father has forbidden the marriage?"

Her words overlapped his. "Someone to prove what?"

"Would somebody like to explain what's happening?" Matilda interjected.

"I didn't go to London after all, Mother." Wesley caught Mr. Oakhurst's eye and gave him a nod. "I went to Gloucester on a matter of personal business and brought back a visitor."

Matilda gave him a puzzled glance. "I don't understand."

Wesley grasped Belle by the hand and pulled her toward the door. "I'll let Mr. Oakhurst explain, while I introduce Belle to her grandfather."

∼

Belle's elation at being reunited with Wesley quickly turned to trepidation as he led her out of the house and toward the garden. "My grandfather?" She clutched at his arm. "I'm not sure if I'm ready to meet him."

"Trust me." He reached out his fingertips and caressed her cheek. "Mr. Heathcliff is really very amiable and I'll be by your side all the while."

"Y-You read my letter?"

"I did. I was too pigheaded to notice the letter at first, but Cavendish brought it to my attention yesterday. Oh, Belle, it made me the happiest man in the world and yet cast me into the pit of despair. I knew I'd do anything to save you from that monster."

"Monster?" Belle was taken aback. "Errol is bad, but I hadn't thought of him as a monster."

"You don't know the half of it. He's your grandfather's stepson."

At that, Belle's head swam and she became dizzy. "What?"

Wesley's strong arms steadied her. "He was after your inheritance. You're Mr. Heathcliff's sole heir."

Too shocked to respond, she allowed Wesley to escort her toward a tall, middle-aged stranger waiting underneath a honeysuckle vine-covered arbor. The man's eyes widened as she approached.

Wesley cleared his throat. "Miss Annabelle Oakhurst, allow me to introduce Mr. Hamish Heathcliff. Mr. Heathcliff, this is your granddaughter."

Belle remembered to curtsy. "It's an honor to meet you at last."

Mr. Heathcliff put his hands on her shoulders. "You look just like your beautiful grandmother."

His eyes moist, Mr. Heathcliff drew Belle into a heartfelt, tender embrace. After a few moments, her arms tightened around him as well.

Cavendish came to stand next to Wesley. "I think it may be a good time for a nice cup of tea, Your Grace."

Wesley laughed. "How very English."

"Precisely."

"In your opinion, Cavendish, is there anything not improved by a cup of tea?"

He frowned. "Only that which is best addressed by a tot of gin, brandy, or rum."

∼

CAVENDISH EXCUSED himself to go unpack Wesley's bags while Matilda ordered tea served on the patio. Belle and her grandfather sat together and soon were immersed in conversation. Although Wesley chatted with his mother and Mr. Oakhurst, inwardly he began to seethe. He couldn't help but dwell on how Errol had insinuated himself into Belle's affections and then blackmailed her into setting a wedding date. *He's an utter cad who deserves to be whipped!*

"I must say, Wesley, you're wearing the fiercest scowl," Matilda said.

"Sorry." He took a deep breath and let it out. "I was just wondering how best to go about apprehending Errol."

At the mention of Errol's name, both Belle and Mr. Heathcliff glanced over.

"Nothing would give me more satisfaction than seeing the scoundrel arrested and charged." Wesley's fingers curled into fists. "And if he resists arrest, all the better."

"The whole operation must be handled with delicacy," Mr. Heathcliff interjected. "If Dickie realizes the jig is up, as they say, he'll flee."

"Well, if I invent some excuse to invite Errol to Caisteal Park, the constable could arrest him here," Wesley said.

"Your Grace, if you invite me to Caisteal Park for dinner tomorrow night, Errol would eagerly consent to be my escort," Belle said.

Wesley shook his head. "You mustn't have any further contact with the man."

Mr. Oakhurst and Mr. Heathcliff spoke at the same time. "I quite agree."

"Be reasonable, gentlemen!" Belle exclaimed. "We must do this quickly, before one of the servants accidentally mentions that Grandpapa is here. The only way to do it is by appealing to Errol's jealous nature."

"No. I don't like it," Wesley said.

"Send Cavendish in a carriage to pick the three of us up," Mr. Oakhurst suggested. "My arm isn't yet up to full strength and he could lend me his assistance in guarding Annabelle."

Wesley's mother gave him a nod. "From what you've told

me, Wesley, Cavendish *has* proven himself adept at hand-to-hand combat."

"It's the perfect plan." Belle stirred her tea. "When we arrive at Caisteal Park, Grandpapa will stay out of sight, the constable will be here as an invited guest, and when Errol is lulled into complacency, he'll be subdued and arrested without any fuss."

Wesley frowned. "I still don't like it. If Cavendish is agreeable, however, I suppose it's our best course of action."

Belle glanced at Mr. Heathcliff. "Grandpapa, since Errol will expect to see Grandmama's ring on my finger, do you mind awfully if I keep it until then?"

"Child, your grandmother would have wanted you to have the ring." Mr. Heathcliff gave her an affectionate smile. "Consider it yours."

She returned his smile with one of her own. "Thank you, Grandpapa. Although I dislike Errol, I've always thought the ring quite beautiful. I'll treasure it, knowing it comes from you."

∽

Belle hummed as she dressed for dinner the following evening in a new off-the-shoulder dinner gown she'd purchased in London. Although her recent weight loss had decimated her curves, the use of bust improvers filled out the peacock-blue taffeta bodice nicely. The housekeeper had helped her dress and had suggested the improvers for maximum—and somewhat indecent—effect.

"What the gents don't know won't hurt 'em." Mrs. Beveridge gave her a wink. "Besides which, once you've got your appetite back, you can dispense with the improvers and use what God gave you."

Belle knew she was blushing but she was grateful for the woman's help. It was paramount that Errol be distracted this evening by any means necessary, but if Wesley should enjoy the view, so much the better.

The chime at the front door rang.

"That's Errol," Belle said. "Tell him I'll be down in a moment."

As the housekeeper went to answer the door, Belle pinched her cheeks to bring out the color. The lovely diamond flower ring sparkled on her finger, and she took a moment to admire it before heading for the stairs.

When she entered the drawing room, Errol was waiting for her dressed in a formal cutaway suit.

Belle forced a smile to her lips. "Y-You look very handsome."

He gave her a heavy-lidded glance. "And you are simply ravishing."

Errol closed the distance between them in two steps and pulled her into a kiss.

Belle leaned back. "Papa will be down any moment."

"But he's not here now."

His kisses trailed down her neck and toward her décolleté.

Belle squirmed and tried to push him away. "We aren't married. Please don't take liberties."

A flash of anger crossed Errol's handsome face. "That ring on your finger entitles me to anything I please. And if you didn't want me to sample your wares, why do you display them so freely?" His eyes narrowed. "Unless they aren't displayed for *my* benefit, after all."

She gulped. "Don't be silly."

He released her. "I'm inclined to beg off dinner this evening. Give my respects to the duke and his mother."

"Oh, Errol, please forgive me." She slid him a seductive

glance. "I'm glad you find me attractive and that *is* the whole point of my toilette. I'm wearing a new fragrance...can you guess what it is?"

He smirked, put his hat down, and resumed his fondling. Belle gritted her teeth, even as she feigned sighs of pleasure. Finally, he stepped back, straightened his clothes, and picked up his hat once more.

"Let's ride on ahead, my pet. My landau is outside."

Belle flinched. "But His Grace is sending a carriage for us."

He shrugged. "Let your father ride in it. Do you find the prospect of being alone with your fiancé for a few minutes so distasteful?"

"Why no, of course not."

As he took her by the hand and guided her toward the front door, Mrs. Beveridge appeared in the hallway.

"Tell Mr. Oakhurst we've taken my carriage to Caisteal Park." Errol smirked. "We'll meet him there later."

∽

THE DARKNESS OUTSIDE was relieved only by the lit oil lamps on Errol's landau. Belle gulped when she realized the convertible top had been raised, and the passenger compartment was completely concealed from view. The uniformed driver sat on the high bench in front, keeping his face discretely forward.

Belle's eyebrows drew together. "It's such a fine night, Errol, wouldn't you like to put the top down?"

"What is the point in that, since we desire privacy?"

Errol gave her a smile as he handed her into the carriage. Although she realized it was a futile gesture, she slid all the way over, to put as much space as possible between herself and her escort. She heard Errol murmur something to his driver, and then he climbed in and sat next to her. As the landau lurched forward, Belle cast about for some topic of conversation to keep Errol preoccupied.

"This is a lovely carriage, dearest. I understand a patent was granted to a German who was working on a horseless carriage. Can you—?"

But Errol silenced her with a passionate kiss.

"I told Johnson to detour to my cottage so we may have a drink before dinner," he murmured finally. "Perhaps an appetizer as well."

Belle tried to direct Errol's hands to more respectable places on her body without revealing her repugnance to his touch.

"Be reasonable, dearest. If we don't arrive at Caisteal Park before Papa does, he'll worry."

"Not if he knows you're with me. Besides which, I have in my pocket a special license to be married, Annabelle. I'll send for the pastor and we can be married tonight."

"No!" She pushed him away with all the strength her arms possessed. "Are you mad?"

"Mad with desire, my love. Married or not, I will have you tonight."

The carriage was picking up speed, and as its wheels hit a small bump in the road, Belle and Errol were jostled apart. They were both obliged to grab onto the hand straps or risk being thrown to the floor.

Errol pounded on the front of the carriage with an angry fist. "Johnson, rein in the horses for pity's sake!"

Apparently the driver couldn't hear Errol's voice over the clatter of horse hooves on the pavement, because the carriage didn't slow.

"I'll have the man's guts for garters!" Errol snarled.

Terrified that the carriage would tip over, Belle kept a firm grip on the overhead strap. Although she was relieved to be free of Errol's lasciviousness for the moment, she was petrified at what awaited her at the end of the journey. The brilliant and reasonable plan hatched the afternoon before had been thwarted by the libertine urges of her erstwhile bridegroom. *Why has everything suddenly gone horribly wrong?*

When the landau finally came to a thundering stop, Belle threw the door open and leaped out. To her relief, she discovered they'd stopped in the Caisteal Park courtyard.

Errol's face was tight with fury as he climbed down from the carriage. "Johnson, how *dare* you behave in such a fashion, and what do you mean by bringing us here!"

With a gracious smile, the driver turned and lifted his hat. "Forgive me, sir, but the name's Cavendish, and I work for the Duke of Mansbury."

Errol's jaw dropped. "Where's my driver?"

The valet smirked. "Indisposed."

Belle edged toward the house just as Wesley arrived on Kelpie. He reined in his horse and dismounted.

"Are you all right, Belle? I've been behind you the entire time."

Her lips felt numb from fear, but she managed to nod.

Wesley gave her a reassuring nod. "Perhaps you wouldn't mind summoning our guests?"

"I wouldn't mind at all." Belle picked up her skirts and fled into the house.

CHAPTER 26
INTREPID EXPLORER

Hostility between Wesley and Errol swirled like a cyclone as the two men circled one another.

"What's the meaning of this?" Errol spat.

"I could ask you the same, Errol. Or perhaps I should call you *Dickie*."

Errol's eyes narrowed. "Well, well, well. The American savage isn't so stupid after all." His jaw clenched in anger as he took a menacing half step forward.

Wesley grinned and raised his fists. "I'm so looking forward to this."

"As I was looking forward to bedding Annabelle Oakhurst tonight. She has so much passion for such a young naïve girl, but then perhaps you've already discovered that for yourself?"

"You're not fit to speak her name."

"And you're going to be sorry you interfered."

Without warning, Errol darted toward Kelpie, mounted the horse, and spurred him forward—directly at Wesley. Out of pure instinct, Wesley dove to one side, narrowly avoiding the horse's hooves. Errol brought Kelpie around for another attempt, but Bartleby drove up with Mr. Oakhurst just then, blocking Errol's way with the carriage. Kelpie reared up on his hind legs in terror, but Errol managed to stay seated. He calmed the horse long enough to deliver one final threat:

"Watch your back, Yankee."

Errol jerked Kelpie's reins to the side, urging the gelding across the lawn and into the darkness. Undeterred, Wesley set off in pursuit. Although the sky was clear, insufficient light was cast from the crescent moon to illuminate his way. Nevertheless, he followed the sound of Kelpie's hooves, muffled as they were by the grass.

∽

As Belle led the duchess, her grandfather, Constable Dremond and his assistant from the house, Mr. Oakhurst was climbing down from a newly arrived carriage.

"Papa!" She hastened to join him.

The constable glanced around, bewildered. "What's happened? Where is Sir Errol?"

"He stole the duke's horse and rode off across the lawn," Cavendish said. "His Grace went after him on foot."

Belle groaned. "Errol is sure to escape."

Cavendish held a kerosene lantern in one hand and a coiled whip in the other. "Not necessarily. His Grace knows that Kelpie will balk at clearing the hedge lining the drive. When Errol is thrown, the duke will have him."

"Even so, Dickie's treachery is without measure," Mr. Heathcliff said. "Young Wesley needs help."

Cavendish raised his lantern. "If the constables will accompany me, I'll light the way."

∽

Wesley's breath came in ragged gusts, but he forced himself to keep moving. He'd covered a half mile at least, but there was no sign of Errol. Worse, he could no longer hear Kelpie's hooves. After a horse whinnied in the distance, however, he rushed toward the sound and saw Kelpie trotting toward him, riderless. Moments later, he heard someone moaning in pain.

"Good boy." He patted the horse's neck and then gave him a sharp tap on his hindquarters. "Go home."

Kelpie cantered off. As Wesley crept forward, a man's hat became visible in the moonlight. While he was scanning the area for signs of the hat's owner, Errol sprang out from behind a bush and tackled him to the ground. Wesley felt fists raining down blows…but it wasn't the first time in his life he'd been waylaid by a thug. He twisted around and used the tip of his elbow to dislodge Errol with a brutal strike to the man's ribs. Then, the two men fought each other in a savage ground fight fueled by raw, animal hatred.

∽

Belle bit her lip as she stood at the edge of the courtyard, watching Cavendish and the constables strike out across the lawn. The glow from the kerosene lantern in the valet's hand bobbed up and down in the dark until even that was swallowed up by darkness.

Her grandfather joined her. "I'm devastated by the trouble Dickie has caused. If it's any consolation, his arrest and conviction may provide his mother the motivation to finally grant me a divorce."

Belle peered at him. "How did you come to marry her in the first place?"

"Maude is a beautiful woman, and it was an idle fancy." He shook his head. "I've discovered the truth in the axiom 'marry in haste, repent at leisure.' At any rate, I apologize for his misdeeds."

"The fault is mine. If I hadn't been so silly, I would never have accepted his proposal." Belle paused. "I must confess something to you, Grandpapa. When I was on the voyage from America, I led my friends to believe you were a baronet."

"A baronet?" The man's frown turned into a chuckle. "Well, I've been called worse."

"I meant no harm, but when your neighbor, Mrs. Stilton, came aboard the *City of New York* from the *Apollo*, she cheerfully laid bare my lie."

"Ah." Her grandfather nodded. "I've never met Mrs. Stilton, but she knows my wife. I've been told by my staff what a dreadful woman she is. Her dog ruined one of my carpets."

Belle averted her gaze. "Although my dear friends forgave me for my lie, I find it difficult to forgive myself. I just thought I should tell you before you heard it from somebody else."

"Hmm." Her grandfather tapped his temple with a forefinger. "If it will please you, I'll apply to Her Royal Majesty for a baronetcy. I happen to be acquainted with John Ponsonby, Her Majesty's Private Secretary. When I'm in London next, I'll speak to him directly. If the baronetcy is granted, you won't have been a liar, you will have been prescient."

Belle turned to him, wide-eyed. "You'd do that for me?"

"Why not? I rather fancy the idea of a baronetcy myself."

∼

SWEAT STREAMED down Wesley's face as he held Errol down with his knee and pummeled the man's face with blow after blow. Out of the corner of his eye he could see the illumination of a lantern coming ever closer.

"Do you yield, sir?" Wesley's words sounded muffled due to his swollen lip.

Errol lay limp. "I yield." His words were muffled as well.

Exhausted from the battle, Wesley struggled to stand. He staggered off a few paces and drew his sleeve across his face. Already the numerous cuts and bruises he'd sustained were beginning to make their presence known.

He managed to grin as Cavendish and the two constables appeared. "He's all yours."

Cavendish suddenly gasped. "Look out!"

Wesley turned just as the blade of a knife swooped down in a deadly arc. He tried to dodge but cried out as the steel sliced into the skin across his chest. Errol's arm drew back once more, but before he could strike, a horse whip curled around his wrist and yanked him sideways. The bloody blade went flying from his hand and disappeared into the darkness.

Cavendish's voice resonated in a commanding fashion. "We'll have no more of that, sir!"

Nursing his wrist, Errol turned to flee, but Wesley grabbed the back of his collar and spun him around.

"Let's finish this, Brooklyn-style."

Wesley's right hook connected with Errol's jaw. The blow snapped the man's head to one side, and he crumpled to the ground in a heap. Wesley bent nearly double as he tried to catch his breath. As Constable Dremond and his assistant hauled Errol to his feet and frog-marched him back toward the house, Cavendish hastened to Wesley's side.

"Can you walk, Your Grace?"

"I think so." Pain began to pierce Wesley's consciousness in earnest. "I must admit, Errol fights like a wildcat."

Wesley straightened, only to discover his waistcoat and shirt were stained red and hanging open where the knife had slashed the fabric.

Cavendish winced. "You're injured, lad. Put your arm around my shoulder."

Although Wesley would have preferred to walk unassisted, the sight of his own blood made him woozy. He gratefully accepted Cavendish's help, and they moved slowly across the lawn. They got as far as the reflecting pool before a groan escaped Wesley's lips and he sank to his knees. The last thing he remembered before he blacked out was Belle's screams.

∼

A WEDGE of pillows behind his back allowed Wesley to sit up without putting pressure on his wound. Gauze bandages circled his torso, visible through his open pajama top.

Belle spooned the last bit of soup into Wesley's mouth and sat back with a smile. "Very good, Your Grace. You've been an exemplary patient." She set the bowl and spoon down on a nearby tray.

"With such a beautiful nurse, Miss Oakhurst, I may be inclined to malinger."

"No malingering allowed! With your house party in seven days, you need to be fit enough to dance with me."

"And so I shall. In fact, the surgeon has finally given me permission to rise tomorrow."

"That's excellent news!"

"Yes, it is. And now that most of my scrapes and bruises are on the mend, I'll no longer look like a ruffian."

"You do seem to get into more fights than anyone I've ever met, but I've decided perhaps it's in the nature of a warrior hero to do so." She smiled. "Speaking of which, I want to show you something."

Belle retrieved a short slender knife with a handle of ornate gold and silver and presented it to Wesley. "One of your gardeners found this on the lawn. Be careful, it's sharp."

Wesley examined the dagger with admiration. "So this is what Errol used to carve me?"

She nodded. "He kept it hidden inside his boot, apparently. I'd no idea he possessed such a thing, but Grandpapa recognized it right away as one of the items Errol stole from Brimstone Manor. This weapon is an ancient Roman artifact and Grandpapa says it's very valuable."

Wesley chuckled. "I suppose that makes my injury a little more elegant, doesn't it?" He gave the knife back to her.

"Grandpapa said he wants you to have it since he already has far too many things as it is." Belle returned the knife to Wesley's cufflink tray and came back to perch on his bed. "Grandpapa had to go home, but he'll be back for the ball. Acceptances have been arriving, and your mother has been working very hard to make sure all our friends will have proper accommodations."

Wesley frowned. "Has Mr. Ley responded?"

"Yes. He wrote to say he was leaving Derby for London but would wrap up his business there in time to attend."

He relaxed back onto his pillow. "Very good."

Belle took his hand. "How did you know what Errol planned to do with me that night?"

"I didn't know for sure, but I didn't trust him. A wise man once advised me to always protect my queen." Wesley brought her hand to his lips for a kiss. "I wasn't about to leave anything to chance."

Belle felt her skin tingle at his touch. "Thank you, Wesley, for being my champion." She paused. "As far as Errol is concerned, however, I behaved more like a court jester than a queen. He certainly played me for a fool. Did you know he used to read to me from Fordyce's *Sermons to Young Women*? I thought him to be a pious and upright man."

"Perhaps an impudent American is more to your liking?"

Belle's lips curved in a smile. "An impudent American is most definitely much more to my taste."

⁂

NEARLY A WEEK after Errol's attack, the long scratch on Wesley's chest was still reddened but at least the wound itself was fully closed. Fresh from his bath, he examined the mark in the mirror with a rueful smile.

"If it's not a sprained ankle or singed hair, it's a scar." Cavendish helped Wesley don a dressing gown. "I hope I'm in for a slight reprieve from damage going forward."

"You're in for a haircut and a shave, Your Grace." The valet chuckled. "You've begun to resemble a Teeswater ram again."

Wesley took a seat and allowed Cavendish to drape a towel around his shoulders.

"I'm looking forward to seeing London for the first time."

Cavendish frowned as he picked up a pair of shears. "Are you certain you feel up to traveling, sir? The Belgravia townhouse is being made ready for you, of course, but I'd advise waiting another day or two."

"With the house party in less than a week, this is my last chance to go shopping."

The valet gave him a hopeful glance. "Perhaps I can go on your behalf?"

"Thank you, but that won't work this time. I need to pick out a ring in person."

"Ah." A pleased expression lit Cavendish's face. "I understand now."

"I'm also going to meet with Mr. Ley while I'm in London."

The valet beamed. "I'm sure he's excellent company."

"And he plays a mean game of chess. By the way, I'm happy to give you time off if there's anyone you wish to visit."

"Alas, no, but perhaps I'll go for a long walk while I'm in town." The expression on Cavendish's face grew thoughtful. "It will be good to see London again."

∼

THE BREAST POCKET of Wesley's coat bulged slightly from a successful trip to Hunt & Roskell Jewelers in Westminster. Buffeted by the crowds in Piccadilly Circus, he consulted the directions written on a piece of paper, headed down a side street, and finally spotted the tavern where he was to meet Mr. Ley. *Esmeralda's* was carved into the shingle hanging over the door, and when he entered the establishment, it was as if he'd walked into an explorer's museum—equipped with a bar and fully occupied tables. Maps from around the world hung on the wooden-paneled walls, along with all manner of weaponry, armor, and tools for navigation. A barmaid behind the bar caught his eye; her youthful beauty was faded, but she was still quite striking and possessed a fine figure.

She raised her voice over the din. "What can I get for you, sir?"

Far from a barmaid's accent, the woman's voice and manner of speech was cultivated and refined.

Wesley bowed. "I'm looking for Mr. Francis Ley."

A flash of recognition appeared in her eyes. "You must be the Duke of Mansbury. Mr. Ley is in the club, Your Grace." The woman came out from behind the bar and led him to a door marked "Private."

She smiled. "Just through here."

"Thank you."

Wesley passed into the large back rooms, which were decorated in largely the same way as the tavern, with the addition of a large number of bookshelves. Here, however, the furniture consisted of armchairs, sofas, as well as tables. Well-dressed gentlemen were playing cards, reading newspapers, or engaged in lively discussions.

A butler approached. "May I take your hat, sir?"

"Oh, yes." Wesley surrendered his top hat and received a claim ticket in return. "Er...thanks."

Mr. Ley hastened over to shake Wesley's hand. "So you found us." He made a sweeping gesture. "This is the Explorer's Club, or what remains of it. Our membership has dwindled since the original founders died and disappeared, respectively."

"Disappeared?"

"Well, that's why I asked you to meet me here. I'd like to introduce you to a few of the members, of course, but I also wanted to show you something I think you'll find very interesting."

After a waiter took Wesley's drink order, Mr. Ley ushered him toward an unoccupied table in the corner. "I wish to tell you a story about the two original founders, Lord Archibald Gotham and Lord James Overton."

"Lord James Overton?" As Wesley recognized the name, the hair on the back of his neck rose. "He was one of my valet's previous employers."

"I never met Mr. Gotham or Lord Overton personally because I joined the club after they'd left. I'm told, however, they were a couple of audacious rebels and very great friends. They traveled the world together and were so fond of adventure they founded this club. Then, as the story goes, they had a falling out over a lady."

The image of Stephen van Eyck and Belle flashed into Wesley's mind. "I can imagine."

"Well, after his argument with Lord Overton, Lord Gotham went on an extended safari in Africa and was killed by a poacher."

"How horrible." Wesley grimaced. "And Lord Overton?"

"He mysteriously disappeared, never to be heard from again. That was nearly thirty years ago."

Wesley frowned. "I was told that Lord Overton died. What happened to the woman?"

"Miss Christianson had been engaged to Lord Overton. After he disappeared, she never married—despite the fact she was rumored to be one of the greatest beauties in England."

Wesley studied him a moment. "This is a very sad tale, Mr. Ley, but I'm curious what this has to do with me."

"Over your shoulder, on the wall just there, is a portrait of Lord Gotham and Lord Overton. I think you ought to have a good look at it."

Wesley turned around to examine the oil painting of two handsome, dapper young men posed side by side with devilish grins on their lips. One man was tall and athletic, with a well-trimmed beard. The other man had a clean-shaven, boyishly handsome face and was slight in stature. He also held a walking stick with a distinctive snake head for a handle.

"Good Lord." Wesley glanced back at Mr. Ley. "Lord Overton is *Cavendish*."

The waiter set down a glass of gin and hastened off.

Mr. Ley shook his head. "I *knew* I'd seen your valet somewhere, Your Grace, but it didn't register until I was sitting here the other day and glanced over at a portrait I'd seen dozens of times before."

Wesley stared into his glass as he recalled all the conversations he'd ever had with Cavendish about his past. The pieces of a puzzle slid into place and his murky history finally became clear.

"Cavendish has taken great pains to hide his identity for some reason." Wesley glanced at Mr. Ley. "I trust you'll keep his confidence."

The man nodded. "You have my word as a gentleman."

"Where is Miss Christianson now?" Wesley asked. "I'd like to meet her."

Mr. Ley chuckled. "You already did, lad...on the way in."

∽

ON THE CAB ride back to his Belgrave Square townhouse, Wesley was pensive. From the moment he saw Lord James Overton's portrait, Wesley had debated with himself on how to approach Cavendish. His instincts had always told him there was more to the valet than the man was willing to disclose, but the reality was much larger than he had imagined. Part of him wanted to ignore the information altogether, so as not to pry into the man's affairs. *And yet, can I pretend as if nothing has happened?* Outside of an overwhelming urge to help Cavendish in some way, Wesley was consumed with the need to know what would cause a man to abandon his title, fortune, and identity in favor of a life of servitude?

Cavendish had not yet returned that afternoon when Wesley reached his townhouse. After he deposited the newly acquired engagement ring in his bedchamber, Wesley went down to the drawing room for a stiff drink.

Just after five o'clock, Cavendish appeared. His cheeks were flushed from his recent walk, and his eyes were brightened by the exercise.

"The housekeeper said you wished to see me, sir?"

"Yes." Wesley beckoned the man closer. "Come have a drink with me, Cavendish."

The man chuckled. "Although I appreciate your regard for me, it wouldn't be appropriate for a duke to drink with his valet."

"Have it your way, then." Wesley smiled. "In that case, I'd like to have a drink with Lord James Overton."

CHAPTER 27
BELLE AT THE BALL

Overton's smile faded. "I'm sorry, sir, I don't know who you mean."

Wesley waved off the man's attempt to dissemble. "It's no good, Lord Overton. I saw your portrait at the Explorer's Club. It's been quite a few years since it was painted, but your appearance has not changed overmuch."

Several long seconds passed before the man replied. "You have my resignation and I'll be gone by morning."

Overton turned to leave, but Wesley bounded from his chair and caught the man by the sleeve. "I don't *want* your resignation. I want the truth."

The baron freed himself from Wesley's grasp. "I don't appreciate your *snooping* into my business, as you Americans say."

"I didn't snoop! As a matter of fact, Mr. Ley is a member of the Explorer's Club, and he figured out who you were first."

"Nevertheless, if my service has been satisfactory, that's all you should have been concerned about."

"I can't force your confidence, but after what we've been

through together, I just want to understand." Wesley paused. "I consider you a friend."

Overton held his gaze a few moments before nodding. "I suppose I owe you that."

He closed the drawing room doors, poured himself a brandy, and then turned to face Wesley.

"When I was a few years older than you are now, I was cocky, arrogant, and convinced of my own superiority. Archie and I were a team, out to conquer the world. We were also the terror of London debutantes...until Miss Esmé Christianson came out into society. Archie and I both fell madly in love with her and were rivals for her affection for a short while. To his credit, when she chose me, he was gracious about it. We largely went on as before until I began to suspect she harbored a secret admiration for him. Archie was a strapping, good-looking fellow, and I envied him. It was unfair and unjustified, perhaps, but I blew up at them both. Archie went off and got himself killed in Africa, and I held myself accountable."

"How could it have been your fault?" Wesley peered at him. "He was murdered by a poacher."

"I should've been there for him! He was always there to watch my back, and because of my jealousy I let him go off on his own. It was then that I realized my money, the barony, and my position in society meant nothing. I pensioned off my long-suffering valet, Cavendish, relinquished my title and estate to my younger brother, and went off to seek redemption. My life as a valet was a chance to be useful, teach myself humility, and perhaps improve my character a trifle." He brought the snifter to his lips.

"The man I see before me bears no resemblance to what he might have been thirty years ago. Isn't it time to resume your former life?"

"Even if I wanted to, I wouldn't know how to begin.

Besides which, I'm quite contented with the way things are. There's a great deal of satisfaction to be had in serving others, and I do it well."

"What of Miss Christianson?"

"Esmé was the most dazzling woman I'd ever beheld. I was never quite sure what she saw in me." A haunted expression passed over the man's face. "At any rate, she's most certainly spoken for."

Wesley shook his head. "She's unmarried and still very handsome. I met her today."

"I'm past my prime and would hold no attraction for her whatsoever."

Wesley made a sound of impatience "I can't say whether you might successfully rekindle your romance or not, but I've noticed women flock to you." He shrugged. "You never know unless you try."

"Stop it, lad!"

The heated reply took Wesley aback.

"Don't you realize how many nights I've lain awake, torturing myself with what could have been?" Overton's voice was raw and filled with pain. "I'm not worthy of her and I never will be! Please, let's not discuss it further."

"You're wrong, but you'll hear no more about her from me."

The baron lowered his brandy snifter to a table. "Do I still have a position as your valet?"

"Only until you can train your replacement."

Overton averted his eyes. "I understand."

"I don't think you do. If you wish to continue working for me, you must have a loftier position and a raise in salary. How does Master Tutor sound?"

"It sounds very well...but why not simply discharge me?" The baron gave him a puzzled glance. "You've every reason."

"We're family, Cavendish…er, Lord Overton. As far as I'm concerned, you may work for me as long as you desire. By the way, since I know who you are, how should I call you?"

"James, if you like."

"I would prefer if you called me Wesley."

"As you wish." The man's eyes took on a bit of their former twinkle. "You remind me a trifle of Archie."

"In that case, remind me never to go on safari." Wesley peered at him. "Now that you are no longer among the missing, can you take back your barony?"

"I never legally abdicated the title to my brother, so the barony is still mine. I merely permitted him to use it in my absence." He checked his pocket watch. "It's time for you to dress for dinner."

"I'll be along directly."

The baron bowed and left the room. Wesley frowned at his glass of port. *James has more than paid the price for any slights he may have inflicted thirty years ago. I won't rest until he takes his former life back completely.*

CAISTEAL Park had been buzzing with activity for days. The Van Eycks, the Stengers, and the Egermanns arrived on the afternoon of the ball, and after they'd had tea, everyone went to their rooms to dress for the festivities. Louise and Stephen stayed behind for a few minutes to speak with Wesley.

"Promise you'll give us a more extensive tour of the place tomorrow?" Louise begged. "It's so terribly splendid."

"We're going to be here a whole week, Louise," Stephen said. "Perhaps Wesley can spread out the tour over several days to prolong our excitement as long as possible."

Wesley gave Stephen a reproving glance. "It *will* take several days to see the entire estate and it's worth it."

Stephen clapped his friend on the shoulder. "Undoubtedly. What I've seen so far has been superlative, and I'm extremely jealous."

"And I'm extremely anxious to see Annabelle." Louise giggled. "I can't wait to show her my new ball gown."

Stephen peered at his sister. "After all that's happened, you're most concerned about a dress?"

"Not *most* concerned, no." Louise beamed. "But I do want her to see it, nonetheless."

Wesley escorted his friends to their rooms and then went to his own. Since he had been unable to hire another valet on such short notice, James had continued with his duties. He'd laid out Wesley's formal attire for the evening, with a black tailcoat and matching trousers, a white waistcoat, white dress shirt, and a white bow tie. Wesley bathed and donned his evening clothes, but as the time drew near for him to go down to the ballroom, he was beset by nerves. While James expertly tied Wesley's bow tie, Wesley took a deep breath to calm his jitters.

"I can't help but notice you seem a bit off." James gave him a worried glance. "Have you overtired yourself?"

"No, it's not that." Wesley's gaze slid to the sparkling engagement ring resting on the dresser. "I've never asked anyone to marry me before."

"Stiff upper lip and so forth." The baron brushed the shoulders of Wesley's evening jacket. "You'll do fine, lad."

"I'm sure it will all work out in the end." Wesley slid James a smile. "I'm glad you've agreed to attend the ball as Lord Overton. It's going to be fun, introducing you to our friends as a baron."

"Your friends will, of course, be shocked." James laughed. "They only know me as Cavendish."

"My friends don't *really* know you at all, do they? Tonight will be your debut and the ladies will be counting on you as a dance partner."

"Speaking of which, I must go dress." James put the brush down. "You know, I'm rather looking forward to being myself for the evening."

"It doesn't have to be just for tonight. You're a legitimate baron, and you can take your barony back."

"You'll be relieved to know I've already written a letter to my younger brother, informing him of my decision to do exactly that. Henry will be extremely put out when he reads it."

"The man blackened your name quite fiercely when Mr. Oakhurst contacted him for a reference." Wesley grimaced. "I take it you two don't get along?"

"My brother has always viewed me as the sole obstacle to his happiness. If I compensate him handsomely for his loss, however, that might waken a bit of brotherly affection."

"I don't understand. Didn't you already give him the entire estate?"

"Only a small fraction, actually. He owns our father's house, and I arranged for him to have a reasonable sum, paid annually."

Wesley stared at him. "Are you telling me you're wealthy?"

"Quite so. I was distraught thirty years ago, not out of my mind. I possess enough money for twenty lifetimes."

"Why you sly boots!" Wesley stood with his arms akimbo. "You could've paid your own way across the Atlantic, couldn't you?"

"I believe I mentioned in our interview that I was exceedingly economical." He winked. "I'll see you at the ball."

With Mr. Oakhurst on one side and her grandfather on the other, Belle sailed through the entrance to Caisteal Park. Even from the courtyard, she could hear the sound music. Anticipation lent energy to her steps.

"This is my first real ball." She beamed. "I'm very excited."

"You're quite the beauty," Mr. Oakhurst said.

"Thank you, Papa! I expect no other girl has two distinguished escorts like I have."

"You flatter me, Annabelle," Mr. Heathcliff said. "But I would prefer that you cover your bodice with your fan at all times."

"Oh, Grandpapa! Aunt Meg picked this gown out for me and I intend to do it justice."

Belle's pearl-encrusted gown was fashioned of ice-blue tarlatan and satin, with a pointed waist and low square neckline. A small Napoleonic ruff drew the eye toward her décolleté, which was barely covered by a modesty piece of gathered tulle. The slightly puffed sleeves, trimmed with satin ribbons, ended just above the elbow. Long white gloves covered her hands and lower arms, and a simple pearl choker completed her jewelry.

A footman escorted the trio to the ballroom, where Wesley and Matilda were receiving their guests. When Belle caught sight of Wesley, her heart soared. *He possesses not only the demeanor of a gentleman, but also the appearance of a prince. I've never seen anyone look more handsome.*

Wesley took her hand in his. "Welcome, Miss Oakhurst."

She dipped down into a low curtsy. "Thank you for inviting me, Your Grace."

He didn't release her hand right away. "Please save the promenade and first waltz for me."

"Gladly."

Wesley greeted Mr. Oakhurst and Mr. Heathcliff, and Belle turned to Matilda. Wesley's mother wore a black and pink striped gown with a pointed bodice and full, puffed sleeves made of chiffon. A generous number of jet beads and sequins on the fabric sparkled under the lights.

"Good evening, Your Grace." Belle gave her an admiring glance. "You look lovely."

"As do you, Miss Oakhurst. Thank you for helping me with the guest list. I'm so pleased with all my new acquaintances from the neighborhood."

As soon as Belle entered the ballroom, Louise hastened over. She wore a gorgeous white broché voile fabric gown with an off-the-shoulder neckline that made the most of her pale complexion and smooth skin.

"It's so good to see you, Annabelle." Louise frowned. "I thought my gown was pretty, but now that I see *yours*, I feel like a mouse."

"Nobody could possibly mistake you for a mouse, Louise. You're perfectly splendid."

"Oh, you're so nice. I got your letter about Sir Errol, and you'll have to tell me all the details! But first come say hello to everyone! We came by train from London today, and it was a very merry journey."

She pulled Belle over to greet Stephen, Carl, Horatio, Stacy, and Eva, and the next few minutes were lost to greetings and animated conversation.

Stephen finally maneuvered Belle to one side. "I heard you broke off your engagement. Does that mean I've got a chance with you now?"

His question was asked in a light-hearted manner, so Belle had no qualms about responding in a similar fashion. "I'm no longer engaged, Mr. Van Eyck, but my affections are still spoken for."

"Pity. Then perhaps you'd do me the honor of introducing me to that girl over there...the one in the pale green gown?"

Belle stifled a laugh. Stephen was staring at pretty Maureen Crane, who was the mayor's daughter—and the unabashed town flirt. "Yes, I think you and Miss Crane will get on well together." *In fact, Maureen just may wrap Stephen around her little finger.*

Just then, Eva gasped. "Is that *Cavendish?*"

The former valet was impeccably attired in evening wear, much the same as the other gentlemen, but he had a certain graceful swagger in his step that attracted admiring glances from several of the local matrons. His mustache and goatee were gone, and his clean-shaven appearance revealed his extreme good looks.

Stacy shook her head. "Wesley explained how Cavendish was Lord Overton now and everything, but he looks so different."

"Lord Overton is devilishly handsome, isn't he?" Louise murmured. "And a baron, to boot!"

"I'm a bit shocked." Belle blinked. "He could almost be mistaken for a rake!"

Stephen lowered his voice. "My heavens, Mother has gone all red in the face. I've never seen her do *that* before."

Horatio snorted. "And my mother is fluttering her fan like a pigeon."

"Mind your tongue, Horatio." Carl was biting back a smile. "It's more like a hummingbird."

Stacy sighed. "I hope Lord Overton asks me to dance tonight. I've never danced better than I did with him."

Eva cast an impatient look toward the orchestra in the

corner. "I wish they'd start the dancing now. I'd love to see who he asks first."

"It won't be *you*, if that's what you mean," Stacy said.

Eva made a face at her sister. "It won't be *you*, either."

∽

As Wesley chatted with James, Mayor Crane, and the mayor's wife, he kept one eye on the ballroom entrance. At last, Mr. Ley appeared in the doorway, along with a handsome older woman dressed in a beautiful gown.

Wesley touched James on the sleeve. "Lord Overton, two special guests have just arrived. Will you help me receive them?"

"It would be a pleasure, Duke."

James accompanied Wesley toward the ballroom entrance, but when he caught sight of Mr. Ley's companion, he blanched and stopped dead in his tracks.

"It's Esmé! Wesley, I can't believe you broke your word to me."

"I only promised not to speak of her to you, and I haven't. As it happens, I met with Miss Christianson again before I left London and she insisted on seeing you. I could hardly withhold an invitation in those circumstances and so asked Mr. Ley to escort her tonight."

"Nevertheless—"

"Give her a chance, James, so you'll have no regrets. Judging from the glances you're receiving from the ladies tonight, I expect Miss Christianson will have nothing to regret either."

As James's eyes rested on his former fiancée, his expression softened. "She's absolutely breathtaking."

Wesley nodded. "You can do it, James. Stiff upper lip and all that."

"Right you are." James threw his shoulders back, strode up to Miss Christianson, and sketched a bow. "It's extraordinarily good to see you again, Esmé."

Even as her eyes sparkled with emotion, a coquettish smile lifted the corners of Miss Christianson's mouth. "It's wonderful to see you, James." She curtsied and extended her hand. "I've been waiting for your return."

～

Wesley appeared at Belle's elbow. "Come walk with me."

His nearness sent delicious shivers throughout her body. "I could use some fresh air."

Unnoticed, they slipped out of the ballroom and into the garden, where polka music from the orchestra serenaded the flowers. Wesley led her into a small gazebo, which was barely illuminated by the lights from the ballroom.

"The ball is a smashing success." Belle smiled. "Congratulations."

"I can't believe your grandfather insisted on dancing the first waltz with you!" Wesley groused. "I couldn't convince him to yield, despite the fact my name was written on your dance card."

Belle giggled. "I'm afraid Grandpapa is not a man to be gainsaid easily."

"Neither am I."

Wesley took her into his arms, and Belle could scarcely breathe for happiness. He pressed gentle kisses against her forehead and then her cheeks. "Do you know how much I adore you?" His lips hovered over hers.

"Show me."

As they kissed, Belle knew she could never get enough of this man...this American duke who'd stolen her heart. She kissed him over and over again, as if trying to memorize the curves of his mouth and the sweetness of his lips. Her senses were overwhelmed with the taste and smell of him and the heady sensation of his body against hers.

Too soon, he leaned back and frowned. "Miss Oakhurst, this is entirely improper, wouldn't you say?"

With pent-up ardor, Belle kissed the frown from his face. "Not at all, Your Grace."

Wesley's voice became husky. "What of your reputation?"

She slid her hands up his back, enjoying the feel of his muscles. "Hang my reputation."

"What? You've made me into a gentleman, Belle, and unfortunately I've become quite chivalrous. We'll just have to marry as soon as possible."

She froze.

"That is, if you'll have me," he added.

Wesley retrieved a ring from his pocket, held up a fiery opal flanked by two mine cut diamonds, and sank to one knee. "Miss Annabelle Oakhurst, will you marry me?"

Despite the burst of joy lifting her spirits skyward, Belle feigned a sigh. "This is all so sudden, Your Grace."

"Sudden? You must be joking." Wesley scowled and got to his feet. "I've wanted to marry you since the first time we met!"

"Nonsense." Belle laughed. "You despised me when we first met but with good reason. I was an awful prig back then."

"A beautiful prig. Besides which, I've grown to love prigs."

"Your compliments will go to my head."

"My compliments are meant for your heart."

She gave Wesley a slow smile. "In that case, I accept your proposal."

"That's more like it." He slipped the ring onto Belle's finger and gathered her into his arms. "The way you look in that dress is giving me some extremely scandalous ideas. Let's go in and announce our engagement before my guests think I brought you into the garden to take liberties."

"Didn't you?" She pouted. "I was really rather hoping you had."

Belle slid her arms around his neck and pulled him into a passionate kiss.

The End

LADY OF A GILDED AGE
BOOK TWO OF THE GILDED AGE SERIES

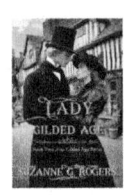

In the wake of romantic disappointment, Stephen van Eyck and his sister, Louise, decide to leave England and return to Philadelphia. When he inherits a property from an earl he barely remembers, however, they delay their departure long enough to visit the cottage. Once Stephen discovers the residence is magnificent, he feels compelled to make amends for his windfall to the earl's heirs. Unfortunately, the beautiful Lady Delphine wants nothing to do with him.

Keep reading for an excerpt...

EXCERPT · LADY OF A GILDED AGE

Delphine sat down in Mr. Regan's office, retrieved a piece of paper from her valise, and put it on his desk. "This is a list of parcels Logan has identified for sale. We intend to sell them one at a time until we reach the amount required to satisfy the tax debt."

The solicitor put on his spectacles before he picked up the list. "What if, after selling these parcels, you cannot raise enough money?"

"I hope that won't happen, but we are prepared to sell more. I would like you to help."

Mr. Regan nodded. "I'll put an advertisement in the newspaper right away."

"Please be discreet and don't use the Wentworth name."

"Of course not. I'll have any interested parties contact my office directly."

"Thank you."

"You may not get any eligible purchase offers right away, Lady Delphine. I don't mean to be overly personal, but are you able to manage your bills?"

"I will be engaging the services of a secondhand furniture company and making as many economies at Weeping Willow as possible."

The solicitor removed his spectacles and laid them on the blotter. "If I may say so, you are very brave, Lady Delphine. Not too many women of privilege have your pluck."

"Logan and I are determined to do whatever it takes to keep our home." Delphine paused. "By the way, I would like to know who owns Wheeler Cottage now."

"He's an American."

"Oh. If he's in America, I needn't worry about meeting him, then." Delphine stood. "You've set my mind at ease."

"He's a young American gentleman who is living in London at the moment, actually. His name is Van Eyck and he has a sister."

"I see." Delphine frowned. "If you'll excuse me, I have an appointment."

She left Mr. Regan's inner office and crossed through his outer office where another client was waiting. The fellow had burnished blond hair, regular features, and a mischievous expression. When she appeared, he shot to his feet and sketched an exceedingly elaborate bow. Although his actions were showy and meant to impress, she could not help but smile. Delphine reached for the door handle, but he beat her to it and held the door open.

Her smile deepened. "Thank you, sir." Oh, why couldn't she be wearing a gown of pink silk and white lace?

He grinned. "The pleasure is mine."

Delphine left the office, puzzled at the fellow's curious accent. It sounded almost American, but she shook off the notion as nonsense. If that handsome young gentleman was the hateful cardsharp who had bested her father, *she* was Princess Beatrice.

SUZANNE G. ROGERS

Bestselling author Suzanne G. Rogers is a California native, but she changed coastlines and now lives in romantic Savannah, Georgia, on an island populated by deer, exotic birds, turtles, otters, and gators. Writing blush-free, young adult fiction is her passion.

Also by Suzanne G. Rogers
Historical Romance

Graceling Hall Series
Larken (Book One)*
Lord Apollo & the Colleen (Book Two)

The Beaucroft Girls Series
Ruse & Romance (Book One)*
Rake & Romance (Book Two)*

The Mannequin Series
The Mannequin (Book One)*
Grace Unmasked (Book Two)
The Star-Crossed Seamstress (Book Three)
A Chance of Rayne (Book Four)
The Substitute (Book Five)

Gilded Age Series
Duke of a Gilded Age (Book One)
Lady of a Gilded Age (Book Two)

Standalone Titles
*Spinster**
A Gift for Fiona
Lady Fallows' Secrets
My Fair Guardian
*Jessamine's Folly**

*The Ice Captain's Daughter**

An American in Paris of the West

Rumer Has It

One Little Kiss

The Glass Heart

The Prettier Sister

Courtship on Eaton Square

*Audiobook available

Also by Suzanne G. Rogers
FANTASY

<u>The Yden Series</u>

The Last Great Wizard of Yden (Book One)

Dragon Clan of Yden (Book Two)

Secrets of Yden (Book Three)

Kira (Prequel to the Yden Trilogy)

<u>Standalone Titles</u>

Dani & the Immortals

*The Dragon Rider's Daughter**

Clash of Wills

Tournament of Chance: Dragon Rebel

Magical Misperception

*Whimsical Tendencies**

Something Wicked in L.A.

Royal Promenade

*Audiobook Available